BEFORE YOUR VERY EYES

Alex George was born in 1970. He is married and lives in London. This is his second novel.

ALSO BY ALEX GEORGE

Working It Out

ALEX GEORGE

BEFORE YOUR VERY EYES

HarperCollins*Publishers*

This novel is entirely a work of fiction.
The names, characters and incidents portrayed in it are the work of the author's imagination. Any resemblance to actual persons, living or dead, events or localities is entirely coincidental.

HarperCollins*Publishers*
77–85 Fulham Palace Road,
Hammersmith, London w6 8jb

www.**fire**and**water**.com

A Paperback Original 2000
1 3 5 7 9 8 6 4 2

A catalogue record for this book is available from the British Library

ISBN 0 00 6513336

Typeset in Perpetua by Palimpsest Book Production Limited, Polmont, Stirlingshire

Printed and bound in Great Britain by
Clays Ltd, St Ives plc

For my mother and father,
Alison and Julian George,
with love and apologies for the language

On me your voice falls as they love should,
Like an enormous yes.

For Sidney Bechet
Philip Larkin

ONE

Simon Teller kissed the card.

It was a hesitant, surreptitious, don't mind me kiss. A small, I'm not really doing this kiss. His lips barely puckered as they brushed against the white cardboard. It felt good. He read the card once more, and then kissed it again. As he did so, he made a 'mwah' noise. Then, feeling rather silly, he put it down on the kitchen table.

'OK,' he said out loud. 'Good.'

He picked the card up again, and walked into the sitting room.

There he cursed silently. That was the problem with these converted flats. The builders had got rid of all the fireplaces. Without fireplaces you had no mantelpieces, and without mantelpieces – well. Where was one supposed to put invitations?

For that was what Simon Teller had been performing his solitary act of osculation upon. An invitation, yes, but the word failed to convey the full import of the rectangle of reinforced card that Simon held. This was no ordinary invitation. This invitation was the key to God knows what, the ticket to God knows where, the introduction to God knows who.

Simon went over to the record player and lifted the

stylus on to the waiting vinyl. Sonny Rollins broke into an effervescent 'St Thomas', his joyful, bristling, honking saxophone reflecting Simon's own mood. Simon propped the card up against the stereo and stepped back to admire it. There was no doubt about it: it looked good. All right, the handwriting was messy, and the green ink had smudged badly. But that didn't matter. What mattered were the names scrawled along the top of the card.

Angus and Fergus.

Yes yes yes.

Angus and Fergus were Simon's neighbours. They lived in the flat immediately above his. They had moved in about two years ago. Since then, Simon had only actually seen them a few times – chance encounters on the stairs, mostly – but he felt that he knew them intimately. For the other draw-back about the building in which Simon, Angus and Fergus all lived, lack of mantelpieces aside, was extremely thin ceilings.

As a result, Simon had witnessed, albeit indirectly, most of the important recent events in the lives of Angus and Fergus. He listened to their rows, and to their drunken reconciliations. But, most of all, he listened to them having sex. It wasn't that Simon was a voyeur, or whatever the aural equivalent of that was, it was simply that he didn't have any choice. Wherever he sat in his flat, the unmistakable sound of heavy-duty bonking would permeate through the ceiling, causing his light fittings to wobble alarmingly. Angus and Fergus enjoyed having sex, and consequently they did it a lot, with as many different girls as they could.

Simon grew to recognize the sounds of the various females who visited the upstairs flat. There seemed, at any given time, to be at least five or six who could be identified. Simon would sit in bed and, recognizing a particular trill or coo, settle back into his pillows, knowing that it was this one or that one who was being entertained that evening. He never got to see any of these women, of course. They would all leave early in the morning, while their performances were analysed in forensic detail by the two flat-mates over breakfast. Simon preferred not to listen to these post-coital discussions. The two men pored over techniques and replayed certain copulatory highlights with the relish of football pundits analysing a questionable penalty decision.

Angus and Fergus led torrid social lives. Most weekends were punctuated by the regular ringing of their doorbell. Simon sat in his flat listening to the parties swell and throb above him with a despairing heart. How he wanted to join in! How he wanted to float and glitter with the Beautiful People! He would listen to the festivities as long as he could, and then would retire to bed with an old pair of socks wrapped around his head as sound insulation.

Simon stared at the invitation again. This was it. His time had finally come. He wrote the date in his diary, and put a big red ring around it.

It was soon after this that the worries began. Simon was out of practice at parties, and hopeless at social small talk. He met people every day at the shop, of course, and could talk to them. But this was quite different. At the party he would meet sophisticated people with beauty and charisma. He would have to sparkle.

It had been a long time since Simon had sparkled.

Keen to make a good impression, Simon instigated

emergency measures to hone his social skills. He spent two evenings watching Wim Wenders videos, hoping that these would see him through any sticky conversational moments. He spent hours smiling at himself in the bathroom mirror, tilting his head this way and that as he listened to imaginary chit-chat.

'Really?' he murmured in his best Sean Connery, as the extractor fan whirred noisily above him. 'How *fas*cinating.' He flashed his eyes dangerously. 'Tell me *more*.'

As the appointed day approached, Simon began cramming information as if he were taking an exam. The problem was that he was preparing himself for the unknown. He had witnessed countless parties through the vibrating medium of his ceiling, but it had been impossible to distinguish specific conversations. All he was sure of was that the conversation must be awfully sophisticated. In the absence of any specific intelligence, he employed the cultural scatter-gun approach, and was ready to discuss – albeit at rather superficial levels – everything from football to Fellini.

On the evening of the party, Simon waited for several people to arrive before venturing up himself. As he climbed the stairs, he could feel his brain bulging with useless information. He clutched an excessively expensive bottle of Montrachet, hoping that it would impress his hosts.

Taking a deep breath, Simon knocked.

The door opened. In front of Simon stood a huge man in jeans and a striped shirt. Angus or Fergus. Simon could not remember which. Suddenly he realized that he had never actually known which of Angus or Fergus was which. The man looked at him enquiringly.

'Hello. Simon from downstairs.' Simon proffered the

bottle of wine as a fleeing refugee might attempt to bribe border guards.

'Oh. Right,' said the man. 'Come on in. We're just getting going.' He took the bottle without bothering to read the label, and turned to go back into the flat.

'You been here before?' asked Angus/Fergus over his shoulder. His voice was ripe with public school fruitiness, and ridiculously deep. He sounded like an aristocratic Darth Vader who had taken testosterone boosters.

'No,' squeaked Simon self-consciously. He cleared his throat and followed his host. The flat was in total disarray. The corridor was lined with piles of magazines, garlanded with dirty socks and crumpled underpants. There were no pictures on the walls. The carpet had been worn bare at several points. There was the unmistakable smell of unwashed laundry, uncleaned toilets, unemptied bins. It was the smell of two men living together.

'Right,' said Angus/Fergus, as they went into the sitting room. 'Here we all are. Let me do some introductions.' He pointed at an equally large man who was sitting at one end of the table which sat in the middle of the room. 'Him you know, obviously.' Simon nodded weakly. This was the other host, whichever of Angus or Fergus that Angus/Fergus was not. Simon swallowed. This wasn't going to be easy. Angus/Fergus continued. 'Next to him is Stella, then Joe. Over there is Delphine, and next to her is Suzy.'

Simon nodded, trying to take everything in. The other people around the table hadn't stopped talking or even looked up.

'Tell you what, why don't you stick yourself there,' said Angus/Fergus, pointing to the empty chair next to

Delphine. He winked at Simon. 'You'll get on well with Delphine. Fantastic bit of totty. French. *Très sophistiquée.*' He lowered his voice to a mild bellow. 'Goes like a shit house door in a hurricane. Drink?'

'Er, thanks,' said Simon.

'Margarita?'

'OK. Fine.'

'Right. Back in a tick.'

As Simon hesitantly sat down next to Delphine, she momentarily half-turned her head towards him and smiled, before turning back to the conversation.

Not much, really, but it was enough.

Delphine was extraordinarily beautiful. She had rich, dark hair which hung down past her shoulders. She wore a sleeveless dress which showed her exquisitely turned arms. From where he sat Simon had a good view of her long and elegant neck, but what he really wanted to see again was her face. In those few moments that she had acknowledged him, he had had the sensation of having the breath knocked out of him. Delphine had huge, beautiful, dark green almond-shaped eyes, which were embellished by the longest eyelashes Simon had ever seen. Her mouth was delectable, too, a perfect oasis of dark, kissable lips.

Simon's brain began to haemorrhage all of the information he had been hoarding so carefully over the past few weeks. He could almost hear the facts whizz out of his ears, and realized that all of his careful preparation had been fruitless. Two minutes of sitting next to Delphine had been enough to empty his head of everything except the knowledge that she was without question the most beautiful woman he had ever seen in his life. Oh great, he thought bitterly. I get to sit next to the perfect woman, and then have nothing to say to her. And she goes like a shit house door in a hurricane. Just my bloody luck.

Simon stared numbly at the table in front of him as the conversation continued without him. Come on, he told himself. Get a grip. He waited for a lull in the conversation, which, to his surprise, was not about Jacques Derrida, but instead was about a popular soap opera. Finally there was a pause, and Delphine turned back towards Simon to pick up her glass.

'Hi,' said Simon, who had now worked out what he was going to say.

Delphine turned her eyes on Simon as she took a sip of her drink. 'Hi,' she replied, smiling.

'Er,' said Simon, who had now forgotten what he was going to say. Delphine's gaze was the equivalent of a cerebral enema. There was immediate and total evacuation of the brain.

Her eyebrows arched. 'I'm Delphine,' she said, her French accent adding to the already alluring cocktail of sensual stimuli she was presenting.

Simon gulped, and wished he had something to do with his hands. 'I'm Simon,' he said. 'Very nice to meet you.'

'Nice to meet you too, Simon,' replied Delphine, and delivered a soul-destroying smile of impossible perfection. Simon felt himself spiritually crumple.

'Who do you –' began Simon, only to see Delphine turn back to the conversation at the other end of the table. He was left once again to contemplate the graceful, swan-like lines of her neck. Well, he thought, that went pretty well, considering that you're behaving like a complete fucking moron.

A few moments later a large glass of off-white liquid was plonked down in front of him. A dusting of salt sat around the rim of the glass. 'There you go,' said Angus/Fergus jovially. 'Get that down you and you'll feel more in the mood.' He released a loud guffaw.

'Thanks,' said Simon, eyeing the contents of the glass suspiciously. It had been a long time since he had drunk margaritas. He took a tentative sip, his mouth puckering involuntarily on contact with the salt.

'Golly,' he said.

'Puts hairs on your chest, doesn't it?' said Angus/Fergus, grinning.

'I dare say,' mused Simon, thinking that he must establish which of his hosts was which before much longer.

There was a crash from what Simon supposed was the kitchen, followed by a tense whinny that he recognized from past nocturnal /performances.

'Fuck,' said Angus/Fergus. 'Clumsy cow. Hang on. Back in a sec.'

From the kitchen came the sound of an argument, the deep tones of Angus/Fergus interspersed with the high-pitched screeches of the unfortunate cook. After a few minutes the door re-opened and Angus/Fergus appeared with a stack of plates. He was followed by a tall, skinny girl with slightly buck teeth, who carried a large Pyrex dish. She put the dish down in the middle of the table.

'Rice?' asked Angus/Fergus irritably.

The girl spun on her heel and flounced back into the kitchen.

'Right then, everyone,' announced Angus/Fergus. 'May I present the traditional gourmet extravaganza. Rice and chilli, from an old family recipe, passed down by word of mouth from generation to generation. We are preserving an important gastronomic tradition this evening. Had a bit of an accident with the casserole, hence this rather unattractive see-through thing, but we rescued most of it off the floor.'

The cook arrived back at the table with a steaming bowl of rice which she slammed down wordlessly before sitting down in the empty seat opposite Simon. Plates were passed around the table, and people began to help themselves.

Simon took another sip of his margarita.

'Hello,' said the buck-toothed girl opposite him. 'I'm Heather.'

'I'm Simon. Do I take it you're the cook this evening?'

'Yes, for all the thanks I get,' said Heather. She whinnied.

Do you know, Simon wanted to ask, that's *exactly* the noise you make when you have an orgasm? Instead he said, 'Well, it looks delicious to me.'

'Don't be fooled,' replied Heather. She nodded sideways at Angus/Fergus. 'He's very particular about what goes in and how it's all done. He stands over my shoulder directing matters. I don't know why he doesn't just do it himself.'

Simon saw his chance. 'You're the girlfriend . . . ?' he nodded towards Angus/Fergus.

'Of Fergus? Yes, for my sins.'

Fergus! Simon settled back into his chair, feeling pleased with himself, and waited for the chilli to be passed around. When the bowl arrived in front of him he dolloped two spoonfuls of the brown and red mixture on to his plate, followed by a large helping of rice.

Simon stuck his fork into the steaming pile of food. He

absent-mindedly swallowed his first mouthful, wondering how to make Delphine realize within the next couple of hours that she really ought to get to know him better.

Such thoughts were abandoned seconds later, as the back of Simon's throat erupted. He gasped as the chilli began its descent to his stomach, charring his tonsils and scalding his epiglottis on the way down. His eyes brimmed with tears. He grabbed his drink and swallowed half of it in one go. He then struggled to restrain the coughing fit that the potent margarita mix provoked.

After a few moments, Simon recovered his poise. Nobody seemed to have noticed his discomfort. On the other side of the table, Fergus and Heather were arguing. Heather looked as if she were about to cry too, although it was not clear whether this was due to the chilli or what Fergus had been saying to her.

'Let me get you another drink,' said Fergus to Simon, abruptly turning away from Heather as she was hissing in his ear. He returned moments later with a large jug and topped up Simon's glass.

'Oh, thanks,' said Simon, wondering if it would be awfully rude to ask for some water. He looked at the hill of rice and chilli on his plate, and the full glass of margarita in front of him. His head had started to buzz gently. Tentatively, he picked up his fork and scooped up a small mound of chilli. He switched the fork to his left hand, and picked up his glass with his right. Almost in one movement, he deposited the chilli in his mouth, swallowed, and then slugged back a mouthful of margarita. The effect was interesting. His mouth went numb, and the chilli's passage southwards was marked by no more than a slight tingling sensation. After a few moments he felt the chilli sitting malignantly in his stomach, sloshing about in a sea of margarita mix. Encouraged, Simon began to address the rest of his plate in the same way.

By the time he had finished his helping, Simon was yabberingly drunk. His mouth seemed only vaguely connected with the rest of his body. When he moved his jaw he felt nothing, as if he'd been given a mammoth local anaesthetic. Now that he had eaten the food, his primary job, he remembered, was to persuade Delphine to marry him.

Simon carefully put his fork down on his empty plate, and surveyed the rest of the table. He noticed that most people had hardly touched their food. Delphine's back was still turned to him.

The discussion was about jobs. Angus, Simon was able to deduce with what was left of his alcohol-decimated cerebral cortex, was an estate agent. He was telling a story about a woman who, he claimed, had tried to seduce him when he went around to value her flat.

'So what did you do?' asked Stella, who was sitting next to Angus, smoking a cigarette.

'Well, what could I do? I shagged her, of course,' boomed Angus.

Stella stiffened. 'I see,' she said.

Angus carried on. 'She wasn't much good, to be honest. Bit saggy, really. Desperate, you know. Quite sweet, but desperate.' He turned to Stella, who was now puffing so hard on her cigarette that she was momentarily obscured by a wall of billowing smoke. 'Nowhere near as good as you, my pet,' he said to her.

Stella ground her cigarette into the ashtray in front of her with a ferocity which suggested that she would rather be grinding it into Angus's forehead. She got up and left the table.

'Oh, for Christ's sake,' complained Angus. 'What's the matter with her?'

From the other end of the table, Fergus raised his eyebrows and drew a suggestive finger across his neck. Next to him Heather stared silently at her plate, saying nothing.

There was an awkward pause, before Fergus said to Simon, 'So, er, what do you do? Get propositioned by desperate women in your line of work?'

Simon shook his head, more to clear it than to indicate a negative response. He tried his mouth. It seemed to work. He was aware that Delphine had now turned towards him again, but rather than risking another look at her face, he looked at Fergus instead, and said, 'Not often, no. I work in a magic shop.'

This was met with a gratifying reaction of disbelief and laughter. Stella came and sat down again at the table. Angus ignored her.

'So you're a magician?' said Delphine.

'Sort of,' said Simon. 'I do tricks. But I sell them rather than perform them.' His head had begun to spin alarmingly with the effort of producing entire sentences.

'Gosh,' said Delphine. 'I'm impressed.' She smiled at him. Simon was momentarily pole-axed, and grinned back at her stupidly.

'Thanks,' he dribbled.

'Show us a trick, then,' demanded Stella sourly. There was a murmur of assent from around the table.

The words echoed around Simon's head until finally he managed to decipher them. 'Oh no, couldn't,' he mumbled.

'Why not?' demanded Fergus.

'Just . . . couldn't,' said Simon. 'Too pissed,' he whispered as an afterthought.

'Go on,' said Heather.

Simon shook his head. 'Sorry.'

'Spoilsport,' complained Angus. 'Go on.'

'Absolutely not,' said Simon.

'*Please*,' said Delphine.

'OK,' said Simon.

Delphine clapped her hands in delight.

'Have you got a fag?' Simon asked the table in general.

'Here's one.' Stella flung a box of cigarettes at him.

Simon took a cigarette out of the packet and held it up in front of him. There was an expectant silence. 'Right,' he said. 'Watch closely.' He turned towards Delphine and beamed at her.

Simon clenched his left hand into a fist and held it up level with his face. Then he slowly inserted Stella's cigarette into his fist and pushed it in until it was completely concealed. He opened his hand to show the cigarette.

'Now,' said Simon, 'watch again.'

He performed the same movement. This time, however, before opening his fist he waved it in the air a few times. Then he lowered his hand and opened his fingers one by one, palm upwards, over the table.

The cigarette had vanished.

'Wow,' said Delphine. 'That's *amazing*.'

Simon's heart thumped.

'All right,' said Stella, 'now bring it back.'

'Can't, I'm afraid,' mumbled Simon. 'It's gone.'

'What do you mean?' demanded Stella. 'What sort of a trick is that? Where is it?'

'It's vanished,' explained Simon.

'Of course it hasn't *vanished*,' replied Stella sarcastically. 'Where is it? I want it back. Give me my fag back. Thief.'

Simon squirmed in his chair. 'I can't,' he said. 'Honest. Sorry.' (The cigarette now lay, out of reach, beneath Simon's chair, where he had surreptitiously dropped it.)

'Well if you were a *proper* magician you could make it come back again,' said Stella sulkily.

'Don't worry, babe,' said Angus. 'You can have one of mine.'

'Oh, sod off, Angus,' replied Stella.

Simon took another long drink of margarita. He had stopped feeling the drink's corrosive effect on his larynx some time earlier.

'I suppose, being a magician, you've heard the story about the boy and the magic coin he found,' said a man on the other side of the table, who up until then had hardly said a word.

There was a collective groan from around the table.

'God, Joe, not again, please,' said Heather.

'I thought Simon might like to hear it if he hasn't before,' said Joe.

Simon shrugged. 'If nobody else minds.'

'No, I suppose we don't mind,' said Angus.

'Right,' said Joe. He addressed himself to Simon. 'There was this young boy called Timmy. He's walking down the street one day when he spots something gleaming in the gutter. So he goes over and discovers that it's a foreign-looking coin, one he's never seen before. So he picks it up and takes it home.'

'OK,' said Simon.

'A couple of days later, Timmy's sitting in his kitchen, and he puts his hand into his pocket and remembers this old coin that's sitting there. He takes it out and wipes it on a bit of kitchen paper. And suddenly this voice comes booming out of nowhere. "Timmy, you may have as many wishes as your heart desires." So obviously it's a magic coin. Well, Timmy is delighted. He has a think, and then says, "OK, I'll have three bowls of chocolate ice cream, then." Just to check out whether this is for real. And sure enough, three bowls of chocolate ice cream appear on the kitchen table. As you can imagine, Timmy can't believe his luck.'

'Right,' said Simon. He noticed that everyone was listening to the story, but that Joe was addressing it to him alone. It felt good to be at the centre of things.

'Well,' continued Joe, 'Timmy is very excited about this, and wants to show off to all his friends. So next day at school he shows them his magic coin and grants them each one wish. Suddenly he's the most popular boy in the school.

'That evening he goes home from school, planning all the things that he's going to ask for. He wants to play football for England, and have a fast car. But most of all –' Joe held up a finger, '– most of all, he wants a shag. He's desperate to lose his virginity. He wants to be the first in his class. So he decides that tonight will be the night.'

'Get on with it,' sighed Stella.

Joe ignored her. 'OK. So. That evening he goes home and has his tea. He's a bit subdued. His mother asks if everything is all right, and he replies, well, no, not really, and says that perhaps he'll have a bath and then go to bed early.

'In fact, what Timmy wants to do is to have a bath so he smells good,' explained Joe. 'He's decided that he's going to wish for Posh Spice to be his first shag, and wants to be as fancy as possible for her. So he runs a bath. While the bath is running he splashes on some of his dad's aftershave, and brushes his teeth.'

'OK,' said Simon, nodding. The rest of the people around the table seemed to lean in fractionally.

'Finally,' said Joe, 'he gets into his bath. He puts his magic coin in front of him by the taps. And all he can think about is Posh Spice coming to visit him later in bed.' Joe put his hands out. 'Naturally, Timmy gets a hard-on. And the thought occurs to him that maybe it wouldn't be such a bad idea if perhaps he has a quick tactical wank now, just to make sure he doesn't come too quickly later on.'

'Right.' Simon took another swig of margarita.

'OK. So there Timmy is, in the bath, happily whacking off. And before too long, he ejaculates. So – he's sitting in the bath, feeling pretty pleased with himself. And you know what sperm looks like in bath water?'

Simon nodded, keen to hear the end of the story. 'Yeah,' he said.

At that point the entire table erupted. Fergus banged his hands on the table in appreciation. Everyone else collapsed into hysterics.

'Hook, line, and sinker,' gasped Stella between breaths.

'Well done, old mate,' said Angus, shaking hands with Joe, who shrugged modestly. 'Extra special.'

It dawned on Simon that something profoundly awful had just happened. Amidst the laughter, his brain replayed the last few exchanges prior to the onset of hilarity. He swallowed. Everyone else around the table had been in on the joke. They had all been waiting to see if he would take the bait. A feeling of intense and abject self-pity washed over him. He chanced a glance at Delphine, hoping that she, at least, would have risen above such juvenile amusement. She was giggling unstoppably. Simon sighed. That was the end of his chances with her, then. He reached for his glass and downed its contents in one gulp.

'That's my boy,' hooted Fergus. 'Drown your sorrows. Mind you, nothing to be ashamed about, masturbating in the bath. Even at your age.'

'At least he came clean,' said Stella, at which the entire party dissolved into fits of laughter again, leaving Simon sitting there, wondering how soon it would be before he could excuse himself and retreat back to his flat. He stared morosely at his empty glass.

'Oh dear,' sighed Heather, wiping her eyes. 'Priceless.'

'Any chance of some more?' enquired Simon, holding up his empty glass. He decided that the only feasible method of survival was to get even more drunk than he already was.

'Coming right up,' replied Fergus, getting to his feet. 'Christ,' he said as he stood up. 'I needed that.'

Simon's embarrassment had raised everybody's spirits, and the party became more animated. Someone turned on some music. Simon began to drink quickly and with determination.

A little while later, someone clapped their hands to get everyone's attention. Simon looked up slowly through the fug of his booze-sodden brain. One of his hosts was standing up. Simon realized that he had again lost track of which was Fergus and which was Angus, but was by now far too drunk to care or to do anything about it.

'Right, everyone,' declared Fergus/Angus loudly. 'It's reached that time of the evening when we move on to the traditional party amusements.'

This announcement was met with a chorus of excited whoops and cheers. It occurred to Simon that he could probably now leave without too much fear of embarrassment. However, he decided to stay where he was for a little while longer. There were two reasons for this. Firstly, Simon realized that if he left now, he would probably never see Delphine again. Secondly, and perhaps more compellingly, he was unable to move his legs. He wondered what form these party games would take. He remembered having pondered this for hours from the sanctity of his own flat as he listened to similar parties go on into the small hours. He had always imagined that they would be terribly high-brow, intellectually rigorous games – having to identify arcane literary quotations, or composing sonnets on topics chosen by the opposing team.

Fergus/Angus went into the kitchen and came out moments later with a large box under his arm. 'Ladies and gentlemen,' he pronounced. 'I give you – Twister.'

This was followed by more cheering and whistles. Heather took the box and opened it. Inside was a large sheet of plastic with different coloured spots on it, which she spread out on the floor. The sheet took up most of the remaining space in the living room.

'You all know how to play, I take it,' she said. 'Two teams of two players each. The players have to put their hands and feet on a particular colour spot, as specified by the spinny thing.' She indicated a coloured piece of cardboard with a pointer mounted in the middle. 'First team to fall over loses. Who wants to play?'

Stella's hand shot up. 'Me,' she shouted, and then turned to Joe, grabbed his wrist, and pulled it into the air. 'Him,' she shouted again.

'Very good,' said Heather. 'Who else?'

Simon shrank back further into his chair, nursing his glass. He had already made a supreme tit of himself in front of all of these people. He was going to stay right where he was.

Heather turned to him. 'Simon?' she asked.

'No thanks,' mumbled Simon.

'I'll have a go,' said Delphine.

'Oh, go on, then,' said Simon. He turned to Delphine. 'Same team?' he suggested.

Delphine smiled. 'Good idea,' she said, as she got up. Simon followed, wobbling a little.

'Good man,' exclaimed Fergus/Angus.

'Listen, er, Fungus,' said Simon, drawing his host to one side. 'Before we start, d'you mind if I ask you a question?'

'By all means.'

'Well.' Simon lowered his voice. 'It's about Delphine, actually.'

'Oh yes. What about her?'

'Well.' Simon looked around conspiratorially. 'Is she, you know, *with* anyone?' He suppressed a hiccup.

Fergus/Angus shook his head. 'Don't think so,' he said. 'Footloose and fancy-free. And French. That's Delphine.'

'*Really*,' said Simon seriously.

'Really.'

'Right.' Simon hiccuped again. 'Thank you. Most helpful.' He turned towards the plastic sheet, now brimming with woefully misplaced confidence.

'Shoes off, please,' said Heather.

Stella squared up with Joe at one end of the mat. Delphine and Simon faced them, each foot on a different coloured spot. Simon looked with loathing at Joe, architect of his earlier misery, who had apparently forgotten his meanness and was now grinning affably at his two opponents, his conscience clearly untroubled.

'Right, everyone,' said Heather. 'Ready?'

Four heads nodded.

'OK.' Heather spun the needle. 'Left foot blue,' she announced.

There was a flurry of activity on the plastic sheet. Stella, Joe and Delphine all swivelled so that their left feet were standing on a blue spot. Baffled by the rapid movement, Simon looked down slowly at his feet. His left foot was already on a blue spot. The dim light of understanding glimmered faintly somewhere near the back of his brain. Delphine had spun around almost one hundred and eighty degrees, and her leg brushed gently against his. Simon could smell her intoxicating scent. She grinned at him. He began to worry about getting an erection while his limbs were splayed all too obviously across the plastic sheet.

'Everyone ready?' said Heather as she spun the needle again. 'OK, right hand red.'

The players went into a crouch. Delphine by now had contorted herself somewhat and was having to stretch to put her hand on a red spot. Simon tried not to stare down her cleavage which had appeared enticingly about eight inches in front of his eyes. Seriously worried now about the impending tumescence in his trousers, he shut his eyes briefly, but opened them again when he found himself losing his balance. Delphine had begun to breathe a little harder, which didn't exactly help. Simon tried to concentrate on staying upright.

After a few minutes, and much to his own surprise, Simon had not fallen over. He was beginning to enjoy himself. A few spins earlier Delphine had finally collapsed on to the floor. She accepted defeat cheerfully, and had gone back to her chair to watch the game continue. This distraction gone, Simon was able to concentrate. He would pursue Delphine properly once the game was over. In the meantime, he had the opportunity to impress her with his prowess at Twister. Win the game, he told himself drunkenly, and you win the girl. Easy as that. By this stage Stella had also fallen over, and only Simon and Joe remained on the sheet. Simon eyed Joe defiantly. This would be a battle to the death, an opportunity to avenge Joe's story about bloody Timmy and his bloody magic coin. Revenge would be sweet. No prisoners would be taken. He braced himself for the next move.

Heather spun the needle again. 'Left foot green.'

Simon groaned. He needed to move his left foot from one side of the sheet to the other. By the time he had completed the manoeuvre, he was turned upwards with his back facing the floor. His arms were braced beneath him, twisted horribly, and his legs were bent, supporting most of his weight.

Immediately next to Simon's face hovered Joe's denim-clad bottom. Simon tried to shift away from it, but he was unable to move. He waited for Heather's next spin.

The bottom moved nearer as Joe tried to get into a more comfortable position. And then, without warning, there issued from it an unmistakable *phhhhhttt*.

Joe had farted, right in Simon's face.

This was no ordinary fart, either. This was a fart born from the enthusiastic consumption of Fergus's chilli. It was a sulphurous, cataclysmic bomb of a fart. It was a bleak fart, a fart without hope.

'Oops,' said Joe over his shoulder. 'Sorry.'

Simon gasped in horror at the untold beastliness of what was happening to him. Then he collapsed, landing heavily on his wrist.

'Ow,' said Simon, just before he fainted.

TWO

Simon woke up, and immediately tried to fall asleep again. His head was filled with a searing, shrill whining sound, not unlike that of twenty or so chain saws going at full throttle. He cautiously opened one eye. The noise got louder. He shut his eye again. It occurred to Simon that he was not, in all probability, surrounded by a posse of lumberjacks. Blinding white light flashed across his beleaguered brain. Simon groaned. While he had been asleep his tongue had been removed and replaced with a large slab of medium-grain sandpaper. The chain saws had by now been joined by a chorus of crashing anvils.

Simon lay back and, against his better instincts, thought. Trying not to move, he mentally did a rapid check of his body. There was a painful throbbing in his right hand, and an even worse one in his left foot, but apart from that, and his monstrous headache, everything seemed to be all right. Tentatively he moved his left hand over to feel his right, and found that it was trussed up in bandages. Frowning, Simon opened his eyes again, and waited for the mist to clear.

He was in a hospital ward. On either side of him motionless figures were humped beneath sheets and blankets. Simon struggled up on to his left elbow, trying to ignore the demonic pounding in his head.

What was he doing here? he wondered. He cast his mind back to the previous evening. The last thing he could remember was being inelegantly spread-eagled on the Twister sheet, waiting for Heather to spin the needle. Suddenly the unpleasant memory of Joe's appalling fart popped into Simon's brain, and he recalled collapsing on to his hand. Simon looked down at his body. He was wearing a pair of pyjamas that he did not recognize, and which bore the unmistakable smell of an industrial cleaning process. Someone had undressed him. Slowly he began to assimilate the possibility that, as humiliations went, he had quite possibly just eclipsed all his previous efforts.

Simon's hangover began to reassert itself as waves of nausea flooded over him. He slumped back on to his pillows and sighed. His left foot throbbed. He stared at the ceiling. This was all very peculiar, and very unpleasant. With Wagnerian hangovers such as this one, there was only one place to be: at home, in bed, within running distance of the nearest toilet. He glanced up and down the ward again. There were no nurses to be seen. He would have to wait to be rescued.

Eventually Simon drifted off into an uneasy sleep. When he woke again, a nurse in a dark blue uniform was standing next to the bed.

'Good morning, Mr Teller,' she said as soon as he opened his eyes.

Simon's brain was still eddying around the fringes of unconsciousness. 'Er, hello,' he replied.

'How are we today?' asked the nurse briskly.

'Not too great, actually,' admitted Simon. 'My hand and foot hurt, and I've got a bit of a headache.'

'Yes, well, I can't say I'm surprised,' said the nurse, 'after all of last night's excitements.'

Simon said nothing, hoping for more information.

'What did you think you were doing?' continued the nurse.

Simon stared back at her blankly. 'I really have no idea,' he answered truthfully. 'I was quite drunk, I think.'

The nurse snorted. 'I think *that* much was obvious,' she said, extracting a thermometer from her pocket and inserting it in Simon's mouth without further pleasantries. She glanced at her watch. 'I gather the board of the hospital have asked for a report to be prepared,' she continued.

'Wur yur moorr terrin mir wur harwen?' asked Simon politely.

'Don't worry, Mr Teller,' said the nurse. 'You'll find out soon enough.' She reached over and extracted the thermometer from Simon's mouth and scrutinized it. She pulled a face. 'Well,' she said, 'your temperature seems fine. May I see your hand, please?'

Gingerly Simon pulled his right hand from beneath the covers and presented it for inspection. The nurse examined the binding. 'Fine,' she said. 'You sprained it quite badly. You'll need to keep the pressure off the wrist for a while. Does it itch?'

'No,' said Simon. 'It just hurts a lot.'

'That's all right, then,' said the nurse. 'That'll wear off soon enough. How is your foot?'

'Painful. Especially when I move.'

The nurse nodded. She walked to the end of the bed and picked up the chart which hung there. 'I'll arrange for you to have an X-ray so we can find out what sort of damage you did to yourself. In the meantime, I suggest you try and keep as still as possible so you don't aggravate things.' She smiled, without humour. 'Here are two aspirins for your headache.'

Simon took the pills. 'Thanks,' he said.

'Please make sure you stay in bed and don't get into any more trouble,' said the nurse.

'Oh, absolutely,' said Simon, who was ransacking what was left of his brain for some small snippet of information, some undeleted detail, about what had happened the previous evening. He could remember nothing after the game of Twister in Angus and Fergus's flat. After that there was a great, depressing, black hole of nothingness. What had the nurse meant about preparing a report?

Unable to ponder more recent events, Simon's mind turned back to the dinner party itself. The brain being the playful organ that it is, he could remember in agonisingly clear detail Joe's story about the magic coin, and shuddered at the embarrassment of it all. He remembered his anguish when he saw Delphine laughing at him along with everyone else. Cruelly, Simon's brain was able to reconstruct Delphine's exquisite face in photographic detail. His spirits spiralled still lower.

What was it with women? Simon wondered. They were a confusing breed. He really couldn't understand why he had been single so long. He had read all the right books and magazines. He knew what women wanted. He could tick every box on the Ideal Man wish-lists that cropped up regularly in *Cosmopolitan* and *Marie Claire*. He had read *Crime and Punishment*, twice. He had Grade 6 piano (with Merit). He was an excellent cook. He liked Jean-Jacques Beineix films, and owned several on video.

Years of gazing critically at himself in the mirror had

persuaded him that physically he wasn't too bad, either. He had dark, curly hair, and green eyes that he suspected might be his best feature. (He had been told this one evening, by his first girlfriend, in between tongue-heavy snogs, and had clung on to the belief ever since. After all, it was quite something even to *have* a best feature.) Overall his face had a pleasing look to it: decent skin, middling cheek-bones, good teeth. His chin had in the past been described as 'strong'; Simon wasn't entirely sure what that meant, but had concluded that it had to be better than having a weak one.

There was no doubt: in the eligibility stakes, Simon was up there with the best of them. He had the lot.

What was more, Simon didn't just regard females as members of another, alien race. He was not an Angus or a Fergus, for whom women were either cooks or sex objects. Women, he knew, wanted to be respected as *people*, to be liked and admired for their minds and not just their bodies or domestic skills. Simon understood this, and behaved accordingly.

And yet they stayed away in droves. It was all very perplexing.

Simon had never had any trouble making friends with women. It stood as testimony to his sensitivity and emotional candour. Women felt able to talk to him openly. They loved him for it. It was just that they loved him like a brother. It would have been nice to find one who would love him like a randy hot-blooded sex machine.

Despite the number of female friends that Simon had had, they never stayed friends for very long. There were two principal reasons for this.

The first problem was his respect for women generally. This meant that he wasn't interested in trying to sleep with a girl before he got to know her properly. The difficulty with this approach was that, by the time Simon felt that they knew each other well enough to progress to the next, more interesting, stage, the girl had either got bored and had given up hope, or they had become such good friends that neither of them wanted to risk the friendship by sleeping together.

Eventually of course the girl would meet someone else and start sleeping with him immediately. She would then gradually see less and less of Simon, until disappearing completely in a frenzy of loved-up happiness.

Secondly, and perhaps more crucially, Simon had an embarrassing habit of falling hopelessly in love with his platonic girlfriends at wholly inappropriate moments. This usually happened just as they had begun to go out with someone else. It was only then, seeing them breathless and giddy with the excitement of new-found romance, that it would occur to Simon that, actually, it should be *him* that they should be getting so breathless and giddy about. There then followed excruciating confrontations, bewildered accusations, sheepish (but hopeful) admissions, scornful rejections, and (if he was lucky) cautious reconciliations coupled with stern warnings that nothing like this must ever happen again, *ever*. It was all rather humiliating.

The few fully functioning romantic relationships that Simon had managed also followed a predictable pattern. Simon was hopelessly, cripplingly, romantic. At the beginning of every relationship he would bombard his new paramour with letters, poems and flowers. He would spend hours composing his wedding speech in his head, and would moon about, unable to concentrate on anything. This clumsy, romantic streak, this desire to fall in love the way they say you should, was beguiling to the girl in question, usually for about a week. After that, the constant attention would begin to unnerve her somewhat, and before long Simon would be treated to the usual, hand-holding chat about slowing down, taking things easy, and giving each other a bit more space, which Simon now recognized as the inevitable precursor to the girl disappearing off the face of the planet. There would then follow a period of intense and histrionic mourning, after which came the hyper-critical self-analysis phase. This would leave him none the wiser, and primed to make all the same mistakes again next time around.

After contemplating this situation for some time and trying not to think about Delphine, Simon sighed, and closed his eyes. He tried to sleep, without success. Sometime later he heard a nearby cough. Simon opened his eyes. Standing at the end of the bed, clutching a brown paper bag, was Joe.

Simon struggled to sit up. 'Hello,' he said.

Joe proffered the bag. 'Grapes,' he explained.

'Oh. Thanks very much.'

There was a pause as the two men looked at each other uncertainly.

'I wanted to see how you were,' said Joe.

Simon shrugged, slightly nonplussed. 'Well, that's thoughtful of you. Thanks.'

'How's your hand?'

'Don't know, to be honest,' said Simon. 'It's all bandaged up so tightly that I can't feel much.'

Joe pulled a face. 'You haven't broken it?'

Simon shook his head. 'Just a sprain, apparently. I suppose that's good news, but it still hurts like buggery. And something else obviously happened last night. My foot is agony.'

Joe sat down on the end of the bed and frowned. 'Your foot? There was nothing wrong with your foot at the party.'

'Exactly. I've no idea what's wrong with it. I'm due to have an X-ray later today.' He paused. 'Actually, Joe, there is something I'd like to ask you.'

'What?'

'Well, this is slightly embarrassing, but can you remind me how I got to the hospital? It's a bit of a blur.'

'We called you a taxi. Don't you remember?'

'Oh yes. I remember now.' Simon felt his cheeks go hot.

'And you didn't want to go.'

'I didn't?'

'Well. First things first. You fell on your hand during that game of Twister, and fainted. When you came round you insisted on staying at the party. You wanted to talk to Delphine.'

Simon groaned. 'Go on.'

'Anyway, your wrist was swelling, and so Fergus called a cab and packed you in it, gave the driver a tenner and told him to get you to the nearest hospital. And here you are.'

Joe opened the bag of grapes and stuck one in his mouth, looking around the ward as he did so.

'So,' said Simon eventually. 'How is Delphine?'

'Delphine? She's fine, I think.'

'Oh good.'

Simon reached across and took a grape himself. 'Nice girl,' he said as he inspected the skin of the grape closely.

'Very nice,' agreed Joe. 'Pretty. Funny too. Apparently, she goes like a –'

'– shit house door in a hurricane, yes, I know,' said Simon miserably.

The bag of grapes was now shuttling up and down the bed between the two men. Well, this is an unusual situation, thought Simon. Here am I, trying to make small talk with this man, when the only two times we have interacted socially were firstly when he humiliated me completely in front of a room full of strangers and secondly when he farted so *badly* that I ended up in hospital. What does one say?

'I thought Delphine was very nice,' said Simon.

'Mmm.' Joe's mouth was full.

Did she, Simon wanted to ask, mention me after I'd gone? Ask for my telephone number, that sort of thing?

He tried a different tack. 'It's hard to meet people properly at those sorts of parties, isn't it?' he said.

'I suppose so,' said Joe.

The grape bag scooted up the bed again.

'Anyway,' said Joe, 'I never pull at parties.'

'Pull? As in pull women?'

Joe nodded. 'Never do it.'

Simon thought about this. 'Neither do I, I suppose. It's terribly difficult, isn't it? It's such an artificial situation. Go up to a girl at a party and start talking to her and you may as well be wearing a sign around your neck saying "Sad Bastard". And women treat you accordingly, which is generally with enormous contempt.'

'Actually, that's not what I meant at all,' said Joe. 'It's amazingly *easy* to pull at parties.'

'Oh,' said Simon.

'You're right, of course,' continued Joe, 'you may as well be wearing a sign around your neck, but that's the beauty of it.'

Simon looked blank. 'It is?'

'Absolutely,' said Joe. 'Look. You're at a party. You see this woman you want to talk to. And, because you're at a party, you *can*. You can just wander up to her and start chatting about any fucking thing in the world, and it doesn't matter – *because you're at a party*. Normal rules don't apply. If a woman goes to a party, she's more or less signed up for the social chit-chat bit. She'll be expecting it. It's all part of the experience. She's not going to tell you to bog off the moment you start speaking to her.'

Simon said nothing.

'Now, if this woman gets bored with you a bit later on, then she can quite legitimately turn around and ask to be left alone. And that's OK, too. That's all part of the deal. At that point, you've had your chance, and you've blown it. But at least you got your chance. The party is a great social leveller. It's a very democratic institution. Everyone has the chance for a go. It's yours for the taking.'

Simon considered this. 'If it's so easy to pull at parties, then why don't you?'

'Because the problem with parties,' replied Joe patiently, 'is that, by definition, in order to be invited, you need to know someone else there. Or know someone who knows someone. Ultimately, unless either you or the woman is a gatecrasher, there will be some sort of connection, however indirect, between the two of you. Mutual friends, that sort of thing.'

Simon frowned. 'OK,' he said. 'What's the problem?'

'Well,' explained Joe. 'Exactly that. If this woman is part of your circle, or part of your circle's circle, then there's always a risk that you'll bump into her again afterwards.'

'Afterwards?'

'Yeah.' Joe winked. 'Afterwards.'

'Oh. I see,' said Simon after a few moments. 'So tell me,' he said. 'If you don't pull women at parties, where *do* you meet them?

'The National Gallery,' said Joe.

There was a pause.

'What?' said Simon eventually.

'The National Gallery,' said Joe. 'It's in Trafalgar Square.'

'I know where it is,' snapped Simon.

Joe reached into the bag and took another grape. 'It's the best place in London to meet women. Although you do need to do research.'

'Research on what, exactly?' Simon asked, distaste and curiosity growing at equal rates.

'The paintings. I've established what sort of women stand in front of what sort of paintings. And then I wow them with some poetry. I've got different poems for each painting.'

'I don't believe this,' said Simon.

'It's true,' said Joe, missing Simon's point. 'If I want to meet a gentle, nicely brought up girl who wears Laura Ashley skirts and reads Jane Austen novels, I go to *Boating on the Seine* by Renoir. Then I hang around until a suitable specimen turns up – I never have to wait more than a few minutes. Bit like buses. Anyway. So I'll wait until this girl has been gazing at the painting for a while. And then I'll step up behind her, and say,

> My soul is an enchanted boat,
> Which, like a sleeping swan, doth float
> Upon the silver waves of thy sweet singing.

'And then she'll turn around, surprised. I look at her shyly. We discuss the formless spontaneity of the picture for a few minutes, then maybe do a quick tour of the rest of the gallery, and then I ask, casually as you like, whether she has time for a coffee. And bingo, you're off.'

Simon sat back on his pillows. Finally he said, 'What was that poem?'

'It's from *Prometheus Unbound*, by Shelley. Gets them every time.' Joe made his hand into the shape of a pistol and shot an imaginary target. 'So, that was Laura Ashley Girl. Clean-living, generally. Usually very good cooks. They always fall for the whole poetry thing. It's just *so* romantic, being approached by a stranger in an art gallery.'

'God,' mused Simon. 'You really have this all worked out, haven't you?'

'Oh yeah. For example,' continued Joe, 'absolutely the best sex, without question, you get in front of the Canalettos.'

'Really?' said Simon in a defeated way.

Joe nodded. 'Don't know why. Maybe there's something in the paintings that appeals to nymphomaniacs. Anyway, with Canalettos, as there are quite a few of them, I tend to stand in front of the painting *next* to the one that the girl is in front of, and then murmur quietly,

Beneath is spread like a green sea
The waveless plain of Lombardy,
Bounded by the vaporous air,
Islanded by cities fair;
Underneath Day's azure eyes
Ocean's nursling, Venice lies,
A peopled labyrinth of walls,
Amphitrite's destined halls.'

Joe looked at Simon. 'Shelley again. Top man.'

'What's Amphitrite?' asked Simon.

'No idea,' said Joe. 'Nobody's ever asked. A woman wouldn't, you see. As long as a poem rhymes, it doesn't matter what it actually says. Here's another example,' he continued, warming to his theme. 'There's a painting by Munch called *Melancholy*. It's of this man sitting with his head in his hands on this beach, and in the background there are two other people hugging each other. Dark squirly skies. Pretty depressing stuff. Now, the sort of people who tend to hang around that painting are either angry students, or women who have just been dumped. Each needs a different approach.'

'Which is?'

'Well, for the students, I've just got this new thing. I'll walk up next to them and stare at the picture as intensely as they are, and say,

A hidden rage consumes my heart
As fuelled by years of wasted time
I close my eyes
And tense myself
And screaming
Throw myself in fury over the edge
And into your blood.'

Simon thought about this. 'Wow,' he said. 'Heavy stuff. Shelley again?'

Joe shook his head. 'The Cure. Works wonders. They just melt. *At last*, they think – a kindred spirit. Somebody else who *understands*. After that, it's easy.'

'So what,' asked Simon, unsure if he really wanted to hear the answer, 'do you do for the recently dumped?'

'Oh well, quite different, of course. There you need compassion, understanding, sympathy. So I usually try a bit of Emily Dickinson:

My life closed twice before its close;
It yet remains to see
If Immortality unveil
A third event to me,

So huge, so hopeless to conceive
As these that twice befell.
Parting is all we know of heaven,
And all we know of hell.

'That tends to get them going a bit, and then I go for the usual drink-round-the-corner routine. Recent dumpees are great, though, because they're either on the rebound and desperate for some love and attention, or they're on the look-out for a revenge fuck.'

'Revenge fuck?' said Simon, blinking.

'Sure. You know. Just to show whoever-he-was. And revenge fucks are usually brilliant, from a sex perspective. It's as if they're performing in front of an audience.'

Simon was silent as he contemplated this.

'So anyway, there you are,' said Joe. 'Why bother with the effort of chatting up people you might meet again when there is an endless source of available women wandering around London's art galleries? I've had a bit of success in front of Tintoretto, too, although they're exclusively history of art students. Nobody else bothers with Tintoretto nowadays.'

Simon stared at his visitor with appalled fascination.

There was a pause.

'I shouldn't have farted,' said Joe after a while. 'Sorry.'

Simon was caught off guard by the abrupt change of subject. 'Amazing the lengths some people will go to, to win a game of Twister,' he said.

Joe grinned. 'Well, I'm sorry, anyway,' he said.

'Apology accepted,' said Simon.

There was another pause. 'I'd better go,' said Joe. He stood up.

'Right. Thanks for coming. It was kind of you.'

Joe shifted awkwardly from one foot to the other. 'Least I could do, in the circs. And sorry again.'

'That's OK.'

There was a pause.

'Yeah, while we're at it, I guess I should apologize too for that story I told,' said Joe. 'About the, er, bath.'

'Forget it,' said Simon, not really meaning it.

The two men looked at each other for a few moments.

'Tell me,' said Joe. 'Where's the magic shop you work in?'

Simon named an address near Victoria Station.

'I know the area,' said Joe. 'Maybe I'll pop by.'

'That would be cool,' said Simon, slightly bemused.

'Right,' said Joe. 'Hope you feel better soon.'

'Thanks.'

'See you, then,' said Joe. He began to extend his hand towards Simon, but then thought better of the gesture and instead thrust it deep into his pocket, before turning and walking quickly out of the ward.

Simon settled back into his pillows. Well, he thought, that was a bit weird. He wondered whether Joe would ever bother to contact him again. He thought it was unlikely. Joe had come to see how Simon was and to apologize, and even that was probably more than Simon had a right to expect. He had seemed nice enough. A cynic when it came to women, of course, but otherwise all right. Despite his behaviour at the party, concluded Simon, Joe couldn't be all bad. Simon checked the grape bag to see if there were any loose grapes rolling around the bottom of the bag. There weren't. His wrist throbbed. He lay back and waited for something to happen.

Nothing did.

Later on that afternoon, Simon had his X-ray.

Soon afterwards, an attractive young doctor appeared by the side of the bed. 'Hello,' she said. 'My name's Dr

Gilbert. We've had a look at the X-ray, and the good news is that it's just a bad sprain.'

'Oh good,' said Simon. He was itching to ask exactly what had happened to his foot, but was too ashamed to ask.

'There's also some severe bruising around the big toe, and that's swollen quite badly as a result. But that should go down in a couple of days.'

'Right,' said Simon, who thought Dr Gilbert was rather pretty.

The doctor put her pen into the breast pocket of her white coat. 'The nurse will come along in a minute and bandage your foot up to keep it nice and firm. After that you'll be able to go.' She paused. 'You're going to need crutches,' she said. 'And I suggest you take things gently at first. They're not as easy to use as you'd imagine. If there's something to hit, you'll hit it.'

'Right,' said Simon again. He flashed Dr Gilbert his best smile. 'Thanks ever so much.'

'Not at all,' said Dr Gilbert. 'Come back in a week and we'll have a look and see how you're doing. And I suggest you keep away from coffee machines for a while.' She winked at him.

Simon stared back at her blankly. 'Er, thanks,' he said. 'I will.'

Dr Gilbert turned away from him and strode down the ward without a second glance. Simon watched her go, perplexed. Coffee machines? What was all that about?

* * *

A little while later Simon Teller stumbled into a taxi at the front entrance of the hospital, his inelegant embarkation surpassed only by an even more spectacular exit twenty minutes later, which left him sprawled on the pavement outside his flat, his new crutches splayed either side of him. Dr Gilbert had been right. The crutches would take some getting used to. Having his hand bandaged up made matters worse.

The taxi driver watched with amusement as Simon picked himself up and hobbled to the window to pay the fare.

'You ought to have "L" plates, mate,' said the driver jovially as he pocketed Simon's money. 'Do someone an injury, heh, heh.'

As Simon opened the door of his flat, relief washed over him. He was home at last. He stood in the hallway and cast his eyes fondly over familiar things. Immediately the pain in his foot seemed to subside a little. He went into the sitting room. Simon sat on his sofa and listened for signs of movement from the upstairs flat. There was silence. Simon wondered whether that meant that Angus and Fergus had gone out, or that they simply had not bothered to get up yet. He looked at his watch. It was six-thirty in the evening. The second explanation was more likely.

Simon saw he had a message on his answer machine. He hauled himself to the other end of the sofa and pressed the button.

'Hi, it's me. Just calling to see how things were, and to check that you're still coming round tonight. There's somebody here who has something she wants to show you. Anyway. Whether that's going to entice you to come or make you stay away, I don't know. Give me a ring. Speak to you later.'

Simon shut his eyes and groaned. Of course. It was Sunday.

THREE

For the past three years, Simon had gone to his sister Arabella's house one Sunday night a month.

Arabella was three years older than Simon. An early lack of affection for each other, due to the usual sibling jealousies, had subsequently been exacerbated by the on-set of prolonged adolescences. The tree of Arabella's teenage years had borne a particularly fruitful crop of loathings and petty rebellions. For eighteen months she said almost nothing to either of her parents or to Simon. Most of that time was spent in her bedroom, where she listened to loud music, sat in front of her mirror applying make-up, and smoked out of her window. From time to time she would swish dramatically down the stairs in a shapeless black shawl, barely recognisable beneath an improbable kaleidoscope of lurid make-up. She would eye her family in silence for a few moments, and then slam the door behind her without saying a word, leaving the rest of the family looking at each other in a bemused way.

Then, a few weeks after her seventeenth birthday, Bella met a boy who played rugby. Overnight she became a picture of femininity, a vision of pastels and pearls.

Simon's own adolescence was a less polished affair. He tried to cultivate an aura of affected loucheness, listening to Southern Death Cult records as he puffed on Sobranie Cocktails. He looked like the pimply love-child of Marc Bolan and Noel Coward.

After a while, though, Simon decided that another approach was needed. Realizing that adolescence was a once-in-a-lifetime opportunity, he did some research, and read *Catcher in the Rye*. The whole point, he saw, was that in order to do the whole teenage angst thing properly, you were supposed to feel alienated. That was the key. You were meant to be *different*.

In an attempt to irritate his father and create some measure of distance between himself and his friends, Simon raided his father's record collection to try and find something different to listen to. (Musical taste was, of course, the principal criterion by which Simon and his peers judged each other, with the possible exception of the pointiness of one's winkle-pickers.) At random he picked out an old Sidney Bechet LP, the unpromising words *Jazz Classics, Volume One* emblazoned down one side of the sleeve in large letters. On the cover was a picture of an old black man, leaning out of a window smoking a cigarette with a contemplative look on his face. Simon took the record back to his room.

Simon did not leave his room for three hours. When he did, it was to go back to his father's record collection to look for more Sidney Bechet. He had listened to the record four times over. Bechet's scorching soprano saxophone cut loose through the old jazz standards of New Orleans' hey-day, wailing and honking with a vibrant and fervent joy. Simon hardly moved except to spin the record from one side to the other. As he sat on his bed, transfixed by the music, he realized that something important was happening, something that would remain with him the rest of his life. As the ensemble floated through *Muskrat Ramble* for the third time, Simon Teller, dizzy with music, fell in love.

After that, everything changed. Simon gave his other records, festooned with skulls and inverted crosses, away. Instead he began to buy jazz records, and soon discovered the music's broad spectrum of colours, textures, and feelings. He started with the brittle modal jazz of Miles Davis, and then spiralled in all directions from the soft, melodic beauty of Bill Evans to the eclectic free jazz of Don Cherry, and the edgy, sophisticated jump of Count Basie.

The music was spell-binding, but Simon's fixation went further than that. He adored the stories, the legends, and the myths that surrounded the charismatic and enigmatic people who played jazz. Beguiled by the faded glamour, in his imagination he immersed himself in the smoky netherworld of jazz clubs, and the musicians who played there, men punctured by their own brilliance. Scenes played themselves out in Simon's mind in the grainy black-and-white of the effortlessly cool photographs of the period. The world he inhabited in his head was unattainable, forty years old and an ocean away. It was a world of flawed genius, dashed hopes, and the cataclysmic ravagings of drugs and self-destruction. It was a world of iconoclasts, dreamers and idealists. And it was his to frolic in as he wished.

Once the heavy chains of teenagerdom had been shaken off, Arabella went to Cambridge to read English, Simon to Bristol to read History. They did not see each other often. Finally both had gravitated to London, like errant moths to the brightest lightbulb. Arabella began a promising career at a small, independent publishing house in North London. Simon, who did not feel that he was quite ready for the responsibility of a proper job, drifted aimlessly between various enjoyable but poorly paid and short-lived careers. Cautiously, bridges between brother and sister began to be rebuilt. Trips were shared to their parents' home in Wiltshire. Invitations to dinner were issued, reciprocated, and enjoyed. After a year they discovered, to their surprise, that they liked each other.

Shortly afterwards, Arabella fell in love with a lawyer called Michael, and they were married the following spring.

Simon's parents stoically did their best to find the good things in Michael, for Arabella's sake, but there was little good to find. Family visits became tense affairs. Michael made no effort to be polite. He treated his new family with teeth-gritted disdain. Arabella and Michael's visits became less frequent, especially after the birth of their daughter, Sophy. When family reunions were unavoidable, Michael could be hostile towards Simon all day, but when pressed to remember specific incidents, Simon couldn't name one. It was the social equivalent of Chinese water torture. Any one individual act seemed innocuous, but cumulatively the effect was devastating. After a while it was decided by tacit agreement that it was easier to avoid each other completely than endure further unpleasantness.

As a result of Michael's behaviour, Simon had not seen Arabella for several months when the telephone had rung one Monday evening in late November, three years previously. It was the North Wiltshire police. There had been an accident.

His parents had been driving home from their weekly bridge club along the narrow hedgerow-lined lanes which latticed the countryside surrounding their village. A car had come too quickly in the opposite direction round a tight corner. The car's back wheels had lost traction. It had spun, and crashed into the side of his parents' car. All three people had been killed instantly. At the inquest, a dour-faced policeman announced that the driver of the speeding car had a blood alcohol content four and a half times in excess of the legal limit.

One drunk driver. That was how tenuous his parents' grip on life had been. His mother had taught English in a local school, and his father was an accountant who spent his spare time building model aeroplanes which he flew at displays on the weekends. They were kind, uncomplicated people. His father would always raise his six o'clock gin and tonic and seriously intone, 'The Fish of God' – his own translation of *Carpe Diem*, Seize the Day. He hadn't finished seizing his days. It was unbearably sad.

To Simon's surprise, his parents' estate had been significant. Despite his professed belief in living for today, Simon's father had been planning for tomorrow. Some prudent investments, a generous insurance policy, their large, mortgage-free family home – when the assets had been realized, there was enough for both Arabella and Simon to pay off their debts and live comfortably off the balance of capital.

The funeral had been terrible. The sympathetic and bewildered condolences of well-meaning friends and neighbours had had to be endured, the telling of interminable anecdotes borne with a polite smile. Throughout the sober-suited canapés after the service, Simon had fought the urge to escape. It was only when he returned to his empty flat at the end of the day that the accumulated grief of the past week finally burst forth. He stood in the middle of the flat that he had longed to escape to all afternoon, and suddenly saw that there *was* no escape. Your parents were not supposed to *die*. They were solidly dependable, a safety net of affection and reliability which had always hung reassuringly beneath Simon and his endeavours. Now the safety net was gone, and nothing was going to bring it back. Simon had wept long, hot tears that night.

Life, of course, went on, albeit in a faltering fashion. For weeks after the funeral, Simon's waking hours were tinged with a despairing sense of unreality. Only slowly did he come to terms with what had happened, the hollow permanence of his parents' absence. Then came the regrets, of the warm words left unspoken, the awkward emotions never expressed.

Finding themselves parentless so unexpectedly had thrown Simon and Arabella back together again. Bella of course had a family of her own, but she had welcomed him into it and slowly they had begun to reacquaint themselves. They established a comfortable ritual of Sunday night suppers; elbows on the table, homely food and warm talk. Their evenings together had become a source of deep comfort to them both.

* * *

Simon looked around his sitting room. The floor was strewn with old record covers, the colourful designs of the Blue Note and Columbia labels migrating in all directions from the record player. Simon had resolutely refused to succumb to the compact disc revolution. There was a magic about sliding the black slabs of vinyl from their musty cardboard sleeves which the clinical silver discs could never replicate. Jazz was about feeling, a sensuous experience which was more than just the sound coming out of the speakers. The cover art, the smell of old cardboard, the anticipatory crackle as the stylus settled into place before the music began – these were all integral parts of the experience. Simon's collection of second-hand records was carefully arranged in alphabetical order, from Albert Ayler to Joe Zawinul. It was to the dust-covered comfort of these records that he retreated when he needed to escape.

The sitting room was dominated by a large sofa, which sat in front of a small television. There were two rattan wastepaper baskets, in opposite corners of the room. They were both overflowing. A Thelonious Monk poster hung on the wall behind the sofa. Over the television was a photograph of a young Chet Baker, his trumpet hanging disconsolately at his side as he moodily contemplated whatever story was unfolding behind the camera.

Usually Simon derived comfort from his flat's messy homeliness (his expression), but that evening he felt a rising sense of claustrophobia as he surveyed the chaos (a more accurate description, possibly) surrounding him. Going to see Arabella in Battersea would be a pain on crutches, but it would be better than hobbling around the flat all evening until it was time to flop into bed.

Simon decided he couldn't face the prospect of London Transport just yet. He pulled on his coat, gathered his crutches, and went back outside to find another taxi.

Half an hour later Simon stood outside the front door of Arabella's house on one of the more fashionable streets running off the north side of Clapham Common. He pressed the doorbell. Immediately there was a chorus of shrieks and barking, the sound of things falling over and footsteps hurtling towards the door. Simon braced himself.

The door opened, and a flash of brown shot past Simon into the front garden.

'Daniel!' shouted Arabella. 'Come back here, you little sod.'

'Hello,' said Simon.

'Hello. What happened to you?' asked Arabella, looking Simon up and down.

'Long story,' said Simon. He raised his bandaged hand a couple of inches. 'I got this because a man farted in my face.'

Arabella regarded her brother evenly. 'Must have been some fart,' she said. 'What about your foot?'

'As for that . . . actually, I don't know,' Simon confessed. 'Nobody at the hospital would tell me.'

Arabella sighed. 'Oh dear,' she said. 'You'd better come in. Does it hurt? How long are you going to have to use those things for? Did you know the guy who farted? Are you insured? I assume you went private. How much does it cost to get that sort of thing done on private health, anyway? Sophy, darling, go and get Daniel, would you, before he tears the whole garden up.'

Simon knew better than to try and answer any of his

sister's questions. If she actually wanted an answer to any of them she would ask again later. He kissed the cheek that Arabella offered, and then bent down towards the small girl who stood next to her.

'Hi, pops,' he said.

'Hello Simon,' said Sophy. 'Are you all right?'

'Bit sore, but apart from that I'm OK.'

'Was it a really nasty one?' asked Sophy.

'What?'

'The fart,' said Sophy.

'Oh. Yes, I suppose it was pretty nasty.'

Sophy thought for a moment. 'Was it eggy?' she asked.

'Sophy,' said Arabella sharply. 'That's quite enough, thank you.'

Sophy pulled a face. 'Just asking,' she said.

'How are you, anyway?' asked Simon. 'Mum behaving herself?'

'She's been all right,' replied Sophy.

'Gee, thanks,' said Arabella to her daughter. 'Right, then. Sophy, you fetch Daniel. Simon, you come in and have a drink and talk to me while I check the moussaka.'

Sophy set off down the steps to look for the dog. Simon followed his sister into the house. In the kitchen Arabella opened the fridge and extracted a bottle of beer.

'So when did this happen?' asked Arabella as she rummaged through a drawer for a bottle opener.

'Last night,' replied Simon. 'I went to a dinner party in the upstairs flat.'

'And how did this man farting cause you to do that to your wrist? I'm intrigued.'

Simon explained what had happened the previous evening.

'Twister,' mused Arabella when he had finished. 'Wow. Remind me how old you are again?'

Before Simon could respond Sophy ran into the kitchen, followed by a springer spaniel, who hurtled into the room and performed a quick tour of everyone's ankles before settling down on a faded square of carpet in the corner of the room.

'Everything all right?' asked Arabella.

'I think so,' said Sophy.

'Is Daniel still trying to escape?' asked Simon.

Arabella was crouching down to inspect the contents of the oven. 'Yes, the ungrateful beast. I can't understand it. Anyone would think we never fed him.'

Daniel looked up and thumped his tail happily against the floor. Daniel the Spaniel. Possibly, thought Simon, the stupidest dog in London.

'Where are the cats?' he asked.

'Oh, off tormenting some of the other dogs in the neighbourhood,' replied Arabella. Her domestic menagerie also included Botticelli and Pissarro, two beautiful Persian cats of uncommon intelligence, elegant creatures who regarded the rest of the animal kingdom, humans included, with an aloof disdain. Whenever they were bored they would tease Daniel mercilessly. Daniel was too good-natured and too stupid to keep the cats amused for long, though, and so in the evenings they would go on forays to find other unsuspecting canine victims. When Sophy was younger she had been unable to pronounce the cats' exotic foreign names, and these had gradually transmogrified into 'Botty' and 'Pissy' – names which were finally adopted by the whole family, to the cats' obvious chagrin.

'Can I go and practise?' asked Sophy.

'Of course,' said her mother. 'I'll call you when supper's ready.' Sophy ran out of the kitchen and up the stairs.

'Practise?' asked Simon once Sophy had gone.

'She's got a new trick for you.'

'Oh. Right.'

'She's been working on it very hard,' said Bella. 'Keeps her occupied. That and looking after Thorald.'

Simon frowned. 'Who's Thorald?'

'Her new pet. He's a woodlouse.' Seeing her brother's blank look, Bella explained further. 'Sophy wanted a pet of her own. So we got her a woodlouse. He lives in a jar in her bedroom.'

'OK,' said Simon uncertainly.

'Problem is, these woodlouses – or is woodlice? – keep dying. Well, to be fair, Sophy killed the first one all by herself. She thought he might be thirsty, and so she tipped a cupful of water into the bottom of the jar. Result – one drowned woodlouse.'

'Oops,' said Simon.

'Quite. So anyway, each time one dies we have to find another one and then we substitute the old dead Thorald for a new, alive version while she's asleep.'

'And she has no idea about this?'

'Not a clue.'

Brother and sister sat in companionable silence for a few moments. Arabella poured herself a glass of wine from an open bottle that sat on the kitchen table.

Finally Simon said, 'No Michael?'

'No,' said Arabella. 'No Michael.'

'Where is he?'

'Working. As usual. He said he'd try and get back for eight, but didn't sound too hopeful. So don't hold your breath.'

Simon wouldn't. He knew how much time Michael spent at the office. During the week, he rarely returned home much before nine or ten o'clock in the evening, and invariably had to work on one, if not both, days of the weekend. Simon knew that lawyers, particularly rich and successful ones, *did* work extremely long hours, but he couldn't believe that Michael could possibly spend all that time at the office. He had a theory – partly engendered, he couldn't deny, by the mutual antipathy that the two men had for each other – that Michael spent at least some of his time away from home not working, but having affairs.

Simon couldn't point to anything that proved that his hypothesis might have even the remotest grounding in fact, but that of course had been no bar to its development from vague suspicion to entrenched and ardent belief. Simon was convinced that Michael was a slimy, low-life lothario. In such circumstances, the absence of evidence was irrelevant. Simon didn't *need* evidence. He had the courage of his convictions.

Simon had never mentioned his suspicions to his sister. She seemed to have resigned herself to the fact that Michael was never there, and always working. Simon, though, was biding his time, waiting to uncover proof that he had been right all along.

'So, anyway,' said Bella, happily unaware of Simon's dark thoughts. 'Apart from your escapades playing Twister, what else have you been up to? What's new in your world?'

Simon thought. 'Very little to report, really,' he said.

Bella looked at him thoughtfully. 'As bad as that?'

Simon shrugged. 'Afraid so. I actually met a beautiful girl at dinner last night, but got farted at before I had a chance to get her number.' He thought about Joe's theory that there was no shame in trying to chat people up at parties. It was an attractive theory, but Simon was not convinced. Even on those rare occasions in the past when he had succeeded in securing a telephone number or a promise of another rendezvous, there had always been another excuse made – the loan of a book, a professed shared interest in a particular playwright, the usual nonsense that gets peddled at parties. The idea of an honest approach – Look, can I see you again? I think you're gorgeous – filled Simon with apprehension. He respected women, yes, but not to the extent of telling them the truth.

'Well,' said Bella. 'I have a question for you. More of a favour, really.'

'OK,' said Simon, trying not to feel put out at the ease with which they had glossed over his romantic difficulties. 'Fire away.'

'It's Sophy's birthday soon.'

'I know,' said Simon. There was a pause. 'Oh no,' he said.

'*Please.*' Bella looked at him imploringly.

Simon shook his head. 'I'm sorry, Bella, but no way.'

'Go on. Just this once.'

'But you know I *don't*. Ever. No exceptions.'

'But it would make her day. She definitely wants a magician at the party, and it would be so much better if it were you. She adores you. She'll never forget it.'

'Look, I'd love to, really I would.'

Bella sat back in her chair. 'Then do it.'

Simon's shoulders slumped. 'I can't.'

Simon loved performing magic tricks. He relished the look of bewilderment on the watcher's face as the miracle was revealed. Unfortunately, however, he turned into a petrified zombie if he had to perform in front of more than three people. Audiences terrified him.

Audience-phobic magicians were, for obvious reasons, unlikely to make much of an impact professionally. Magicians are performers, after all. They cannot operate in a vacuum. Taking the audience out of the equation was rather like being a doctor who hated being around sick people. You became somewhat redundant. This was why Simon worked in a magic shop: it gave him the opportunity to be paid for doing tricks all day without having to undergo the gruesome ordeal of standing up in front of a crowd of strangers.

Bella was asking him to perform in front of perhaps the most demanding audience of all – a crowd of over-excited children at a birthday party. Simon shuddered. He had customers who made a living out of it. They were embittered, ferocious men, whose cheery professional personae hid the fact that the last vestiges of sympathetic character had long ago been eradicated by over-exposure to squealing, fractious children. It was, without question, the hardest job in show business.

'I'm sorry, Bella,' said Simon. 'I can't. You know it's not that I don't want to. I just – can't.'

'What if I told you that I'd already told Sophy that you'll do it?'

'You'd never do that,' said Simon sharply.

Bella shrugged. 'Oops. Sorry.'

Simon sighed. 'For Christ's sake, Bella. That is so unworthy of you.'

'I know,' agreed Bella, without any apparent remorse.

'God.' Just when the weekend couldn't get any worse, it suddenly did.

There was a pause.

'So you'll do it?' asked Bella.

'I'll do it,' sighed Simon. 'I don't see that I have very much choice, do I?'

'Good boy,' said Bella, stretching over the kitchen table and planting a kiss on the side of his head.

The oven pinged. Bella got up and went to the kitchen door. She shouted up the stairs, 'Sophy! Come down, please, once you've washed your hands.' There was an immediate rush of small footsteps, and a few moments later Sophy tore breathlessly into the kitchen.

'How did the practice go?' asked Simon, trying to forget about the weaselly trick Bella had just played.

'Really well,' said Sophy. 'I can't wait to show you.'

'Well, I can't wait to see it,' replied Simon.

Sophy grinned at him. She turned to her mother. 'Where's Daddy?'

Arabella was pulling the moussaka out of the oven. 'He said he was going to be a bit late tonight, darling,' she said as she carried the dish to the table. 'He's very busy at work at the moment.'

'He's *always* busy at work,' complained Sophy.

'Well, you've got Simon instead,' said her mother, as she began spooning the food on to plates.

Sophy looked at Simon. 'Well Simon's very nice, so that's good,' she said kindly. 'You're more interested in magic than Daddy, anyway,' she added.

'Well, not everyone understands the importance of magic,' said Simon. 'It's a craft.' As he said this he realized that with his hand in plaster eating was not going to be easy. He picked up his fork in his left hand, and carefully speared a slice of aubergine.

Arabella noticed the problem. 'Are you going to be all right with that?' she asked. 'Do you want me to cut it up for you?'

Sophy giggled. 'Like a baby,' she observed.

'*Thank* you, Sophy,' said Arabella.

'Or a very old person,' said Sophy.

'*Sophy*.'

'Er, yes please,' said Simon. 'That would be great.'

'Right.' Arabella briskly took Simon's plate away and began chopping the food into manageable, bite-sized pieces, ignoring Sophy's sniggers.

Arabella's chopping made it easier to execute the short journey from plate to mouth, but still a certain amount of moussaka flew off Simon's fork. By the end of the meal a small pile of mince, cheese, and assorted vegetables had amassed in his lap.

While they ate the conversation centred around Sophy and what she had been doing at school, who her best friends were this week, and what she wanted to do during the forthcoming holidays, at the mention of which Arabella went slightly pale. She seemed distracted, half an ear turned to listen for the twist of Michael's key in the lock. By the time they cleared away the dishes, Michael had still not appeared.

As Bella came back to the table with two coffee mugs and a cafetiere, Sophy looked at her expectantly.

'Can I do it now?' she whispered.

Bella sighed. 'Go on, then.'

Sophy slithered off her chair and was gone in a lightning movement. Daniel the Spaniel lazily got up and padded off to see where she had gone. Simon and his sister were alone again.

'Thanks for doing this,' said Arabella. 'You're very patient with her.'

'Not at all,' shrugged Simon. 'I enjoy it. *She* helps *me* sometimes, when my enthusiasm for the wonderful art of prestidigitation wanes a little.'

Bella poured the coffee. 'Well, I still say you're very kind.'

'I would have said the same about you until you pulled that stunt about her party,' said Simon.

Sophy ran back into the kitchen. She carried with her a glass and a pack of cards. She looked at her mother. 'Can I use milk this time?' she asked.

Bella nodded. 'You can this time, as it's Simon, as long as you promise to drink it afterwards.'

Sophy nodded.

'All right, then. In the fridge.'

Sophy turned and went to the fridge, pulled a carton of milk from inside the door, and returned to the table.

'This trick,' she announced, 'is magic.'

'OK,' said Simon. 'Good start.'

Sophy picked up the pack of cards and tried to spread

them into a fan as best as her tiny hands would allow. 'First of all,' she said, oddly formal, 'please choose a completely ordinary playing card from this completely ordinary pack.'

Simon took a card.

'Thank you,' said Sophy. There was a pause.

'Shall I look at it?' prompted Simon.

'If you like,' replied Sophy.

'I will, then,' said Simon, and glanced at the card he had chosen. It was three of diamonds. He held the card to his chest.

'Now give the card to me,' said Sophy, who had put the rest of the pack back down on the table.

'What,' said Simon, 'just like that? On its own?'

Sophy nodded. With a shrug, Simon handed it over. Sophy took the card and turned it over. Hang on, Simon wanted to say, that's cheating. Instead he asked, rather petulantly, 'Now what?'

'And now, the miracle,' announced Sophy. She opened the carton of milk and poured milk into the glass until it was full to the brim. Simon realized which trick she was going to do. He relaxed.

'As you can see, I have poured this completely ordinary milk into this completely ordinary glass,' explained Sophy.

'Indeed,' said Simon.

'Now, I shall take this completely ordinary playing card that you have chosen and place it over the glass of milk.' Sophy carefully slid the card over the rim of the glass so that it covered the mouth of the glass completely. As she did so her tongue stuck slightly out of the corner of her mouth in concentration. Simon waited. Sophy moved around the table next to where he sat. 'Now watch very carefully,' she said. She placed one hand over the playing card, and turned the glass upside down. The milk stayed in the glass, kept there by the pressure of the card which Sophy was still holding in place. Simon applauded as best as he could with one hand.

'*Amazing*,' he said.

'Hang on,' said Sophy, edging a little closer, her eyes fixed firmly on the glass. 'Do you want to see something *really* amazing?'

'More amazing than that?' asked Simon, who knew what was coming next.

Sophy nodded.

'Go on then,' said Simon.

Very slowly, Sophy took her hand away from beneath the playing card. The card, and the milk, stayed where they were, apparently defying the laws of gravity.

Thank God, thought Simon, and said, '*Wow*.'

Sophy beamed. 'Do you like it?' she asked.

'Like it?' said Simon. 'It's the most extraordinary thing I've ever seen. You're a genius. Superb.'

Sophy smiled and took a step towards him. 'Thank –' she began. Before she could go any further, her movement disrupted the finely-balanced principles of physics that the trick relied upon, and the card fell away from the mouth of the glass, swiftly followed by the milk itself, most of which landed on Simon's lap.

'*Sophy*!' cried Arabella. She moved quickly to fetch a roll of kitchen paper. Seconds later the mopping up process had begun.

'Sorry,' said Sophy, who was still clutching the empty upside-down glass.

'Are you all right, Simon?' asked Arabella.

'A bit wet, but I'll live.' The milk had begun to seep through the material of his trousers, which were now cold and clammy against his skin.

Arabella groaned. 'I'm sorry. I should have made her be more careful. Sophy, say sorry to Simon.'

'I just did,' Sophy pointed out.

'Then say it *again*.'

'Sorry, Simon,' said Sophy.

Simon smiled grimly. 'That's all right, Soph. It was still a good trick.'

Arabella was joined under the table by Daniel the Spaniel who began to lap up the remaining milk with his over-sized tongue. When he had finished he lifted his nose into the air, and, smelling more milk, unceremoniously put his snout into Simon's groin and began licking again.

Simon pushed Daniel away as quickly as he could, and put his bandaged arm down to shield his groin from further canine investigation. Some weekend, he thought. It began with the promise of new social frontiers being conquered. It ended fending off offers of oral sex from a mentally retarded household pet.

Arabella sat back down at the table, the clean-up completed. 'Sorry about that,' she said.

Simon shrugged. 'Don't worry.' He looked at his watch. He was feeling tired, and wanted to take his trousers off. 'I'd better go,' he said.

Arabella looked at him sadly. 'All right,' she said.

'Thanks for dinner.'

'You're very welcome. Sorry Michael didn't make it.'

'Oh God, don't worry,' said Simon. Secretly, he

was pleased. He stood up stiffly, leaning against the table.

Arabella handed him his crutches. 'There you go,' she said. 'I'd offer to drive you home but Michael has the car today.'

Simon shrugged. 'I can find a taxi. It'll be quick at this time of night.'

'Back soon?' asked Arabella.

Simon nodded. 'Yes please.' He bent down to his niece. 'See you then, sweet pea.' He kissed the top of her head.

'All right,' said Sophy.

'Bye then,' said Simon. As he opened the door, Michael was walking up the steps.

'Well,' said Michael dryly. 'It's Merlin the Magician. What a nice surprise.'

'Merlin was a wizard, actually,' said Simon.

'*Merlin was a wizard, actually*,' minced Michael. 'I do apologize. How ignorant of me.'

'Hard day at the office?' asked Simon pointedly.

Michael looked at him suspiciously. 'Very,' he replied. He pointed at Simon's crutches. 'Oh dear,' he said. 'Had an accident?'

'Sort of,' said Simon cautiously.

'Sorry to hear that,' said Michael, who didn't sound sorry in the slightest. 'Were you just going?'

'I, er, yes,' said Simon, resisting the urge to clobber Michael over the head with one of his crutches.

'Excellent. Well, goodbye, then.' Michael turned to go into the house. With an apologetic wave, Arabella followed him inside.

Simon stood on the porch, alone. For a few moments

he remained there, staring unseeing at the darkening sky. He felt robbed, the intimacy and comfort of his Sunday evening violated by Michael's brief but brutish intrusion.

Finally a blaring honk from an irate motorist further down the road woke Simon from his dream. He hobbled off to find a taxi.

FOUR

Ah, Mondays.

Mondays mean different things to different people, but one thing that you can generally be sure of is that, whatever that meaning is, it is bound to be *bad*.

For Simon Teller, Mondays meant, amongst other bad things, long queues at the tube station. There was an almost tangible excitement on Monday mornings at Highbury and Islington station as the crowds of commuters waited in line for their weekly travel passes. Frustration and impatience simmered beneath the surface of their bland, just awake faces. One day somebody was going to crack, pull out a semi-automatic machine gun, and mow down the queues of waiting people. It was just a matter of time. In order to add a little spice to proceedings, on Monday mornings London Underground made sure to employ only their slowest and most unhelpful ticket sellers. The atmosphere of chaotic inefficiency contributed richly to the start of everyone's week.

Simon arrived at the station at the usual time. He had not had a good start to the day. With his right hand bandaged up, he had had to shave with his left hand, and the operation had not been a success. When he had finished there were still several tufty outposts sprouting from peculiar places around his jaw, and his face was dappled with dark red pinpricks of blood. As a result, his face was now festooned with small squares of damp tissue.

His foot had also been itching terribly, and when he tried to get dressed (itself a complicated process with only one hand available) he discovered that the trousers he had worn the previous day were the only ones he owned which could accommodate his newly enlarged foot. The trousers were, however, unwearable: the remnants of Arabella's moussaka and Sophy's disastrous milk trick had dried into a brittle crust. Five minutes' scrubbing established only that scrubbing was not going to help, and created an ominous dark patch over Simon's groin. Trying not to think about it too much, Simon had pulled them on anyway and set off cautiously for the station.

The line for the ticket machine seemed even longer than usual. Simon shifted uncomfortably on his crutches. After a few moments, when there appeared to be no movement in the queue, he peered to see what was going on.

His heart sank. The queue was full of Novice Tubists.

Uninitiated users of the London Underground system were the bane of every Londoner's life. Everything they did seemed designed to irritate their fellow passengers as much as possible. They stood on the left hand side of the escalators rather than on the right, creating chaos and congestion behind them. Coming up behind these people on the escalators, of course, Londoners never said anything. Instead they would just begin to sigh loudly. The second loudest noise on the Underground system after the sound of the trains shuttling in and out of stations was the sound of disgruntled Londoners sighing at people on escalators.

There was also a painful routine which every Novice Tubist would follow when they stood in front of the automatic ticket machine:

1. Look at ticket machine for several moments as if it is quite unlike anything you have ever seen before.
2. Scan the machine desperately for a clue as to where to begin. Above all, avoid eye contact with the small digital display which is patiently suggesting that first of all you should select your ticket type.
3. Finally decide, after about a minute and a half, to select your ticket type.
4. Engage in lengthy conversation about what sort of ticket type you require with your travelling companion.
5. Press ticket type you require.
6. Wait patiently in front of machine. Ignore sighs coming from the growing queue behind you.
7. Realize that you must then select destination. Look at machine in confusion, before realizing that the names are conveniently listed in alphabetical order.
8. Engage in lengthy conversation about what destination you require with your travelling companion.

9. Press appropriate destination button.

10. Realize that, as this is a commercial transaction, money must be tendered before the required ticket will be issued. Peer at screen and read how much is needed.

11. Frown.

12. Point at screen and ask your travelling companion whether that figure can *possibly* be right.

13. Assured that it is indeed correct, begin to look for purse or wallet, shaking head and muttering quietly to yourself.

14. Spend several minutes locating your purse/wallet.

15. Finally extract purse/wallet, during which time the machine has got bored of waiting and has reverted to 'Select Ticket type' position.

16. Fail to realize this.

17. Insert money. When nothing happens, after another lengthy consultation with your travelling companion, go back to Step 2.

18. Finally secure your ticket. Stand aside whilst your travelling companion begins at Step 1.

After twenty minutes or so, Simon finally got to the front of the queue. He had the exact change ready, and moved off smoothly after a few seconds, ticket in hand, half hoping for an appreciative round of applause from the passengers behind him. None came.

His journey down to the platform was less smooth, however. Simon had never attempted to use public transport on crutches before, and the ticket barriers, escalators and sheer weight of people all conspired to make it a dispiriting experience. As he hobbled forwards, he was aware that the usual flow of humanity was being hampered by his lumbering progress. To his humiliation he heard a chorus of sighs start up behind him, as ominous to him as a tribe of African huntsmen ululating before a kill. Simon's face reddened with shame. He tried to move a little faster, and in doing so almost scythed down an old lady who was going even more slowly than he was.

Simon reached the platform just as a train was pulling out. He watched it go with mounting despair. The platform was still full of people, and the next train, announced the electric notice board, was not due to arrive for another six minutes. Simon looked worriedly at his watch. He was going to be late.

By the time the next train arrived, the platform was dangerously full. As the train doors opened, the waiting crowd shuffled forwards, poised for action. When the thin line of disembarking passengers had trickled dry, there was a sudden flurry of movement as everyone tried to climb on board at once. Simon was caught somewhere near the back of the throng, but with some judicious prodding with the ends of his crutches he managed to cajole the people immediately in front of him further into the carriage, leaving him just enough room to push himself in before the doors closed behind him.

Simon stood with his face pressed into a man's back. His left cheek rubbed uncomfortably against the fabric of the man's suit. The crutches poked painfully into his armpits. He twisted his neck as best he could and looked around. Next to him stood a man wearing dark glasses, who wore an over-sized pair of headphones and was nodding vigorously. It sounded as if he was linked up to a particularly noisy fax machine. In the nearest available seat sat a tired-looking woman dressed in washed-out leggings and a shrunken T-shirt which advertised her well-advanced pregnancy. The words 'I'm with this Prat' were emblazoned over her chest above a large arrow which pointed at her neighbour, a gumless old woman who was clinging on to a wicker shopping trolley, which she moved occasionally so that its corners prodded into the buttocks of the unfortunate commuters standing immediately in front of her, keeping them at bay.

At King's Cross, a lot of people got out. Simon's immobility made it difficult for him to avoid the oncoming rush of passengers as they poured off the train, and he nearly went down like a skittle under the onslaught.

When the train finally reached Victoria twenty minutes later, Simon positioned himself near the doors, and when they opened he allowed himself to be swept along in the maelstrom of human movement which surged towards the exit. He was jostled and shoved along the platform, prodded and pushed up the escalator, and was only finally left alone once he had struggled through the automatic ticket barrier, where he collapsed on to his crutches, exhausted. The other passengers streamed past him, up the stairs and into the new London morning.

After a few minutes a man in a guard's uniform approached him.

'You can't stop there,' said the guard.

'Don't worry,' said Simon. 'I'm just getting my breath back.'

'All the same,' said the guard, 'you can't stop there.'

Simon looked up at the man, breathing heavily as he did so. 'I'll only be a couple of minutes,' he said. He gestured towards his crutches. 'I've been having a bit of trouble with these things.'

The guard looked at the crutches, unimpressed. 'I dare say,' he replied. 'But you can't stop there.'

Simon looked at the guard in irritation. 'Why on earth not?' he asked.

'You're blocking the thoroughfare, see,' answered the guard. 'Interrupting the flow of passengers.'

'For Christ's sake,' said Simon, 'can't you see I'm on crutches? Give me a break.'

'Whatever,' observed the guard philosophically. 'You're still going to have to move.'

'Anyway,' said Simon, 'what flow of passengers? I'm well out of the way.' He gestured towards the seething mass of grim-faced commuters who were swarming through the ticket machines. Simon had positioned himself to one side of the stampede.

'Look,' said the guard. 'Rules are rules. You're technically blocking a potential thoroughfare for passengers, right? And if you don't move, pronto, I'll have you arrested.'

'Arrested?' cried Simon. 'What for? Being a cripple?'

'Being a cripple in a potential thoroughfare for passengers,' elaborated the guard.

'Oh, for God's sake,' muttered Simon, and swivelled on his heel to go, just before remembering that his foot was bandaged up and therefore not best equipped for swivelling.

'Are you all right?' asked the guard a few moments later, as he bent down to help Simon up.

'Fine, thanks,' muttered Simon. He grabbed his crutches. 'Right. I'll go. Thanks *so* much for all your help.' He glared at the guard.

'Quite all right,' said the guard. 'Mind how you go on those things.' The guard nodded casually at Simon's crutches before sauntering off into the melee of human bodies. Just before he was lost from view, he turned and called, 'And if you're still there in two minutes, I'll call the Transport Police, OK?' and gave a big thumbs-up sign.

Seething with self-righteous indignation, Simon arranged himself carefully on his crutches, and headed for the station stairs and the waiting summer sunshine.

As Simon made his faltering way towards the shop, a man leaned against a wall, watching him approach. When Simon came level with him, the man whipped a magazine out from behind his back.

'*Big Issue*, sir?' asked the man gruffly.

'Do me a favour, Bob,' said Simon. 'Not today, all right? I'm late.'

'Aw, come on, Simon,' said the man. 'I can always rely on you. And things have been slow over the weekend.'

Simon sighed. 'God. All right. Hang on.' He leaned his

crutches against the wall, and, balancing on his good foot, delved into his pocket with his good hand.

'What happened to you, then?' asked the man as he watched.

'Don't ask,' replied Simon. 'I got farted at, as a result of which I fell over and hurt myself.' He handed over a pound coin.

'That's disgusting,' said the man, giving Simon a copy of the *Big Issue*. 'You should sue. You have rights.'

'What, the right not to be farted at?'

'Yeah, something like that. You never know. You might get damages.'

Simon looked at Bob with exasperation. Bob had been selling the *Big Issue* on that particular spot for about a year now, and early on in his tenure he had spotted Simon for the easy sell that he was. Bob's aggressive selling technique and shameless guilt-mongering had resulted in Simon being corralled into buying a copy of the magazine every day, despite the fact that new issues only came out once a week.

In addition to being an extremely effective salesman, Bob was also a devout Buddhist, or at least he claimed to be. His grasp of the religion was vague, to say the least, and Simon often got the feeling that he was making stuff up as he went along, mixing a smattering of the real thing with hippy mantras and anything else that popped into his head. Somewhat incongruously, Bob also possessed a ruthless materialist streak. His devotion to hard cash seemed to sit ill with his professed religious beliefs. Simon noticed that Bob was wearing a pair of extremely well-made and expensive shoes. He didn't smoke and, being a Buddhist, never drank (he had once explained that drinking was in direct contravention of a holy edict issued by the Prophet Bud, which was ironic given that Bud had had a beer named after him).

'I'm not really sure if I'd win any damages,' said Simon.

'You never know,' said Bob.

'I'm not that badly hurt, anyway,' said Simon.

'But it's got to be worth a go, hasn't it?' persisted Bob. 'I mean, you're hobbling round on them bloody things.' He pointed at the crutches. 'That's got to be worth a bit of moolah, surely?'

Simon shrugged.

Bob held up a finger. 'The Prophet says: "Catch each stone flung at you along the road of life, for you never know when you may need those stones to build a wall."'

Simon frowned. 'Are you sure about that?' he asked.

Bob looked affronted. 'Absolutely. And building walls is the path to enlightenment.'

Simon tried to hide his scepticism about this unlikely and arguably confusing dictum – it would be disastrous, after all, if you unwittingly built the wall *across* the path to enlightenment. He looked at his watch. He needed to get to work. He was already late.

'I have to go,' he said.

'Fair enough,' said Bob. 'Stay well. Preserve your karma.' He made a peace sign.

'Er, thanks. Preserve yours, too.' Tucking his *Big Issue* into his trouser pocket, Simon hobbled off.

A few minutes later, Simon arrived in front of a shabby-looking shop. Large yellow letters proclaimed 'STATION

MAG C' above the front door. In the middle of the window display, a toy rabbit flopped forlornly over the rim of a battered top hat. It was surrounded by wilting plumes of fake flowers, and tubes and boxes covered in metallic glitter. There were old black and white photographs of men in dinner suits chopping limbs off smiling, bikini-clad girls. The display had not changed for years, and it showed. Simon pushed the door open and went inside. Behind the glass counter stood Brian Station, the shop's owner. He was a short man with badly dyed hair. He wore a bright and rather horrible waistcoat.

'You're late,' he said as Simon shut the door.

'Hello, Brian,' said Simon. 'Sorry.'

'What the fuck happened to you?' asked Brian, as he looked at Simon's bandages and crutches. 'You look a mess.'

'Slight accident over the weekend,' explained Simon, who really didn't want to have to explain the whole story again, particularly not to Brian, who he knew would be less than sympathetic.

Brian regarded Simon critically. He pointed at the bandage on Simon's hand. 'How the fuck are you going to be able to do anything with that bloody thing wrapped around your hand?' he demanded. 'You'll be no use at all.'

Simon hadn't thought about this. Brian was right: with his hand bound up he would be unable to demonstrate any tricks. 'You're right,' he said.

'Of course I'm bloody right,' said Brian. 'I'm always bloody right. Someone has to be.' He looked resentfully at Simon, as if he suspected that he had done this on purpose. 'Fuck,' he said, after some moments' thought.

'I could just do the stock room stuff and accounts,' said Simon.

'But that means *I'll* have to work in the shop,' said Brian.

It had always struck Simon as odd that for someone who owned a magic shop, Brian hated to sell tricks. The problem was, on a more profound level, that Brian hated anything that involved contact with other people. He was the most misanthropic person Simon had ever met. It was possible, in view of this, that a career in the entertainment industry might have been ill-advised, but it was all a bit late now.

Brian was at least democratic about his dislike of his fellow men. He was hateful to everyone. Simon had long ago learned to speak to him only when strictly necessary, and never to dispute anything he said. Anybody who dared to enter into the argumentative fray with Brian always lost. An argument is a series of structured consequential statements or propositions leading to a logical conclusion, not a flat denial followed by a torrent of foul-mouthed and unanswerable abuse. On that analysis there were no arguments to win, only dignity to lose.

Things were worst during the summer months. Throughout the day the shop thronged with tourists, who paid no attention to the exotic magic effects which were on show in the display cases, but instead went straight for Brian's impressive collection of fake breasts, stink bombs, and plastic spirals of dog shit. Business was good, but Brian resented being little more than a glorified joke shop, and this did little to improve his temper.

'Dean!' Brian shouted.

There was the sound of heavy footsteps approaching.

Finally a short, rather fat man with red hair appeared from the back of the shop. He wore a T-shirt with a dragon on it and a dirty pair of jeans. 'Yeah?' said Dean.

'Evel Knievel here has buggered up his hand,' explained Brian, pointing at Simon, 'so you and me are going to have to work extra hard today.'

Dean shrugged. 'OK,' he said.

'And the next day,' added Brian.

'OK.' Dean looked at Brian and Simon affably. There was a pause. Brian snorted in irritation. Dean annoyed Brian hugely. He meandered through life without worrying about other people very much. He lived in his own world, which, as far as Simon could tell, consisted principally of thrash heavy metal bands and billiard balls. Dean could perform acts of dexterity with his podgy hands that defied belief. He was a prodigiously gifted manipulator, a talent born through hard graft and the unshakeable belief that he never wanted to do anything else. Dean's favourite items to manipulate were billiard balls. Once he had shyly shown Simon his collection. Some were made of wood, some of marble, some of ivory. Simon remembered staring at this extraordinary array, lost for words. It stood as testimony to the all-embracing intensity of Dean's obsession. Ever since, Simon had felt an affinity with him: here was another man with a fixation which left him dislocated and detached from the ordinariness of modern life. Simon sought sanctuary in his jazz records, Dean in his beloved red balls. It was essentially the same escape route.

Dean's ability to make things appear and vanish with his bare hands did not, unfortunately for him, correspond with his ability to interact socially with other people. His astonishing manipulative gifts were balanced by an apparently complete absence of charisma, personality, or luck, and this was why he was working in a magic shop near Victoria Station rather than playing to glittering audiences in Las Vegas, which was what his extraordinary talent probably deserved.

Dean had accepted his lot without rancour. He got on with his own life without bothering others too much, and he expected others to do the same to him. Brian, however, was reluctant to do this. Jealous of Dean's ability, Brian tormented him mercilessly. The more Dean failed to respond, the harder Brian tried to provoke a reaction.

Brian was now in full flow.

'Well,' he said. 'Sure you don't mind working on the shop floor all day while Hop-Along here dosses about doing nothing?'

'Nah,' said Dean equably. 'S'all right.'

'Well I bloody mind,' said Brian.

'I won't be doing *nothing*,' protested Simon. 'I'll do all the accounts and stuff.'

'Heaven preserve us,' muttered Brian.

'Look,' said Simon, 'if you prefer, I'll stay out front. I'd rather. I just won't be able to actually perform any tricks. But Dean's better at that sort of thing anyway.'

'All right,' said Brian. 'You do that.' Simon breathed a sigh of relief. The three of them had established a precarious means of working together harmoniously, the central tenet of which was that Simon and Dean kept as far away from Brian for as long as possible.

At half past nine they opened the doors and immediately the shop was invaded by a scrum of chattering teenagers. They crowded around the counter demanding to be shown fake cigarettes and pepper sweets. Brian quickly disappeared behind the velvet curtain at the back of the shop, muttering darkly to himself.

Later that morning, as Simon and Dean sipped mugs of tea in companionable silence, the bell over the front door rang. Both men turned to face the new customer, a young woman in jeans and a white shirt, dark glasses thrust up into her hair and a heavy-looking bag slung over her shoulder. She glanced an unseeing smile towards the counter and then began to inspect the display cabinets with interest. While she did so, both Simon and Dean watched her curiously. It was unusual to see women in the shop unless they were wives or mothers patiently indulging their husbands or sons. Magic seemed to be a largely male hobby. Simon had always supposed this was because the magician alone knows the secret of the trick he is performing. On the basis that knowledge is power, the magician is therefore more powerful than his audience. Power, of course, is an aphrodisiac, so the logical conclusion was that men did tricks because it made them horny.

The woman, though, seemed to be too interested in the contents of the display cases to be shopping for somebody else. Simon hid behind his mug of tea, eyeing her appraisingly over its brim. As she looked, her button nose wiggled slightly. Simon noted with approval how her bottom fitted snugly into her jeans. Her hair was blonde and cut just above shoulder length in what Simon guessed was a deliberately messy way. Her face was delicately put together, and was pretty, rather than beautiful.

Finally the woman completed her tour of the shop and approached the counter with a pleasant smile. 'So,' she said, 'have you guys finished staring at my butt yet?'

Simon almost choked on his tea. 'I, er, what?' he spluttered. Dean wisely said nothing, although he continued to stare.

The woman cocked her head to one side. 'Come *on*. I saw you. You were checking me out.' She spoke with an American accent.

Dean still stood, immobile, his mouth hanging slightly open, and so Simon felt obliged to answer. He realized that something urbane and sophisticated was needed to defuse the situation, make the customer feel more relaxed.

'No we weren't,' he said.

'Yes you were,' said the woman in a matter-of-fact way. 'So.' She slapped her behind like a cow-girl. 'What do you think?' Simon realized that so far he had not had the best of the exchange. He decided to ignore the question.

'Look,' he said. 'Sorry if you thought we were, er, doing that. We weren't, obviously. It's just that it's quite unusual for us to have lady customers.'

'Well,' replied the woman, 'here I am, a lady customer. Are you going to be able to serve me, now that you've got over the shock of seeing me in your shop?'

Simon nodded dumbly.

'Good.' The woman put her bag down on the counter. 'My name is Alex Petrie,' she said. 'I'm working at a restaurant near here for a few weeks.' She vaguely waved a hand behind her. 'They're doing a series of close-up magic promotions. You know the sort of thing – I wander around the tables cutting up people's credit cards, pulling coins out of the soup, that sort of thing.'

'Right,' said Simon, surprised. She was a professional.

'I've come over from New York especially for this gig,' she said. 'And I want some new stuff.'

Simon and Dean beamed.

Half an hour later, Alex Petrie had spent a lot of money.

As Dean rang up the purchases on the till, Alex Petrie smiled at Simon. 'I must say,' she said, 'you two do a good sales routine.'

'Thanks,' said Simon.

'I like the way you do the talking and the little guy actually does the tricks.'

Simon raised his bandaged hand. 'Talking is about all I can do at the moment.'

'You do it pretty well.' She looked at Simon. 'Look,' she said, 'this might seem forward of me, but this is the first time I've been to London, and I don't know anybody here. I gather that there's some good stuff to see. So I was wondering, if you're free, if you wouldn't mind taking some time to show me around a little.'

Simon stared back at her, speechless.

Dean bustled up with the credit card slip. 'Sign there,' he instructed, jabbing a stubby finger at the dotted line at the bottom of the slip of paper. Alex Petrie did so.

Once Dean had gone back to the till she returned her attention to Simon, who was still staring at her mutely. She looked at him questioningly for a moment, and then picked up her bags. 'Don't worry,' she said. 'Forget it. You've probably got some uptight English girlfriend, right? Sorry I asked.' She turned to leave.

Simon was jolted out of his silent reverie. 'No, no, actually I don't. Have a girlfriend, that is.'

Alex Petrie turned back towards Simon. 'I only asked you to show me around, for Christ's sake. It's not as if I asked you to have *sex* with me.'

'Sorry?' said Simon.

She leaned over the counter and hissed in Simon's ear. 'You probably imagine all American women think Englishmen are cute, don't you?'

'No, absolutely not, look, um,' said Simon. 'You're wrong. That's not what I think at all. Quite the opposite, in fact. Sorry about not saying anything straight away, but it was just that I was slightly –'

'What is it with you *English* people?' demanded Alex Petrie angrily. 'You're all so *stuck up*.'

Simon made a last effort as she turned to leave. 'Look, I'd love to show –'

'Forget it.' With a dismissive wave of her hand she pushed open the shop door and stormed out on to the street.

Simon and Dean looked at each other for a moment.

'Blimey,' said Dean.

'Shut up,' said Simon.

The rest of the day passed quickly. There was a constant stream of customers and so Simon did not have time to consider the episode with Alex Petrie in much detail, which was probably no bad thing.

At half past five Simon locked the front door and twisted the small cardboard sign to read 'Closed'. As he hobbled back to the counter, Dean began to cash up.

'I'm glad that's over,' said Simon. His foot had begun to itch horribly again beneath the bandage. Dean did not reply. His head was bent over the cash register. Simon sighed. He knew better than to try and engage Dean in conversation while he was trying to add up.

Brian came out from behind the velvet curtain. 'All right, boys?' he asked. 'Good day?'

Still Dean said nothing. He leaned fractionally closer to the pad of paper he was scribbling numbers on. 'Pretty busy,' reported Simon.

Brian grunted in satisfaction. 'Excellent.'

Simon glanced over towards Dean, who was now bending so low over the counter that it looked as if his pencil was stuck half-way up his nose.

'Anyway,' said Brian. 'I've got some good news for you. You're going to be getting some help for a while. It's my turn to look after Vick again while her mother goes on holiday with her bastard boyfriend. So she'll be here for the next few weeks to help you out.'

Dean's body jolted as the lead in his pencil snapped. Simon stared at the floor. Vick was Brian's teenage daughter. Her presence was capable of extinguishing good cheer like a fire blanket over a small flame. Brian always made her work whenever her mother went off on holiday, and this did not put her in the best of moods. This of course was precisely the point. After a few weeks of working in the shop, Vick was in such an atrocious mood (even by her standards) that she would make life insufferable for her mother when she came back from her holiday. (Brian's divorce, some years earlier, had been an acrimonious affair. His ex-wife had invested heavily in the nastiest legal advice she could afford, and Brian had been left with only the shop – which his ex-wife had not wanted – and very little else. They had also fought bitterly about who was to have custody of their daughter, but that battle, at least, Brian had won: Vick lived with her mother.)

Finally Simon regained his power of speech. 'Great,' he said. 'It'll be good to see Vick again. Won't it Dean?'

Dean began to mutter to himself, gnawing on the end of his now useless pencil. Dean hated Vick.

There was a knock on the front door.

'Bollocks,' said Brian. 'Tell whoever it is that can't read the sign that we're closed. They can come back tomorrow.'

Simon went back over to the door. He unlocked it and opened it a crack.

'Sorry –' he began, and then stopped.

'Hi,' said Joe.

'Hi,' said Simon, trying to hide his surprise.

'Fancy a drink?'

FIVE

Simon and Joe went to a large, sprawling pub near the station. It was full of commuters who weren't yet ready to face the journey home on their crawling trains. The dark, low-ceilinged room was full of sombre men sitting by themselves, nursing half-drunk pints of beer and staring into space or studying a rumpled newspaper. For a place so full, there was little noise. The air was thick with cigarette smoke which hung in the still air, catching the late afternoon sunlight as it fell through the pub's windows.

Simon was relieved to have an excuse to delay his journey back to North London. It was the height of the rush hour, and if anything the crush would have been worse than it had been that morning.

Simon and Joe went up to the bar. Joe then stuck his hands into his pockets and waited.

'Right,' said Simon eventually, 'what can I get you?'

'Oh, cheers,' said Joe. 'Pint of lager. And some dry-roasted peanuts, if they've got them.' He took his hands out of his pockets.

Trying to hide his irritation, Simon ordered the drinks.

A few minutes later they found a table and sat down. Both men drank silently for a few moments.

'God,' said Simon as he put his glass back down on the table. 'I needed that.'

'Bad day?' asked Joe.

'Average, I suppose. Which is bad enough.'

'Ah.'

'How about you?'

'Oh, my day was fine. I'm on holiday at the moment. I'm a teacher.'

'What do you teach?'

'Brats.'

'What subject?' tried Simon.

'Oh. English.'

'Whereabouts?'

Joe named a famous private school nearby.

Simon whistled. 'Very posh.'

'Yeah, well. They're all arrogant little twats. I hate them.' Joe took a swig of beer. 'And their parents aren't any better. Patronising bastards, the lot of them. On parent-teacher evenings, they talk to you as if *you're* the retarded one, not their precious little pile of snot.'

'I've always thought teaching must be a rewarding career.'

Joe snorted. 'Rewarding in what way?'

'Fulfilling, I suppose. You know, watching your charges grow and develop intellectually. Having the opportunity to help them on their way in life, perhaps to impart some knowledge that will stay with them the rest of their life.'

Joe leaned forward across the table. 'Bollocks,' he said. 'They don't listen to anything I say. They think they know it all already. The only way my job is rewarding is that I get long holidays.'

There was a pause as the two men looked at each other. Simon desperately tried to think of something else to talk about. 'Anyway, sorry,' said Joe after a few moments. 'Didn't mean to get started on the iniquities of private education. Rant, rant. How are you? How are the war wounds?'

Simon pulled a face. 'I'm getting used to them, I suppose. They make life at work a bit difficult. I can't do much with this.' He waved his right hand at Joe.

'Did you find out what happened to your foot?'

'No,' said Simon. 'Nobody would tell me.'

'That's weird.'

'Mmm.' It certainly was weird, and also rather uncomfortable. Simon had been doing his best not to think about his foot and its mysterious fate.

'How's getting around?' asked Joe.

'Terrible. The tube was a nightmare. I mean, the tube is *always* a nightmare, but this was even worse. People make you feel as if you've ruined their day just because you're not going as quickly as they are.'

Joe looked sympathetic. 'Poor you. In the summer, too,' he said. 'I hate the Underground in the summer. It's too hot and too full. And of course there are the tourists.'

Simon thought of the massed ranks of Novice Tubists and nodded. 'They are a problem,' he agreed.

'The foreign schoolchildren are the worst,' said Joe. 'Marauding about the underground system in their horrible anoraks.'

'Oh yes,' said Simon. 'They *are* particularly bad.'

'Why doesn't somebody do something about them? These kids invade carriages and then lower the quality of everyone else's lives with the efficiency of a well-drilled fighting unit. I've watched them.

'Go on.'

'Well, once they've installed themselves in a carriage, one or two pirouette a few times and knock over a few old ladies with their rucksacks. Then someone at one end of the carriage decides to start up a conversation with his best friend, who of course has entered through the door at the other end of the carriage. Everyone else then gets treated to a high-decibel exchange of adolescent squawking in a language nobody understands.'

'Mind you,' said Simon, 'that's probably no bad thing. I don't suppose their conversations are particularly edifying.'

Joe nodded thoughtfully. 'Still,' he said, 'I derive some comfort from the fact that these kids are uniformly ugly, even for teenagers. They all have yellow teeth and acne. It's horrible. And they have dreadful halitosis. And terrible bum fluff.'

'Of course,' said Simon, 'the boys are even worse.'

Joe grinned. 'The boys have got additional problems.' He took another swig of beer. 'None of them seems to have heard of deodorant.'

Simon grimaced in recognition. 'At least I didn't encounter any of *them* this morning,' he said.

'I never use public transport unless I have to,' said Joe.

'So how do you get around?'

'I bike. Cycle everywhere. It's quick, efficient, and cheap. It's good for the environment too, but although I'd like to say that I give a toss about that, I don't.'

'Where do you live?'

'Kennington,' said Joe.

'So are you on your bike this evening?'

Joe shook his head. 'Not tonight. I actually came on the tube – it's not so bad in the afternoons – but with any luck I shall be going home in my mode of transport of choice. A nice cosy taxi.' He looked at his watch. 'I'm meeting someone here, actually. She works nearby. I thought I'd get here a bit early and see you too.'

'"She"?' said Simon. 'This isn't one of your National Gallery conquests, by any chance?'

Joe grinned. 'As it happens, yes. We met in front of *Bathing at Asnières*, by Seurat. I said something about the grandiose scale of the picture elevating the proletariat bathers to the ranks of heroes, and wasn't that cool. That was it. Bingo.' He paused. 'I'm just hoping I won't have to talk about politics all night. I hope she's not going to turn out to be a socialist.'

'Why not?' asked Simon.

'Socialists are so bloody *boring*,' replied Joe. 'I've nothing against Socialism itself, mark you. It's the people who believe in it that I can't abide. Bleeding heart liberals, and insufferably self-righteous. They make me feel queasy.'

'God, absolutely,' said Simon, mentally making a note never to discuss politics with Joe.

'Anyway, it's not the talk I'm interested in.' Joe winked.

'Are you going to sleep with her?' asked Simon.

'Not too much, I hope.'

'Just like that,' mused Simon, a shade wistfully.

'Well, yes,' said Joe. 'Why else would you spend an evening with a girl?'

'Conversation does have its own merits, you know,' said Simon.

Joe chuckled. 'Yeah. Right.'

'All right, then,' said Simon. 'What makes you so certain that *she* wants to sleep with *you*?'

'Look,' said Joe. 'We met in a museum. She doesn't know me. We got on well, and when I asked her to go for a drink, she agreed.'

'Which means?'

'Which means that she fancies me.' Joe rubbed his hands together.

Simon thought. 'How can you be so sure?' he asked.

'Jesus,' said Joe. 'It's pretty obvious, isn't it? Why else would she have agreed to go out with me? She doesn't *know* me, after all. She won't have said yes just to be *nice*. We're strangers. At the moment.' He winked again.

Simon could see the logic of Joe's reasoning, but was baffled by his self-confidence. This was, he recognized, one of his own big problems. He had never had the self-belief required to approach strangers and start talking to them, confident that they would actually want to talk to *him*.

To make matters worse, Simon was spectacularly inept at reading the signals. He thought about Alex Petrie, who had asked him, a stranger, to show her around London. Did that mean that she wanted to go to bed with him? Evidently not – she had actually said as much. Simon's lack of confidence, coupled with his suspicions about his ability to interpret female signals correctly, meant that he was always paralysed by fear when faced with the decision as to whether or not to take the plunge, and lunge. He was not a gambling man. Rejection was too awful to contemplate. Simon was only interested in dead certs. And even then he would agonize – sometimes, fatally, for too long – before making that crucial, no-going-back leap of faith into the amorous void. The vision of Delphine's face floated into his brain once more. Simon sighed.

'Tell me,' he said. 'Does it ever occur to you that you might have misread the situation? That, actually, a woman *doesn't* fancy you?'

'God, of course,' replied Joe. 'Happens quite often. That can be a bit embarrassing. But it's all part of the fun. The way I see it, chasing girls is a bit like playing cards. It's a percentage game. You have to accept that there will be times when things don't work out. That's life. But do the maths. The more you try, the more success you'll have.'

The logical corollary of which, thought Simon, was that if you never try, your chances of success are a big fat zero.

Both men had finished their pints. Simon waited. After some time Joe reluctantly asked, 'D'you fancy another?'

'Go on then,' said Simon.

Joe returned a few minutes later with the drinks. He sat down opposite Simon and looked him in the eye.

'You don't really approve of me, do you?' he said.

Simon was about to take his first swig, but put his glass down. 'What do you mean?'

'You don't approve of me. You don't like my attitude towards girls. How I go after them. You think I should treat them with more respect.'

Simon opened his mouth to reply, but nothing came out, so he shut it again. 'It's not,' he said carefully after a few moments, 'that I *disapprove* of you. It's just not the way that *I* go about things.'

Joe looked at Simon curiously. 'So how *do* you go about things, then?'

'Well, I . . .' Simon began. That was a very good question. 'I *talk* to women,' he ended uncertainly.

'Is that *all*?' asked Joe.

'What do you mean, is that all?'

'Well, don't you shag them too? After you've talked to them?'

Simon sniffed. 'Not usually, no.'

'Is this because you respect women, or something?' asked Joe suspiciously.

'There's no need to say it in that tone of voice,' said Simon. 'And yes, actually, it *is* because I respect women.'

'Christ,' said Joe.

'Have you got a problem with that?' asked Simon.

'No, not at all. Doesn't bother me. I think *you* may be the one with the problem, if I may say so.'

'Well thank you very much, Doctor Ruth,' snapped Simon.

'You *do* disapprove of me.'

Simon shook his head. 'It's your choice. You can do what you like.'

Joe leaned over the table. 'Listen. It's OK to sleep with lots of people. It doesn't make you a bad person. A little superficial maybe, but not *bad*.'

'That's your opinion,' said Simon, heartily wishing that it was his, too.

'Bear in mind that women enjoy sex too.' Joe paused. 'The female orgasm does exist, you know,' he said. 'I've seen one. So *they* don't mind, *I* certainly don't mind, and nobody gets hurt.'

'So you think that we should all just shag as much as possible?' said Simon, his nose wrinkling.

'Absolutely,' said Joe. 'You're only young once, blah blah blah. Women want it, men want it, so why not do it? The problem is that too many men nowadays have become sensitive and considerate. They spend too much time reading women's magazines. And that's the real problem. Those magazines are run by a cartel of militant lesbians who are trying to subvert the heterosexual hegemony of today's society. They know how many men surreptitiously read these magazines, and so they peddle this nonsense about how women want their men to be quiche-baking fops who are in touch with their spiritual side. And of course men, stupid bastards, actually believe it. As a result women are screaming with frustration, waiting for these spineless ninnies to ravage them, but today's man is more likely to rustle up a seafood risotto and want an earnest conversation about the latest Milan Kundera novel than ask for a shag.'

Simon thought. He read women's magazines avidly. 'One of my problems is that I never get to meet anyone new,' he mused.

'Oh bollocks,' answered Joe. 'There are women everywhere. All desperate for it.'

Simon thought again about Alex Petrie. He shut his eyes in frustration.

'Look,' said Joe, 'if you really think that's a problem, I'm sure I can introduce you to some people.'

Simon put up his hand. 'No thanks. I'll be fine.'

'Wait,' said Joe. 'I've thought of the perfect person for you.'

Despite himself, Simon was curious. 'What's she like?' he asked.

'Oh, lovely,' replied Joe. 'She's called Lucy. Very nice.'

He paused. 'She's got a great personality.'

'Forget it,' said Simon at once. 'She's ugly.'

'No. Not at all.'

'What does she look like, then?'

There was a pause. 'Well. I suppose you might describe her as Rubenesque.'

'Oh, great. Ugly and *fat*.'

Joe shrugged his shoulders. 'Well, the offer's open if you change your mind.'

'Thanks a million.'

Joe looked at Simon critically. 'By the look of you, I reckon you could do with a good shag,' he said. 'It would help you to relax.'

'Really,' said Simon, who was now bored with the subject.

'Really.' There was a pause. 'Tell you what,' said Joe. 'What you need is something to work towards. A challenge.'

Simon frowned. 'What sort of challenge?'

'What do you think? A challenge to shag, of course.' Joe took a swig of beer.

Simon looked at his new friend with distaste. 'Oh, *please*,' he said. 'Grow up.'

Joe looked at Simon, bewildered. 'What? What did I say?'

'*A challenge to shag*? Listen to yourself. You sound like a hormonally unbalanced fifteen-year-old. I'm not going to indulge in such puerile games.'

'Oh, OK,' said Joe, settling back in his seat. 'I see.'

'What?' demanded Simon.

'You're scared,' observed Joe.

'Don't be ridiculous,' said Simon. 'It's just that the

whole thing, the idea of a *challenge*, is offensive. Women aren't *sport*.'

'Yes they are,' said Joe.

'Look, Joe, the answer's no. I'm not interested. I have better things to do with my time.'

'What, like sitting around *talking*, I suppose?'

'If you like,' said Simon defensively.

'Well, I still say that you should give it a go. I think you should give yourself a target of, say, a month, by which time you should have had meaningless sex with at least three women.'

'*Three*?' exclaimed Simon, momentarily forgetting his aloof disdain for the subject.

Joe shrugged. 'Less than one a week. Shouldn't be too hard if you apply yourself.'

'That's ridiculous,' said Simon.

'You'll never know unless you try,' observed Joe.

'Well, thanks very much, but I think I prefer to remain in a state of blissful ignorance, if it's all the same to you.'

Joe frowned. 'It's the people who are having lots of sex who are the blissful ones. Sex makes people calmer, more at peace with themselves.' He paused. 'It's a great thing, sex. It's a totally natural high. No additives, no preservatives, no chemicals. Everybody's doing it. Well,' said Joe, gesturing at Simon, 'almost everybody. The birds. The bees. Educated fleas.' He paused. 'Fish do it. Although therein lies a question I've always wondered about.'

'God, you're obsessed,' observed Simon.

Joe nodded. 'Undoubtedly. It's natural, though. I was made this way. It's all to do with survival of the species.'

'No, Joe, you're not talking about *pro*creation. You're talking about *re*creation. Sex as a hobby.'

'Well, I can think of worse. It keeps you fit. Gets you out and about. You get to meet lots of nice people.'

Simon sighed.

'Anyway,' said Joe. 'About these fish. I've always wondered whether there's a way of telling the difference between a lady fish and a gentleman fish. Because there's obviously a difference, right? The female fish lays the eggs and then the male comes along and fertilizes them.'

'That sounds right. I'm not an expert on aquatic mating rituals, though.'

'So, my question is, how do you tell the difference between male and female fish?'

'God, I don't know.'

'I mean, they don't actually *shag*, do they, fish, so I suppose there's no need for any external differences at all.'

'I suppose not,' said Simon, defeated.

Joe's face suddenly broke into a wide grin. 'There she is,' he said. Simon turned, and saw a stunning girl approaching them. She was very tall, and walked like a model. As she crossed the pub, every pair of male eyes in the room was fixed on her. Simon sighed. This really wasn't very fair. Joe got up and gave her a kiss on both cheeks. She sat down opposite Simon. Joe squeezed in beside her. The girl looked at Simon questioningly.

'Simon, this is Claire,' said Joe. 'Claire, this is my friend Simon, who works nearby.'

'Hello, Simon,' said Claire, flicking her hair out of her face with a well-practised manoeuvre. She had a low, gravelly voice which sounded extremely sexy.

'Hi,' squeaked Simon.

'Anyway, mate,' continued Joe. 'Nice to see you again. Thanks for the drink. I'll see you soon, yeah?'

'Oh. Right,' said Simon. He was being dismissed. Joe handed him his crutches.

'There you go,' he said. 'Safe journey home. Just clobber anyone who gets in your way. Hope you're feeling better soon.' Joe gave Simon a wink. 'And have a think about what I said. That little challenge. I'll be in touch.'

'OK,' said Simon, as he hauled himself on to his crutches. 'Have fun this evening.'

'Oh, we will,' said Joe.

'Bye, Claire,' said Simon.

'Bye, Simon,' rumbled Claire.

Simon hobbled out of the pub. He decided to take a bus home, rather than face the escalators and inhuman crush of the Underground.

Some minutes later, he was safely installed on a number 38 as it pulled out into the Victoria traffic, where it immediately stopped and remained stationary for several minutes. Simon sighed. It was going to be a long journey home.

SIX

'Hi there. Fancy a drink?'

No.

'Hi. I've got a whole lobster back in my flat. Interested? In me or the lobster?'

Christ. No.

'Hi. I don't know whether or not you've read about this, or whether you're at all interested, but there's this really good Bavarian film on at the moment about existential florists and, well, I was wondering whether or not that would be the sort of thing you might be interested in going to see, with me, or not, no, probably not, look, never mind, it wasn't very important, just a thought, really.'

Nooooo.

Simon sighed.

He stood up and hobbled across the sitting room. He carefully flipped over the Miles Davis record on the turntable, and replaced the stylus on the spinning vinyl. After a brief crackle of static, Miles, John Coltrane, and Cannonball Adderley began their lilting 6/8 blues. James Cobb's brushes caressed the melody onwards. Beneath the wistful horn lines sat Paul Chamber's robust, gently propelling bass. And somewhere, the ethereal piano of Bill

Evans shimmered and sparkled, cementing the music into one hypnotically beautiful whole.

Simon sat back down, closed his eyes, and listened to the music for a few moments. As Miles's laconic solo peeped out of the speakers, edging cautiously forwards, Simon's worries left him. He immersed himself in the music.

Thousands of notes later, the turntable glided to a stop. Reluctantly Simon opened his eyes. He had to concentrate on the problem at hand.

The problem at hand was that Simon had been thinking.

Since their drink, Simon had tried hard not to think about Joe's theories about women. In many ways, Joe had been right: he *did* stand for everything that Simon disapproved of. His callous, selfish, and old-fashioned attitude represented everything that Simon had always tried to avoid. Despite this, though, Simon had been unable to ignore the fact that, complete absence of ethical integrity notwithstanding, Joe was obviously having an enormous amount of fun.

Simon thought about the challenge that Joe had thrown down in the pub. Sex with three women in a month. He snorted to himself contemptuously. Such a childish idea was indicative of Joe's emotional immaturity in general. Turning sex into a competition! Honestly.

Still.

Perhaps the time has come, he told himself, to face facts. The Women Are People Too approach has got you nowhere. Sensitive men are obviously out. Testosterone is in. He grimaced at the thought, but the empirical evidence seemed undeniable.

Perhaps, thought Simon cautiously, he might give Joe's

technique a go. Just to see what happened. Not that he was remotely interested in Joe's stupid challenge; of course not. But maybe three women in a month might be a useful benchmark to judge his performance by. On a purely unofficial basis.

The question, then, was how to proceed from here. Clearly a more proactive approach was required. He couldn't just wait for opportunities like the one Alex Petrie had presented him with to fall into his lap every day. He would have to go looking for them.

Simon thought about how Miles usually picked up his women. If he saw a beautiful woman in the audience during a gig, he would just point at her coolly and beckon her backstage. They never refused. Well, they wouldn't, would they? He was Miles Davis. Simon Teller, however, was not.

Simon sighed and rubbed his eyes. He had been trying to work out how to ask a girl out without sounding either (a) like a smarmy prat, (b) like a predatorial prat, or (c) like a geeky, nervous prat. He was coming to the conclusion that such a thing was actually impossible. Pratdom, in some shape or form, seemed unavoidable. So it was then a question of which option was the least awful. Simon had decided to go with option (a), the smarmy prat. Even having reconciled himself to this, though, he was still having difficulty. He didn't want to be *too* smarmy, nor indeed too much like a prat. The chat-up lines he had come up with so far suffered from such a hob-nailed lack of subtlety that, whilst they sounded just about bearable when spoken to the bathroom mirror, he knew he would die of embarrassment if he ever tried to say them to a real person.

Another difficulty was establishing which lucky woman

to pursue. Simon had given this a lot of thought. He had briefly considered asking Angus or Fergus for Delphine's telephone number, but had reluctantly decided that it probably wouldn't be a terribly good idea. He wasn't yet ready to face either of his neighbours after his performance the previous Saturday evening, and (more importantly) wasn't sure whether he would be able to look at Delphine's face, let alone the rest of her, without succumbing to another attack of inarticulate mumbling. Also she was French, and Simon had always had the dread suspicion that French men actually *are* quite good at sex. Better than the English, anyway. No, he had concluded: Delphine represented an altogether too insurmountable (in every sense) target for his first foray into meaningless sex. Besides, he wasn't sure whether sex with someone as beautiful as Delphine could ever be meaningless. Miraculous, yes.

The American, Alex Petrie, would have been perfect, he knew. She was pretty enough, and hadn't seemed to mind too much that he had been looking closely at her bottom. And *she* had asked *him* to show her London. He wouldn't even have had to undergo the trial of asking her out. Not for the first time, Simon sighed in frustration. He reluctantly concluded that the safest option would be to take pot luck and ask a complete stranger. This was easy in theory, but more complicated in practice. Simon had no idea where to start looking. He certainly wasn't going to start loitering in the National Gallery.

He sighed. Perhaps he should just forget the whole thing and carry on as he always had. Let people like Joe have their fun, but he wanted nothing to do with it. It was all too complicated.

The telephone rang. Distracted, Simon picked it up.

'Islington Hostel for Lost Souls, can I help you?'

'Simon! Still as cheerful as ever, then.'

Simon grinned into the receiver. 'Kate. How are you?'

'Not bad.'

Simon looked at his watch. 'What time is it?'

There was a pause at the other end of the telephone. 'Hang on, not quite sure. It's about, what, five thirty.'

'In the *morning*?'

'Uh-huh. I've just got in, and thought I'd give you a ring.'

'Well, I'm touched,' said Simon.

'I'm a bit pissed, to tell you the truth,' admitted Kate.

The fact was that Kate only ever called Simon when she was extremely drunk. Since she had left London eighteen months ago, Simon could not remember ever having a conversation with her when she was sober. She had elevated the practice of Drinking and Dialling to an art form. After enough Australian lager, Kate would suddenly develop acute homesickness and would immediately pick up the phone and ramble incoherently for hours at whomever she called.

These calls were generally welcome, except when Kate had been drinking during the afternoon and decided to call when it was the middle of the night in England. She had never really come to terms with the principle that Australia was twelve or so hours ahead. Simon had spent several nights listening to Kate talking, rubbing his eyes, and trying not to look at his bedside clock. Kate was unique. She was the one female friend that Simon had managed to hold on to over the years. She had never seemed particularly interested in men. She enjoyed her freedom to do as she pleased, and so preferred to remain single rather than submit to the compromises of romantic entanglements. Perhaps because of this, Simon had avoided the usual embarrassing ill-timed infatuation with her, and so they had remained close, united in their unattached states. She was the person to whom Simon would always turn when he needed a shoulder to cry on, an ear to bend, a soul mate to laugh with. As the years progressed, they had become inseparable.

It was perhaps inevitable that someone as free-spirited as Kate should eventually seek to escape the constricting atmosphere of London life. One night, over supper, she had gently told Simon that she was becoming stifled by the routine she had fallen into. She had resigned from her job, and had applied for a visa to go and work in Australia. Simon had nodded uncomprehendingly.

So it was that the closest friendship of Simon's adult life was now conducted telephonically, when one of the protagonists was always three sheets to the wind. It was not an ideal situation.

'So, how are you?' asked Kate breezily.

'OK, I suppose,' replied Simon. 'Busy contemplating the minefield of meaningless sex, as it happens.'

'What? Doesn't sound like you.'

Simon explained briefly Joe's theories about women.

'And you're thinking of having a go?' said Kate incredulously.

'Just thinking about it,' said Simon sheepishly. 'No definite plans, as yet.'

'Well, I think you should go for it,' said Kate.

Simon frowned. 'You do?'

'Absolutely. Best thing for you. I reckon you could do with a good shag.'

Simon blinked. His conversation with Joe seemed to be repeating itself. 'Oh,' he said eventually. 'OK.'

'I mean, it'll help you relax a little. Sex is fun.'

'Sorry, what?' said Simon. 'Is this the proudly single, resolutely abstemious Catherine I'm talking to?'

There was a sigh down the telephone line. 'Simon, darling, there is a world of difference between proudly single and resolutely abstemious. I was always one, never the other.'

'What are you saying?' asked Simon.

'What I'm saying is that I may have been single for a very long time, but that hasn't stopped me getting my oats on a regular basis. I enjoy a good hump as much as the next person.'

'But you never told me,' said Simon, rather miffed.

'If I may be blunt, I didn't really think it was any of your business.'

Simon thought. 'And was this the case even when we –'

'Back in England? Of course.'

Simon's shoulders slumped. 'I see,' he said. This was a bit much. Even Kate had been at it, and he had never known. Well, he thought, if it's good enough for Kate, it's good enough for me. 'All right, then,' he said. 'Answer me this. If I'm going to do this, how do I go about meeting the right sort of girl?'

'No idea,' replied Kate cheerfully. 'Although you could always try going to bars, like other people.'

'God. I'd rather have my teeth pulled.'

Kate yawned. 'Well,' she said, 'I'm sure you'll think of something.'

'Fat lot of good you are.'

'Sorry. Look, I think I may call it a night. I have to go to work in three hours' time.'

Simon exhaled. 'Fair enough. Will you call me if you have any bright ideas?'

'Sure. And let me know how you get on, all right? I'm proud of you, Simon. Congratulations. You're about to join the human race at last. And remember: you're supposed to enjoy it.'

Simon pulled a face. 'Right. I'll try not to forget. Wish me luck.'

'Good luck, sweetheart. See you soon.' Kate put the phone down.

Morosely Simon picked up the television remote control. He tried not to feel hurt that Kate had been shagging so enthusiastically all the time they had known each other without ever mentioning it to him. Still, he told himself, that decides it. I'm going to give it a go. If I can find the right woman, of course. Or women. He switched on the television. On the news there was a report about under-funding in the National Health Service. On location in a hospital, a reporter delivered his piece to the camera while in the background doctors and nurses carried on their business, wheeling trolleys back and forth and talking quietly with each other.

Suddenly Simon had an idea. He was due to go back to the hospital in a couple of days to have his wrist and ankle checked. What was the name of that doctor? Simon tried to remember. Dr Gilbert. She had been nice in an efficient, doctorish way, and really quite attractive.

Dr Gilbert. Yes.

* * *

Victoria Station had looked better. She was slouching against the shop's counter as Simon pushed open the door the following morning. Her physical appearance had deteriorated since last year's visit. She had slipped deeper into the greasy trough of adolescence. Knobbly florets of acne blossomed on her chin. Her mouth was a cat's cradle of gleaming metal tracks, rubber bands and plastic plates. She wore a dirty, over-sized T-shirt with the words 'Rabid Sluts of Mogodon' on the front.

'Hello, Vick,' said Simon. 'Good to see you again.'

Vick delivered a look of pure contempt in return and slouched off behind the velvet curtain without saying a word.

Victoria Station had every right to be pissed off. Her parents' choice of name for their baby daughter had been a singularly brutal act of mental violence. Naming her after a large, dirty public space suggested that perhaps she had not been a welcome addition to the family.

As a result of this monstrous act of cruelty, Victoria Station had suffered more than most at the hands of her school friends. There are few creatures as dazzlingly repellent as adolescent girls. Victoria had correctly identified Brian as the principal architect of her misery. Subsequent relations between father and daughter had always been frosty.

For years, Victoria had insisted that everybody call her Vick. Simon supposed that a medicinal chest rub was a better bet than a railway station, although not by much.

Simon stood in the middle of the shop, looking around him and contemplating the day ahead. Suddenly Vick's face re-appeared from behind the curtain. 'Actually,' she said, 'it's not "Vick" any more.'

'Oh,' said Simon. 'OK.'

'Yeah. From now on it's "V".'

'V. Right. Noted.'

'And it's not V for Vick, either,' said Vick.

'It's not?' said Simon.

Vick shook her head.

'What's V for, then?'

'Vixen,' said Vick.

Simon blinked. 'Ah. Right. OK. V it is, then.'

Vick disappeared again in a bad-tempered swish of velvet. Simon went behind the counter and propped his crutches up against the wall. Dean appeared from the stock room.

'All right,' said Dean cautiously.

'Hi Dean,' said Simon.

'Have you seen her yet?' asked Dean.

'Oh yes,' replied Simon. 'She's in there.' He pointed behind the curtain. Even Vick's presence couldn't spoil Simon's good mood. Having decided to pursue the lovely Dr Gilbert, he was looking forward to the adventure. The prospect filled him with fear, but it was an exhilarating, heart-rushing fear. He was feeling irrepressibly cheerful.

'Look,' he said. 'I'm bored. Let's play a game. OK?'

'OK,' said Dean.

Simon looked at the displays around the shop. He reached up and plucked a large pair of fake breasts off the wall. As he did so the latex wobbled dramatically. Rather than slip them on to his chest, Simon placed them over his head so that the breasts stuck outwards on each side. They looked like exotic ear-warmers.

'So,' said Simon, turning to face his friend. 'Who am I?'

Dean shook his head. 'Dunno,' he said flatly.

'Well at least have a guess,' said Simon irritably.

Dean shrugged. 'Dolly Parton?' he tried.

Simon stared at him. 'No,' he said after a moment. 'Guess again.'

Dean looked pained. 'Samantha Fox?'

Simon snorted in disgust. 'It's Brian.'

'Brian?' Dean looked baffled.

'Yes. Brian. Now you have to guess why.' He pointed at the latex breasts.

'Er, what, he's a complete tit?' asked Dean a little hesitantly.

Simon slapped his hand on the counter. 'There you go,' he said. 'That wasn't so difficult, was it?' He went off in search of some more props.

Dean had begun to look around nervously.

'Right.' Simon put on a set of Groucho Marx glasses which had huge fake eyebrows attached to the top of the rims and a moustache fixed beneath a large plastic nose. 'So go on. What does this mean?' he asked.

Dean looked at Simon uncertainly. 'Brian's as silly as the Marx brothers?' he guessed.

'Try again.'

Dean's face was a picture of concentration. Finally his face crumpled in defeat. 'I don't know,' he said.

'It's obvious,' said Simon. 'The moustache is the thing. It means Brian is a fascist.'

'What? The moustache says that?' said Dean.

'Of course.'

'So Groucho Marx was a fascist?'

'No, *Hitler* was a fascist,' said Simon impatiently.

'But that doesn't look anything like Hitler's moustache,' said Dean.

'Look, if you're going to be pedantic about it, this is going to be no fun at all,' said Simon. The large latex breasts wobbled as he shook his head.

'Sorry,' said Dean.

'Now.' Simon began rummaging again. After a few moments he reappeared with a plastic dog turd, which he carefully placed on top of his head, in between the breasts as they sagged sideways. He turned towards Dean. 'Any ideas?'

'He's got shit for brains?' said Dean.

'You're getting the hang of this,' said Simon.

'I think Brian might be coming,' said Dean.

Simon ripped off the breasts, dog turd and Groucho glasses and threw them on to the counter top. A few moments later the curtain was pulled back and Brian came into the shop, followed by his daughter. 'Good, you're here,' said Brian.

'Er, yes, hello Brian,' said Simon, sweeping the remains of his performance to one side as casually as he could.

'Vick's here, as you can see,' said Brian.

'It's "V",' said Vick.

'Oh, that's right,' said Brian. He waved a finger at Simon and Dean. 'It's V, now, so don't you forget.' He turned to his daughter. 'Right, you remember all this from last year, I'm sure.' Vick looked at her father in a bored way and said nothing. Simon tried cracking another small grin. Vick looked at him and sighed deeply. 'I thought maybe, er, V could work in the stock room today,' continued Brian, 'sorting out the new delivery of novelty party items.' He still couldn't bring himself to call them jokes.

'All right,' said Simon. 'That seems like a good idea.' Vick in the stock room was a more attractive prospect than Vick on the shop floor. The further away she was, the better.

'Right,' said Brian sourly. 'Let's not waste any more time, then, shall we?' He disappeared behind his curtain.

About an hour later, Simon went down into the stock room to offer Vick a cup of tea. She was nowhere to be seen. He stood in the middle of the floor for a few moments, wondering where she had got to. Suddenly a plume of white smoke shot upwards from behind a stack of cardboard boxes.

'Hello?' said Simon.

Vick emerged from behind the boxes, a half-smoked cigarette cupped behind her hand. 'All right,' she said. 'I was just having a quick break.'

Simon looked at her, shocked. 'Does your father know you smoke?' he asked.

Vick scowled. 'No. But he doesn't care, anyway.'

Simon looked at her fierce, defiant face. 'You shouldn't smoke,' he said.

'Yeah, I know. I go to school. We have the lectures. Every term they show us slides of the insides of a smoker's lung and all that shit.'

'And?'

'And what?'

'Doesn't that mean anything to you? Don't you worry about what it's doing to your body?'

'Look,' said Vick. 'I'm fifteen years old. I'm *supposed* to smoke.'

Simon frowned. 'Well, what do you think your father would say? I'm sure he wouldn't approve.'

Vick sighed. 'OK. First of all,' she said, 'he doesn't

know. Second of all, even if he did, he's not *meant* to approve.'

'So shall I tell him what you're up to, then?' asked Simon.

Vick took another long drag. 'Please yourself,' she said.

'Well, I'll overlook it this time, but if I catch you again, then I'll definitely tell your Dad,' said Simon. There was a pause as the two of them looked at each other.

'Anyway,' continued Simon, 'smoking down here is a fire risk. All these cardboard boxes would go up in a flash. Fake fried eggs are highly inflammable.'

'I'll risk it,' said Vick, dropping the butt on the floor and extinguishing it with the heel of her trainer.

Simon shook his head, baffled by this hard little girl. Vick looked at Simon thoughtfully. 'You couldn't do me a favour, could you?' she said suddenly.

Simon was immediately on his guard. 'That depends,' he said. 'What is it?'

'Well,' said Vick. 'Would you mind getting me some more fags?'

'Yes, I would bloody mind,' said Simon.

Vick sighed. 'Please.'

'No way,' huffed Simon.

'Go on,' said Vick.

'Absolutely not,' said Simon. 'Do it yourself.'

'Oh,' said Vick. 'I see.' She looked at her shoes. 'That's a pity. Well, I'm sure Dad would be interested to hear about your little performance in the shop this morning. Remind me what the dog turd meant again. Shit for brains, wasn't it?'

'I, er, no, that is, how did you know about that?' stammered Simon.

'I watched you,' said Vick smugly. 'From behind the curtain. You were so busy showing off you never noticed me.'

'Well, look,' said Simon disloyally, 'it was Dean who said the thing about shit for brains, not me.'

'Sorry.' Vick shook her head. 'I saw it. You're the one who started it.'

'This is blackmail,' said Simon.

Vick nodded. 'So will you get them for me?' she asked.

Simon thought briefly, and then held out his hand. He didn't seem to have much choice. 'Go on,' he said. 'Just this once.'

Vick reached into her jeans and handed Simon some money. 'Twenty Benson and Hedges,' she said. 'And a box of matches.'

'Twenty Benson and Hedges,' repeated Simon sourly. 'Right.'

Half an hour later, Simon hobbled to the nearest newsagents. He prowled around the shop for a few minutes, waiting for the other customers to leave. As he waited, Simon scanned the ranks of magazines on display. There was a bewildering range of subject matter, from home interiors to taxidermy, from topiary to pregnancy tests. Simon looked to see whether there was a magazine for single men approaching middle age without the remotest prospect of ever having sex again. There were several, of course, all on the top shelf.

Finally Simon was alone in the shop with the girl behind the counter. As he approached, the girl scratched her armpit.

'Hello,' said Simon. He ostentatiously took a chocolate bar from the display in front of him and put it by the till. The girl cocked her head to one side to read the price tag on the bar and rang the figure up. 'And twenty Benson and Hedges, please,' said Simon quickly. 'And some matches.'

The girl put the cigarettes on the counter next to the chocolate and rang up the till again. The total figure appeared in green neon on the till's display screen. The girl pointed at the display, to save herself the trouble of having to open her mouth and speak. As Simon handed over Vick's money the bell over the shop's door trilled.

'Hello,' said Brian, coming up to the counter. 'What's this? Unscheduled break? Early lunch?'

'Brian,' said Simon shrilly. 'I, er –'

Brian nodded at the cigarettes on the counter. 'Didn't know you smoked.'

'I don't really,' said Simon. 'Just every now and then, you know. I, um, got a craving for one this morning.'

Brian tsk-tsked. 'Terrible habit,' he said. 'Disgusting.'

Simon nodded. 'I know. But there are times when I can't help myself.' He grinned weakly. The girl handed over his change. He turned to leave.

'Hang on a sec,' said Brian, who had chosen this day of all days to be effusive. 'I won't be a moment. We can walk back together.'

'OK,' said Simon, mortified.

Brian turned to address himself to the girl behind the counter. He bought two packets of extra strong mints. As he turned to leave, he gestured to Simon to lead the way.

On the pavement, Brian turned to Simon, and said,

'Well? Aren't you going to light up?'

'What?' said Simon.

'Your fag? The one you have such a craving for? Aren't you going to smoke it?'

'Oh. Well, no, I thought I might wait a bit,' muttered Simon desperately.

'Nonsense,' said Brian. 'You go right ahead. After all, can't have you smoking in the shop, can we?' He laughed heartily. Simon joined in as best he could, his heart beating blackly as he thought of Brian's daughter puffing away in the stock room. Seeing no alternative, Simon peeled the plastic wrapping off the cigarette packet. Cautiously he extracted a cigarette and put it between his lips. Simon had last smoked at around the time he had made that first discovery of his father's Sidney Bechet record. Now was not the time to begin again. As Brian watched, he balanced precariously on his crutches, struck a match and lit the cigarette.

Simon drew as gently as he could on the cigarette. A familiar warmth filled his mouth. He held the smoke in for a few seconds and then exhaled through pursed lips. Well, that wasn't so bad, he thought. He relaxed slightly as he took another drag. Smoke shot into his lungs, scratching the back of his throat on the way down. Immediately Simon was overcome with the urge to cough, but he knew that this would look suspicious. Instead he fought to keep his composure, lungs heaving and eyes watering, until the maelstrom in his chest subsided and he was able to breathe more easily again. It occurred to Simon that he should probably look as if he was enjoying it.

'Ah,' he said, totally without conviction, 'that's better.'

Brian looked on. 'Don't know how you can stand to

smoke those things,' he said. Simon said nothing. He took a few more tentative puffs, doing his best not to inhale, as they walked along the pavement in silence. As soon as he felt able, Simon threw the cigarette on to the pavement and stepped on it with relief. When they arrived back at the shop, Simon went into the stock room to deliver his booty.

'Here you are,' he said sourly to Vick, handing her the packet.

Vick looked at the box, and opened it. 'Hold on,' she said. 'Did you nick one?'

'I had to. Your father made me smoke one in front of him.'

'Caught you, did he?'

'Red-handed. And you'll be glad to hear that he definitely doesn't approve of smoking.'

Vick looked unsympathetic. 'Well, you should pay me for that one you smoked,' she said.

Simon looked at her levelly. 'You're joking, of course,' he said.

Vick shook her head. 'Course not. Deadly serious. Come on.' She held out her hand. 'Cough up.'

It was an unfortunate choice of words. 'It's not as if I enjoyed it,' complained Simon. 'I feel sick now.'

'Ah, diddums,' said Vick, unimpressed. 'Come on. Twenty pee. Otherwise I'll tell Dad about this morning.' She made a fascist salute and silently clicked the heels of her trainers together.

Simon closed his eyes. Vick really was impossibly obnoxious. There was, he realized, a principle at stake here, but in the circumstances it was probably prudent to concentrate on a more pragmatic approach.

He stuck his hand into his pocket and pulled out a coin.

'*Thank* you,' said Vick, snatching the coin.

Simon turned to leave the stock room without saying another word. He tried not to think about the prospect of having to put up with Vick in the shop for another two weeks. So far she had been there for about two and a half hours.

That Friday evening Simon went back to the hospital. He was feeling nervous, but not because of the medical check-up: he was going to ask Dr Gilbert to go and see a film. He had thought hard about what would be the safest proposal for a first date – safest in terms of (a) offering the smallest chance for rejection and (b) presenting the fewest potential awkward moments over the course of the evening.

Simon had therefore focused on events that would require their participation as audience members, thereby reducing the need to interact with each other too much, at least until afterwards, when they would of course have Something to Talk About. Several options presented themselves: a film, the theatre, an opera maybe, or a jazz gig. Gradually Simon had worked backwards through this list, eliminating each one in turn. Jazz was too risky. Opera too pretentious. A play seemed like a safer bet, but again there was a danger of appearing slightly too flash, or trying too hard. No, he concluded, a film was the best way forward. It was also, quite by coincidence, the cheapest.

Next came the question of which film to see. This was crucial in terms of creating the right impression. Nothing too obscure, but nothing too cheesy. He scanned the review section of the newspaper to find a suitable choice. Finally he had chosen a film by a famous director – the idea being that this would be his (patently transparent) lead-in to the invitation itself:

He: Of course, the guy I really like is Pedro Marimba. He's fantastic.
She: Oh God. Absolutely. Did you see *Teeny Tiny Toes*?
He: Twice.
She: The man is a genius. So funny. So *relevant*.
He: Actually, his new one has just opened if you fancy going to see it.
She: Oh, yes, I'd love to! But only if you sleep with me afterwards.

Simon wasn't actually expecting Dr Gilbert to accept his invitation. He had resigned himself to the fact that there would undoubtedly be several failures along the way as he honed his technique. It was best to get these out of the way as quickly as possible. He remembered what Joe had said about playing a percentage game. Rejections were, if you believed Joe, all part of the fun. A cold shiver of dread passed through him. Simon didn't want to waste any time getting his first rejection under his belt and familiarizing himself with abject humiliation. His fingers beat a rapid tattoo on the side of his chair. He ran through his lines silently to himself. Let this be quick and painless, he thought.

Simon had to wait for forty minutes before Dr Gilbert appeared. She looked, if anything, prettier than the last time Simon had seen her. This time she wore black-rimmed glasses. Simon had always fancied women in glasses.

'Hello, Mr Teller,' said Dr Gilbert.

'Simon, please,' said Simon. Beads of sweat immediately began to prickle out all over his skin.

'Follow me, please.' She led him to a small, brightly lit room. 'How are you feeling?' she asked as she closed the door.

'Very well, thank you, doctor,' replied Simon. He waited for her to insist that he call her by her first name. She didn't. He pressed resolutely on. 'My foot itches a bit, and I had a few teething problems with the crutches, but apart from that, I've been fine.'

Dr Gilbert was looking down at her clipboard. Simon surreptitiously checked to see whether she was wearing a ring on her left hand. She wasn't.

'Well,' said Dr Gilbert, not looking up, 'that all sounds encouraging.'

'Um, look,' said Simon. 'I would really appreciate it if you would tell me what happened last Saturday evening. You know, with my foot.'

'Goodness me,' said Dr Gilbert, 'have you still not remembered that little story?'

'No,' said Simon. 'So I was wondering whether you would mind terribly just giving me some sort of idea about what went on.' He smiled feebly. 'Just to put my mind at rest.'

'I'm not the best person to ask, really,' said Dr Gilbert. 'I wasn't actually on duty that evening.'

'But you've obviously heard one or two things,' said Simon.

Dr Gilbert snorted. 'Oh yes, I should say so. Sit on the bed, please.'

As she examined his wrist and ankle thoroughly, Simon

tried to rein in his frustration. She obviously wasn't going to tell him what had happened. He tried to compose himself. There were more important things to worry about.

Once she had examined him, Dr Gilbert consulted her clipboard again. 'Now,' she said, 'would you mind just doing a few tests for me, please?'

'Absolutely not,' said Simon gallantly.

'Stand up, please, and lift your left arm above your head.'

Simon did so. He took a deep breath. Here we go, he thought. Once more unto the breach, and all that jazz. 'I read somewhere last week that more people are going to watch films now than ever before,' he said.

'Really,' said Dr Gilbert.

'Yes, which I thought was interesting.'

'Really,' said Dr Gilbert again.

'Especially when you think how popular videos are nowadays,' continued Simon. There was a pause.

'I don't own a video,' said Dr Gilbert eventually.

Aha! thought Simon. She doesn't own a video! Obviously she *only* goes to the cinema, and she is telling me this because she wants me to ask her to see a film! Progress!

'So do you like films, then?' he asked.

'Not really. Now can you shut your eyes and turn right around until you think you're facing the same direction as you are now?'

Simon did so. As he spun he wondered what to do next. He came to a halt and opened his eyes. Dr Gilbert was standing in front of him.

'Very good,' she said.

'I don't like films much either,' said Simon. He paused.

Suddenly inspiration struck him. 'But I do enjoy going to art galleries.'

'Do you?' said Dr Gilbert. 'I can't stand them. Boring. And full of tourists. Now would you put your arms out to the side for me?'

'Well, yes,' agreed Simon, 'there is that. They *are* full of tourists. You're right.'

Dr Gilbert pulled a small hammer out of her coat pocket. 'Now,' she said, 'Don't move for a few moments.'

'Of course,' tried Simon, 'what I really like is going to the theatre.'

'I don't like plays,' said Dr Gilbert.

'Absolutely,' agreed Simon, shaking his head in agreement and confusion. 'Me too. Either. Neither. Ghastly things, plays.' Well, he thought, this is going pretty well, so far. He had now completely given up hope and just thought he might as well give each invitation an airing to see how they sounded. 'Actually,' he said, 'what I *really* like is eating.'

'Oh yes. Me too.' Dr Gilbert thumped Simon's right elbow quite hard with the hammer. Simon jolted with surprise, both from the hammer blow and her response.

'You do?' he said.

'Of course. I love food. Who doesn't?'

'Well, quite.' Simon decided to crank the bullshit machine up a notch or two. 'There's nothing quite like having people over to dinner, you know, and enjoying good food and wine and sparkling conversation.'

'Oh, I agree,' said Dr Gilbert, taking a well-aimed swipe at his left elbow. Simon suppressed a yelp. There was a brief pause as she lined herself up for her next shot with the hammer. Simon gulped. It was now or never.

'Well, if you really like that sort of thing, perhapsyou-shouldletmecookdinnerforyouonenight,' he blurted out.

There was a long pause.

'Yes, all right, then,' said Dr Gilbert, and then administered her hardest blow yet.

Simon blinked back tears of pain. 'I mean, when I say, you know, cook you dinner, if you prefer we can go out. To a restaurant.'

'No. I'd rather *you* cooked,' said Dr Gilbert.

'Oh. Right,' said Simon. There was a pause. 'Are you sure?' he asked.

'Of course I'm sure,' said Dr Gilbert.

'Oh. Well. Good.' Simon suddenly found himself in uncharted waters. He wasn't sure what to do next. There was a pause.

'When do you want me to come?' asked Dr Gilbert.

'When *can* you come?' asked Simon.

To Simon's relief, Dr Gilbert put away her hammer. 'Well, I'm off on holiday in about two weeks. If you want to do it before then, then how about a week tomorrow, if you're not busy?'

Simon pretended to think. 'Let me see. Next Saturday.' He pursed his lips in simulated concentration. 'OK,' he said after a considered pause. 'I think I can do that. That would be great. Thanks.'

'I think,' said Dr Gilbert, 'that I'm the one supposed to be thanking you.'

Simon grinned. He suddenly felt rather pleased with himself. He wondered what on earth he had been so nervous about. 'Well,' he said. 'You're very welcome.'

'Good. I'll look forward to it. As for your health, I'm pleased to say that you seem fine,' said Dr Gilbert. 'We'll have the bandages off you before too long. But you'll need to stick with the crutches for a while longer.'

'Excellent,' said Simon.

There was another pause.

'Where do you live?' asked Dr Gilbert. Simon gave her the address. 'Great,' she said simply. 'What time do you want me?'

'About eight?'

'OK. See you then.' Dr Gilbert disappeared through the door, leaving Simon rather dazed. Bloody hell, he thought. You actually did it. He smiled smugly. He'd show Joe. Challenge, indeed. Ha!

Right, he thought. Now what?

SEVEN

The next eight days were busy.

Simon was an excellent cook. The problem was choosing what to cook for someone you don't know but whom you wish to seduce. There were a few obvious requirements:

It should taste good.
It should look good.
It should look *difficult*.
It should be excessively, flagrantly, expensive.
It should contain alcohol; *or*
It should be an effective aphrodisiac.

Over that weekend Simon scoured his collection of cookbooks, trying to find something suitably impressive which would make Dr Gilbert melt into his arms at the appropriate juncture. By late on Sunday evening, he had come up with the following informal menu:

Ballotine of Guinea Fowl stuffed with Pan-fried Foie Gras served on a comfortable bed of Radicchio and

Endive leaves with home-made Croutons al forno and drizzled lightly with a Piquant Dandelion Vinaigrette

followed by

Lobster in a Cream and Chilli Sauce enhanced with Truffles and Pistachios with a White Wine and Basil Mousse and flavoured by a Soupçon of Air-Dried Saffron

accompanied by

Gratin of King Edward Pommes de Terre with a Hint of Braised Fennel

followed by, after a discreet pause,

Light Pear Mousse with Crisp Twills and Kirsch

(and)

petits fours and coffee served with a hopeful smile and a nervous twitch

Simon spent the next week in a daze, his mind a blancmange of recipes and possible topics of conversation. He ambled through his days at the shop distractedly, performing his double-act with Dean without paying much attention.

The following Saturday, Simon woke at five o'clock in the morning. He was so nervous that he realized that he would never be able to go back to sleep again. Instead he got up and prepared an extremely long shopping list.

Most of the day was spent in frantic culinary preparation.

Simon was so busy cooking that he didn't have much time to think too much about the evening itself, and so he approached it with the studied insouciance of a headless chicken.

An extremely expensive bottle of champagne sat on the top shelf of his fridge. Simon tried not to think about Joe's assertion that women didn't care about the quality of the food or wine on these occasions. Simon was a firm believer in the principle that you have to speculate to accumulate. On that basis, he stood to accumulate a *lot*.

At about four o'clock in the afternoon, Simon realized that the flat was in chaos. For the first time he considered panicking properly. He spent half an hour trying to clear up some of the more obvious mess in the flat, scooping up used coffee cups, emptying rubbish bins, arranging books and records into neater piles on the floor.

As he surveyed the sitting room a little while later, Simon suddenly realized that if things went according to plan he would need to tidy up the bedroom, too. And, even worse, the bathroom. With a sigh, he started work.

The cleaning done, Simon brushed and flossed his teeth, and then anointed himself liberally in *Rhino pour Homme*, a new after-shave he had bought that morning. The packet had announced that this was a sophisticated new fragrance for Modern Man, with a Woodsy, Light-Hearted Impression but with Brooding, Oaky Undertones and High Notes of Cinnamon and Vanilla. Simon had been intrigued. As the fragrance settled on his skin, however, the over-powering impression was not woodsy, or light-hearted, but more redolent of a latrine which hadn't been cleaned for several weeks. Simon did his best to wash it off, but try as he might, he couldn't eradicate the Subtle Whiff of Piss that still lingered after five minutes' vigorous scrubbing.

Simon was worried about what he and Dr Gilbert were going to talk about. This was the problem with the fast-track seduction process. Where invitations were issued under some other sneaky pretext, some ostensible reason other than bald lust, it provided the perfect excuse to skirt discreetly around the real issue until both parties were feeling suitably relaxed, or sufficiently drunk. But things became decidedly more awkward where there was no common ground. He picked up the telephone and called Joe.

'Hello, mate,' said Joe. 'How's things?'

'I wanted to ask your advice,' explained Simon. He outlined the position so far with Dr Gilbert.

There was a loud whistle down the phone line. 'Fuck me,' said Joe. 'You actually did it. Good for you.'

'Nothing to do with that stupid challenge of yours, of course,' said Simon hastily.

'Oh, of course,' agreed Joe.

There was a pause.

'The thing is,' said Simon, 'I wanted to pick your brains.'

'Fire away,' said Joe.

'I don't know what to say to her,' said Simon. 'What do we talk about?'

'I thought you were the one who advocated conversation as an honourable pastime,' said Joe wryly.

'That was then,' replied Simon. 'This is now.'

'Ah,' said Joe. Simon heard a high female laugh

somewhere in the background. 'What have you talked about so far?'

'My injuries, mainly.'

'Nothing else?'

'Well, I've established that she doesn't like films or plays.'

'OK, so try and find out what she *does* like. You know, ask her what she does in her time off. What are her hobbies? Get her to do all the talking. Ask her stuff. What was her most memorable meal? Does she like being a doctor?'

Simon sniffed. 'That's not very original,' he said.

'Well, no,' admitted Joe. 'It's not. But there's no need to be original. You're not getting marks for *originality*. Some women don't even like it. It catches them off-guard, makes them have to think. Your best bet is to stick with the tried and tested stuff.'

'OK,' said Simon. 'So what else?'

'Ask her what her dreams are. You know, her hopes, aspirations and ambitions. That's usually a good one.'

'Dreams,' said Simon. 'Are you sure?'

'Trust me,' said Joe. 'Women love that shit.'

'OK,' said Simon uncertainly. 'Dreams. Right.'

'If you've got some good stories you can tell against yourself then that's always a helpful stand-by. A bit of self-deprecating humour is good. Shows you don't take yourself too seriously.'

Simon thought of Joe's story at the dinner party two weeks earlier. Now *that* would make a great story to tell a girl you were trying to impress. He sighed. 'All right. Stories. I've got enough of those.'

'Apart from that, I think you should just go with the

flow, see where the evening takes you,' said Joe. 'You'll always find something to talk about until you start taking each other's clothes off.'

Simon shut his eyes in apprehension. 'Thanks, Joe,' he said. 'I think.'

'Not at all. Give me a call tomorrow, yeah? Let me know how it all went. And good luck. It'll be one down, two to go.'

'No, I've already explained –' began Simon, before he heard the buzzing in his ear. Joe had hung up.

Simon didn't know whether to cackle hysterically or cry. This was madness, utter madness. On the message pad next to the telephone he wrote down, 'Hobbies, Memorable Meal, Doctor, Dreams. Stories against Yourself.'

Simon put on his nicest shirt. He laid the table in the sitting room, and lit two candles.

Finally, with fifteen minutes to spare before his guest was due to arrive, Simon fell on to the sofa, exhausted. He had put on a record of the Modern Jazz Quartet, playing tunes from *Porgy and Bess*. The calm, controlled performances soothed Simon's over-anxious mind. He took a few deep breaths, and began to relax. This had better be worth it, he thought darkly.

Suddenly a chill went through him. Despite all his careful preparations and planning, he had forgotten one crucial thing.

Condoms.

Simon struggled off the sofa and scuttled to the bathroom where he began to rummage frantically through the cabinet in the vague hope that he might find a long-forgotten prophylactic from a distant campaign hiding beneath the detritus of pill boxes and razor blades.

There was nothing. Simon glanced at his watch as he tried to stem the feeling of panic that was rising in his throat. She was a doctor, for heaven's sake. Surely if she had sex in mind then she would bring her own supplies? Probably, but it would look bad if he didn't have his own. Presumptuous. Arrogant. Above all, stupid. Or would it look charming? Simon wondered hopefully, as if the possibility of an end-of-evening tumble had simply not occurred to him. Probably not, he concluded. He sighed. There was no avoiding it. He would have to go and buy some. He went to look for his crutches.

As retail outlets go, Simon's local shop was a peculiar place. Certain ranges of items were more fully represented than others. If you wanted to buy a fresh chilli, it offered one of the finest selections in London. It was also pretty good on some of the rarer varieties of kumquat. If you wanted bread or margarine, however, that was more likely to be a problem.

The shop was long and thin. The walls didn't really have a colour as such; they were too dirty for that. Apart from a grimy window at the front of the shop and two dim strip-lights, the largest source of light was the bright neon glow from inside the glass-topped freezer compartment which stood in the middle of the shop, flanked by dried pasta on one side and cartons of crisp packets on the other. The over-powering smell in the shop was of curry powder.

Charlie, the shop's owner, was stationed behind his old cash register, as always. He greeted Simon with a broad wink. 'All right,' he said.

'Not bad,' said Simon. Charlie liked to share his own brand of home-spun philosophy with his customers, and it was possible to get trapped for some time if he was feeling in a loquacious mood. 'Listen, Charlie,' said Simon by way of pre-emptive strike, 'I'm in a bit of a rush.'

Charlie spread his fat hands in front of him. 'Whatever it is, I'll help if I can,' he said.

'OK, good. The thing is, right, that actually I need a packet of condoms.'

Charlie's laughter rattled up and down the shop, causing the other customers to look up for a moment. Simon stood in front of the till, looking pained.

'You?' said Charlie a few moments later.

'Is there a problem?' asked Simon stiffly.

'A problem? No, there's no *problem*. It's just – well.'

'Well what?'

'Well. What do you want condoms for?'

'I would have thought that was pretty bloody obvious,' snapped Simon.

'But you've never bought *condoms* before. Are you turning over a new leaf, or something?'

'Look,' said Simon, who was eager to get back to the flat. 'Are you going to sell me some or not?'

'All right, keep your hair on,' said Charlie mildly. 'What sort do you want?'

'What?' Simon looked blank.

'What sort? You can have ribbed ones, coloured ones, flavoured ones, ones with funny pointy bits on the end, big ones, little ones. You name it, I've got it.'

'God. I don't know. You choose.'

'Can't do that,' said Charlie. 'Too much responsibility, man.'

'Well, all right then, do you have any normal ones?' asked Simon.

Charlie looked disappointed. 'Suppose so.'

'Then I'll have a pack of those, please.'

'Three, six, twelve, eighteen or twenty-four?'

'Jesus. Three.' Simon paused. 'Make that six.'

'Good boy. Hope you've been drinking your milk.' Charlie rang up the condoms on the till. 'Would you like a bag, sir?' he asked, trying to hide his sniggers.

'No thanks,' said Simon, and snatched the box. He thrust it into his pocket and began to hobble back to the flat.

As Simon turned the corner back into his street his spirits performed a curious stretching manoeuvre, soaring and dipping at the same time. Dr Gilbert was standing by his front door, waiting. Simon looked at his watch. It was exactly eight o'clock. What sort of a woman is on time for dinner appointments? he wondered. The sort that wants to get things over with quickly, perhaps, suggested the gloomier part of his brain.

'Hi,' he called.

Dr Gilbert turned towards him and flashed him a relieved smile. 'Hi,' she said. 'I was beginning to think I had got the wrong day.'

'No, no,' said Simon, pulling his keys out of his pocket. 'I just had to run to the shop to get some last minute supplies.'

Dr Gilbert looked at him appraisingly. 'Didn't they have what you wanted? You haven't got any bags.'

'Oh. Er, no. They didn't.'

'What was it you needed? Was it important?'

Simon shut his eyes in frustration and tried to think.

'Not really,' he said. 'Just something for a garnish. We can live without it.'

'Sure?'

'Sure I'm sure.' Simon smiled weakly. 'Come on in.'

EIGHT

Inside, Simon took Dr Gilbert's coat and hung it up.

'So, er . . .' he said.

She looked at him. 'It's Rachel,' she said. She produced a bottle of wine from behind her back. 'This is for you,' she said.

'Wow,' said Simon. 'That looks *great*. Fantastic,' he said, conscious that he sounded as if he had never been given a bottle of wine before. 'Thank you very much. So, Rachel. Welcome. Thanks for coming. What can I get you to drink?'

'What have you got?'

Simon decided not to pull his punches. 'How about some champagne?'

Rachel smiled. 'Champagne sounds perfect. Thank you.' She wrinkled her nose. 'What's that smell? Do you have a problem with your drains?'

'Yes, yes I do,' said Simon hastily, regretting his liberal hand with *Rhino pour Homme* earlier in the evening. 'The plumber's coming next week. Look, come in and have a seat. Make yourself at home.'

Simon went into the kitchen and pulled the champagne from the fridge. He followed Rachel into the sitting room where the MJQ were still playing gently. Suddenly a slow,

steady thudding sound began to echo through the
from Angus and Fergus's flat. Oh no, thought Simon. Great timing. He poured two glasses, and handed one to Rachel. They looked at each other for a beat too long.

'Right, cheers,' said Simon, and necked half of his drink in one needful swallow.

'Cheers,' said Rachel, taking a more dainty sip. She looked around. 'Nice place.'

'Thanks,' said Simon, his stomach a knot of nerves.

'What's that noise?' asked Rachel, pointing at the ceiling. The thudding had got louder and faster.

Simon shrugged affably. 'No idea,' he said, gesturing Rachel towards the sofa. He wracked his brains for something to say. All of Joe's advice had flown from his head. 'Busy day?' he finally blurted.

'Pretty busy,' said Rachel. 'Sorting things out for my holiday. Buying sun tan lotion, books, that sort of thing. Not very exciting. You?'

'Oh. Busy-ish, I suppose,' lied Simon. 'Equally boring, really. A bit of shopping. Knocking supper together.'

'What is this awful music?' asked Rachel.

There was a brief pause. 'It's the Modern Jazz Quartet,' said Simon.

'Would you mind if we put something else on?' asked Rachel. 'It sounds like elevator music.'

'Oh. OK.' Elevator music? Hiding his horror, Simon switched off the record player. 'Perhaps you'd like to choose something,' he said.

'Yes, good idea,' said Rachel.

'Do you like jazz?'

'God. No. I hate it. It's all pillocks who think they're cool just because they wear dark glasses in smoky night

music, if you can call it that, is just lots of
and squeals and too much drums. Yuk.'

Well, that's certainly one opinion,' said Simon, aghast. 'I'll leave you to choose, then. Back in a tick.' He moved off back to the kitchen, leaving her peering at the spines of his record collection.

In the kitchen he drew in a couple of deep lungfuls of air. The woman was a philistine. Well, he thought, that's one problem out of the way. At least you know there's no danger of falling in love with her. Just get through the meal, have the sex, and then be over with it all. Simon arranged the first course decoratively on two plates. When he walked back into the sitting room, Rachel was still looking at his records.

'Not much here I recognize, to tell you the truth,' she said, straightening up.

'How about Mozart?' asked Simon. 'Will that do? It's not jazz, anyway.'

'Don't you have *anything* decent?'

'Mozart's not bad,' protested Simon.

'Matter of opinion,' sniffed Rachel.

'Well it's probably the best I can do,' replied Simon, drawing his record of Mozart's clarinet concerto out of its sleeve and placing it on the turntable. There was a pause as they both listened to the opening bars of the piece, trying to ignore the insistent banging from overhead which was now going at break-neck speed. Simon casually wandered over to the stereo and turned up the volume.

Suddenly what was unmistakably Heather's whinny echoed shrilly through the flat, accompanied by a supporting chorus of chortling grunts from Fergus. Rachel looked suspiciously at the ceiling. A few moments later, the thudding stopped.

There was an awkward pause.

'So, Rachel,' began Simon, his cheeks hot. He stopped. What was it he was supposed to say next? That was it – hobbies. 'Tell me a little bit about yourself,' he continued, trying not to sound like a game-show host. 'Any hobbies?'

Rachel took another sip of champagne. 'Well,' she said, 'I enjoy toxophily.'

Simon nodded slowly. 'Right,' he said. 'Interesting.' What on earth was toxophily? Presumably something to do with poisons. 'Toxophily,' he repeated, rolling the word around his mouth, trying it out. 'So. Why that? Presumably because you're a doctor.'

Rachel frowned. 'Well, in a way, I suppose. I do it with other people from the hospital.'

Simon nodded. Weird hobby, he thought. 'Where do you do it?' he asked.

'In Kent. Near Tonbridge.'

'Really? Why so far away?'

'Well, you need a big field, and we found one in Kent.'

'A field? You do this *outside*?'

Rachel looked at Simon oddly. 'Of course we do.'

'So, what, do you practise on animals? Random bits of wildlife roaming around?'

'On animals? Good grief, certainly not. Do you think we're monsters?'

'No, no, of course not,' said Simon hastily. 'So what do you use?'

'Well, targets, of course, like everybody else.'

It began to occur to Simon that he might have been

mistaken about the poisoning thing. Targets. He thought quickly. 'And do you have your own . . . stuff? To use, er, with the targets?' he fished.

'The bows and arrows? No. We hire them all when we get there.'

Archery. Why couldn't she have just said so? He tried to think of something interesting to say about it. 'Are you any good?' he asked.

'Not really. I'm just a beginner. I'm better at small bore rifle shooting.'

Simon sat up. 'You shoot small boars?' he asked, shocked.

Rachel nodded. 'Since I was at school.'

'I see.' Simon shifted uncomfortably. What was this obsession with shooting things? He hoped he hadn't unwittingly chosen to sleep with a psychopath. He wanted to shift the conversation away from maiming and killing, and tried to think what else was on the list of topics Joe had suggested. 'Hobbies, Memorable Meal, Doctor, Dreams. Stories against Yourself.'

'So,' he said. 'Tell me about your dreams.'

Rachel shut her eyes momentarily. 'I don't dream,' she said. 'I suffer from acute insomnia.'

'Oh,' said Simon. 'Actually, when I said dreams, I meant more –'

'Which may be no bad thing in my job,' continued Rachel bitterly, 'given the hours that we're expected to work.'

There was a pause. Simon realized that he should show some sympathy. 'Oh, poor you,' he said.

'What do *you* do?' asked Rachel suddenly, looking at him directly for the first time since she had sat down.

'Me? Oh, I – nothing much,' stammered Simon, suddenly ashamed of his insubstantial way of passing his days. You save lives, I sell stink bombs. 'Tell me about your insomnia,' he suggested, eager to steer the subject away from him.

'It's awful,' said Rachel. 'I flop into bed, totally exhausted, and then stare at the ceiling all night, unable to get a wink of sleep.'

'Isn't there anything you can do about it?'

'There are various things like hypnosis, although I've never tried. The one thing that always works for me is getting drunk.'

'Ah,' said Simon.

'At which point I suffer from narcolepsy.' Seeing Simon's blank face, she explained: 'That's when you fall asleep when you're not supposed to.'

'*Ah*,' said Simon again. What a peculiar woman, he thought. 'Er, right,' he said. 'Hungry?'

Rachel smiled at him. 'Ravenous.'

'Excellent.' Simon gestured towards the table. 'Have a seat. I'll be through in a minute.' He returned to the kitchen.

Simon set a pan of water at a rolling boil on top of the stove, and added the lobster to it, setting the timer for twenty minutes. He inspected the first course critically, and allowed himself a smirk of self-congratulation. It looked perfect. He carried the plates into the sitting room and proudly set one down in front of Rachel.

'Voila,' he breathed.

There was a brief pause while Rachel inspected her Ballontine of Guinea Fowl stuffed with Pan-fried Foie Gras served on a comfortable bed of Radicchio and Endive leaves with home-made Croutons al Forno and drizzled lightly with a Piquant Butternut and Dandelion Vinaigrette.

Finally she said, 'Oh.'

'What?' asked Simon.

'It's my fault,' said Rachel. 'I should have said.'

'Said what?' asked Simon.

'I'm a vegetarian,' explained Rachel. 'Sorry.'

Simon's mouth opened and closed a few times.

'It certainly looks nice, though,' said Rachel.

'Are you a very conscientious vegetarian?' asked Simon.

'Oh, absolutely, afraid so.'

Simon shut his eyes in despair. Suddenly he thought of the lobster sitting in the saucepan on the stove. 'What sort of a vegetarian are you, exactly?' he asked, trying not to panic.

'What do you mean?'

'Do you eat fish, that sort of thing?'

Rachel nodded. 'Oh yes. I *love* fish. I'm a lacto-ovo-pesco-vegetarian.'

'Good,' said Simon. 'We're safe for the main course, anyway.' He looked at Rachel's plate. 'Can you pick around the meat?' he asked. 'The rest of it is quite nice even just on its own.'

Rachel shook her head firmly. 'I can't. It's been polluted. It's been sitting on the same plate.'

Simon looked at Rachel in disbelief. 'My salad is tainted?' he managed to say.

'I'm afraid so.' She looked at him with disdain. 'Don't worry. You go ahead. I'll have more room for the main course. Do you mind if I have some more champagne instead?'

'Of course, help yourself,' said Simon, cursing himself

for failing to keep her glass full. At this rate they would both need to be paralytic if anything was to happen later.

Simon ate as quickly as he could. He could hardly taste the guinea fowl. As he shovelled food into his mouth, he got Rachel to talk about her imminent holiday to Greece.

Finally he finished. 'Right,' he said, still chewing his last pleasureless mouthful as he stood up. 'Let's see if I can do a bit better for the main course. Help yourself to more champagne. I won't be long.' He checked his watch as he went back into the kitchen. The lobster was just about done. All he needed to do was to heat up the sauce he had prepared earlier and administer the culinary coup de grace, which would give the whole dish a bit of a zing. Simon reached into the fridge and took out a small, red, and very potent fresh chilli. He chopped the chilli up into tiny pieces, swept it into the sauce and began to stir.

Simon pulled the lobster out of the boiling water. It was bright red. He arranged the lobster pieces on the plates, and spooned the white wine and basil mousse into artful heaps next to them. The cream sauce was simmering gently. Almost there, he thought. This was going to be good. The way things had gone so far, it *had* to be good.

'We're nearly ready,' he called. 'Shan't be a moment.' He went to the bathroom for a pee.

As he stood in front of the toilet he awarded himself a pat on the back. Whatever else had gone wrong so far, and even if she was a vegetarian philistine who hated jazz, the lobster would redeem things. It was an impressive and delicious dish. If that and the champagne weren't enough to get Rachel Gilbert into his bed, then nothing would.

Suddenly Simon was aware that something wasn't quite

right. An uncomfortable feeling had begun to manifest itself around his genitals. A moment or two later, the uncomfortable feeling was gone, replaced instead by an unholy pain. His penis felt as if it was on fire. It was as if a red hot needle had been rudely shoved up his urethra.

Simon stifled a howl of agony. In the absence of any useful alternative, he began hopping up and down on the spot, clenching his teeth in an effort not to make any noise. His penis flopped up and down as he jumped, but even such efficient exposure to the cooling air failed to relieve the burning sensation. It was as if he had dipped his member into a saucepan of boiling water. He suddenly understood how the lobster must have felt.

Then Simon realized what had happened. The chilli. He had forgotten to wash his hands after he had chopped the little bastard up – hands which had now pawed his hapless penis. Tears began to well up at the corner of his eyes. The pain was excruciating. It felt as if a swarm of belligerent wasps had settled on his foreskin.

With the caution of a bomb disposal expert, Simon carefully placed his aching member back into his underpants. Bent almost double, he scrubbed his hands furiously and hobbled back to the kitchen.

'Are you all right?' called Rachel from the sitting room.

'Fine,' muttered Simon.

'I've helped myself to some more champagne,' said Rachel. 'Hope that's OK.' She giggled. 'Oops. Champagne on an empty stomach. Silly me.'

Simon shut his eyes. The evening's priorities had suddenly shifted dramatically. Now the last thing that he wanted to do was to let Rachel anywhere near his private parts. What he really wanted to do was to stick his penis into a bowl of ice cubes. Trying to ignore all sensations below his waist, Simon spooned the cream and chilli sauce carefully over the lobster.

'OK,' he called. 'Here I come.' He picked up the two plates and gingerly made his way back into the sitting room. As he put the plate down in front of Rachel, he saw that the champagne bottle was almost empty.

Rachel inspected her plate. 'This looks nice,' she said.

'Thank you,' whispered Simon. The pain had not diminished.

'What is it?' asked Rachel.

'Lobster,' replied Simon. 'With truffles and pistachio nuts and stuff like that. Hope you like it.'

Rachel looked at Simon. 'I'm really sorry, Simon,' she said sadly, 'but I can't eat this.'

Simon looked at her, lost for words. Finally he said, 'But you're a lacto-ovo-pesco-vegetarian. This is seafood. It's fine.'

'I'm Jewish, you clot,' said Rachel, not unkindly. 'It's shellfish. I'm not *allowed* to eat this.'

Simon looked at his guest in dismay. 'You didn't say anything about *shell*fish.'

'Well, you didn't ask.'

Simon slumped into his chair. A Kosher vegetarian. Unbelievable luck, from a culinary perspective. The pain in his groin seemed to have been somewhat eclipsed by this news. 'What are we going to do now?' he asked.

Rachel sat back in her chair, looking at her plate of untouchable food. 'Have you got some salad I could have?' she asked.

'I suppose so.' Simon stood up again and picked up her plate.

'I'll need a clean plate, of course,' she said. 'And if you've got any more wine, that would be good.'

'Right,' muttered Simon. This, he could see, was a very good plan. They should both get drunk. This would have the additional and not inconsiderable benefit of anaesthetizing his groin. He went to the fridge and pulled out a plastic bag of washed lettuce, and plonked it unceremoniously on to a clean plate. There was little point in trying now. He took the plate and a bottle of pre-made Italian vinaigrette into the sitting room and set it down in front of Rachel.

'How's that?' he asked.

Rachel inspected the lettuce. 'Seems fine,' she said.

'Good.' Simon fetched a bottle of wine and the bottle opener from the kitchen and opened the bottle. Food would have to wait. He poured healthy measures of wine into their glasses, and began to drink.

The meal, such as it was, was conducted more or less in silence. Rachel inspected each leaf carefully before putting it in her mouth. Simon did his best to enjoy the lobster, but he had lost his appetite. His penis was still throbbing painfully, and he sat with the lower half of his body as motionless as possible. To make matters worse, his foot had begun to itch. The clarinet concerto had finished, but Simon didn't dare move to put on any other music.

Simon looked at Rachel, who had eaten hardly any of her salad but was matching him glug for glug on the wine. The doorbell of the upstairs flat rang, and Simon and Rachel listened to the enthusiastic exchange of greetings and noisy air kisses. Angus and Fergus knew how to entertain properly, thought Simon miserably. 'Everything all right?' he asked politely.

'Fine. You?'

Simon nodded. 'Oh yes. Absolutely fine.'

'Good.'

There was a pause.

'More wine?' said Simon.

Hours later, neither Simon or Rachel had moved other than to drink. They had barely spoken to each other.

Simon had been desperately wracking his increasingly muddled brain in an attempt to find something to talk about. The party upstairs was now in full swing, and the sound of music, laughter, and general festivities filtered down into Simon's flat as a dramatic counterpoint to the nightmarish awkwardness that had descended there. As each cork was popped, as each joke was met by peals of laughter, Simon felt his soul shrivel a little more. He wondered whether Delphine had been invited again. Delphine! His heart fluttered. What was he doing here with Rachel, for heaven's sake?

There was also, of course, the small matter of Simon's genitals, which were still unspeakably sore. As he hobbled to the kitchen to fetch the bottle of wine that Rachel had brought, a thought occurred to him. Rachel was a doctor! Surely she would know what to do about his penis. He realized though that he should have asked her about it straight away. To go back into the sitting room now and solemnly declare that, actually, and he couldn't think why he hadn't mentioned it before, his cock felt as if it was on fire, and would she mind taking a quick look? would look suspicious at this stage of the evening.

That was another thing. What on earth was Rachel still doing here, anyway? She had been fed virtually nothing and they had exchanged scarcely more than a few words all evening. She should have got up and made her excuses a long time ago. It was well past the time when she could have escaped without embarrassment. And yet she was still here, knocking back the wine as if oblivion couldn't come quickly enough.

A worrying thought tripped into Simon's brain. What if, said the thought, she's after what you're after? What if she's waiting for sex?

Simon gulped. It would explain a lot. It would explain why she had accepted his artless invitation in the first place, and why she was still sitting at his table after such an atrocious evening. Simon thought of Joe's remark about the irrelevance of food to the seduction process. Well, he thought ruefully, I think we've established that beyond any reasonable doubt. He looked at his watch. It was past midnight. The tubes had stopped.

Simon slumped against the wall of the kitchen and wondered what on earth he should do. The idea of Rachel going near his genitals in anything other than a strictly medical capacity made him weak with apprehension. He would just have to fend her off as best he could, he supposed. Simon walked gingerly back into the sitting room. Rachel had, ominously, moved to the sofa.

'*Hi*,' she said.

'Er, hi,' replied Simon.

'I thought we should move over here,' explained Rachel. 'Get a bit more, you know, *comfortable*.'

Simon gulped. 'OK,' he said. He reluctantly sat down on the sofa and began to pour wine into their glasses. Rachel watched him with renewed interest as he did so.

'Mmm,' she said. 'Lovely.'

Simon said nothing. The transformation from taciturn alcoholic to seductive temptress was unnerving. Rachel flashed her eyes coquettishly. 'So,' she said. 'This is nice.' She inched closer towards him. Simon's penis began to scream in alarm.

'Goodness me,' he gasped. 'It's late.' He made a great show of looking at his watch. 'Doesn't time fly when you're having fun?' This was supposed to sound sarcastic but instead for some reason sounded sincere.

'Far more fun to be had yet,' murmured Rachel lasciviously, recommencing her advance up the sofa.

'Shall I, er?' asked Simon, before catapulting out of his seat and moving over to the record player. He scanned his music for something wholly inappropriate which would shatter the mood. For the first time in years he found himself wishing he hadn't given away all his Southern Death Cult records.

'Put on something mellow,' suggested Rachel.

Simon shut his eyes. 'OK,' he said meekly. He pulled out a record of Satie solo piano pieces. The wistful chords of the first Gymnopédie floated into the room. Simon hobbled back to the sofa, thinking furiously.

Rachel nodded at him in approval. 'Very nice,' she said. His genitals cranked up the pain an extra notch. Simon sat back down on the sofa and took a long swig of his wine.

'So,' he said.

'So,' Rachel agreed.

Simon abandoned the subtle approach. 'Shall I call you a taxi?' he asked.

A frown flickered over Rachel's face. 'I didn't think we were quite finished yet,' she said.

'Oh?' said Simon. As soon as he said it, he realized he had made a terrible mistake. What had been required was a brisk, Afraid so, busy day tomorrow, thanks for coming, perhaps I'll see you soon, bye, and instead he had said 'Oh?' in what, he saw miserably, might even be construed as a *hopeful* tone of voice. For God's sake, he thought. You can't do *any* of this stuff right.

Rachel put down her wine glass purposefully. Jesus, here we go, thought Simon. His penis continued to throb in apprehension.

'Now,' said Rachel, 'I've had a very nice evening so far.'

'Oh good,' replied Simon uncertainly, wondering what a bad evening was like.

'And I would very much like to continue things for a little bit longer.' Rachel's eyes flashed again and her tongue emerged slightly from her mouth. Simon gulped.

'And I think,' continued Rachel thickly, 'that we should get a bit more . . . intimate.' With this she lunged at Simon across the sofa, effortlessly negotiating the small fortification of cushions that he had been casually trying to erect between them. Simon watched helplessly as his guest hurtled towards him, primed and loaded with amorous intent. As she approached, Simon opened his mouth to protest, which (in retrospect) was a tactically naïve move: Rachel took the opportunity to insert her tongue into it before he could say a word.

Half a second later, the rest of Rachel's body arrived,

slamming unceremoniously into Simon's side. For a small woman she had managed to build up quite a bit of momentum and Simon was half-winded, leaving him prostrate on the sofa like a limp rag-doll as he struggled to regain his breath. Rachel took this absence of active protest as encouragement, and ran one hand through Simon's hair and placed the other on his crotch.

It was at this point that Simon recovered enough to realize that now he had no choice but to react – Rachel had begun to paw the top of his trousers, and the consequent doubling of pain in his nether regions jolted him into action. He tried to protest, but his tongue just slapped against Rachel's and all he could manage was a few muffled moans. Rachel began to moan a little herself to show that she, too, was having a good time.

After a few more moments of this unedifying and slightly unequal struggle, Simon managed to push Rachel off. Rachel sat back on the sofa, her pupils dilating and her breath heavy.

'Wow,' she breathed.

'Um,' replied Simon.

'That,' said Rachel, 'was *nice*.' She sat back and reached for her wine glass. Watching her drink, Simon had an idea.

He adopted a bug-eyed face.

'Is something wrong?' asked Rachel.

Simon gripped the arm of the sofa tightly. He said nothing, but looked stricken.

'What is it?' demanded Rachel.

Simon rose unsteadily to his feet. 'I'm sorry,' he stammered. 'I don't feel too good, all of a sudden.'

Rachel frowned. 'What –?' she asked, before Simon,

judging his moment to perfection, hurried out of the room with a suitably theatrical gasp, holding his hands up to his mouth. He went into the bathroom. He stood with his back against the door, and took a few deep breaths.

Simon began to make the loudest retching noise he could manage. He called up reserves of phlegm that he didn't know existed. He coughed, he gurgled. He sat on the toilet, staring miserably at the ceiling, as he created a rich aural tapestry of someone being violently, horribly sick. And, he had to admit, it sounded pretty good.

There was a quiet knock on the door. Simon quickly kneeled down in front of the toilet and opened its lid. 'Hello?' he groaned.

The door opened a crack and Rachel peered in. 'Are you OK?' she asked.

Wow, some doctor you are, thought Simon. He turned towards her and raised his best puppy eyes to her face. 'Not so good,' he replied. 'Actually, I've been a bit sick.' He wiped his mouth with his shirt sleeve. He hoped Rachel's professional interest wouldn't prompt her to inspect the vomit, and he moved slightly to block her line of vision to the pristine toilet bowl.

'I heard,' said Rachel. 'It sounded bad.'

Simon nodded sadly. 'It was. Is. That is, I don't think I've –' He turned quickly and stuck his head deep into the bowl of the toilet, and began heaving.

'I think I'll just leave you to it,' said Rachel before shutting the door behind her.

Simon stood up again, and began to produce puking noises of real flamboyance while he gazed morosely at himself in the bathroom mirror. How long, he wondered, would he have to keep this up before Rachel's ardour had been extinguished completely?

Some minutes later, Simon emerged from the bathroom. He didn't have any further backup plan in the event that Rachel hadn't been totally grossed out by his performance in the bathroom. Nervously he peered into the sitting room.

Rachel Gilbert had fallen asleep on the sofa.

NINE

There was a loud explosion as a car engine choked and backfired.

One eye.

A squadron of fat-chested birds began chorusing outside the window. A child's scream rose from the pavement.

One and a half eyes.

The BOOM BOOM BOOM of a neighbour's bass bin rattled the window frames.

Two eyes.

Simon's head remained motionless on his pillow as memories of the previous evening flooded back into his brain. He groaned. At least the pain in his nether parts had disappeared. The relief that this news would ordinarily have engendered, however, was muted somewhat by the ferocity of Simon's hangover, which felt as if the front part of his brain was encased in a tightly-wound wrench. Cautiously he turned over. The bed was empty. Simon hauled himself out of the bed. He peered around the cdgc of the doorway into the sitting room. The sofa was empty.

Simon heaved a sigh of relief. Rachel Gilbert had gone. He went into the kitchen and switched on the kettle. By the sink were some folded pieces of paper. On top of them was a page from the message pad by the telephone. A note had been scrawled on it.

Hi Simon. Thanks for an interesting evening. Hope you're feeling better today. Sorry I fell asleep on you. Anyway. Thought you might be interested in this.

Rachel

P.S. Sorry I never got to hear any 'Stories against Yourself'. That sounded quite interesting.

Frowning, Simon picked up the note and inspected it. On the other side were the words 'Hobbies, Memorable Meal, Doctor, Dreams. Stories against Yourself' that he had scribbled down after his conversation with Joe. He threw the note into the bin. Then he picked up the other papers Rachel had left and began to read.

St Botolph's Hospital and Trust

Internal Memorandum

Strictly Private and Confidential

To: Head of Personnel
Secretary of Trust staff
Surgeon in Chief

From: Hospital Administrator

Re: Saturday 10 July

I have been asked to prepare a report about the incidents that took place in the Accident and Emergency Department at the Hospital on the evening of Saturday 10 July.

Mr Simon Teller arrived at the A and E admissions desk at approximately 11.15 p.m. Nurse Bagnall, who was on duty at the time, saw immediately that Mr Teller was experiencing a certain amount of difficulty speaking. Nurse Bagnall believed that this might be a symptom of earlier concussion, and paged a doctor to perform a preliminary check on the patient.

The examination was performed by Dr Cooper, who established that Mr Teller was merely extremely drunk. Mr Teller had also suffered a sprain in his right wrist (see attached medical report).

Having established that there was no immediate danger, Dr Cooper instructed Mr Teller to wait in the out-patient area until a doctor was able to examine his wrist. Mr Teller duly returned to the waiting area at approximately 11.45 p.m.

The next incident took place by the automatic coffee vending machine in the A and E waiting area at approximately 12.30 a.m. Mr Stuart Booker had taken exception to the way in which Mr Teller had earlier spoken to his girlfriend, Anita Hulse, and had followed Mr Teller to the coffee machine in order to confront him. There he accused Mr Teller of using suggestive and offensive language towards Miss Hulse. When subsequently questioned about these accusations Mr Booker alleged that Mr Teller had started talking to Miss Hulse about what semen looks like in bath water.

It appears that as a result of the confrontation

at the coffee machine, Mr Booker shoved Mr Teller, causing Mr Teller to be propelled backwards into a hospital trolley, which was occupied by Mrs Ida Matthews. Unfortunately the trolley's wheel locks had not been set, causing the trolley, with Mrs Matthews on it, to roll backwards on impact with Mr Teller.

The coffee machine in the A and E department is situated next to the stairs leading down to C block and the mortuary unit. Mrs Matthews's trolley was positioned at the top of those stairs and the momentum created by the collision with Mr Teller caused the trolley to topple over the top of the stairs. Fortunately the trolley's descent was halted before it reached the bottom of the stairs and so Mrs Matthews did not suffer any adverse effects other than a degree of distress caused by her precipitous descent to the mortuary unit. The trolley was stopped by Mr Liam Thrush, who had just identified his mother's body in the mortuary and who was therefore in a somewhat highly-strung emotional state. Having stopped Mrs Matthews's descent, Mr Thrush saw Mr Teller leaning against the wall at the top of the stairs. Seeing this, Mr Thrush concluded that Mr Teller had pushed Mrs Matthews's hospital trolley down the stairs as a prank.

This is the reason that Mr Thrush has given for his subsequent behaviour. He began to chase Mr Teller through the waiting area, and was joined in his pursuit by Mr Booker.

Mr Teller began to run through the hospital in an attempt to escape his two pursuers. As he turned the corner at the top of Staircase 3, however, he collided with Orderly Hughes, who was making his way to the operating theatre. Orderly Hughes was carrying a heart which had been recovered from a fatal car accident in the West Midlands. As members of the Board will know, hearts are carried in aluminium flight cases. On colliding with Mr Teller, Orderly Hughes dropped the aluminium case. Fortunately, the case's fall was broken by landing on Mr Teller's big toe.

Having picked up the box again, Orderly Hughes was able to continue his journey to the operating theatre. The heart was not damaged by the incident, and the transplant operation was subsequently successfully completed. The impact of the aluminium case caused serious bruising to Mr Teller's big toe.

Mr Teller was so drunk that he did not appear to notice the damage that had been sustained by his toe, and he continued to run in an effort to escape Messrs Thrush and Booker. Finally he came to a dead end, in the corridor leading towards E wing (whose doors have been locked since the bacterial alert last Spring). There were several empty trolleys at the end of the corridor. As Mr Thrush and Mr Booker approached, Mr Teller clambered on to the nearest trolley and began to direct kicks at the two men. In doing so, he lost his balance and fell off the trolley, and on landing twisted his left ankle, resulting in a further strain.

At this point staff arrived at the scene in time to persuade the other two gentlemen that there was nothing to be gained by attempting to perpetrate further violence against Mr Teller.

Mr Teller was taken into treatment straight away in order to avoid the possibility of any further attacks. He was discharged on Sunday afternoon.

RJT

Simon re-read the report twice. So. His toe had been bruised by a heart. That was ironic. Usually in the past it had been his heart that was bruised from being given the boot. As he wandered around the flat looking for aspirin, he began to understand why the nurse had been so cagey but so near to hysterical laughter at the same time. Well, he thought. You really have hit the lowest of the lows. Simon hobbled to the bathroom and was promptly very sick, for real.

Some hours later, things had not improved much.

Simon surveyed the kitchen. It was an utter mess. By the sink sat the untouched second helping of lobster, quite ruined now. Simon retreated back to bed.

Midway through the afternoon, Simon finally pulled on some clothes and began to clear up the detritus of the previous evening. This done, he went out to buy a newspaper. Reading about other people's problems had to be better than further broody introspection, he reasoned.

Back in the flat and installed on the sofa, Simon skimmed through several of the newspaper's many sections, but was too distracted to assimilate much. He looked at his watch. It was now late afternoon. The day was going too slowly, eking out his misery. He switched on the television and flicked through the channels. All of the programmes were either about religion or antiques. There was one about religious antiques. He turned the television off.

Simon had never felt so lonely.

He debated whether to call Kate. He tried to work out what time it would be in Australia. Very early on Monday morning. She would either be fast asleep, or out carousing with the locals.

Finally Simon's mind drifted back to his conversation with Joe in the pub. He thought of Joe's insouciant approach to one night stands. He'd done his best, but hadn't managed more than a one night crouch. What was Joe doing that was so right? Or, more to the point, what was Simon doing that was so wrong?

He stared at the telephone for a long time before finally picking it up.

TEN

The Pillock and Pineapple, Pint 1

'Cheers.'

'Cheers.'

'Oh, fantastic. Peanuts. You're a mind-reader. So what happened then?'

'Well, nothing. That's it. I came out of the loo and she'd fallen asleep on the sofa.'

'Didn't you try and wake her?'

'God, no. It was perfect. Thank God for narcolepsy. She was out like a light.'

'And in the morning?'

'In the morning she was gone. Vanished.'

'And your todger?'

'Seems fine now. No side-effects to speak of, as far as I can see.'

'Fully operational, then?'

'Looks like it.'

'Shame your doctor didn't hang around so you could try it out.'

'I'm sure she couldn't get out of there quickly enough. I did a pretty good job with the puking noises. I sounded as if I'd got bubonic plague. And we didn't exactly have a successful evening, anyway.'

'That was bad luck about the food.'

'Unbelievable. Look, thanks again for coming out.'

'God, don't mention it. Not exactly a struggle, is it, drinking beer and eating peanuts.'

'Well, I appreciate it. I needed to get out of my flat. I was close to over-dosing on aspirins and self-pity.'

'You're very welcome. Anyway, I wanted to be the first to hear all the juicy gossip.'

'And was it worth it? Was it sufficiently juicy for you?'

'Well, I have to admit, I haven't heard a story quite like that in a long time.'

'No, I don't suppose you have.'

'Oh, come on, cheer *up*. I've heard worse.'

'You have?'

'Well, all right, not exactly worse, but just as bad.'

'I find that hard to believe.'

'Look, Simon, I realize it didn't go quite according to plan, but you can't let that get you down. I mean, after all, she actually did want to go to bed with you, didn't she?'

'Well, it certainly looked like that, but I wasn't going –'

'Exactly. *She wanted to shag*. OK, you didn't actually get round to it, but you did the tricky stuff. Despite all the disasters with the food, she was attracted to you. She wanted sex.'

'What's your point, Joe?'

'My point *is* that you should take heart from last night, instead of getting depressed about it. You were a success. She was gagging for it.'

'I don't know. I just feel this whole enterprise is fated. I can tell that I'm going to make a tit of myself at every available opportunity. I just know it. So that's it for me. No more adventures. My career as a lothario is officially over.'

'But *why*? Just because of one small upset like that?'

'Just *because*, OK?'

'Well, it's hard to argue with such untrammelled logic.'

'Oh, fuck off, then.'

'All right. Calm down.'

'Sorry. I'm just depressed.'

'I can see that. And I'm trying to cheer you up.'

'It's not working.'

'Why did you ask me out for a drink, then?'

'I don't know. Because this is all *your fault*, perhaps?'

'Oh, come on, that's hardly fair.'

'Fair? Who said anything about *fair*?'

'Look. You have to cheer up. Don't be so down on yourself. You can't just give up because of one unlucky night. Look on it as a learning experience.'

'Just what am I supposed to be learning, exactly?'

'About women.'

'Jesus. I'm thirty-one years old.'

'Well, you were put back a few years in school because of all this Women Are People Too nonsense.'

'Seriously, Joe, it's all too little, too late. I don't see how pursuing this any further could possibly be worth it.'

'Of *course* it's worth it. All you need is a bit of luck to start you off and before you know it you won't be able to move for available women. I promise. You'll see.'

'Couldn't I just have one nice one rather than a whole crowd?'

'Do I deduce from that wistful tone of voice that you have someone in mind?'

'Of course not.'

'Thought so. Anyone I know?'

'Don't be stupid.'

'Wait. I know. That French girl. At that dinner party. What was her name?'

'God, you can be impossible.'

'*Delphine*. That's right. It's her isn't it?'

'Oh, sod off.'

'No, no, look, excellent choice. She's gorgeous.'

'Mention shit house doors or hurricanes and you die.'

'The thought never entered my mind. So if you fancy Delphine, why haven't you got in touch?'

'Oh, come on. You might as well suggest I climb the Himalayas in my underpants. It's just not going to happen.'

'Why not?'

'She's *way* out of my league.'

'Simon. Nobody, and I do mean *nobody*, is out of anyone else's league. Look at Billy Joel.'

'What about Billy Joel?'

'Well, he's an ugly bastard, isn't he? But he still married Christie Brinkley.'

'What, and because Billy Joel can, I can?'

'Absolutely.'

'There is one small difference between me and Billy Joel that you've forgotten about.'

'What?'

'Well, Billy Joel is humungously rich.'

'And?'

'Well, come on, you can't deny that it might have had something to do with it.'

'OK. Maybe you've got a point. But the fact is that the ugly guy got the beautiful girl.'

'And I should derive comfort from this?'

'Of course.'

'Well, that's *very* inspiring.'

'Thank you. I aim to please.'

'By the way, I meant to ask. How did it all go with that girl? The Seurat girl. What's her name?'

'God. Can't remember. Claire?'

'That's the one.'

'Yeah. It was fine.'

'What did you do?'

'We had a couple of drinks and then went back to my place. Then we did *everything*.'

'What? Just like that?'

'Simon, you really have to get it into your head that everyone else operates on a different timetable to you. You have to get on and get the job done as soon as possible. No time to waste.'

'So you keep telling me.'

'It's *true*. If you carry on like you've been doing you're never going to have sex again, ever.'

'All right. Just suppose – *suppose* – that I decided to carry on with this little experiment, what would you suggest I do differently next time?'

'Well, don't paw your dick while you've got chilli juice all over your hands, for a start.'

'Apart from that.'

'Apart from that, not much. You did all right, didn't you?'

'Well, I hardly felt relaxed. It would be nice if I could maybe do some of this without feeling so uncomfortable all the bloody time. I mean, if I remember correctly, it's not unreasonable to expect to *enjoy* it. That's rather the point, isn't it?'

'Do you know what might help?'

'What?'

'A change of image.'

'Really? What's wrong with the one I've got?'

'Oh, nothing, nothing at all. It's just that you might benefit from a change. You know. A change is as good as a rest, that sort of bollocks.'

'What have you got in mind?'

'Well, your hair, for starters.'

'What's wrong with my hair?'

'Nothing's *wrong* with it. It's just a bit – I don't know. You could do with a bit more of a funky cut.'

'This is fantastic. A funky cut. Are you being serious?'

'Absolutely. Look, I know a hairdresser. He's Iranian, I think. He's good. I've been going there for years.'

'And you really think this is going to help?'

'No question. Well, look, it can't hurt, can it? His name's Corky. Have you got a pen?'

'Here.'

'Here's his address. Try him.'

'I might. No promises.'

'Suit yourself. I'm just trying to help.'

'I can't believe I'm even contemplating this.'

'Oh, come on. It'll be fun.'

'All this in pursuit of meaningless sex. I must be mad.'

'No, you're just being *normal*.'

'I don't know what's normal any more. I mean, with the greatest of respect, you're completely obsessed.'

'Well, maybe. Did you know that there's a town in Switzerland called Gland?'

'Really?'

'Honest. Imagine living there. *Gland*. Now *they* must be obsessed.'

'Actually, Joe, there is something I've been meaning to ask you about all this.'

'Fire away.'

'Well. It's not the sixties any more. Sex is a bit scary nowadays. You know, what with all the diseases around. There is a responsibility that goes with it all that wasn't there before, don't you think?'

'Oh sure. You have to be careful nowadays.'

'So you always wear a condom?'

'Jesus. Of course I do. I haven't had unprotected sex for years now.'

'And before that?'

'Well, it was generally with, but sometimes without. It was at the stage when people still believed that AIDS was just a disease for gay men, drug addicts and haemophiliacs.'

'But don't you ever worry?'

'I *was* worried. Well, not so much worried. Terrified, actually. I used to sit in the bath and think about all of the women I had slept with, and then wondered who they had slept with, and who *they* had slept with. It used to make me ill just thinking about it.'

'You seem pretty calm about it all now.'

'Well, I had a test.'

'You did?'

'Sure. I was losing sleep from worry. Not because I'd been particularly stupid, but just *because*. It was the not knowing that was so awful. I just wanted to be sure.'

'God. So what was it like?'

'Awful. The results took a few days to come through. Those days weren't much fun. I couldn't concentrate on anything. All I could think was: this will change your life for ever. This may be a day you will remember for the rest of your life, the day when everything changed. Forget death – I was thinking about the rest of my life. By the time I arrived at the clinic, I was a gibbering mass of nerves.'

'But everything was all right.'

'Yeah. It was fine. I was quite proud that I didn't burst into tears of relief on the spot.'

'You were brave to have done it at all.'

'Well. Maybe. But I *had* to for my own sake, to stop me worrying. It was worth a week of hell to clear my mind.'

'I'm not sure I could go through all that.'

'Simon, mate, it doesn't sound as if you need to, the rate you've been going.'

'All right. Don't rub it in.'

'Time for another one?'

The Pillock and Pineapple, Pint 2

'Thanks. Did you eat tonight?'

'No. It's a waste of time, eating, if you're going to have a drink later on. It just slows down the whole process of getting drunk.'

'I rather thought that was the point.'

'Well, it depends on your point of view. Do you go

out to the pub to enjoy the company of your friends, the warm atmosphere of your chosen hostelry, and the witty repartee and banter of conversation, or do you go to sing obscene songs and get arse-biting drunk?'

'Why would anyone want to sing obscene songs? It's such a loutish way to behave.'

'Have you ever tried it?'

'Christ. No.'

'Aha. Then there's no way you could know what jolly good fun it is.'

'Well, all right. But isn't it possible to do a mixture of just the witty repartee and the arse-biting drunk stuff?'

'Of course you can, but if arse-biting drunk is the ultimate goal then your best bet is to drink on an empty stomach. Much more efficient. Cheaper, too.'

'I'm surprised you're prepared to admit it.'

'Why?'

'Well, most people wouldn't. And if they do, it's usually in a surprised voice at the end of the evening. You know, they come up to you, clamp a hand on your shoulder and whisper, "Actually, I reckon I'm quite *pissed*," as if this was somehow unexpected after seven pints of beer.'

'But Simon, that's all part of the fictional world men inhabit. Look at the facts. One: If you drink enough beer, you get drunk. This we know. Two: The more beer you drink, as a man, the more respect you get from your mates. Why? Largely because of Fact One. But for some reason the one thing you absolutely mustn't do is admit that Fact One *exists*. Everyone is in denial about the whole alcohol thing, until you actually collapse dead drunk into the gutter, at which point everybody applauds you as being a great sport and a bit of a character.'

'That sort of behaviour is so stupid, though. Collapsing into a gutter in public. It's like the obscene songs. It's disgusting. I suppose that's why I'm surprised that you actually *admit* to wanting to get drunk.'

'Well, life's too short for macho posturing. I'm on holiday at the moment. I don't need to get up and go to work tomorrow. What do I care if I have a hangover in the morning?'

'So do you never eat if you're going out drinking?'

'Well, it depends. On a big pub night I generally won't. If it's been a good evening then come closing time you can usually rely on somebody to suggest an après-pub detour to the local Taj Mahal for some poppadoms and a beef vindaloo.'

'Ugh.'

'Ugh is right. For some reason the idea of a curry has huge appeal when you're sitting over your last pint in the pub. And even as you're spooning huge globs of that runny mint sauce over your onion bhaji and talking in a fake Indian accent it still seems attractive. It's only when they stick the plate down in front of you with a pile of sticky rice and a steaming heap of unidentifiable *meat* that it occurs to you that maybe this wasn't such a good idea after all.'

'So why do you keep doing it?'

'I don't know. Perhaps men have a small gland in their brain somewhere like the one women have which erases the memory of the pain of childbirth straight after a baby is born.'

'I'm not sure I follow.'

'Well, this gland women have is a biological necessity, otherwise nobody would ever have more than one child. And it's only when they go into labour the next time that they think, "Oh *shit*. Now I remember how much this bloody *hurt*." But by then of course it's too late. And I reckon men have a similar memory-erasing organ when it comes to eating curry. You just don't remember how much you regretted doing the same thing last time. If it weren't for this little quirk of the male brain most of the curry houses in Greater London would have gone out of business years ago.'

'I'm not a big curry fan myself.'

'Neither am I. Mind you, people don't go to curry houses because they like curry.'

'They don't?'

'God, no. They go because they can carry on drinking beer after the pubs have shut. But more importantly, they go for Trial by Vindaloo.'

'Which is?'

'Good grief, you really have missed out, haven't you? Basically, the way it works is that each bloke tries to eat the hottest, most inedible curry in the restaurant, without crying. Whoever wins may scar his taste buds irreparably, but he will have gained the admiration and respect of his peers.'

'Rather like the man in the gutter.'

'Precisely. Actually, it's often the same person.'

'Delightful.'

'I knew someone whose vindaloo was so hot that he actually had to go to hospital the next day, he'd done so much damage to his digestive system. Now he can't eat anything stronger than a mild prawn korma.'

'Truly, Joe, you're a mine of seductive anecdotes.'

'Thank you.'

'Maybe I'm being thick, but I just can't see the appeal.'

'There *is* no appeal. It's more to do with tradition and a male sense of self.'

'It sounds positively Neanderthal. Do you go around thumping your chests and pissing on the upholstery when you've finished eating?'

'Only sometimes. Depends who paid the bill.'

'Jesus. What fun.'

'Don't knock it. You should try it some time.'

'It's hard to believe that I should have reached this stage of my life without ever experiencing what is clearly such a rich and fulfilling way of passing the time.'

'It's never too late to start. Time for one more?'

'Twist my arm, then.'

The Pillock and Pineapple, Pint 3

'There you go.'

'Lovely. Thanks.'

'When do your holidays end?'

'School starts again in mid-September.'

'Do you enjoy it?'

'Yes and no.'

'Intriguing. Go on.'

'It's difficult to explain. I enjoy teaching. I think I'm quite good at it. And I have no political or philosophical problems with private education. If I did, I'd be a hypocrite to work where I do. If people want to waste their money on their children's education, then that's their business. My objections are based more on the empirical results of the system.'

'Meaning?'

'Well, look, these places are businesses, like any other. In order to be successful they need to fill their order books. How do you do this? You need a product to sell. What is the product? It's the children you spew out at the end.'

'OK.'

'Well, it's much easier to sell a product if they're all more or less the same. You know, you need brand identity, or some such. So these schools have turned into factories, churning the same bland stereotype off the conveyor belt and bludgeoning any individuality into submission.'

'Doesn't sound very healthy.'

'It's not.'

'Mind you, I went to a school like that.'

'There you go. You, Simon, are the exception that proves the rule. Anyway. Tell me about *your* job. How did you get involved in magic?'

'I was given a box of magic tricks one Christmas. My parents didn't see me for the rest of the afternoon. I didn't come out of my bedroom until I could do every trick in the box. I suppose I must have been about nine. Of course, having made my family's Christmas by spending all day in my room, I then spoilt it all by making them miss half of the Agatha Christie film by insisting that they watch me do every single trick. They were very good about it, though. I think they'd seen the film before.'

'And then?'

'Well, it just went on from there. I began sending off for catalogues, buying books, and pestering my dad to take me to magic shops whenever we went up to London for the day. After a while I had amassed quite a respectable collection of tricks. I used to spend hours practising. I would stand in front of the mirror, look myself in the eye, and talk to myself as I produced handkerchiefs from nowhere. It was the sad person's equivalent of playing air-guitar. Most people back then dreamed of being in the Sisters of Mercy. I just wanted to be Paul Daniels.'

'So were you actually any good?'

'Not really. It was just a hobby. I mean, I always wanted to do it professionally, but at that age I also wanted to play for Arsenal and be a racing driver. It was a problem of deciding which glamorous career to concentrate on. Needless to say I stopped doing any magic at all as soon as I hit adolescence. No way was I going to do *that* any more. Not nearly cool enough. So all my tricks lay underneath my bed for years until one holiday when I was back from university. I was bored one afternoon, and began mucking around with them. I went back at the start of term with lots of tricks and started to bore all my friends rigid. It was just like that first Christmas all over again. After university I came to London and did all sorts of completely boring jobs. All I knew was that I didn't want a proper job until I was at least thirty-five.'

'Sounds like a sensible plan to me.'

'Well, one day I passed the magic shop where I work now, and there was a sign in the window advertising for a sales assistant. So on a whim I went in. And I'm still there, two and a half years later.'

'Ahh. I love a story with a happy ending.'

'Well, you say that, but it's not exactly fulfilling. I mean, magic is an amusing way to pass the time, but it's not going to change the world, is it?'

'Well what is?'

'Good question. I don't know.'

'So, what would you really like to do?'

'Oh, that's easy. I'd run a jazz club.'

'Really? I didn't have you down as a creature of the night.'

'I'm not. I've never understood why people think they can only listen to live jazz after two o'clock in the morning.'

'You like jazz?'

'Hah. Sort of. I'm a bit obsessive about it, to tell you the truth.'

'I've never really got into it myself.'

'Oh, you should. There's something about jazz that makes it about much more than just music. It transcends it. It's weird. It's as if it creates this direct link between the musician and the listener. It's electrifying. Listen to a great jazz solo – Miles, Ben Webster, Clifford Brown – and you just *know*. You know. And all this without a word being said. And the other amazing – what is it?'

'Sorry, Simon, you lost me way back there.'

'Oh.'

'It was interesting, though.'

'I can get a bit carried away, I suppose.'

'We should open a jazz club together.'

'Now *that's* a good idea.'

'It would be perfect. You could organize the music and do magic tricks in between sets, and I could get up and deliver lectures on *Henry IV Part 1*.'

'Sounds like a winning combination.'

'We could get pissed every night and not have to get up until late the next day.'

'And have the best musicians in the world who would want to play there because it was the best club in London.'

'And it would all be really exclusive and we'd only let famous and beautiful people in and there'd always be paparazzi outside waiting to see who was going to turn up.'

'And we could make jazz truly popular and increase its exposure so more and more people would enjoy the music.'

'And everyone would want to know us and beautiful women would sleep with us just to get into the club.'

'We should do it.'

'Yeah.'

'No, really. We should. It would be brilliant.'

'All right, then. Let's. Do you fancy going somewhere different for one more first?'

The Faggot and Gherkin, Pints 4 and 5

(As one)

'My oneskin lies over my twoskin
My twoskin lies over my three
My threeskin lies over my foreskin
So pull back my foreskin for me

PULL BACK
PULL BACK
Pull back my foreskin for me
For me

PULL BACK
PULL BACK
Pull back my foreskin for me!'

O'Malley McShamrock's Genuine Irish Hostellrie, Pint 6

'Look, fancy a quick curry once we've finished this one?'

'Yeah! Great idea!'

The Bombay Balti Brasserie, later

'There are your beers, gentlemen. Can I take your food order now?'

'Let's see. They do a good chicken tikka masala here.'

'Sod that. I want a – what did you say it was?'

'Beef vindaloo?'

'That's the one. *That's* what I want.'

'Are you sure?'

'Course I'm sure. Don't you think I can handle it?'

'No, Simon, it's just – oh, never mind.'

'Right. One beef vindaloo and some popalongs, please.'

'Poppadoms, sir?'

'Right.'

'And for you, sir?'

'Oh, I'll just have a prawn korma, please.'

The Bombay Balti Brasserie, even later

'Simon, are you all right?'

'Er, yeah.'

'Sure? You look a bit – odd.'

'No, it's all right. It's just a bit –'

'Quick, have some more beer.'

A Gutter, later still

'Simon. Simon? Are you OK? Can you get up? Simon? Can you hear me?'

ELEVEN

'Blimey,' said Dean the next morning as Simon gingerly pushed open the door, half-an-hour late. 'You look awful.'

'Bit of a hangover,' whispered Simon. 'I had quite a night last night.'

'Yeah?' Dean looked impressed. 'What did you get up to?'

'Just went for a few drinks with a mate of mine. Then we went for a curry.'

Dean looked surprised. 'I didn't have you down as the curry-eating type.'

'Oh yes,' said Simon. 'I love a good curry.' In fact he was having a certain amount of difficulty speaking due to several lacerating ulcers that had appeared on the roof of his mouth, caused by five mouthfuls – all he could manage – of his scalding beef vindaloo. He had resolved never to go near a curry house again.

Simon leaned against the counter and closed his eyes. He had an astronomically bad hangover. Instead of the usual guilty self-recriminations over a glass of water fizzing with pain-killers, though, today was different. Simon was actually in a very good mood. For the first time in his life, Simon was actually *enjoying* a hangover.

He was celebrating: last night he and Joe had got drunk. They had talked, they had caroused, and yes, they had sung obscene songs. Some of the conversation, he was prepared to accept, had been less than edifying and one landlord had asked them to leave (which was in itself a new experience for him), but overall they had had a great evening, of that he was sure.

In the past Simon had tended to go drinking with girls, and nights out were less raucous, more refined affairs, even if the drinking was more determined. Last night, though, he'd been out in a *gang*. A gang of two, admittedly, but there was an undeniable satisfaction at the manly camaraderie he and Joe had enjoyed. At long last, Simon felt as if he *belonged*. Life had stopped happening just to other people; he was finally getting his turn. Even the disastrous episode with Rachel Gilbert had been eclipsed by the success of the previous evening.

Simon at last understood why men behave like morons when they go out drinking together: it was actually quite good fun.

'How about you, Dean,' asked Simon. 'Good weekend?'

'Yeah, not bad,' said Dean.

'Do anything nice?'

'Not much.'

'See anyone nice?'

'Not really.'

'But a good weekend.'

'Yeah, not bad,' confirmed Dean.

Simon changed tack. 'Looking forward to another week of magic and mayhem?'

Dean pulled a face. 'Not really,' he said.

'No,' agreed Simon. 'Can't say I blame you.'

Vick had emerged from the stock room, and was listening to their conversation. Both Simon and Dean were unnerved by her presence, and soon they fell into an uneasy silence.

'Simon,' said Vick.

Simon turned around. 'Yes?'

'Can I have a word?'

'Right,' said Dean. 'I'm off.'

'Where are you going?' demanded Simon.

'Er, you know, off,' replied Dean, before hurrying into the stock room, leaving Simon to fend for himself.

'OK, I'm all yours,' said Simon reluctantly. He braced himself.

'You're a bloke, aren't you?' said Vick.

Simon shrugged.

'OK, well answer me this, then,' said Vick. 'Why, as a bloke, would you take a girl out a couple of times, do all that romantic stuff, you know, and then disappear off the face of the earth?'

'Oh dear,' said Simon. 'Young love's course not running smoothly, then?'

Vick frowned. 'What?' she said irritably.

'Boyfriend problems?' tried Simon.

Vick nodded. 'If he *is* a boyfriend.'

'What's his name?'

Vick looked at Simon suspiciously. 'Russell,' she said.

'And what exactly is the problem?'

'He's stopped calling me.'

Simon suppressed a smile. It was comforting to know

that he wasn't the only one with romantic difficulties. He pictured the unfortunate Russell, his teenage face festooned with acne and embroidered with bum-fluff.

'Go on, then,' he said. 'Tell me about Russell. Where did you meet, for a start?'

'At a club,' said Vick.

'What, drama club? Athletics club?'

Vick looked at Simon oddly. 'A night club in Brixton,' she said.

'Oh,' said Simon. 'What were you doing there?'

'It's on every other Thursday. It's called "Lunge". Wicked flava and jungle. With DJ Roadkill.'

Simon pressed on. 'So, OK, you met at this "club". When was this?'

'About three weeks ago.'

'OK. And you've seen him since then?'

'Once or twice. We've gone to other clubs, stuff like that.'

'And now he's not calling?'

Vick shook her head. 'We were supposed to be meeting up last Thursday at a new one-nighter in Camberwell, and he just never turned up. And since then I've heard nothing, no apology, nothing.'

'Well, maybe he couldn't make it and he's too embarrassed about it to call you.' Simon imagined Russell's parents sternly wagging their fingers and imposing an eleven o'clock curfew on school nights.

Vick didn't look convinced. 'But he should have called,' she whined.

'Can't *you* call him?'

Vick looked shocked. 'Don't be stupid,' she said.

'Well, all right, then,' said Simon, whose good spirits

had put him in a generous mood. 'If you want to get him back, you have to make him want you.'

'And exactly how am I supposed to do that?'

'Perhaps you should make him feel jealous.'

Vick looked doubtful. 'How?'

Simon thought. 'You could pretend to be going out with someone else. Someone far cooler than he is.'

'And exactly how do I do that?'

'Easy. You lie.'

Vick considered. 'OK. So let's say I do that. Then what?'

'Then you wait. Once he starts hearing these stories about you and this other guy, then maybe he'll realize what a mistake he's made, and he'll come crawling back to you, begging for you to have him back. And then you both live happily ever after.' This last bit, thought Simon, was possibly somewhat unlikely.

'Interesting,' said Vick thoughtfully. 'I might give it a go.'

'So tell me a bit more about this Russell,' said Simon encouragingly.

'Well,' said Vick, 'his name is Russell Square.'

'Oh,' said Simon. Russell Square and Victoria Station. It was perfect. Two London Underground stations thrown together in love. Simon could see why the two had been attracted to each other. They probably both came in for a fair amount of teasing in the playground and so had sought refuge in each other. Simon looked down at his shoes and tried not to laugh.

'Funny, is it?' said Vick.

'Not at all,' said Simon, keeping a straight face. 'Perfectly good name.'

Vick looked slightly mollified. 'Well. Anyway. Thanks for the advice.' She thought for a moment. 'I may just pop out for a minute,' she announced. 'Might make a quick call.'

'Fine,' said Simon. 'No time like the present.'

Vick eyed Simon beadily. 'Right,' she said. 'Back in a bit.' She turned and nearly ran out of the shop.

A minute or two later, Dean emerged from the stock room, glancing nervously about. 'Has she gone?' he asked.

Simon nodded. 'The coast is clear.'

'What was all that about?' he asked.

'Boy trouble,' explained Simon.

Dean pulled a face.

'Listen,' said Simon. 'You won't believe what this poor guy is called.'

Dean crossed his arms. 'Amaze me.'

Simon's eyes sparkled with mirth. 'Russell Square.'

There was a pause.

'Russell *Square*,' repeated Simon. 'You know, as in the place. The tube station.'

Dean frowned. 'What about it?'

'Well, don't you think it's funny? Victoria Station and Russell Square?'

'There's nothing funny about being named after a place,' said Dean.

'Oh, come on,' retorted Simon. 'It *is* pretty funny.

'*My* name is Dean Street.'

There was a long pause.

'Of course,' said Simon, 'not all place-names sound ridiculous. And Dean Street's in Soho. So your name is cool. Unlike Russell Square, which is just stupid.'

Dean was still looking hurt. Simon began to wonder

how he could have worked with Dean for two and a half years and never have learned his surname. He tried again. 'Look, Dean, I'm sorry. I didn't mean it.'

Dean sniffed and turned away to wipe an imaginary speck of dust off the cash register. 'Forget it,' he said shortly.

Simon sighed. It was going to be a long day.

The rest of the morning was quiet. At one point while Dean had gone to make the tea, Simon surreptitiously pulled a small bit of paper out of his pocket and examined it. On it was written the address of Corky, the hairdresser that Joe had recommended the night before.

Simon had decided that he would go and visit him. It was about time he had his hair cut anyway. He certainly wasn't going just because Joe had suggested it. Of course not.

Simon hadn't really thought much about his hair since he had been fourteen. (Then, of course, he had thought about it a lot. In those days, peroxided hair was considered, amongst fourteen-year-old fashion cognoscenti, to be the quintessence of chic. During chemistry lessons he had siphoned off small amounts of hydrogen peroxide to anoint his head with later, to no avail.) His hair was brown and rather boring. If left to grow for too long it would assume a worrying wave-like effect, which made him look like a professional footballer, but that was avoided easily enough by regular visits to the barber. No: hair was not an issue for Simon any more. It was still all there, and he was grateful for that, but that was the extent of his interest.

Corky's salon was in Mayfair. At lunchtime Simon

caught the tube to Green Park. When he arrived at the address Joe had given him, he saw an old fashioned barber's pole painted in red and white diagonal stripes attached to the wall outside. Simon carefully went down the steep stone steps and pushed open the door. As he stood in the doorway, his nostrils were assailed by the pungent aroma of pomade, which reminded him of the barber at his school, who would listen sympathetically as unsuspecting schoolboys issued precise instructions about how their hair should look, before mercilessly shearing them all so that they looked like miniature American marines.

The salon didn't look as if it had changed much for decades. On the walls there were some fading photographs of men in shirts with very large collars. Their hair shone brilliantly. So did their teeth. The floor was covered by faded and battered linoleum, which had begun to curl up at the edges. Down one side of the room was a long orange sofa. In front of it sat a small table covered in old colour supplements from the *Sunday Express*.

On the other side of the room were two barbers' chairs, all chipped chrome and battered leather, which faced two large mirrors. In front of each mirror was an old-fashioned sink, the porcelain cracked from years of use. In one corner of the room sat a small radio, out of which came the sound of a man talking quickly in an unintelligible language.

Simon stood on the doorstep of the shop, taking all this in. It wasn't quite what he had been anticipating. He had been expecting a brightly-lit salon with loud music, assistants rushing back and forth with frothing cappuccinos for clients, and stylists in tight black T-shirts who shrieked a lot. Instead, standing side by side in the middle of the room, two men in blue nylon coats watched Simon wordlessly.

Both wore magnificent moustaches, thick and black and enormous. Simon felt as if he was being scrutinized by a pair of walruses. Neither said a word.

Simon stepped into the room. The linoleum squeaked in protest as he landed on it. 'Er, hello,' he said. 'I'm looking for Corky.'

The two men looked at each other silently. The slightly smaller of the two raised his hand. 'Thass me,' he said.

'Oh good,' said Simon. 'You've been recommended to me by a friend, so I thought I'd come and see what you could do with my hair.'

'OK,' said Corky. He gestured towards one of the leather chairs.

Simon sat down. He looked at himself in the mirror. Corky fetched a nylon sheet and swung it in front of Simon, fastening it around his neck. Then he gazed critically at Simon's hair, his head cocked to one side. His moustache twitched. 'You haff good hair, strong hair,' he opined, running his hand through it a couple of times.

'Thanks,' said Simon politely. He waited.

'What you wan?' asked Corky. 'How you wan me to cut?'

'Well, I was hoping you might be able to give me some ideas, maybe suggest something a little different,' said Simon.

'Huh?' said Corky.

'I'm looking for a cut which is a bit more up to date,' explained Simon.

'Huh?' said Corky again.

Simon ploughed on. 'I suppose I'd like something a bit more, er, funky.'

Corky exchanged a glance with his colleague. The other

man shrugged. Corky scratched his tousled, grizzled head. 'Hees OK,' he said. 'I know wha I'm gonna.' He took a pair of scissors out of the breast pocket of his nylon coat and began to snip the air purposefully. Simon shifted uneasily in the chair. The other man stood to one side, watching proceedings with an inscrutable look on his face.

Corky performed a few more air snips with the scissors before putting them back into his pocket. He took an electric razor off the shelf, and switched it on. It buzzed ominously.

'You wan I thin out the back?' he asked Simon.

'Er, all right,' said Simon.

Corky thrust Simon's head forward and began to run the razor up the back of his head. Simon stared at his knees, wondering whether this had really been such a good idea. Corky began to whistle quietly to himself. Soon he pulled Simon's head upright again and began to work his razor along the sides. Simon looked at himself in the mirror. 'Not too short around the sides, please,' he said.

Corky shook his head. 'No worries. I do you a good cut. You see.' He completed one side and moved around the chair to begin the other. Simon risked a quick look. It seemed fine. Good and short, a sensible length. He relaxed a little.

When Corky had finished the second side, he went round to inspect the side he had completed first. In the mirror Simon saw him frown. Simon tried to move so that he too could examine Corky's handiwork, but as he did so Corky's hand swiftly descended on to his head in a gentle but secure grip so that he could only look straight ahead. Maintaining his grip, Corky began to speak to his colleague urgently in a language Simon couldn't understand.

The other man walked over to the chair and inspected both sides of Simon's head. When he had done so, he grunted, took a step towards Corky, and then cuffed him hard on the back of the head. The resulting sound suggested that Corky's head was entirely hollow. Corky spun round and the two men began to shout at each other, gesturing angrily towards Simon. Simon turned his head fractionally each way. He wasn't entirely sure what the argument was about. His hair seemed all right to him. After a few more ill-natured exchanges, the other man approached the chair.

'Am sorry,' he said. 'My brother, ees not so hot today. He make fuck up with your hair.'

'Are you sure?' asked Simon. 'It looks fine to me.'

'Yes, but that coz you don know what you see,' explained Corky's brother patiently. 'But he make *big* fuck up with your hair.'

'OK,' said Simon uncertainly. 'Now what?'

'Now he sort it out.' He turned to Corky and muttered something to him. Corky approached the chair cautiously.

'Sorry 'bout dat,' said Corky. 'I do small mistake.'

'Big fuck up,' corrected his brother.

'Small mistake,' insisted Corky, 'and now I make good, OK?'

'All right,' said Simon. 'Will it take long?'

Corky shook his head vigorously. 'Oh no,' he said. 'No time.' He picked up his electric razor and bent down to inspect the side of Simon's head, and after a few moments began to attack it again.

'What are you doing?' asked Simon. 'It was fine as it was.'

Corky waved a dismissive hand. 'No, ees no fine. You don't mind, I fix, OK?'

'Er, right, OK,' said Simon doubtfully.

Corky busied himself with the electric razor, which hummed and rasped in his hand. He would stand gazing at Simon's hair for a minute or two, and then apply the buzzing razor so delicately to the side of his head that Simon was sure that it had had no effect at all. Having done this, Corky would then move to another area of Simon's head and perform the same manoeuvre.

Some time later, Corky stood back and admired his work. 'There,' he said. 'Now ees even. Ees good.' He released Simon's head from his grip and Simon was finally able to turn his head both ways.

'Oh, bollocks,' said Simon quietly.

Whilst the individual snips and swipes of Corky's razor were on their own insignificant, the cumulative effect was devastating. Simon wasn't quite bald around the sides, but very nearly. He had been scalped.

'So,' said Corky agreeably. 'We done that bit. Now wha?'

Simon regarded what was left of his hair numbly. He shrugged. 'You'd better cut the rest of it pretty short, I suppose,' he replied. 'Only not,' he added hurriedly, 'quite as short as what you've done already.'

Corky nodded, and pulled out the scissors from his coat pocket again. He proceeded to hack what remained of Simon's hair into an immaculate flat-top, about a quarter of an inch off his skull. By the time he had finished, the top of Simon's head looked smoother than a putting green.

Corky fetched a mirror and held it behind Simon's head. Simon looked at his hair with resignation. He looked like the Action Man that he had cherished when he was six.

He hauled himself out of the chair. It was time to go back to work. As he walked back to the Tube station, he did his best to avoid looking at himself in shop windows. There was a slight summer breeze passing through the tops of the trees in Berkeley Square. Simon felt it whistle past his scalp.

When Simon arrived back at Station Magic, Dean, Brian and Vick were all in the front of the shop. Dean was demonstrating a card trick to a man and his young son, who were both peering intently over the glass counter top. Brian was looking on from behind the sanctuary of the velvet curtain. Vick was giving some of the displays a desultory flick with the end of a brightly coloured feather duster. As Simon stood in the doorway, there was a momentary silence. And something happened that Simon had never seen before.

Victoria Station laughed. And laughed. And laughed.

TWELVE

Things were not going particularly well.

Simon's attempts to liven up his sex-life could not exactly be described as unqualified successes. The episodes with Rachel Gilbert and Corky had done little more than cause horrendous embarrassment.

Perhaps the largest cloud that was looming over Simon's personal horizon, though, was the imminent prospect of having to stand up in front of a crowd of Sophy's young friends to perform magic tricks for them at her birthday party. The party was the following Saturday afternoon, and Simon was still reduced to gut-wrenching terror every time he thought about it. Consequently he had done his best not to think about it at all, and so still had no idea what he was going to do. This, of course, made him feel even worse.

At least he was no longer using the crutches. The bindings on his wrist and foot had been removed by his local GP – the prospect of another return to the hospital being now so fraught with the danger of cumulative embarrassments that Simon could not contemplate it. The doctor had reluctantly agreed to return the crutches to the hospital for him as well.

* * *

One morning later that week as Simon walked to the shop, he stopped as usual to buy a copy of the *Big Issue* from Bob, who was in an expansive mood.

'How goes it, my friend?' he asked as Simon delved into his pocket for change.

'God. Don't ask. Awful, just at the moment. If I could just borrow someone else's life for a while so I could forget about the mess mine's in, I'd jump at the chance.' Simon handed over his money.

Bob looked at Simon critically. 'You always have the ability to change things, you know. Your destiny is there to be shaped. If you don't do it, other forces will. But it's in your hands, first and foremost.'

'I don't know, Bob,' replied Simon bitterly. 'I get the feeling that those other forces are already in the driving seat. I lost control of my destiny a long time ago. I just get swept up in everyone else's mess.'

'Nonsense. You can always get control back.' Bob handed over the magazine. 'Look at me. I was a complete mess until I found Buddha and saw the light.'

Oh what, thought Simon meanly, and now you're sorted, homeless and standing on street corners selling magazines?

'I realized that I had to change myself completely,' continued Bob, 'so I took a new name, and set out on a new road.'

Simon frowned. 'You changed your name when you became a Buddhist?' he said.

Bob nodded. 'You're supposed to. You know, Cassius Clay became Mohammed Ali. That sort of thing.'

'OK. And you changed yours to Bob?'

Bob nodded.

'What was it before?'

'Phil,' said Bob.

There was a pause.

'Right,' said Simon.

An electronic trilling sound broke the silence. 'Sorry,' said Bob, and reached into his back pocket. He extracted a small mobile phone. 'Hello?' he said. 'Yes. Yes. All right. Sounds good. Yep. And tell him, it has to be *good*. OK. Right. Yes. OK. Cheers. See you later.' He briskly flipped up the flap and put the phone back in his pocket.

'You have a mobile phone?' said Simon.

Bob shrugged. 'How else am I going to keep in touch?' he asked.

'What's wrong with a normal phone?'

Bob looked at Simon strangely. 'You seem to forget that I'm *homeless*. I can't *have* a normal phone. That's why these things are a God-send.' He tapped his back pocket. 'I can be contacted twenty-four hours a day, seven days a week. Brilliant.'

Simon shook his head in bewilderment. 'Er, right,' he said. 'I'd better go.'

Bob waved a serene hand. 'Catch you later,' he said. 'And remember. Take charge of your life. Enshallah.'

It was a fairly quiet day in the shop. Brian was out for most of the morning, and Vick was keeping very much to herself in the stock room.

Simon was still worrying about Sophy's party. He decided to seek Dean's counsel. Dean suggested three or four tricks that were low on magic but extremely high on audience participation, with particular emphasis on screaming and dialogue of the 'Oh-no-it-isn't-oh-yes-it-is' variety.

'And balloons,' said Dean.

'Really?' said Simon, his shoulders sagging.

'Absolutely,' confirmed Dean. 'Kids love balloons. You can do all that stuff, can't you?'

'I used to,' said Simon. The idea was that the magician would take a long, straight balloon, and with a few deft twists would transform it into a rough approximation of a giraffe or a sausage dog. 'It was a long time ago, though.'

'Better get practising then, hadn't you?'

At that moment Vick walked into the shop from the stock room. She smiled at Simon, who was immediately on his guard.

'Hello,' said Vick cheerfully.

'Er, hello,' replied Simon.

'Remember what you said to me about Russell?' said Vick.

'Yes,' said Simon cautiously.

'Well, I thought you might like to know that I took your advice. I told everyone who knows him that I'm seeing someone new. He'll probably have heard by now.'

'Well, good for you,' said Simon. 'You watch. He'll be ringing you up in no time.' Simon wondered whether this was in fact true. It was quite within the bounds of possibility that Russell would be whooping with joy and relief when he heard the news.

'Hope so,' said Vick. 'Anyway, guess who I've been telling everyone I'm seeing now?'

'No idea,' said Simon. 'Who?'

'You,' said Vick.

'*What?*'

'You,' repeated Vick.

'Tell me you're joking,' said Simon, aghast.

Vick shook her head. 'I've told everyone you're this gorgeous guy I work with. I thought you'd be flattered,' she added, after a pause.

'Oh, well, obviously I *am*,' said Simon quickly. 'It's just that – well. I don't know.' It was just that he didn't want to get any more involved in Vick's love life, whether on a fictional basis or not. He thought of the hoards of school children who would now be whispering his name, fingering him as the one who had broken poor Russell's heart.

'I think,' he said carefully, 'I'd prefer it if you didn't mention me any more. Use someone else instead.'

Vick shrugged. 'Fair enough. Mind you, it's a bit late now.'

'Yes, well. For future reference.' He pictured the pimply Russell Square hatching dreadful plots of revenge. Oh come on, he reprimanded himself. How much damage can a schoolboy do?

'Anyway,' said Vick, 'I'll let you know how I get on, shall I?' She beamed.

'Er, OK,' said Simon.

As Vick went whistling into the stock room, Simon reflected that he preferred her sullen and moody. Better the devil (quite literally) you know, he reasoned.

That evening, Joe rang.

'Are you up to anything tonight?' he asked.

'Not really,' said Simon cautiously.

'Good. Come on, then. Get your dancing shoes on.'

'What?'

'And your fin.'

'My fin?'

'You and me are going dancing and sharking,' said Joe.

'Oh God,' said Simon.

'Listen. There's this bar called Slick Tom's. They have live music every night.'

Simon pulled a face down the telephone. 'I don't know,' he said. 'It sounds terrible.'

'It *is* terrible,' agreed Joe cheerfully. 'It's full of twats in suits who can't dance and gorgeous drunk girls from Spain and Sweden who are over here on holiday.'

Simon thought about gorgeous drunk girls, and then about his disastrous haircut. 'Absolutely no bloody way,' he said.

Forty-five minutes later, Simon was standing in the queue outside Slick Tom's, waiting for Joe to arrive. In front of him stood a gaggle of women, smoking cigarettes and adjusting their bra straps. Whenever a man walked past they poked each other in the ribs, rolled their eyes, and dissolved into gales of ribald laughter. There then followed what appeared to be a complex ritual of digital inter-communication, as fingers were flashed silently at each other, sometimes with one hand, sometimes with two. This would cause further sniggers, and the occasional jeer. Simon realized that they were awarding the men marks out of ten. A chill went through him. He stared at his shoes and wondered whether this was such a good idea.

A few minutes later Joe joined him in the queue. 'Bloody hell,' he said as he approached. 'It's Vanilla Ice.'

'Ha ha,' said Simon.

'What happened to your hair?'

'That, Joe, was the fine work of your mate Corky.'

'Shit. It looks awful.'

'Yes, I know. Thanks.'

Joe clapped his hands together and rubbed them vigorously. 'So,' he said. 'Are you ready for this?'

Simon shook his head. 'Probably not,' he said.

'Come on,' said Joe. 'It'll be a hoot.'

Simon remained unconvinced.

Eventually they passed under the heavy stare of the two enormous doormen in black bomber jackets and purchased two tickets to get into the subterranean bar. As Joe pushed open the large double doors at the bottom of the stairs, a huge wall of sound rolled out and seemed to buffet them physically. Simon stared in horror. In the middle of the large, low-ceilinged room was a four-sided bar, which was surrounded by baying packs of drinkers, in crowds at least five deep. The rest of the room was only marginally better in terms of human congestion. All Simon could see was a seething mass of bodies. Everybody was shouting at everybody else. The noise was phenomenal. Above the extraordinary human racket a song which Simon didn't recognize was playing through the loud speaker system. Beyond the bar area Simon could see another larger room, also filled with people. At the back of that area was a stage, in the middle of which sat a drum kit. Four men stood on one side of the stage, smoking, looking a little apprehensively at the crowd in front of them.

Joe looked at the chaos before them with satisfaction. He leaned sideways and shouted directly into Simon's ear.

'God,' he bawled, 'I haven't been here for a while. Always a happy hunting ground.'

Something in Simon's inner ear shattered as Joe shouted at him and he winced in pain. He began to feel dizzy. Joe gestured into the melee. 'Shall we?' he shouted. Simon nodded, braced himself, and set off after his friend into the throng. The journey to the bar did not take very long, as they arrived at a halt when they were still a good ten yards away from it. Above the heads of the people in front of them, Simon could see two bar staff who were slowly serving people and doing a successful job of ignoring the hundreds of other punters who were desperate to buy a drink. As they stood waiting, Simon was prodded, poked and shoved from all sides. Cigarette smoke hung heavily in the air, and soon his eyes began to water. After a few minutes the front row of a rugby team moved in behind them and slowly started to push forward, crushing Simon and Joe against the backs of the people in front of them. Simon was still feeling unbalanced from the trauma Joe had inflicted on his left ear. The cramped conditions at least meant that he didn't need to worry about falling over. There was nowhere for him to fall.

Joe turned to Simon. 'Isn't this great?' he asked.

Simon looked at Joe. 'Fantastic,' he shouted. 'I haven't had this much fun since I stepped on a wasp in my bare feet.'

'Believe me,' said Joe, 'it'll be worth it.' As he spoke, a girl with a three-inch band of lycra wrapped around her chest eased past him, clutching six bottles of beer above her head. Joe turned away from Simon and shouted something in the girl's ear as she went by. A wide grin spread over her face. She looked at Joe archly, and nodded, before moving on. Joe turned back to Simon, grinning.

'What did you say to her?' asked Simon.

'The usual old bollocks,' shrugged Joe. 'I'll see if I can find her later. She was quite fit, wasn't she?' He turned and cheerfully watched the complete lack of progress at the bar. The three enormous men behind them edged fractionally closer. Simon had begun to sweat.

A loud drum roll came across the loud speakers, followed by an unsavoury cough. 'Evenin' all,' said a disembodied voice. 'Our name is Zurich, and we are your entertainment for the evening. Are you all having a good time?'

Everyone continued shouting at each other as before, taking no notice.

'I *said*: Are you all having a good time?'

This time there was a muted wail from the crowd in front of the stage.

'Orright. We're going to start you off nice and gentle with a couple of slow numbers, give you a time to get good and pissed before we liven things up a bit later on. This one is from R.E.M.'

With that the band started to play, extremely loudly. The most noticeable consequence of this was that the entire crowd queuing at the bar began to nod in unison. After a minute or two, the nodding had mutated into a fully-fledged dance, as the crowd rose up and down as one. The music crashed through the speakers. Simon tried not to listen. When the song finally ended, everyone around him began cheering.

The next song was even louder than the first, and was obviously popular in rugby clubs, as the massive trio behind Simon began shouting the words at each other, accompanying themselves with manly and percussive slaps on each other's backs.

Thirty minutes later, Simon and Joe finally reached the bar. Simon, who by now was completely exhausted, leaned with relief on the counter and tried to catch the bartender's eye. The barman served the people on their left, and then on their right, and then he turned away and started to serve people on the other side of the bar. Finally he sauntered back across the bar and casually raised an inquisitive eyebrow towards Simon.

There was a sudden thump as an enormous hand landed on the bar next to him. It was one of the rugby players. The barman's eyes flicked immediately upwards to a spot just behind Simon's head.

'Six pints of Guinness,' barked a very loud voice into Simon's right ear.

The barman nodded and set to work.

Hang on, Simon wanted to say. There is a fucking queue. He had however been momentarily incapacitated by the rugby player's brutish yell. Something had gone ping in his ear, as another integral part of Simon's auditory system disintegrated. As it did so, Simon suddenly found that he had regained his sense of balance: equal damage had now been inflicted on both ears. Unfortunately for him, Simon was still able to hear properly, which meant that he could hear the gravelly, out-of-tune honks of a saxophonist who had got up on stage to join the other musicians. Simon winced. Everybody else still seemed to be enjoying the music though, as they continued to rock back and forth.

Simon looked around him. Everyone was smiling and shouting. He could only assume that they had already been there for some time. There were certainly a lot of attractive girls about. There were also the promised twats in suits, who leered at every female in sight, pulling hard on their cigarettes as their mean eyes flitted across the room.

Simon turned back to the bar and watched the barman slowly line up six pint glasses on the counter top. The man yawned as he lazily flicked the switch behind the pump and watched the black liquid trickle into the first glass. Simon watched anxiously, appalled at the slowness of it all. When the first glass was half full, the barman turned off the tap and waited for the liquid to settle in the glass. Oh perfect, thought Simon bitterly. It's a fucking *Irish* pub. That meant that Guinness had to be poured in the correct way, which took, approximately, for ever. He sighed and glanced at Joe, who had turned away and was chatting to the girl standing next to him.

Very slowly, full pints of Guinness began to appear on the counter. Joe tapped Simon on the shoulder, and gestured to the girl he had been speaking to.

'Simon,' shouted Joe. 'This is Corinne.'

Corinne smiled and waved. She was wearing a tight T-shirt beneath a pair of dungarees that were too big for her. The tightness of the T-shirt and the bagginess of the dungarees provided the optimum eyeful of her ample bosom for the casual onlooker whilst maintaining some semblance of propriety. She was very pretty.

Simon smiled back, unsure what else to do. Was he supposed to talk to her? If so, how?

'Hello,' he bawled.

Corinne smiled blandly back.

'Corinne's from Canada,' shouted Joe. Corinne nodded in confirmation.

'Really? Canada?' Simon was flummoxed. 'That's nice,' he said. Suddenly he felt himself being pushed forcefully downwards as an immense arm reached over his shoulder to pick up the glasses of Guinness. Simon managed to squeeze himself sideways just in time to avoid being hammered like a pile-driver through the floor. The giant behind him began to distribute drinks to his friends, two pints each.

Joe leaned over. 'Listen, can we get Corinne a drink too? What d'you reckon?'

Simon shrugged. 'Sure. We should get served – oh bollocks.' The barman had now wandered off to the other side of the bar again.

Some time later – although how much later Simon was unable to tell, as he had by that stage lost all track of time – Simon, Joe and Corinne were finally served. They pushed their way to the side of the stage and watched as the band blasted its way through 'Play that Funky Music'. Simon sipped his drink very slowly. The prospect of going back to the bar again was too ghastly to contemplate. Joe was talking to Corinne while scanning the passing crowd, presumably for the girl with the lycra top he had spoken to earlier. Conversation was not helped by an artless and screeching saxophone solo which seemed to go on for ever.

'So,' shouted Simon to Corinne. 'Are you here on your own?'

Corinne shook her head. 'I'm meeting two friends. They're really great. They're Canadian, too. Debbie and Bryony.'

Joe did a not very subtle thumbs-up sign behind Corinne's back.

Simon sighed, and looked at the over-crowded dance floor. People were singing, dancing, and waving their drinks in time with the music. From where he stood Simon could count at least four couples who were snogging openly, ignoring the surrounding whirl of dancers. There was an atmosphere of brazen lust floating through the room. Acres of nubile female flesh were on display, shimmying and shaking to the music. Lips pouted, eyes flashed, breasts heaved. Trousers bulged. Next to Simon a young couple stood with their faces stuck together and their hands planted firmly on each other's buttocks. From where he stood the only movement that Simon could detect was a hollowing out of their cheeks and a slight circular movement of their heads. Simon turned away. All this palpable horniness was out there on the dance floor and he could do no more than watch from the sidelines. He took a parsimonious sip of beer and wondered how long he would have to wait before he could go home.

Simon glanced idly towards the bar area. As he did so the crowds parted for a moment and he saw something that brought his glass to a halt half-way to his lips. Standing by the bar was another twat in a suit, who was bending down leerily over a young blonde. The girl was leaning towards him, gazing up into his eyes. Then the crowd swarmed back to obscure Simon's line of vision, leaving him to contemplate what he had just seen.

The twat in the suit was Michael, Simon's brother-in-law.

Simon simultaneously felt the conflicting emotions of extreme anger, at the all too apparent betrayal of his sister, and a warped sense of elation that his suspicions about Michael's infidelities had finally been proved right. He knew he had to do something. He might never catch Michael red-handed again. Simon turned to Joe and Corinne. 'I've just seen someone I know,' he shouted. 'Back in a tick.' He turned and pushed into the crowd.

Simon shoved his way back towards the bar. He found his emotions in a state of free-fall. Part of him was hoping fervently that he had been mistaken, and that the twat in the suit was not Michael at all. Arabella was happy in her ignorance, after all, and much as Simon despised Michael, he did not want to be the architect of their failed marriage. But Bella deserved to know the truth, didn't she?

Finally he reached the spot where the couple were standing. The man's back was now towards Simon and he had to negotiate some more drunken revellers before he was in a position to get a proper look at the man's face.

The man was bending down, speaking so closely into the girl's ear that he could quite easily have nibbled her earlobe. When he looked up briefly and saw Simon watching him, his face drained of colour.

It was Michael all right.

With a swift movement of his right arm he smoothly pushed the girl aside without giving her another glance and moved towards Simon. The girl looked at Michael in annoyed surprise for a few moments, before disappearing into the crowd, shaking her head.

'Simon, good lord. What a surprise. Get you a drink?'

Simon shook his head. The last thing he wanted to do was to stand talking to Michael for half an hour while they waited to get served. 'No thanks,' he said.

'What are you doing here?' asked Michael.

'I'm here with a friend.' Simon pointed towards the stage.

'Right, right. Excellent.' Michael did his best to pretend that seeing his brother-in-law was the best thing that had happened to him so far that evening. He actually looked mortified.

'What about you?' asked Simon.

'Me?' Michael held a hand up to his chest. 'Oh, well, I'm, er, here with clients, actually.' He paused. 'Not my sort of place, frankly,' he continued. 'Awful, in fact.'

'Indeed,' said Simon. He waited.

'Yes,' said Michael, looking around desperately.

'Who was your friend?' asked Simon.

'Friend?' Michael had a peculiar look on his face.

'The one you were talking to just now.' Simon pointed at the crowd into which the girl had disappeared.

'Oh *her*,' said Michael. 'She's not a friend. No idea who she is. She wanted to know what the time was.' He laughed a little too forcefully.

'Good of you to explain it to her in such detail,' observed Simon. Michael shot him a look of naked hatred.

There was a pause. The music crashed on and people swarmed past them on all sides. 'So where are your clients?' asked Simon conversationally.

Michael frowned. 'My clients?' he asked. 'Oh, my *clients*. They're, er, in the loo.'

'What, all of them?'

Michael nodded eagerly. 'They tend to go about in packs. Inseparable. It's quite sweet, really. Japanese bankers. Lovely, *lovely* men.'

'Why do they like it here, do you think?'

Michael shrugged affably. 'The live music, perhaps.'

'And it seems quite a lively atmosphere,' observed Simon.

'Er, yes,' agreed Michael cautiously.

'Well, look,' said Simon, who had seen enough, '*great* to see you again. I'll leave you to wait for your, ah, *clients*. I wouldn't want to impinge on your professional entertaining. I know it's a serious business.'

Michael's face brightened in ill-disguised relief. 'OK,' he said. 'Nice to see you, anyway.'

Simon smiled flatly. 'Have a good evening, won't you? Be good.' With that he turned and fought his way back to where Corinne and Joe were standing, trying not to think about what he had just seen.

In his absence, progress had been made. Corinne was so close to Joe she was almost standing on his toes. Her arm was wrapped around his neck, and Joe clung on to her midriff with his beer-free hand, although it looked as though this was more to maintain his balance than a display of affection. Joe looked at Simon with relief as he approached.

'All right, mate,' he said, interrupting Corinne, who was speaking in full flow into his left ear. 'Was it who you thought it was?'

'Oh yes,' said Simon. 'It was him all right.' He fell into a thoughtful silence.

'Look! It's Debbie and Bryony. They're here,' squeaked Corinne suddenly, and began to wave frantically at someone by the door. From the bustling crowd there emerged two human behemoths of such singular unattractiveness that it occurred to Simon that they might have something of a problem on their hands. Simon glanced at Joe. His mouth was hanging open in undisguised horror. Corinne's friends were both grossly overweight, and the small, sharp features on their chubby faces were squashed together in a disastrously unattractive way.

Debbie and Bryony waved at Corinne as they waddled over. Corinne went to greet them, and after exchanging some ostentatious kisses, began to point excitedly at Joe and Simon.

'Oh, fuck a duck,' muttered Joe. 'What have we done?'

'Give me the duck any day,' said Simon, before reaching deep into his soul to extract a broad smile with which to greet the approaching trio of Canadians. The band, with exquisite timing, broke into Stevie Wonder's 'Isn't She Lovely?'

Corinne made the introductions, then deliberately moved in between Joe and Simon, and began to lean on Joe's arm. Joe had begun to watch the surrounding crowds even more desperately than before.

Simon smiled blandly at the two new arrivals as they exchanged news with Corinne. One of them caught his eye and gave him an awful, skewed-toothed grin.

Simon was suddenly grateful for the intrusive presence of the band, whose music was so loud it made it impossible to talk much. Joe turned his attention to the girls. He pointed at them. 'You haven't got a drink,' he said suddenly. 'That won't do.' Bryony giggled coquettishly. Simon saw Corinne deliver a terrifying stare of warning. Joe continued. 'What would you like? I'll go.'

Debbie and Bryony asked for bottled beer. Corinne did the same. Joe turned to Simon. 'Mate? For you?'

Simon looked at Joe suspiciously. Something was going on. Joe looked affably back. 'I'll have a pint, thanks,' he said. 'Look, Joe, why don't I come and help you with those?'

Joe shook his head. 'Wouldn't hear of it,' he said. 'You stay here and entertain the ladies.'

'That's right,' said Debbie. 'We need you here to look after us and to protect us from all the men in this place.'

Simon smiled weakly. 'Please,' he said to Joe. 'I don't mind helping.'

If Joe saw the desperate pleading in Simon's eyes, he chose to ignore it. 'No, don't worry,' he said. 'I shan't be long. So that's three bottled beers and one pint. Right. See you in a tick.' With that he turned and dived into the surrounding mash of bodies.

Corinne watched him go wistfully. Debbie nudged her in the ribs. 'Reckon you're in there, girl,' she hooted raucously. Bryony cackled in sisterly collusion. Corinne blushed.

The band had now started to play 'Mustang Sally', and the guitarist was embarked on a futile effort to get the inebriated masses on the dance floor to sing the chorus. Most of the dancers had by now drunk so much that the words 'Ride, Sally, Ride' were too syntactically complex for them to remember.

The amorous couple next to Simon had now begun to dry hump enthusiastically. The girl had spread her legs slightly and the man was thrusting his groin into hers in time to the music. The girl's head was tilted backwards, and she stared at the ceiling, her mouth slightly open, while her partner sucked at her neck.

'Fantastic band,' shouted Debbie.

'Fantastic,' agreed Simon, as he turned towards the

bar to see if he could spot Joe. He was nowhere to be seen.

'Nice place,' said Debbie, looking around.

'Great,' said Simon.

There was a pause.

'Fantastic band,' said Debbie again.

Simon was growing concerned about Joe. He seemed to have disappeared completely. He looked towards the bar, but the throng of people made it impossible to see what was going on. Corinne was also looking in that direction, tugging anxiously on the strap of her dungarees.

'I think I might go and see if I can give Joe a hand with those drinks,' he shouted at Debbie, swivelling to leave as he spoke.

To his horror, Debbie grabbed hold of his hand. 'I'm sure he can look after himself,' she said, winking at him. Simon felt momentarily sick from the nauseating hue of Debbie's eye shadow.

'I, er, OK,' he said.

'Tell me, Brian,' said Debbie, who had not relinquished her hold of Simon's hand, 'do you like to dance?' She gestured towards the crowds on the dance floor.

Simon shook his head. 'Not really,' he said.

Debbie smiled coyly at him. 'You're shy, aren't you?' she purred, no mean feat given the volume at which she did it.

'No,' said Simon defensively.

'Oh, Brian,' sighed Debbie, finally letting go of Simon's hand so that she could peer into her handbag and extract a packet of cigarettes. 'You're such a typical Englishman. It's so sweet.'

Simon's eyes scanned the crowd while Debbie smoked

her cigarette. Suddenly he saw the girl with the lycra strip across her chest that Joe had been searching for earlier on. She was on the other side of the room, laughing and chatting and swigging from a bottle of beer. The person she was speaking to was slouching against a table. The girl said something in his ear, and he turned to look at the band. Simon froze. It was Joe. *Bastard*, thought Simon.

There was a gasp from next to him. Corinne was looking across the room. She had also spotted Joe, and was staring at him, her face a black mask of fury. Simon looked back towards Joe. Lycra Girl said something, and they both leaned back laughing. Corinne leaned across to say something to Bryony, and then picked up her bag and left without another word.

'Is everything all right?' asked Simon, wondering whether he should go and warn Joe that he had been found out.

'Don't worry, Liam,' said Bryony. 'Corinne just spotted your mate on the other side of the room.' Bryony did not look particularly put out by this news nor very upset on her friend's behalf.

'Is she going over to talk to him?' asked Simon nervously.

Bryony shook her head. 'She's going home. She's fed up.'

'So,' said Debbie alluringly, 'looks like it's just the three of us, then.'

'Great,' said Simon bravely.

'I suppose we'll have to get our own drinks now,' said Debbie. She shot a meaningful look at Bryony.

'I'll go,' said Bryony reluctantly after a brief pause.

'No, look, that's absurd,' said Simon, seeing his opportunity. 'Let me go. I insist. Man's prerogative and all that.'

An iron grip descended on his arm. 'No way,' said Debbie firmly. 'Bryony's going.' Bryony looked less than happy, but she nodded in agreement.

'What do you want, Liam?' she asked.

Simon gave up. 'Pint of lager, please,' he said miserably.

Bryony turned to go. 'Right,' she said. 'See you guys later. Be good.' She winked. Debbie stuck her tongue out.

There was a small pause. Debbie and Simon turned to watch the band. Debbie had not relinquished her grip on Simon's arm. He risked a brief look at her face. She really was quite horrifically ugly. Debbie caught the movement and turned to face him.

'So,' said Debbie.

'So,' agreed Simon.

'Do you live near here?' asked Debbie.

'Pardon?' said Simon.

'Your home. Is it nearby?'

Simon spluttered a little. 'Not particularly,' he managed to say.

Debbie pulled a face. 'Mine neither. How far away are you?'

'Look,' began Simon nervously, 'I'm not sure quite what –'

'Oh come on, Brian,' interrupted Debbie. 'Let's not pretend we don't both know what's going on here.'

Simon's panic was momentarily punctured by a flashing, crystallised moment of resentment of Joe for his gutless desertion. He would not forgive him for this, he told himself. Debbie winked at him. Simon desperately began to concoct escape plans. He looked around. To his left, the humping couple had progressed. The man had done his best to remove the girl's skimpy top and his hands were now roving freely over her chest. Her hands were no longer clutching his bottom, and Simon could only guess where they might be and what they might be holding now. He blinked, and turned away.

Bryony finally arrived back with the drinks. 'There you go, lovebirds,' she said.

'Thanks,' muttered Simon, who immediately gulped down half his pint.

The band finished its song, and once the applause had died down the guitarist announced into his microphone, 'Thanks very much. If you have a request you can always come and ask. We probably won't be able to play it, but you never know, miracles do happen.'

Suddenly Debbie clapped her hands in excitement. 'Something Canadian!' she squealed. 'Let's ask for something Canadian!'

Simon looked at her blankly.

Bryony nudged her. 'Go on.'

Debbie clapped her hands again. 'Back in a sec. Don't let him out of your sight,' she said to Bryony as she set off towards the stage.

There was an edgy silence as prisoner and guard watched Debbie go. She reached the front of the stage and Simon saw the guitarist bend down to speak to her. He nodded a couple of times and then straightened up. 'Right,' he announced. 'We do have a request, for a certain Mr Bryan Adams.' A cheer went up. Simon's soul shrivelled a little. He had reached his musical nadir.

The guitarist continued. 'We've been asked to dedicate this song to – what's your name? – *Debbie's* new boyfriend, who is hiding at the back of the room there. So this one is for Brian. Big hand for Brian.' Simon stood frozen against the wall. This is just a horrible dream, he told himself. Shut your eyes and it will all go away.

The guitarist was obviously having a certain amount of difficulty believing that someone as hideous as Debbie actually *had* a boyfriend, or perhaps he was merely curious. 'I want to see this guy,' he said into the microphone. 'Where's Brian? Come on Brian, make yourself known.'

Simon's brain had by this stage more or less shut down. This couldn't, just *could not*, be happening. He was not a bad man. So what had he done to deserve this? Why this relentless humiliation? He stood rooted to the spot, petrified into inactivity, his brain frozen in catatonic shock.

Suddenly he felt his arm shoot into the air as Bryony grabbed it with a grip even stronger than Debbie's and thrust it upwards. There was a grunt of satisfaction from the stage. 'Ah-hahh!' cried the guitarist, pointing at Simon in case anybody had missed him. 'There he is. Lucky man,' he commented, shaking his head thoughtfully. 'Right. Well, Brian, this is for you and, er, Debbie.' With that he began attacking his guitar as the opening notes of 'The Summer of '69' roared out of the speakers.

Bryony let go of Simon's arm. Simon leaned against the wall, dazed. He saw Debbie approaching at speed, and braced himself.

'Come on!' she shouted, grabbing his hand. 'Isn't this cool?'

'Er, where are you, we, that is, going?' stammered Simon.

'To dance, of course. Come on. This is our song!'

It is extraordinary, thought Simon a few moments later as he stood in front of Debbie, cautiously waving his arms about and shifting his weight occasionally from one foot to the other, how just when you have convinced yourself that things can't get any worse, they do. The one thing worse than having to listen to a Bryan Adams' song was having to *dance* to a Bryan Adams' song. This, though, he said to himself, is surely it. I can go no lower. He looked at Debbie. OK, he thought, so technically I *can* go lower. But I won't. He began to look around furtively. He was stabbed viciously in the back by the elbow of a woman who was spinning like a whirling dervish.

Finally the song finished, and Simon went back to where Bryony was standing on the edge of the dance floor. Bryony looked at him, amused. 'Having fun?' she asked.

'Oh yes,' gasped Simon, slightly out of breath.

'Just you wait,' said Bryony ominously as Debbie approached.

'Shall I get the drinks in?' asked Simon hopefully. 'I'm thirsty after all that exercise.'

Debbie looked at him appraisingly. 'Tell you what,' she said. 'I'll go with you. Keep you company while you queue.' She turned to Bryony. 'That all right with you, Bry?'

Bryony nodded in a resigned way.

Suddenly Simon had an idea. 'Tell you what, Bryony. There's a chap over there at the bar who's a mate of mine.' He turned and pointed towards where Michael was standing. Bryony stood on tiptoe to look.

'The tall guy? I see him. Cute.'

'Well, he's just the sort of person who would like you very much,' said Simon.

'Really?' said Bryony doubtfully.

'*Really?*' echoed Debbie, perhaps a touch jealously.

'Really,' said Simon. 'You're just his type. I know this guy very well. He's almost family.'

'Why don't you bring him over here, then?' asked Bryony.

Simon thought. He didn't want to talk to Michael again. He just wanted him to suffer. 'Actually, he's very shy,' he said. 'You'd be better off going over there and introducing yourself. Be bold, though. If you wait for him to make a move you'll be there 'til Christmas. I suggest you just jump in and really go for it.'

Bryony shrugged. 'Fair enough. See you.' She turned and pushed off into the crowd.

'Right, then,' said Simon, as he watched her go with satisfaction. He turned to Debbie. 'How about those drinks?'

Debbie took Simon's arm once more and steered him towards the bar. They joined the back of the crowd waiting to be served. Debbie nudged him in the ribs.

'Saucy bastard,' she said. 'Getting rid of Bryony like that so we can be alone. Not exactly subtle.'

'Oh,' said Simon, suddenly worried. 'You misunderstand. That wasn't –'

'D'you live on your own?' she asked.

'Yes,' answered Simon automatically, before realizing that this might have been a serious tactical error. 'That is,' he began, before seeing the futility of a belated denial, 'er, yes, yes, I do.'

'Excellent. Look, I might as well tell you this now. The thing is, I'm on.'

Simon frowned. 'You're on?' he said. On what? Acid? Steroids?

Debbie rolled her eyes. 'You know,' she said. 'I've got the painters in.'

'Painters?' repeated Simon blankly.

Debbie nodded. 'It's rag week.'

'Rag week?' said Simon.

'Yeah,' said Debbie. 'You know, Dracula's tea-bags.' She winked again.

Suddenly Simon understood what Debbie was talking about, and was momentarily too horrified to speak. Debbie didn't seem to notice. 'That OK with you?' she asked.

Simon nodded dumbly.

'Actually,' she continued, quite impervious to the mortified look on Simon's face, 'that reminds me. Do you have any condoms?'

This time Simon was able to kick start his mouth. 'No,' he said firmly, with relief. 'Sorry.'

'Right, well never mind,' said Debbie. 'I saw a vending machine in the ladies', so that'll see us right. Actually, why don't I go and get some now before we forget? It would be awful to get home and then realize we'd left it too late.'

'Right,' said Simon, 'good idea.'

Debbie squeezed his arm again. Simon began to wonder what it would look like in the morning. Covered in bruises, he suspected. 'Will you be all right on your own?' asked Debbie.

'Of course,' said Simon.

'OK. Back in a tick.' For one awful moment Simon thought that she was going to try and kiss him on the cheek, but instead she just moved away and began to barge her way through the crowd. Simon watched her go, mesmerized.

He waited for a few seconds and then began threading his way through the surrounding drinkers until he reached the periphery of the crowd. Taking a deep breath, he broke cover and made a run for the door.

Simon pushed the door open and ran up the stairs back to street level. As he passed the bouncers, a refreshing blast of cool air hit him in the face and he immediately began to feel better. He walked away from Slick Tom's as quickly as he could without actually breaking into a run.

THIRTEEN

The following day, Simon decided to go for a stroll at lunchtime. He was still feeling a little shaken after his narrow escape from the amorous clutches of Debbie the previous evening. The polluted air around Victoria was better than the shop's musty atmosphere. As he closed the front door, he noticed a sleek silver Porsche parked immediately outside.

Simon was thinking about Sophy's party. He was debating whether he could bring himself to call in sick on Saturday and avoid the ordeal. Had it been anyone other than Sophy, he would have done so without thinking twice. Lost in thought, Simon failed to notice that the silver Porsche had started crawling alongside the kerb right next to him, until the driver hit the horn, waking him from his reverie. Simon stopped and turned to look at the car. As he did so, the tinted window smoothly lowered, revealing a well-dressed man in his late twenties, with a thick-set jaw and closely cropped hair. He wore a pair of wrap-around sunglasses, despite the absence of any sun. The man looked at him without smiling. He leaned out of the window.

'Simon Teller?' he asked.

'Yes,' said Simon, frowning.

The driver of the Porsche burst out of the car, grabbed

Simon by his jacket, and pushed him up against the nearest wall. His face was about four inches away from Simon's when he began to speak.

'Right, you toe-rag.'

Simon coughed. He was having some difficulty breathing.

The man continued. 'Me and you, we've got some business to attend to.'

'We have?' choked Simon.

'Yeah,' nodded the man, hoiking Simon further up the wall, and then staring at him intently. The malice was etched clearly into his features.

Simon was struggling to get air into his lungs. Finally he managed to gasp, 'Who *are* you?'

The man relaxed his grip until Simon was able to breathe more or less normally again. 'I,' he said menacingly, 'am Russell Square. Ring any bells?'

Simon's eyes boggled. This was Vick's boyfriend. Russell Square was supposed to be a pimply adolescent, not a muscular thug in a sports car and a snappy suit. Vick's decision to use Simon as a romantic stalking horse now took on a more serious aspect. 'Ah,' said Simon finally. 'You know Vick.'

'It's "V", actually,' said Russell Square, 'and yes, I do, or rather I *did*, until she decided to take up with you.'

'Right, well, it's funny you should say that actually, because it's not true,' stammered Simon.

'Yeah, well, you would say that, wouldn't you?' snarled his aggressor.

'No, look. Honestly. I haven't gone near her. I *wouldn't* go near her,' added Simon truthfully.

Russell looked unconvinced. 'That's not what I've

heard,' he said. 'I heard you've been shagging like randy bunnies every chance you get.'

Simon was genuinely appalled. 'Not true,' he gasped. 'She made it up.'

Russell sneered. 'Fucking weed. Haven't even got the balls to stand up for yourself. She deserves better than you, for Christ's sake.'

Simon couldn't have agreed more. 'Listen. She made it up, I promise.' He paused. 'I told her to.'

'What?'

'I told her to make those stories up. Although not about me, obviously.'

Russell Square continued to stare into Simon's face. 'Why did you do that, then?'

'She was upset that you hadn't called her. I told her that one way of getting your attention was to make you jealous, you know, invent a new boyfriend.'

'Bollocks,' opined Russell after a moment or two.

'Well, look, why *didn't* you call her?' answered Simon, deciding that attack might be the best form of defence.

'Because my *fucking* mobile wasn't *fucking* working,' said Russell, increasing the pressure of his arms.

'Couldn't you use a normal phone?' squeaked Simon.

Russell Square looked at Simon oddly. 'Don't be stupid,' he said.

Simon thought it prudent not to pursue the point. He tried to think.

'Look, it's quite simple,' he said. 'I told Vick to pretend that she was seeing someone else and to make sure that word got back to you.'

'And that someone *just happened* to be you,' commented Russell.

'Well, I didn't know she was going to do that.'

'You have to admit, it does look suspicious,' said Russell.

'Maybe,' conceded Simon cautiously. 'But all I ever wanted was for you two to get back together.'

'What, and you thought the best way of doing that was for her to pretend to be going out with some other fucker?'

'Basically, yes,' agreed Simon.

'Right. Well, by my reckoning, that makes you a prize arsehole,' said Russell, hoiking Simon a little further up the wall.

'I was only trying to help,' whined Simon.

Russell's face scrunched up as he tried to think. As he did so, Simon dangled helplessly. Finally Russell shook his head. He lowered Simon to the ground and let go of his jacket. 'Nah,' he said, as Simon brushed himself down.

'What?' said Simon, relieved to be back on his feet again.

'Nah,' said Russell again. 'It's bullshit.'

'What is?'

'Your story. Bullshit. Bollocks. Fucking *bollocks*. You're making it up.' Russell's face had started to turn red.

Simon spread his hands wide in supplication. 'No, look, honestly –'

But Russell had made his decision. He grabbed hold of Simon and slammed him into the wall again. 'You little toe rag,' he breathed. 'You little toe rag *fucker*.' Simon had been winded by his impact with the wall and was bent forwards, unable to speak. 'I'm going to teach you a lesson you won't forget in a hurry,' said Russell, as he waited for Simon to regain his breath. 'I'm going to hit you so bloody hard you'll –'

'Hey, man.'

Simon felt Russell's grip loosen as he turned to face the intruder. 'Can't you see I'm busy? Fuck off.'

'No way. You're never going to resolve anything by violence. Bad karma all round.'

It was Bob.

'Look, pal,' said Russell, turning to face Bob, 'I'm not going to tell you a second time.'

Bob held up a finger. 'For he who listens not when the time has come to listen will have no more use for his ears but to hear the screams of the unfulfilled,' he proclaimed solemnly.

Russell frowned. 'What?' he said.

'I was basically agreeing with you,' explained Bob.

'Oh, right,' said Russell, trying to remember what he had said. 'Good.'

Bob nodded. 'See? Peaceful accord is the only way for man to live with man.'

'You reckon?' asked Russell, who was looking at Simon, still crumpled on the pavement.

Simon peered upwards fearfully just in time to see Russell roll up his right sleeve. He gulped. Bloody Vick, he thought.

Bob laid a hand on Russell's arm, shaking his head. 'Listen, guy. The prophet says, "He who raises his hand in anger shall suffer each blow he casts a thousand-fold in the next life." It's true. The true path is the path of peace.'

'What, like the Paul McCartney song?' asked Russell.

'Er, yeah,' answered Bob.

'Who the fuck are you, anyway?' said Russell.

Bob drew himself up. 'I am the voice of your conscience, man. I am the sole voice in the wilderness, proclaiming the truth, directing others towards the light. I am the sole journeyman on the road to enlightenment.'

Simon sighed. He was sick to death of the bloody road to enlightenment.

'You're a fucking nutter,' said Russell, perhaps not entirely unreasonably.

Bob shook his head sadly. 'Madness manifests itself most clearly in those who may not see it in themselves.'

Oh-oh, careful, thought Simon.

Russell let it go. 'So you reckon I should let this little dick-wipe go, do you?'

Bob nodded. 'What is it exactly that he's supposed to have done?'

'He's been sleeping with my girlfriend,' said Russell.

Bob burst into laughter.

'I don't think it's very funny,' said Russell, his eyes flashing dangerously.

Bob carried on rocking with unsuppressed mirth. 'No, generally not, I agree. But *him*?' Bob pointed at Simon. 'Not him, pal. Believe me. I know him. He wouldn't do something like that.'

Simon looked at Bob gratefully.

Russell looked suspiciously at Simon. 'Why not? What's wrong with him?'

'Nothing's *wrong* with him,' replied Bob, apparently oblivious to the waves of undisguised menace that were rolling off Russell like bad aftershave. 'All I'll say is that I think it's *highly unlikely* that this bloke has slept with your bird.'

'OK,' said Russell, still not sounding convinced.

'And the road to enlightenment is not lined with the broken bones of old disputes, but with the flowers of reconciliation.' Russell's eyes clouded over. Bob sensed he was losing him. 'So, anyway,' he continued hastily, 'I suggest that the best thing to do is to talk to your bird, and check that it was really this guy who she's been having it away with. And if it really was – well, at that point you have to look to your conscience and reflect on your spiritual karma.'

'So, what you're saying, is ask questions first, fight later?' said Russell.

'Bingo,' said Bob.

'That's not normally the way I go about things,' admitted Russell.

'Life is change, change is life,' observed Bob philosophically. 'Do something a bit different. Try it. You never know. You might like it.'

Russell stared at Simon and came to a decision. 'If I find you've lied to me, you squeally little runt, I'll do you twice as bad.' He turned to go back to the Porsche. 'If there's one thing I cannot fucking *stand*, it's shits who won't take what's coming to them. No fucking honour. Makes me sick.' He opened the car door and climbed in. 'I'll talk to V,' he called through the open window. 'And maybe we'll speak again.' He turned the ignition and sped off with a squeal of rubber, leaving a cloud of dust behind him.

Simon and Bob watched him go wordlessly.

'Thanks, Bob,' said Simon after a moment or two.

Bob was still looking longingly in the direction of the now vanished Porsche. 'The Prophet has a saying,' he remarked. 'Show me a man with a flash motor, and I will show you a man with a profound worry about the size of his genitals.'

'Very up-to-date, this prophet of yours, isn't he?' said Simon.

Bob shrugged. 'I'm paraphrasing slightly.'

'I didn't sleep with his bloody girlfriend, you know,' said Simon.

'Whatever.' Bob winked. 'Judge not your brother's keeper.'

Simon frowned, trying to work this one out. 'Anyway,' he said. 'Thanks for getting me out of that fix. I really appreciate it. Anything I can do to help, let me know.'

'Well,' said Bob. 'Couldn't spare me twenty quid, could you?'

Simon returned to the shop to confront Vick. She was slouching against the cash register, inspecting the chipped black polish on her well-chewed finger nails. Simon wondered why on earth a Porsche-driving young man would be at all interested in such an unprepossessing specimen of the female species. No accounting for taste, he reasoned.

Vick was obviously in a bad mood. She scowled as Simon approached. As she bared her teeth, the mash of orthodontic metal that was normally kept hidden by her sullen expression glinted menacingly beneath the shop's lighting. Simon involuntarily drew back a step.

'Guess who I've just met,' he said.

Vick yawned. 'Couldn't give a rat's arse,' she said.

Simon continued, undaunted. 'Your boyfriend. Russell.'

Immediately Vick's eyes lit up, and she almost – almost

– stopped slouching for a couple of seconds. 'You did?' she asked.

Simon nodded. 'Yup. He came looking for me.' He paused. 'He wasn't very happy about the stories he's been hearing.'

'Was he really angry?' she asked.

'Really angry is one way of putting it. Insanely, violently angry is another.'

Vick clapped her hands together. 'That's *fantastic.*'

'Actually,' said Simon, 'I'm pleased you're pleased, of course, but it's not that fantastic for me. I meant what I said about the insane violence bit.'

Vick nodded. 'Yeah. He's got quite a temper on him, hasn't he?'

'He certainly has,' agreed Simon ruefully.

'So you think he does care after all?'

'Judging from the performance I've just seen, most definitely.'

Vick beamed. 'That,' she said, 'is fucking *superb* news.'

'Yeah, well, anyway, when you see him would you mind awfully telling him that you made up all that stuff about me and you? Because otherwise he's coming back for me.'

Vick, though, seemed too excited about the prospect of a delirious reunion with Russell to worry much about Simon's problems. 'So you definitely think he'll come back?' she asked dreamily.

'He never went away, apparently,' said Simon. 'He claims his mobile wasn't working.'

'Oh.' Vick nodded wisely. 'That explains it, then.'

'So you'll tell him, then?' asked Simon nervously. 'About us. Or rather, that there wasn't any us.'

'Hmm?' Vick's mind was elsewhere; quite where Simon didn't really want to contemplate. 'Oh, right. Yeah, I'll tell him.'

'Sure? Because I'll be in trouble if you don't.'

'God, Simon, just *relax* for once in your life,' said Vick irritably. 'I'm off for a fag.'

Simon watched Vick slope off towards the stock room stairs. You're welcome, he said to himself. Don't bloody mention it.

FOURTEEN

The condemned man did not have much of an appetite.

The day of reckoning had finally arrived. He morosely pushed his last meal around his plate, too fearful of the impending ordeal to be interested in his food.

The condemned man stood up. With a sigh, he went to the corner of the room and picked up his implements. Trying not to think of what awaited him at the end of his last journey, with a last regretful gaze at the room, he turned to go.

Half an hour later Simon arrived outside Arabella's house. A yellow balloon had been tied to the front door, bobbing in the mild summer breeze. From within Simon could already hear the shrieks of over-excited children. His stomach began to churn with apprehension. Reluctantly he rang the doorbell.

After a few moments, the door was opened by a woman Simon didn't recognize. She was in her late thirties, and seemed to be dressed for a glitzy night out rather than a children's birthday party in the middle of the afternoon. She gazed at Simon with interest.

'Hello,' she said after a moment or two.

'Hello,' said Simon. 'I'm Simon.' He held up his bag of tricks. 'Uncle and magician for the day.'

The woman's eyebrows went up. '*Ah*,' she breathed. '*You're* Simon. Well, how lovely to meet you at last. I've heard so much about you.'

'Really,' said Simon as neutrally as he could.

The woman gestured Simon into the house. 'My name's Monique,' she said, following him down the corridor. Monique had sprayed herself liberally with a pungent and over-powering scent, apparently about five seconds before she had opened the door.

'Nice to meet you,' said Simon politely.

'Nice to meet *you*,' purred Monique. 'I'm here in my official capacity as Piers' mother,' she continued. 'Arabella asked if I wouldn't mind helping out. The little horrors *are* quite a handful.'

'Er, quite,' said Simon, who was already feeling sick with nerves at the prospect of performing in front of the children and did not need reminding of the trial he was about to undergo.

'Bella tells me you're quite an expert at all this magic stuff,' said Monique. She flung her head back and for no apparent reason laughed a wholly unconvincing laugh.

'Oh, not really,' said Simon. 'I don't perform much.'

'I find that hard to believe,' said Monique, flashing her eyes meaningfully at him.

'So, er, where are they all, then?' said Simon hurriedly.

'In the garden, playing Statues.' Monique pointed a purple fingernail out of the window.

'Well, I suppose I should go and say hello,' said Simon affably, and fled.

As he opened the door to the garden, the volume of the screaming increased dramatically. Simon pressed on. There was no turning back now, especially with Monique lurking predatorily behind him. He walked down the side of the house and turned the corner into the garden. On the lawn in front of him stood about fifteen small children, all dressed in white. In front of them stood Bella and Michael. Bella saw Simon and waved cheerfully. The small figures in front of her did not move. Disquietingly, though, they continued to scream in high-pitched excitement as they held their poses, waiting for the game to continue.

Simon walked up to Bella and Michael. It was the first time he had seen Michael since their encounter at Slick Tom's. As Simon approached, Michael beamed at him nervously over his wife's shoulder.

'Michael. How's tricks?'

'Oh, absolutely *wonderful*,' gushed Michael. Bella turned and glanced at her husband quizzically, before moving forward and giving Simon an affectionate kiss on the cheek.

'Hello, you,' she said. 'What happened to your hair?'

'Mad barber with insufficient English,' explained Simon.

Bella winced. 'Thanks for coming,' she said.

'How are they all?' asked Simon.

'Behaviour is moderate to poor at the moment,' reported Bella. 'But I think we should expect standards to lower dramatically once they've tasted my strawberry jelly. It's disgusting. Well below acceptable standard. We'll have a riot on our hands.'

Simon swallowed. 'Marvellous,' he said. 'I can hardly wait.' He looked at the motionless children in front of him. Sophy, resplendent in a white tutu, saw him and waved excitedly.

'Oh, Sophy, you moved,' said Michael irritably. 'That means you need to go to the back.' Seeing Sophy's face begin to crumple in disappointment, Michael clapped his hands together and adopted a different tactic. 'OK,' he said. 'That was brilliant. Shall we stop the game and play something else instead?'

The white figures all began moving at once. As if drawn by some magnetic force, within ten seconds they had formed a fairly creditable rugby maul, an indistinguishable mass of small bodies, heads, and limbs.

'What's with the costumes?' asked Simon.

'Oh, that's Sophy's idea,' explained Bella. 'She wanted to have a fairy party, and insisted that everyone had to come dressed as a fairy. I did try and suggest that perhaps the boys could come as elves instead, or munchkins, or something, but she was adamant. It had to be fairies or they wouldn't be invited. I wasn't sure quite what the mums would think about that, so rather than have any awkwardness I took an executive decision and lied.'

'What did you say?'

'I told the boys, or rather their mothers, that it was an angel party, so they should come dressed as angels.'

'Brilliant,' said Simon.

'I'm not sure, actually. Stephanie from two doors down called at lunchtime to say that her son Jonathan has just come down with a virulent strain of some unidentified but very contagious disease. I think she thought the whole thing was a bit morbid. Either that or deeply sacrilegious.'

'And Sophy doesn't know?'

Bella shook her head. 'As far as she's concerned, they're all fairies.'

Simon looked at the assembled crowd of children.

The boys seemed quite unconcerned about the more obvious fairy-related accessories sported by some of the girls. Angels, after all, didn't generally carry pink plastic wands covered in glitter. Luckily, both the fairies and the angels had wings, albeit of varying sizes. One boy wore a white linen caul over his head, and looked eerily like a tiny member of the Ku Klux Klan.

'Where's Daniel?' asked Simon, looking around.

'We had to lock him in the shed,' explained Arabella. 'He got far too excited with all the kids running about and ended up peeing on someone.'

'Oops,' said Simon.

'Indeed,' agreed his sister. 'Anyway, luckily we had a spare pair of spangly tights, so not too many tears were shed.'

'Who's that strange woman inside?' asked Simon.

'Monique? Yes, I was meaning to tell you about her.'

'Sounds ominous.'

'For you, maybe. She's the mother of Piers, who's the cherub over there pinching Tinkerbell's bum.' Bella pointed towards a boy with a blond mop of hair which flopped over his face as he twisted hard on his victim's nylon-clad buttock. 'Don't be deceived by the pretty face,' she advised. 'He may look angelic, but he's a vicious little bastard.'

'Right, noted,' said Simon. The fairy whose bottom had been pinched began to wail as Piers glided calmly away from the fracas with a smug grin on his face. 'So why is Monique dressed up to the nines and smelling like the cosmetics department at Harvey Nichols?' he asked.

Bella sighed. 'She's recently divorced.'

There was a pause.

'And?' prompted Simon.

'Well, what else do you need to know? When I told her you were coming to do some tricks she rather foisted herself upon me as a helper and has been here for hours, waiting for you to arrive and checking her make-up every thirty seconds or so.'

'All that display is for *me*?' said Simon, dismayed.

'I hope you don't mind,' said Bella. 'I thought you might enjoy the diversion.'

'Christ,' said Simon. 'I may be desperate, but I'm not *that* desperate.'

Bella shrugged. 'Suit yourself,' she said. 'In any case, consider yourself warned. She'll devour you if you let her.'

Simon pulled a face. He looked at his watch. 'When am I on?' he asked.

'Well,' said Bella. 'I think we've just about exhausted our selection of games, so I suppose we'd better give them their tea. You can get ready in the living room while they're stuffing themselves.'

Sophy broke away from the scrum and ran towards her mother. 'Mummy, mummy, what's next, I'm hungry, hello Simon, can I have some cake yet?' she babbled, her small face flushed with excitement.

'Hello Sophy,' said Simon. 'Happy birthday.'

'What happened to your hair?' asked Sophy.

'Remind me how old you are again?' said Simon, ignoring the question.

'I'm six,' said Sophy.

'Wow,' said Simon. 'Very grown up.'

Sophy nodded. 'I think,' she said judiciously, 'that I'm the most grown-up person here.'

Bella raised a sardonic eyebrow. 'You may be right, kiddo,' she said softly, stroking her daughter's hair. After a moment she looked up and saw her husband about to be backed into a bank of azaleas by the assembled mob of angels and fairies. 'Right,' she shouted, clapping her hands together as she did so. 'Time for tea.'

With a cheer the mob immediately stopped harassing Michael and instead moved as one down the garden and into the house, expertly marshalled by Bella. Simon was left alone in the garden with Michael. He looked at him coolly. He had not yet decided what he was going to do about his discovery of Michael at Slick Tom's.

'Well,' said Simon.

'Well,' agreed Michael anxiously.

'Good to see you, *again*,' said Simon.

'Ghastly place, that, wasn't it? I sometimes wonder whether my clients have any taste at all. Imagine going to a place like that to *enjoy* yourself.'

'You looked as if you were having an OK time,' said Simon.

Michael gestured expansively. 'Well, one has to look as if one is enjoying it all, however tedious it may be. It's bad form to look bored. Clients take it terribly personally. They're very sensitive souls, you know.'

'Did you meet my friend Bryony?' asked Simon.

Michael frowned. 'Bryony? I don't remember –'

'She was Canadian,' interrupted Simon. 'And, er, fat.'

Michael's face crumpled gratifyingly as he remembered. Suddenly he looked suspicious. 'You knew that – that –?' he stuttered.

'Absolutely,' said Simon. 'I saw you there, looking so miserable, and so *bored*, and I sent her over to you to introduce herself. Thought you could do with the company. Did you get on?'

Michael's face had gone an interesting colour. His mouth opened and closed a couple of times.

'You bastard,' he finally hissed.

'No need to thank me,' said Simon, and walked off towards the house.

Back in the kitchen, chaos reigned. Fifteen mouths were all open, but rather than food going in, an awful lot of noise seemed to be coming out. Simon crept into the living room and began unpacking his tricks behind Arabella's sofa. As he was bending down, a familiar aroma wafted past his nostrils, seconds before Monique's face appeared over the top of the sofa.

'*Hi*,' she said, looking down on Simon.

'Oh, hi,' mumbled Simon.

'What are you up to down there?' Monique licked her heavily rouged lips.

'Just getting ready for the big performance,' replied Simon, returning to his tricks. He took a wooden cut-out of a rabbit and placed it in a grey top hat.

'Mmm,' oozed Monique. 'Can't wait.'

Simon looked at her. She wasn't actually a bad-looking woman, he thought. She just needed to take off about half of the make-up and stop acting like a randy teenager. 'I shouldn't get too excited if I were you,' he said. 'It's very much for the kids. The grown-ups aren't going to be especially amazed.'

Monique tipped her head back and performed her peculiar laugh again. She pointed at some long strips of rubber that lay on the floor by Simon's knee. 'Are those what I think they are?' she squeaked in excitement. 'You naughty boy!'

Simon smiled weakly. 'They're modelling balloons.'

'Oh.' Monique sat back on her heels and stuck her tongue into her cheek as she considered Simon carefully, a glint in her eye. 'So, each of those little things needs to be blown, then?' she said, pointing at the balloons.

'Er, that's right,' muttered Simon.

'I know how they feel,' murmured Monique, one hand trailing languorously through her hair.

At that moment the children rushed into the room. To his surprise, Simon found himself heaving a sigh of relief. Facing these children would be easy compared to fending off Monique. At Bella's direction, the children sat in well-ordered rows in front of the sofa. When they were all settled, Bella stood in front of them and said, 'Now, as a very special treat, we have Sophy's uncle Simon, who is going to do some brilliant magic tricks for us.'

She turned and gave Simon a thumbs-up sign. Simon looked at the children, who were sitting cross legged in front of him, staring up at him in complete silence. At the back of the room, Monique applauded politely. Simon was momentarily dumbstruck.

Finally one of the little boys at the back of the group nudged his neighbour and said, 'Rubbish name.' The other little boy nodded in agreement.

'What's wrong with my name?' demanded Simon, stung. He recognized the boy who had spoken as Piers, Monique's son.

'Well,' said Piers, 'it's not much of a name for a

magician, is it? We had a magician at *my* party and his name was Cosmo the Clown.'

'And I had one called the Great Bolivari,' piped up the boy next to him.

'Well, my name's Simon, and so we'll just have to make do with it,' replied Simon as heartily as he could. He could see Bella leave the room, shaking her head as she went. Monique, though, remained where she was. Simon swallowed, and tried to begin.

'Now, boys and girls, for my first trick, I'm going to tell you the story of Robert the Rabbit.'

'Oh,' sniffed Piers, 'I know this one.'

To his credit Simon resisted the urge to walk over and wallop Piers on the back of the head, and instead he ploughed on with the trick. Before long he had the children happily screaming at him, getting more and more excited as the (somewhat implausible) story gradually unfolded. Robert the Rabbit finally made it back to his home and snuggled up in bed for a good night's sleep – lines delivered by Simon while staring anywhere except at Monique. He pressed on with the next trick.

'Boys and girls, what you are about to see will astound you,' announced Simon. 'Watch closely.' He balled his left hand into a tight fist and began to stuff an orange handkerchief into the top of the fist with his right forefinger. Fifteen pairs of eyes unblinkingly followed every move. Once the handkerchief was completely hidden, Simon held his hand with the handkerchief in above his head.

'And now, boys and girls, prepare to be amazed,' said Simon. Finger by finger he opened his fist, revealing that the handkerchief had vanished. Simon was using a fake flesh-coloured plastic thumb. It was hollow, and the perfect size for hiding a small handkerchief. The reaction of the children was muted, to say the least. Some twisted their heads to look quizzically at their neighbours. Others frowned.

Piers, though, looked bored. 'I can see how you did it,' he said.

'It's *magic*,' snapped Simon. He closed his empty hand into a fist again, and with the thumb and forefinger of his right hand, reached into the fist and started to withdraw the handkerchief.

'You've got a fake thumb thing,' said Piers loudly.

Simon had pulled the handkerchief out of his hand and was showing it off to the audience. 'Nonsense,' he said, quickly depositing the orange handkerchief, and the plastic thumb, in his pocket.

'You *have*. You've got a fake thumb,' insisted Piers. 'Your trick's rubbish.'

'I don't have a fake thumb,' replied Simon. He held up his hands to the audience.

'It's in your pocket now, obviously,' said Piers.

'No it's not.'

'Show us, then,' said Piers.

There was a pause. 'Why should I?' asked Simon petulantly.

'I knew it,' said Piers with grim satisfaction.

'Anyway,' continued Simon, a little desperately, 'now I'm going to do something which you'll all love.' He reached behind the sofa before Piers could proffer another opinion and picked up the uninflated balloons. He waved them at the children, who stared back at him wordlessly. 'All right,' he said. 'Here are some balloons.' Monique snorted audibly and held up a hand to cover her mouth.

Simon suddenly remembered that the gobby brat Piers was her son. He shivered involuntarily and tried to concentrate. He looked at Sophy, who was sitting with her legs crossed in the front row, immediately in front of him. 'All right, Sophy, as you're the birthday girl, you can go first. What do you want me to make for you? I can do a sausage dog, a poodle, or a giraffe.'

Sophy thought for a moment. 'Can you do a cat?' she asked.

Oh thanks very much, thought Simon bitterly. 'Sorry, Sophy,' he said. 'Can't do cats.'

Sophy's face crumpled heart-breakingly. 'Not even a small cat?' she whispered.

Simon could sense that the other children were becoming a little restless. 'Why don't I see what I can come up with?' he said, and then quickly blew up the balloon. Fully inflated, the balloon was long and thin and curved away from Simon in a rather obscene arc. By this time Monique was laughing so much that she had had to sit down. Mercifully none of the children noticed. They stared transfixed at the balloon as Simon began to twist and pull the rubber, forming it into a weird, three dimensional shape which didn't actually resemble anything.

'There!' he exclaimed triumphantly, handing it to Sophy.

'What is it?' asked Sophy, examining her sculpture curiously.

'It's a, er, very special sort of magic wand for fairies,' improvised Simon.

Sophy frowned. 'Are you sure?'

'Absolutely. Now, who else wants a special wand?' This was going to be much easier than doing giraffes, Simon saw. He'd be able to perform extemporaneous balloon sculpture, not working within any set parameters, free to go where the urge took him. It was the children's entertainment equivalent of Free Jazz. He was the Ornette Coleman of balloon modelling. Simon became quite excited.

Thirteen hands shot up, each accompanied by a squeak of pleading. Simon held up his hands. 'All right. You'll all just have to wait your turn. Now, who's first?' More hands, more squeaking.

'I don't want a magic wand,' said Piers. 'Why would an angel want a magic wand, anyway?'

Sophy turned round to address him. 'You're not an angel,' she told him. 'You're a fairy.'

'No,' said Piers – reasonably enough in the circumstances, Simon had to concede – 'I'm an angel. Aren't I, mum?'

Monique was about to agree when she caught sight of Sophy's face, which was awash with the unmistakable warning signs of an impending tantrum. 'I think,' she said, 'that everyone is a fairy, because you're all magic, and that everyone is an angel, too, because you're all as good as gold.'

Both Piers and Sophy seemed satisfied by this dubious piece of maternal sophistry. They nodded and addressed their attention back to Simon, who shot Monique a grateful look. She winked at him. This caught Simon slightly off-guard, and in his anxiety he twisted the balloon he was holding a little too tight, causing it to burst with a loud bang.

The little girl who had been waiting patiently to receive the sculptured balloon immediately burst into inconsolable hysterics. Thirty seconds later, every child in the room was crying, except for Sophy, who was waving her new balloon at her friends, thus exacerbating the problem, and Piers, who was watching proceedings with a disdainful look on his face.

Arabella rushed into the room. 'What's going on?' she demanded.

'I burst a balloon by mistake,' explained Simon. 'I think everyone got a bit of a shock.'

'Well, can you start the next one, then?' asked Bella.

Simon shrugged. 'Sure.'

'Tell you what,' said Bella, surveying the bawling mass in front of her. 'We'll get them all outside again playing some more games. Can I leave it to you to make a –' She stopped. 'What *is* that?' she demanded, pointing at Sophy's balloon. 'Doesn't look like any animal *I've* ever seen.'

'It's a special magic wand,' explained Simon defensively.

'And I said that angels don't have wands,' piped up Piers.

'Of course they do,' retorted Bella briskly. 'How else do you think they fly?'

Piers didn't reply, and remained sulkily silent. Simon was impressed. Clearly forthright denial and aggressive counter-questioning was the best way to deal with obnoxious children. Simon made a mental note.

'Right,' said Bella. 'Come on everyone. Let's leave Simon alone to make your special wands. Let's go and play some more games.' Rolling her eyes at Simon, Bella herded the children back out towards the garden. 'I'll leave you to it,' she said. 'Good luck. Hope you've got enough puff.'

Simon was left alone in the sitting room with Monique, who got up from her chair and approached him.

'Quite a show,' she purred.

'Pretty awful, wasn't it?' said Simon.

'I thought it was *great*,' said Monique. 'I love it that you do this for your niece. What a nice man you must be.'

'Not really,' said Simon. 'But thanks,' he added a moment later, not wishing to seem rude. 'Right, I suppose I'd better get started on all these balloons.'

'Do you want a hand?' asked Monique.

'Aren't you needed outside?' asked Simon hopefully.

Monique waved a hand. 'They'll manage. Let me help you. It's been a while since I've handled quite so much rubber in such close proximity to an attractive man.'

Simon swallowed.

Half an hour later, the sitting room floor was littered with various abstract balloon sculptures. There was no real unifying theme, other than perhaps the wish in the creator's mind to make sure that nothing he produced was even remotely sexually suggestive. Monique had proved herself startlingly adept at concocting lewd *double-entendres*, and she had also demonstrated just how overtly pornographic the act of blowing up a balloon can be made to look. By the time he had finished, Simon was exhausted.

He surveyed the debris in the sitting room with some satisfaction. 'That's me done, then,' he said. He had already packed his other tricks into his bag, and was hoping to make a quick escape before anyone complained about their balloons, and also before Monique got bored of waiting for him to proposition her, and propositioned him instead.

He went out into the garden. Piers was standing in the middle of the lawn with his hands over his eyes. Behind him stood Bella. 'Hide and Seek,' she explained to her brother as he approached. 'Piers is it.'

Piers was also cheating by peeking through his fingers.

'I thought I might shoot off,' he said.

'All right, Piers, time's up! Go and see who you can find.' Piers shot off round the side of the house with the determined certainty of one who knows exactly where he's going. 'Sure you won't stay?' asked Bella.

'No thanks.'

'Exhausting, aren't they?'

Simon nodded.

'Well, thanks again for you help,' said Bella. 'Did you do the balloons?'

'Every last one.'

'And you're in one piece?'

'Just about. Monique managed to restrain herself.'

'Hmm. Jolly good.' There was a pause. 'I like this game,' said Bella. 'The great thing about hide and seek is that everyone keeps as quiet as possible.' After the constant noise, the silence was rather eerie.

'I'll pop off, then,' said Simon. 'Say bye to Sophy for me.'

Bella nodded. 'Shall do. And thanks again, Simon.' Brother and sister exchanged kisses.

Simon had a thought. 'Tell me,' he said. 'You remember when you asked me to do this party?' Bella nodded. 'You hadn't told Sophy at all, had you?'

'Of course not. That would have been terribly unfair on you. Do you really think I would actually put you in such an intolerable position? I'm your *sister*, Simon. I would never do that.' She grinned at him. Finding it impossible to be angry, Simon stuck his tongue out and left her standing in the middle of the lawn.

Just as Simon was opening the front door, Michael emerged from the downstairs loo, looking self-conscious. 'Er, Simon, just before you go,' he whispered.

Simon turned and put his bag down. 'Yes?'

'Look, sorry about that comment earlier. Didn't mean it, obviously. Just got a bit hot under the collar, you know. I think it's all these kids. They can get on your nerves a bit after a while.' Michael did his best to eke out a smile.

Simon couldn't restrain his curiosity. 'So, tell me, Michael, what happened with Bryony?'

'It was *horrible*,' said Michael. ' There I was, minding my own business – with my clients, obviously – and then before I know what's happening, this, this *thing* is all over me.' The horror of the moment was being replayed on Michael's face. Simon almost felt sorry for him.

'What did your clients do?' he asked.

'Well, obviously it was all a bit awkward,' said Michael. 'I had a job convincing them that I'd never met the girl before.'

'Embarrassing for you, though.'

'God, yes. She was so ugly.'

'Actually, I meant with you being married,' said Simon.

'Oh, right,' said Michael. 'Yes, yes, of course. Absolutely. Being married.' There was a pause. 'Anyway,' he continued, 'I just wanted to say thanks very much for doing your tricks today.'

'You're very welcome.'

'And I'm sure Bella wouldn't be terribly interested in that whole episode in that bar last week.'

'Oh? You don't think so?'

Michael shook his head firmly. He leaned towards Simon conspiratorially. 'If anything, to be honest, she might well get the wrong end of the stick.' He paused. 'You know, what with me being in that sort of place at all. As I say, though, if that's what the client wants, then that's what the client shall get.'

Simon looked at Michael. 'Don't worry,' he said. 'I won't say anything.' Michael's face broke into a cautiously relieved smile. 'For the moment.' Simon turned and let himself out of the front door.

FIFTEEN

Simon spent the rest of the weekend trying to decide what to do about Michael.

His euphoria at catching him in Slick Tom's had long since evaporated. Simon now wished he had never seen him. He didn't know what to do. Should he tell Arabella what he had seen? What exactly would that achieve? Bella would be devastated, their marriage perhaps put in peril. Simon doubted whether he could stomach the responsibility for turning Sophy into another statistic about one-parent families.

There was also the question of proof. Simon hadn't really seen anything other than circumstantial evidence. Talking to a young girl at a bar didn't necessarily mean that Michael was cheating on his wife. Perhaps there really *had* been a posse of insecure Japanese businessmen with a love of terrible rock music in the lavatories. Simon hadn't thought to go and check.

It was all very difficult. The problem weighed heavily on Simon's conscience as he tried to decide what to do. Shouldn't Bella be told what was going on? Simon wasn't sure whether he had a right, or a duty, to protect his sister from the knowledge of her husband's sordid behaviour. Arabella was more than capable of looking after herself.

Simon spun in a frenzy of indecision. He was incapable of sorting out his own problems and certainly wasn't equipped to start playing God in other people's lives.

Towards the end of the following Monday morning, while Simon and Dean were enjoying a quiet moment in the shop, discussing a new trick which made it look as if you had chopped off your leg, Brian stuck his head around the velvet curtain with a scowl on his face, brandishing the telephone.

'It's for you,' he said, thrusting the receiver into Simon's hand.

'Hello?' said Simon.

'Simon? It's Joe.'

'Joe,' said Simon. 'The very man. Long time no hear.'

'How are you?' asked Joe.

'Fine. Abandoned and left to fend for myself against three Canadian mooses, but otherwise fine, no thanks to you.'

'Yeah, sorry about that,' said Joe. 'I just happened to see that girl, you know, and we got talking, and suddenly I just ended up with her and I didn't get the chance to get those drinks.'

'I'm not worried about the bloody drinks, you moron. I only narrowly escaped a near-death experience with the luscious Debbie, who was hell-bent on seducing me.'

There was a pause as Joe remembered Debbie. 'God,' he said eventually. 'Sorry.'

'You should be. I'm lucky to be alive.' Simon paused. 'I can't believe you've waited almost a week to check I was all right. For all you knew I could have got trapped beneath one of them and died of starvation. Or asphyxiation.'

'Sorry,' said Joe again.

There was a pause. 'Anyway,' said Simon. 'Did you have a successful night with Lycra girl?'

'Oh yes,' said Joe. 'Her name was Melanie.'

'Well, that's fantastic. I'm delighted for you.'

'Look,' said Joe, 'let me make it up to you. Are you up to anything tonight?'

'Nothing special. Why?'

'Come and have dinner. My treat.'

'No dancing?'

'No dancing. I promise.'

Simon thought. He was still angry with Joe for his desertion at Slick Tom's, but there seemed little point in holding a grudge. 'OK,' he said. 'Where and when?'

'About eight? I thought we might try Mango.'

Simon whistled. 'Great.'

'I'll see you there,' said Joe, and rang off.

Mango was, simply, the *only* place to eat in London that summer. The restaurant had opened in Chelsea some months earlier in a blaze of publicity. Everybody was talking about the cheekily eclectic wine list, the recherché interior design touches, and the couture-designed staff uniforms. Nobody was talking about the food. After all, people didn't go to restaurants to *eat* anymore. At Mango, form didn't just triumph over substance. At Mango, form kicked substance's head in and jumped up and down on its flailing body.

Just before eight o'clock Simon arrived at the restaurant, where he was greeted at the door by two huge men dressed in black, who looked at his hair critically for a few moments. After exchanging a brief glance between themselves, the larger of the two hauled open an enormous stainless steel door to let him in. Inside, a glamorous crowd of people were milling aimlessly about, chatting to themselves. Everyone was dressed from head to toe in black, and they all seemed impossibly beautiful. Wow, thought Simon, it's true what they say about this place, then. After a moment or two Simon spotted an awkward-looking couple cowering in one corner, looking apprehensive. They were ignored by the beautiful people in black. Suddenly Simon realized that the glamorous crowd were staff, and that the hesitant couple in the corner were customers. He approached a desk of quirky post-industrial design. Three young women stood behind the desk, dressed in black. The trio looked at Simon as if he had just farted.

'Help you?' said the girl on the left with a small sneer.

'I'm meeting someone,' explained Simon. 'We've a table booked for eight.'

'For eight people?' said the girl, surprised. Simon probably didn't look important enough to be able to book a table for eight people.

'Er, no,' said Simon. 'For two people. Me and my friend. For eight o'clock.'

'Oh. You've booked a table *for* two, *at* eight,' said the girl, shaking her head at Simon's inability to get even the simplest things right.

'Right,' muttered Simon.

'Name?' demanded the girl in the middle with a slightly bigger sneer.

'Er, Joe?' suggested Simon.

Elegantly cut fringes flopped forward as three heads went down to scrutinize a large sheet of paper before them. 'No Joe,' said the girl on the right, who effortlessly out-sneered both her colleagues with a derisive curl of the lip that Billy Idol would have been jealous of.

'OK,' said Simon. 'How about Browning?'

Down went the heads again. 'Oh,' said the one on the left. 'We have a Browning for two at eight.' The disappointment was audible. 'He's not here yet. Do you want to have a drink at the bar while you wait?'

'Why not?' said Simon. The three women looked at him as if they were all itching to give him several reasons.

'Giuseppe will show you the way,' said the girl in the middle, pointing to a swarthy male model, dressed in black, who was hovering by the desk. Giuseppe stepped forward, his thickly oiled hair shining glossily. Simon tried not to think about his own haircut. Giuseppe solemnly gestured to Simon to follow him.

Simon followed Giuseppe into a room the size of an aircraft hangar. The ceiling soared above the heads of the assembled crowd. There were a number of enormous skylights through which the early evening light flooded. Simon could see endless lines of tables stretching off into the distance. The echo of several thousand people eating and talking ricocheted like bullets off the nattily distressed walls.

Giuseppe led Simon to the large bar, behind which Giuseppe's twin brother appeared to be waiting. Simon clambered cautiously up on to a chrome and leather bar stool.

'Hello sir, welcome to the Mango bar,' the barman said, giving Simon a flash of his perfect teeth. 'My name is Pedro. Would you care for something to drink?'

'Er, yes, gin and tonic, please,' said Simon, suspecting that ordering a pint of lager here would have resulted in another outbreak of sneers.

'Very good, sir,' purred Pedro, and he spun away.

On the zinc bar surface was a hand-painted Italian ceramic bowl full of peanuts. Simon stuck his hand into the bowl and began to munch contentedly. After a few moments Pedro presented Simon with his gin and tonic, discreetly leaving a bill face-down on a hand-painted Italian ceramic dish. Simon took a sip of his drink. He remembered that he didn't like gin and tonic much.

Simon looked around the bar area. There were mostly couples, who stood or sat so close together that their heads were almost touching. At first Simon thought that they were just canoodling, until he realized that it was the only way they could make themselves heard above the extraordinary noise. Around the low tables which were dotted around the periphery of the bar area there were groups of men in big pin-striped suits, who leaned backwards in uncomfortable-looking chairs, smoking. They addressed the problem of ambient volume by shouting at each other. They all looked supremely self-satisfied, lounging about as if they had large Italian salamis stuck down their bespoke trousers.

Overall, thought Simon, the customers were attractive, but nowhere near as good-looking as any of the staff.

Simon looked at his watch. It was almost eight o'clock. Taking another sip of his gin and tonic, he flipped over the bill that Pedro had left for him. The figure at the bottom of the scroll of paper was so large Simon nearly fell off his bar stool. He beckoned the bartender over to him.

'Another drink, sir?' oozed Pedro.

'Actually, I wanted to ask you about this,' said Simon, holding the bill up.

One of Pedro's eyebrows arched skywards. 'Sir?'

'Well, I ordered one gin and tonic.'

'Yes, sir.'

'How can that possibly come to that much?' Simon prodded the piece of paper.

'Well, sir,' began Pedro, his distaste at having to discuss such matters evident, 'that sum there is for the gin and tonic.' He pointed at the bill.

'Christ. Go on.'

'That sum there is for the *cacahouettes*.'

'The what?'

'The peanuts, sir.' The translation dripped with contempt.

'You're charging me for the peanuts? They were just sitting there. I didn't realize I would have to pay for them.'

'Well, sir, if you pluck a single rose from a florist's display, you would expect to pay for that, wouldn't you?'

Simon blinked in disbelief. He didn't feel equipped to deal with this cod retail philosophy. 'Never mind,' he grumbled, before picking up the bill again. 'So what's this figure at the bottom, then? A charge for the oxygen I've been breathing?'

'That is your service charge, sir.'

'That's ridiculous,' said Simon. 'All you did was pour me a drink.'

A really quite good sneer materialized on Pedro's face.

'Sir,' he said, 'if you can't afford to pay the service charge, it is in theory optional.'

'I didn't say I couldn't afford it,' said Simon. 'I just don't see why I should.'

Pedro gestured to all of the other drinkers around the bar. 'Well, sir, all of these other ladies and gentlemen don't seem to have a problem with it.'

Suddenly Simon felt awfully mean. He had been swept up in a tide of tight-fisted pettiness which he now regretted. Above all, he wanted Pedro to go away and to stop looking at him as if he had just mooned at the assembled customers. He took out his wallet and put a twenty pound note on the bar. Pedro performed a deeply sarcastic bow, and took the money. He returned a few moments later with the change, which he set before Simon on another hand-painted Italian ceramic dish. He remained in front of Simon, waiting to see whether he would take all of the money in the dish. This is crazy, thought Simon. Am I expected to tip him *again*? He looked at the money, and then at the bartender, who was eyeing him expectantly.

Suddenly a hand landed on his shoulder.

'Hello stranger.' It was Joe. 'Come on in. Our table awaits.'

Simon slid off the bar stool and scooped all of the money in the dish into his hand. There was an audible in-take of breath from Pedro as he did so. Clutching his drink, Simon followed Joe to their appointed table somewhere in the middle of the aircraft hangar. The waitress who showed them to their table, all superb bone structure and pneumatic breasts, handed them laminated plastic menus and batted her eye-lashes in a vacuous way before leaving them to choose their food.

'So. How're you?' asked Joe once they had settled in.

'All right, I suppose,' said Simon. 'I've just about forgiven you for running off without me last week.'

'Those girls *were* awful,' said Joe.

'I know,' said Simon pointedly.

'Why didn't you just leave?' asked Joe.

'I couldn't. Debbie saw what you had done and after that she kept a vice-like grip on my bloody arm. I was half expecting her to whip out some handcuffs.'

'Ooh, kinky.'

'Jesus.' Simon held his head in his hands. 'I don't even want to think about it.'

'Anyway,' said Joe. 'What do you fancy eating tonight?'

'Bloody hell,' said Simon, who had begun to look at the menu. 'The prices are a bit steep.'

Joe waved a dismissive hand. 'Don't worry about it,' he said. 'This is my treat.' He picked up his own menu, and suddenly went very quiet.

The menu was rather strange. In contrast to its swanky interior, Mango specialized in very ordinary food. Everything on the menu was deliberately mundane and bland, and would have been more suited to a motorway service station in Hertfordshire than the snappiest restaurant in London. Ah, thought Simon, post-modern irony. He chose a prawn cocktail followed by toad in the hole. No extras were included in the price. The rustic French rolls were £1.90 each, butter was an extra 50p, and all vegetables came at a swingeing additional charge. Simon scanned the menu to see whether they needed to hire knives and forks separately.

After what felt like an eternity, a waiter sauntered up and asked if they were ready to order.

'What's the *soupe du jour?*' asked Joe.

The waiter looked at him. 'It's the soup of the day, sir,' he said slowly.

Joe looked as if he was considering punching the waiter in the face. 'And what,' he asked, 'is the soup of the day?'

'Oxtail.'

'OK. I'll have that and then the steak and kidney pie with instant mash potatoes.'

The waiter listened to their orders silently, and then strode off, shaking his head.

Joe looked around him with satisfaction. 'This is great,' he said. 'I've been wanting to come here ever since it opened.'

'Why?' asked Simon.

'Just because it's the coolest place,' replied Joe. 'Look. Isn't that Lavinia Dauphinois over there?'

Simon swivelled in his chair and saw a vaguely familiar platinum blonde spoon a mound of mushy peas into her mouth.

'Who's she?' asked Simon.

'Lavinia Dauphinois? You don't know?'

Simon shook his head.

'She hosts that cookery programme, *Sex and Food and Rock and Roll.*'

'God. Sounds ghastly.'

'You should watch it. You might learn a thing or two. It's all about what to cook for that special seductive evening in. But it goes further than that. It also suggests appropriate music to listen to while you eat.'

'What, pasta with putanesca sauce and Paganini, that sort of thing?'

'Well,' said Joe, 'it's more cheese on toast and Celine Dion, actually, but yeah, that's the general idea.'

'If she presents a cookery programme, what on earth is she doing here?' asked Simon. 'The food looks indescribable.'

'Just because she presents a cookery programme doesn't necessarily means she knows anything about cooking,' said Joe.

'It doesn't?'

'God, no.'

Simon turned again to see Lavinia Dauphinois's collagen-inflated lips pucker as she threw her head back and shrieked with laughter, loud enough to ensure that anyone who hadn't noticed her yet would do so now. Just then their waiter returned and unceremoniously plonked plates in front of them. Simon's prawn cocktail came in a small martini glass. There appeared to be about five tiny prawns in it, hiding in a forest of shredded iceberg lettuce.

'Well,' said Simon. 'This looks interesting.'

'Mmm,' said Joe, staring at Lavinia Dauphinois and wisely paying no attention to his soup.

'So, go on,' said Simon, chewing a tasteless and rubbery prawn. 'I'm still not convinced. Explain to me why you like this place. Tell me more.'

'It's *the* place to be,' said Joe. 'There's a trendiness-by-osmosis principle at work here. If you're here, and everybody who's anybody is here, then that makes you anybody, too.'

Simon frowned. 'Were you not somebody before?'

'I was *never* somebody.'

'No?'

Joe shook his head. 'Oh no. Lavinia Dauphinois is *somebody*.'

'How can she be somebody if I've never heard of her?' asked Simon.

'Well, I suppose nobody can be somebody to everybody,' answered Joe philosophically. 'Or, to put it another way, everybody will be nobody to somebody.'

Simon frowned, trying to keep up. 'And sorry,' he said. 'What was it you wanted to become?'

'Oh,' said Joe, 'I just aspire to be anybody.'

'As opposed to somebody.'

'Correct.'

'I see,' said Simon, who didn't.

'Of course,' said Joe, 'I'm not really anybody either, but it's good to pretend for a while. And this place lets you do that.'

'So, if you're not anybody, who are you?'

Joe looked at Simon pityingly. 'Nobody.'

Simon prodded about the martini glass looking for a sixth prawn. There wasn't one. 'I'm off to the loo,' he announced. He stood up and made his way back towards the entrance.

In contrast to the hectic and noisy restaurant, the lavatory was an idyll of calm. Classical music was piped from hidden speakers. A forest of potted ferns had been planted about the room. The floor, walls and ceiling were all covered in black marble, and illumination was provided by discreet spot-lighting. Along one side of the room stood a bank of gleaming stainless steel sinks. Tungsten taps looped over the bowls, and a stack of fluffed up white towels sat on the counter. A vast mirror covered the entire wall so customers could admire themselves while they washed their hands. Standing at the far end of the line of sinks was a man dressed in black.

'Good evening, sir,' said the man, as Simon walked in. 'My name is Julio. Welcome to the Mango toilets.'

'Er, thanks,' said Simon.

'What would you like to do?' asked the man.

'I beg your pardon?'

The man gestured to a row of glistening black marble urinals, and then to a line of doors. 'Stand-up or sit-down, sir?'

'I think I'll just go over here, thanks,' muttered Simon, and made his way to the most distant of the urinals.

'Very good, sir,' said the man. 'Enjoy.'

Simon stood in front of the urinal and unzipped his fly. This was, he thought, taking customer service a bit too far. There was nobody else in the toilet except for the attendant, and Simon could feel the man's gaze rest squarely between his shoulders. After a few moments of contemplation of his own shoes, it dawned on Simon that something was wrong. Nothing was happening. His bladder, which a few moments earlier had been bulging insistently, seemed to have magically emptied itself. Simon stared disbelievingly downwards. His penis was dangling nonchalantly, unaware that this outing was for anything more than just a breath of fresh air. Simon fought manfully with his urethra. After what seemed like an eternity of inaction, there was a pointed cough from the other side of the room. Galvanized by panic, Simon rose on to his tiptoes and with a supreme effort managed to squeeze a trickle out.

He tried to make the most of it. He began by creating delicate yellow rivulets which shimmied smoothly down the black marble. Half-way down, their progress was halted by Simon's next manoeuvre, controlled squirts which interrupted the downwards flow. The noise, whilst not exactly ear-shattering, was sufficient. A few moments later he turned to go, relieved that the ordeal was over.

'Sir?' called the attendant as Simon made his way towards the door.

Simon stopped and turned around. 'Yes?'

The man gestured towards the row of sinks. 'Wouldn't you like to wash your hands before you go back to your table?' he asked.

'Oh. Right,' said Simon, blushing furiously. He walked towards the nearest sink. By the time he had got there, the attendant had glided up the row of sinks and switched on the taps for him. Simon began to wash his hands as the man stood next to him, watching him keenly.

'Soap, sir?' he asked after a few moments.

'What? Oh, no thank you,' said Simon, before catching a disapproving look in the attendant's eye. 'Go on, then,' he capitulated meekly. The attendant produced an ornate soap dispenser from behind his back and pumped a small coil of liquid soap on to Simon's waiting hands.

Silently Simon continued to wash his hands. The attendant watched his ablutions closely. When Simon finally felt it safe to pull his hands from the stream of water, the attendant immediately produced a small towel with a flourish.

'There you are sir,' he said, taking one step backwards to give Simon just enough space to dry his hands.

'Thanks,' muttered Simon.

The attendant responded by discreetly pushing a small hand-painted Italian ceramic dish along the counter towards

Simon. As he dried his hands, Simon peered curiously into the dish. In it he saw a pile of pound coins and one or two five pound notes. He looked up at the attendant, who was now beaming heartily at him. Simon blinked. This intrusive, aggravating service did not come without a cost. Simon was expected to tip the man for helping him with a fairly standard operating procedure which he had been performing unaided since he was two.

Simon stood drying his hands, debating what to do. He didn't want to give the attendant a tip. He hoped that someone else would walk into the room to distract Julio's attention, but the door remained resolutely shut. The attendant edged slightly closer to him – not easy in the circumstances – and fixed him with a beady stare.

'Finished with that now, are you sir?' he asked, nodding at the towel. His hand rested next to the small hand-painted Italian ceramic dish. Simon's hands were by now quite dry, but he carried on rubbing the towel between them, buying himself some more time.

Broadly, Simon's views could be summarized as follows: having a pee was a biological necessity. Trying to shame customers into paying for the privilege was an appalling wheeze. Simon knew that this was hardly the attendant's fault, even if his hectoring condescension hadn't exactly helped. He didn't make the rules up. And these tips were probably the only money he made. Some vague socialist sense of affront stirred within Simon. To tip would, in one sense, merely condone the restaurant's cynical exploitation of the largesse of the customers. Should he show solidarity with this suppressed worker by tipping him, or register his more fundamental disapproval of the regime which forced this systematic indignity upon them both by flouting the accepted convention?

The suppressed worker coughed meaningfully. Simon clung on to the towel, paralysed by indecision. Ignoring the broader socio-economical issues for a moment, another problem was that the attendant hadn't actually *done* anything, except to squirt some soap on his hands.

'Is there anything else, sir?' asked the attendant, a menacing edge creeping into his voice.

Simon looked at the hand-painted Italian ceramic dish with despair. Reluctantly he handed his towel to the attendant. He made a decision. There was a compromise position. He stuck his hand into his pocket and felt around for a fifty pence piece – half the going rate. His fingers found a large coin and pulled it out. To Simon's dismay, the coin he had grabbed was a ten pence piece. The attendant stifled a small gasp of indignation. Hurriedly Simon put the coin back into his pocket and delved for another. He and the attendant eyeballed each other as Simon searched the corners of his pocket. There were no other coins; all there was, Simon realized with a sinking heart, was a crumpled five-pound note. The attendant's left eyebrow had started to twitch. Simon shut his eyes for a moment, and produced the note. With a pang of anguish, he put it into the dish and quickly turned to walk out of the toilet, just as another unsuspecting customer was walking in.

As Simon pushed open the door, he heard the attendant say, 'Good evening, sir. My name is Julio. Welcome to the Mango toilets.' Simon sighed. Perhaps Julio deserved every penny he got.

Simon made his way back through the crowds to his

table. As he rounded the corner, to his surprise he saw Joe laughing. And then, two steps later, the world stopped for a few moments.

Standing next to Joe, holding a blue silk handkerchief, was Alex Petrie.

Simon's first instinct was to run. Remembering her last withering look as she had stormed out of the shop a few weeks earlier, another confrontation with the toilet attendant seemed a more attractive proposition. As he was trying to decide what to do, Joe caught sight of him and beckoned him over. Simon took a deep breath and began to walk back to the table.

Alex Petrie was also laughing as she began to poke the handkerchief into her clenched right fist. She looked up as Simon approached. Instantly the smile disappeared.

'Simon,' said Joe. 'You have to see this trick. It's amazing.' He turned to Alex Petrie. 'Please do it again for my friend.'

'Oh,' said Alex Petrie. 'It's you.'

'Hello again,' said Simon as he sat down again in his chair. 'Nice to see you.'

Alex Petrie regarded him levelly. 'What happened to your hair?'

'D'you two know each other?' asked Joe.

Alex Petrie turned back to Joe. 'Not really. I'm American, you see. Not good enough for stuck-up Englishmen like him.' She re-addressed herself to the handkerchief.

'She came into the shop,' explained Simon to Joe. 'Bought lots of stuff.' He turned to Alex. 'How is it all?' he asked politely.

'Just fine, thanks awfully,' replied Alex in a mock English accent. 'How's the stuck up girlfriend?'

'Look,' said Simon, 'I already tried to explain –'

'*Girlfriend?*' interrupted Joe, laughing more heartily than was strictly necessary. 'Simon doesn't *have* a girlfriend.' Joe managed to make the very idea sound utterly absurd. 'No, Simon hasn't had a girlfriend in absolutely bloody *ages*,' he said.

'Oh.' Alex looked at Simon appraisingly. 'What's wrong with him, then?'

'There's nothing *wrong* with him,' said Joe. 'Well, nothing that can't be fixed.'

'Such as?' asked Alex.

'Well, he's shy,' said Joe, not looking at Simon, 'and, between you and me, I think he's a bit desperate.'

'Excuse me,' said Simon.

Joe and Alex turned to look at him.

'I'm not desperate. I don't have a girlfriend and, all right, I will admit to being shy. But I *would* still very much like to show you around London while you're here, and I'm sorry I managed to make such a tit of myself when you came into the shop. Stage struck, I suppose. It's not every day that a beautiful woman asks me out. Call it my British reserve or something, if you must. So, if the offer's still open, then, yes please, I would very much like to show you around.'

Alex Petrie was looking at Simon, her head cocked to one side. 'That's sweet,' she said. 'I almost believe you mean it.'

'I do,' said Simon.

Joe leaned across the table towards her. 'I know him,' he said. 'And he really does.'

Alex looked between the two men. Her eyes finally settled on Simon. 'OK,' she said. 'I'll bite.'

'See?' said Joe with a smirk. 'I knew that haircut would work.'

SIXTEEN

The taxi swerved dangerously as a motorbike surged past, impossibly close.

'Wanker!' shouted the taxi driver, gesticulating uselessly at the disappearing back of the biker.

'Charming,' said Alex Petrie.

'London taxi drivers spend three years learning to talk like that,' said Simon.

'In New York you're considered fortunate if you can find one who can swear in English,' said Alex.

Simon settled back into his seat. 'So,' he said. 'Tell me. Taxi drivers aside, what do you think of our great city?'

'I think it's perfectly fine,' replied Alex primly. 'Old, and maybe a bit dirty. But I've had a good day. Dinner was delicious, and the company was excellent.'

Simon grinned. It *had* been a good day. There was, he reflected, something to be said for intricate planning.

Simon had agonized at some length about the approach he should adopt to his day with Alex, now that his longed-for second chance had come. Part of him wanted to try a different, devil-may-care approach, to play everything by ear and see where the spirit took them. Ultimately though, his pathological need for order and the fear of potential disaster won out over the less structured approach. By the time the following Sunday arrived, every minute had been rigorously accounted for. They had arranged to meet at midday in front of the National Gallery.

1130 hours: Simon arrives at the National Gallery for a quick preliminary recce of the premises. He checks the postcards in the gallery shop, and chooses one at random, a painting by Degas, which will be his Favourite Picture for the day.

1155 hours: Simon presents himself at the front steps of the Gallery after a last-minute self-inspection in the downstairs toilets.

1205 hours: Simon begins to get bored watching the crowds flock across Trafalgar Square. He reflects that Nelson's Column is a rather uninspiring title for a column with a statue of Nelson on top of it.

1207 hours: Simon tries to remember all of the battles in which Nelson fought in an effort not to become unduly concerned about Alex's non-appearance.

1214 hours: The last vestiges of hope vanish as Simon looks at his watch for the hundredth time in nineteen minutes. He ruefully tells himself that he really should have known better.

1215 hours: Alex Petrie skips up the steps and kisses him on the cheek. She apologizes for being late, claiming that she had been led to believe that the English regard punctuality as being somewhat vulgar. Simon is too relieved to mind.

1216 hours: Alex and Simon go into the museum. The elegant rooms of the gallery are heaving with a babbling swarm of tourists, laden with guide-books and cameras, flocking blindly past Picassos, Rembrandts, and Hogarths, chattering shrilly. Simon leads Alex to the quiet, darkened room where Leonardo da Vinci's fragile cartoon of the Virgin and Child sits behind a sheet of glass. Alex stares transfixed at the picture for some minutes, saying nothing, her face shining with excitement. Simon tries not to think about Joe, and his own particular enthusiasm for the museum.

Finally Alex turns to him and motions that they should leave. They walk into the brightly lit room outside. Alex looks at Simon.

'Wow,' she breathes. 'Some cartoon. It beats Bugs Bunny.'

Simon grins.

1302 hours: Simon takes Alex to the museum shop and expresses surprise and delight at seeing a postcard of his Favourite Picture, a Degas, which he insists on buying as a gift for her. She is suitably impressed.

1320 hours: They go to a nearby café for a small lunch – nothing too showy, right sort of price, absolutely no pressure. Animated chat ensues.

1425 hours: Alex graciously allows Simon to pay the bill, and thanks him demurely. Simon's spirits rise.

1435 hours: Simon leads Alex past Charing Cross station and towards the river. They cross Hungerford Bridge. The sun is shining, brilliantly illuminating London's landmarks. In the middle of the bridge they stop and gaze eastwards. The sunlight plays on the swift surface of the Thames, shooting reflected shafts of light into their wide eyes. Even the rigid, poker-faced buildings of the City seem softened in the afternoon haze. A fresh wind cuffs up the water beneath them and cools their faces. Simon has never seen London looking so good.

They make their way through the concrete jungle of the South Bank Centre and fall upon the Sunday afternoon second hand book stalls beneath Waterloo Bridge. They browse contentedly, recommending reads, brandishing old copies of long-forgotten novels. Simon buys Alex a dog-eared copy of *Middlemarch*, declaring it his Favourite Novel. Alex laughingly asks him to write a dedication to her on the front page. As he does so, Simon thinks that he really must get around to reading it one day.

1450 hours: They begin to walk eastwards. They pass a street-dancing festival and the huge bulk of the Tate Modern. They walk by the Globe theatre and the Golden Hinde. Beside them the river gleams.

1515 hours: They arrive at Tower Bridge, and continue on down Shad Thames. After a brief tour of the Design Museum, they sit down at the neighbouring café to enjoy a cup of latte-macchiato-frappucino with frothed sheep's milk and a dinky snip of lemon rind. Simon is perplexed to discover that this doesn't taste remotely like coffee, but still can't help feeling rather pleased with himself at how well everything is going.

1600 hours: In his one concession to tourism, Simon hails a taxi and they drive to the Marylebone Road and join the queue for Madame Tussaud's.

1615 hours: Queue moves forward six inches.

1633 hours: Simon makes joke about the loud yellow checked trousers worn by the American gentlemen immediately in front of them.

1634 hours: Simon apologizes profusely to Alex for

expressing such bigoted opinions, and makes a mental note to remember whom he is talking to.

1642 hours: Queue moves forward another six inches. Simon is surprised to discover that he does not mind the wait in the slightest, for Alex Petrie is good company. She is funny, assured, and confident. It occurs to Simon that this is perhaps hardly surprising as she makes her living going up to strangers and interrupting their expensive meals to cut their credit cards in two. As they wait in line, Alex and Simon talk. Tentatively at first, they begin with safe subjects – magic, of course, and London. Gradually, as they relax, the barriers drop. They speak of past loves, future hopes, their beliefs, both fervent and indolent. They tell jokes, swap favourite films. To Simon's delight, Alex Petrie is a jazz fan. She regularly goes to some of the venues in New York that Simon has pictured so vividly in his head – the Village Vanguard, Sweet Basil's, Smalls. She has seen many of the greats play. Simon listens, rapt.

1654 hours: finally inside the museum, Alex insists on having her photograph taken with Saddam Hussein and Ayatollah Khomeini. Simon tries not to think too hard about this.

1854 hours: Another taxi is hailed, this time to Monmouth Street, Covent Garden. This, Simon knows, is the big one. He has booked a table for two at his favourite restaurant. This is something of a risk, tactically, as it is a more overt declaration of intent. Alex accepts. Simon tries to hide his relief.

2220 hours: Coffee. The conversation has not stopped or faltered over three courses. 'That was a wonderful day,' says Alex, as she stirs her espresso.

Simon smiles. 'It was.'

'Thank you. I'm glad I got to give you a second chance.'

'So am I. Thank *you*.'

They grin at each other. Simon glances at his watch. 'Still,' he says, 'all good things must come to an end, I suppose.'

Alex Petrie sips her coffee implacably. 'Must they?' she asks.

Simon tapped on the window in front of him. 'Here's fine,' he said to the driver.

Trying not to look as smug as he felt, Simon paid the taxi driver, then turned to Alex and smiled. There was no doubt what was going to happen next. Alex was nothing if not forthright. Over coffee she had told Simon exactly what she wanted to do to him, and what she expected in return. Simon had nodded thoughtfully at this, trying to maintain some semblance of a cool exterior, leaning into the table so that nobody would notice the bulge that had appeared at the top of his trousers. This time, he told himself as he pulled his keys out of his pocket, nothing can go wrong.

As he opened his front door, Ringo Starr's voice was echoing through the flat.

Simon stepped quietly inside, listening. Alex followed him in and took off her coat. Simon held a finger to his lips. Ringo's flat Liverpudlian drone seemed to be coming from the sitting room. Motioning that Alex should remain where she was, Simon inched forwards into the flat.

The lights in the sitting room were all on. Cautiously

he put his head around the doorway. Then he blinked in disbelief.

Sophy looked up from the television. 'Hello, Simon,' she said. She reached for the remote control, and pressed a button. Ringo stopped in mid-irritable vowel. On the screen Thomas the Tank Engine froze.

'Sophy, you almost gave me a heart attack. What are you doing here?'

Sophy stood up and handed Simon an envelope which had been sitting on top of the television. 'Daddy said to give you this,' she explained.

Alex walked into the room. 'Who is this?' she asked sharply.

'Alex, this is Sophy. Sophy, say hello to Alex.' Simon, distracted, began to open the envelope.

'Hello, Alex,' said Sophy.

Alex turned to Simon. 'Is the kid *yours*?' she demanded.

'Hmm? Oh, no, not exactly,' said Simon, as he read the note that Michael had written.

Simon –

Sorry to burden you with Sophy but I have an unavoidable business meeting tonight and Bella is nowhere to be found. She just left a message saying that she would be 'out' without bothering to check if I was free or not. Anyway, all babysitters seem to be busy and so I thought I'd leave her with you. We have a spare key to your flat and so we let ourselves in. Hope that's OK. She's eaten. Someone will come round in the morning to pick her up.

Michael

P.S. Thanks.

'Excuse me,' said Alex, prodding Simon in the ribs, 'but what does "not exactly" mean?'

'She's my niece,' explained Simon unhappily, aware that once again the moment was slipping away from him. The atmosphere was now decidedly unromantic, not to say frigid. Not to say arctic.

'Are you Simon's girlfriend?' asked Sophy.

'No,' said Alex pointedly, ice-cold gusts whooshing across the room.

Simon's shoulders drooped. He turned to Alex. 'Look, stay for a while. Sophy is going to go to bed, anyway.'

Both Alex and Sophy looked at him with expressions of disgust.

'Do I have to?' asked Sophy.

'Yes you do.' Simon looked at his watch. 'It's late. You should have been in bed hours ago.'

Sophy collapsed sullenly back on to the sofa.

Alex put her bag on to her shoulder. 'I'm sorry,' she said. 'I'm going to go. I don't do kids well. Except professionally.' She smiled, without much humour. 'I'm a whizz at children's parties.'

'Well, some other time, maybe,' said Simon hopefully.

'Yeah,' said Alex. 'Some other time.'

As Simon opened the front door, Alex turned to him, and said, 'I had a great time today. Thank you. You're a good host.'

Simon smiled weakly. 'You're welcome. Sorry about Sophy.'

Alex brushed her cheek against his. 'Forget about it. You're sweet. Go and look after the kid. And call me. Let's do it again sometime.'

'Safe journey home,' replied Simon, and he watched her walk down the street before closing the front door. When she had vanished from view, Simon went back into the flat. 'Right, young lady, time for bed,' he said.

'But this is almost over,' complained Sophy, pointing at the television.

'Sophy, it's a *tape*,' said Simon. 'You can finish it tomorrow.'

'*Simon*.'

'No arguments, please. Bed, now.'

Sophy marched off to the bedroom, and Simon rescued his pyjamas and some blankets. As he spread the blankets out on the sofa and arranged the cushions to create a make-shift pillow, Simon contemplated this turn of events. It was, he concluded, a sign. He really should just give up now. He was obviously destined never to have sex again, ever.

Simon didn't feel particularly sleepy, and began aimlessly flicking through the channels in an attempt to distract himself. It didn't work. Finally he picked up the telephone to call Joe. He had to talk to someone before he descended into a funk of righteous indignation.

Joe wasn't there. His recorded voice echoed tinnily down the line, inviting Simon to leave a message. After the beep, Simon began to talk.

'Joe, hi, it's me. You won't believe this. We had a really good day today. Me and Alex. We did the National Gallery, walked along the Thames, dinner, the whole thing. It went very well. And then we got home, you know, game on as it were, only to discover my niece sitting in the middle of the sofa, watching a video. Which is a bit of a passion killer, to say the least. Alex was out of here like lightning.

My wanker of a brother-in-law left Sophy here while he went out, without bothering to ask me first. Anyway. I thought I'd call as I know you always appreciate a good story. I'm in need of consolation, so give me a ring when you get in, if it's not too late. Speak to you later.'

Simon put the phone down and sighed deeply.

'What's a wanker?' asked Sophy.

Simon shot out of the sofa in fright. 'How long, er, hello, are you all right, how long?' he said.

'I need some water,' explained Sophy.

Simon calmed down. 'Oh. Right. I'll fetch some for you.'

'What's a wanker?' asked Sophy again.

Simon looked at his niece despairingly. 'Did you hear all of that?' he asked.

Sophy nodded. 'So what *is* a wanker?' she persisted.

'Well, first of all, it's not a word you should ever *ever* use,' said Simon cautiously. 'It's not a very nice word. So you mustn't ever let Mummy hear you say it.'

'But what does it *mean*?'

'Right. Well.' Simon thought. 'Basically, it means, er, someone with a big nose,' he said, conscious that this was possibly a little unfair.

Sophy considered this information thoughtfully. 'A big nose?' she mused. 'So Postman Pat is a wanker, then?'

'Er, yes, Sophy, he is, but you must absolutely *promise* me that you'll never use that word. It's very naughty and you'll get into a lot of trouble if Mummy hears you.'

Sophy seemed unfazed by the prospect of maternal fury. 'Can I have my glass of water now?' she asked.

'Not before you promise not to use that word.'

Sophy sighed. 'All right. I promise.' She paused. 'If it's such a bad word, why are you allowed to use it?'

'Because I'm a grown-up,' replied Simon, before walking briskly into the kitchen. He thought of the number of times he had been presented with this explanation when he was a child and remembered his helpless rage at its transparent unfairness.

Sophy, though, was obviously used to the lazy, underhand tactics of adults. 'I see,' she said without rancour, taking her glass of water from her uncle. 'Thank you for the water. Good night.'

'Night. Sleep well.'

Sophy went back into the bedroom and closed the door behind her. Simon flopped back down on the sofa and thought about Alex Petrie, now doubtless back in her hotel room. After a few moments he walked to the turntable and pulled out an album of piano pieces by Bill Evans. On the back cover there was a photograph of Evans at the piano, his head tilted to one side, studying the keyboard before him. A cigarette hung from one side of his mouth. He looked thoughtful, lonely. The melancholy opening notes of 'Danny Boy' filled the room. Simon relaxed a little. As always, Evans' gentle touch soothed out some of the wrinkles in Simon's life. Jazz music could be visceral or gentle, funny or sad, but above all it could be beautiful. There was a simple purity in Evans' playing which made tingles fly up and down Simon's spine like an electric current. His playing was free of glossy pyrotechnics or snappy time-signatures. He allowed the piano and the music to speak for themselves. Faced with such naked, unadorned beauty there was little one could do but to allow oneself to be swept along.

Simon lay back on the sofa and allowed his mind to empty. Just as he was falling asleep, the telephone rang.

'Simon?'

'Bella. What's going on?'

'Is Sophy there?'

'Of course she is.'

'Everything all right?'

'Yes, she's fine. She's asleep.'

'Thank God you're there. I could murder Michael. I don't know what he thought he was doing, leaving her there like that with just a note for you. When did you get home?'

'A while ago.'

'I'm sorry. So sorry. So will Michael be, when he gets home from wherever he's disappeared to. I hope it didn't spoil your night.'

Simon thought again of Alex, alone in her hotel bed. 'Don't worry,' he said. 'Where were you?'

'Out.'

'Out?'

'Out.'

'OK,' said Simon.

'Look,' said Bella, 'I'd offer to come and get her now, but the truth is, I've had a bit to drink.'

'That's OK. It's probably better that she sleeps now, anyway.'

'You're an angel.'

'I don't know about that, but maybe there'll be some sort of reward for me in the next life,' said Simon. 'Special turbo wings, extra good quality cat gut for my harp, something like that.'

'How are we going to do this?' asked Bella, her thoughts

back firmly with her daughter rather than Simon's heavenly fringe benefits. 'When should I come and pick Sophy up?'

'Well, I have to go to work tomorrow,' said Simon. 'Why don't I take her to the shop and you can come in and pick her up from there? Save you the trek to North London. And she'll enjoy going to the shop.'

'That,' said Bella, 'is a fucking *great* idea.'

'I don't think I've heard you swear for years,' said Simon, surprised.

'That's because you probably haven't seen me out of earshot of Sophy for years.'

'Ah. That would explain it.' Simon thought guiltily of Sophy eaves-dropping on his telephone message to Joe.

'I do still have a life, you know, Simon,' said Arabella after a few moments. 'I'm a mother first, true, but there is a second, third and fourth there somewhere, just waiting for the chance to escape.'

'I know.'

'Trouble is, look what happens the moment I try and be anything other than a mother. Disaster strikes.'

'Hardly a disaster,' said Simon. He thought of Alex's face when she saw Sophy sitting on the sofa. Well, perhaps a small disaster, then.

'Well, no, I suppose not, thanks to you. But I'm still . . . incandescent with rage.'

'Wow. Four syllables worth of anger. That's bad.'

'You bet. Thank you for looking after my darling daughter, Simon.'

Simon smiled into the telephone. 'You're welcome.'

Bella emitted a long sigh. There was a pause. 'It's not always easy, this motherhood stuff, you know,' she said.

'You seem so good at it,' said Simon.

'Well, I have my moments. But there are times when it can all get a bit much.'

'Well, I don't know about motherhood, but I can recommend uncle-hood,' said Simon. 'The perks are great.'

'Families are hard work sometimes,' said Bella.

Simon said nothing. He wondered whether she already suspected Michael of something. 'Do you know where Michael had to go tonight?' he asked cautiously.

'Some work thing, as usual. It seems crazy, on a Sunday night.'

'I'll say,' agreed Simon. Crazy to the point of being completely unbelievable.

'I wish he'd slow down a little,' she said. 'He's not getting any younger.'

'I wish he'd slow down, too,' said Simon with feeling.

There was a pause.

'I miss mum,' said Arabella after a moment.

'I know,' replied Simon. 'Me too.'

'Goodnight.'

'Night.'

Simon put the phone down, arranged the blanket neatly on the sofa, and went to sleep.

SEVENTEEN

The next day Simon took Sophy to work. He discovered that with a small child in tow people on the Underground were significantly more sympathetic towards him than they had been when he was on crutches. Perhaps children were regarded as more of a handicap.

Sophy was very excited about going to the magic shop. Simon, though, was more circumspect about the prospect. He was worried about how Brian might react.

As the train headed southwards beneath the city, Simon tried not to think about the previous evening's near-miss with Alex Petrie. Instead he thought about the romantic entanglements of Victoria Station and Russell Square. Exactly how, he wondered, had he managed to get caught up in that little episode? He wanted to be sure that Vick had explained to Russell that Simon's alleged role in the matter was entirely a figment of her imagination. The last thing he wanted was to be pursued by a violently-inclined psychotic thug with forearms the size of tree trunks, out for revenge.

On their way from the station to the shop, Bob was not in his usual place. Instead there was another man, who kept his stack of magazines in a tattered plastic bag. He bounded up to Simon and Sophy as they approached.

'*Big Issue*, mate?' he demanded.

'Where's Bob?' asked Simon.

'Holiday,' said the man.

'Holiday?' repeated Simon. 'Where's he gone?'

'The Algarve, I think,' replied the man.

'The Algarve? How long for?'

'Two weeks. He's granted me a sub-franchise for the whole period. He negotiated some tough terms, but there you go. That's business, innit? *Big Issue*?'

Simon automatically reached into his pocket for a pound coin and took the proffered magazine.

When they reached the shop, Brian and Vick were standing behind the counter. They looked up warily as Simon and Sophy entered.

'Hello,' said Simon. 'I realize that Bring your Niece to Work Day isn't officially until next week, but I thought I'd avoid the rush and bring her this morning. This is Sophy. Her mum is coming to pick her up later, but until then she's going to spend some time with us, if that's OK.' He nudged Sophy.

'Hello,' said Sophy politely.

Vick glanced at her in a bored way. Brian, though, was staring at her, transfixed.

'Sophy is actually very keen on magic,' continued Simon, looking worriedly at Brian. There was a pause.

'Brian?' said Simon. 'Are you all right?'

'What? Oh, yeah. Fine,' said Brian absent-mindedly. 'Sorry. It's just that she reminds me of Vick when she was that age.'

'Oh. I see,' said Simon. That explained the haunted look. 'So is it OK?'

Brian continued to stare at Sophy and nodded absent-mindedly. Finally he shook himself out of his reverie when

Dean bustled in carrying a large cardboard box of spinning bow ties. 'Hello,' said Dean cheerfully to Sophy. 'What's your name?'

'Sophy,' said Sophy.

Dean put down his box. 'What a pretty name,' he said. 'Have you had it long?'

Sophy giggled.

'Tell you what,' said Dean. 'I bet you don't know why clowns have red noses.'

Sophy considered this. 'I don't,' she said.

'If you come over here,' said Dean, 'I'll tell you a story that's so amazing you won't believe it.' Simon made a thumbs-up sign. Sophy and Dean went into a corner and Dean began to entertain her with tricks and jokes and silly stories.

Simon prepared for business. There were no customers for the first thirty minutes and so Simon watched Dean's impromptu performance. Sophy was captivated. Eventually a thin trickle of people began to come into the shop, and Simon was soon too busy explaining and demonstrating himself to watch Dean. Occasionally a peal of Sophy's delighted laughter would float through the shop. Dean and Sophy finally returned from their corner, all smiles.

Brian was demonstrating a trick to a spotty boy in an anorak which involved pulling multi-coloured handkerchiefs out of his ear. Sophy pointed at Brian. Specifically at his nose. Then without warning she declared, 'That man is a *wanker*.'

Victoria Station, who was standing by the curtain with a cup of tea, burst out laughing. Simon was beginning to realize that he preferred her sullen and miserable. So far her laughter had always heralded disaster of some sort.

Brian's face froze for a moment, before it began to turn an interesting shade of purple.

'*What* did she say?' said Brian. As he spoke, he put his hands on the counter, leaving a green handkerchief hanging somewhat incongruously out of his left ear.

'Oh, nothing,' said Simon.

Sophy tugged on sleeve. 'I did,' she said. 'I said he was a wanker.' Vick hooted in disbelief, shaking her head as she went into the stock room. The boy in the anorak had also begun to snigger. Brian shot him a sour look.

'*Sophy*,' said Simon. 'What did we say last night? About not using that word?'

'You said I shouldn't say it in front of Mummy,' said Sophy.

'Oh. Well, what I meant was that you shouldn't say it at all,' said Simon, wishing that his niece didn't have such a literal bent. He glanced at Brian, who was still standing, thunderstruck, behind the counter, and grinned a mortified grin. 'Sophy, apologize, please.'

'Sorry,' said Sophy.

Brian looked at Simon and Sophy suspiciously, unsure whether this was some sort of pre-planned joke at his expense. He scratched his ear in confusion, and found the green handkerchief that was still hanging there limply. Hastily he pulled it out and put it in his pocket.

'All right,' he said eventually.

The teenager who had been watching Brian's trick with the handkerchiefs was still smirking to himself. Brian looked at him. 'Yes?' he snapped.

'You were showing me that trick with the handkerchief,' said the teenager.

'Well, it's not for sale,' replied Brian. 'Not to you, anyway.'

'But that's not fair,' said the teenager.

'Life isn't fair. Now sod off.' Brian turned and went behind the velvet curtain, leaving the hapless teenager standing in front of the counter. Eventually he left the shop, shaking his bewildered head as he went.

'Simon,' said Sophy.

'What?' asked Simon, exhausted.

'What does "sod off" mean?'

About an hour later Arabella arrived at the shop, her eyes hidden behind large dark glasses. Sophy was exploring the stock room with Dean.

'Hello,' said Simon as his sister approached the counter. 'How's things?'

Arabella began to shake her head until she thought better of it. 'Not good,' she mumbled. 'Bad,' she elaborated after a few moments. 'I have something of a hangover.'

'Good night, was it?'

'Depends on your point of view, really. An old friend from my publishing days called up out of the blue and we went to a wine bar on Lavender Hill, where we proceeded to set the world to rights with the help of three bottles of wine. Or it may have been four.'

'Ah,' said Simon. Bella was not a big drinker. 'Did you have any success in sorting the world and its problems out, at least?'

'Not really. We got stuck on where to take young children on holiday. Never got on to world famine, cracking down on drug smuggling or the illegal arms trade. And then I came home to discover that Michael had left Sophy alone in your flat. I could have killed him. I *would* have killed him, if he'd been there.' She paused. 'And if I'd been able to stand up straight unaided. Which apparently I wasn't.'

Simon looked at his sister, concerned. He'd never seen her like this before. It seemed that her usual exterior of more or less cheery stoicism was crumbling. Was something going on? Did she suspect Michael? Bella looked around the shop. 'Haven't been in here for a while. Nothing changes, does it?'

Simon shook his head. 'Nothing at all,' he agreed.

'And where is the apple of my eye?'

'The apple of your eye is presently in the stock room tormenting one of my colleagues,' said Simon. 'Hold on. I'll go and fetch her.' He turned and called to Sophy, who duly appeared, followed by an exhausted-looking Dean.

'Hello, darling,' said Bella, bending down to give her a hug.

'Hello,' said Sophy. 'Why are you wearing sunglasses?'

God, thought Simon, does she ever stop asking bloody questions?

'Well, I think it might be sunny later, sweetheart,' replied Bella with the assurance of one who knows that it is not so much what you say, as how you say it.

'Oh,' said Sophy, and left it at that.

'Well,' said Bella, hoiking her bag on to her shoulder, 'we should be getting on our way, I suppose. I'll give you a call during the week. Fix up another Sunday.'

'That would be great.'

'See you,' said Bella.

'Bye Simon,' said Sophy.

'Bye, sweet pea.'

'Bye, Dean,' she said.

'Bye, Sophy,' panted Dean.

As the door shut behind mother and daughter, Dean retreated with relief back to the stock room and Simon went to switch on the kettle, humming a Charlie Parker tune to himself, 'Ornithology'. It was a demanding piece, with chord changes twice a bar, which Parker used to play at a ferociously quick tempo. Sometimes his side men could only just keep up with him as he flew through the tune before launching into electrically charged solos, taking the melody and turning it inside out, shredding it and restoring it again, all with a dazzling fluidity and musical logic that was seamless, perfect. Ornithology. The study of birds. Well, it was a complicated subject, of that there was no doubt. Simon felt like one of Parker's sidemen, always trying to keep up.

His mind drifted back again to Alex Petrie, and the day they had spent together. It had been almost perfect. Almost. He regretted not ending the evening with a rapturous sexual performance that they would both subsequently agree had been the most memorable experience either of them had had, like, *ever*, but in a way he was glad that they would have to wait a while for that. The delights of anticipation, he was discovering, were rather intoxicating, if you knew that something, or someone, was a sure thing.

The kettle clicked off and Simon made himself a cup of coffee. He briefly allowed himself to imagine flying over to New York to see Alex, conducting a glamorous transatlantic love affair. There would be snatched weekends in Manhattan, occasional breaks to an exotic Long

Island resort. Simon had never been to New York, but he had dreamed about it for years – particularly the famous jazz clubs, now defunct, that lined 52nd Street back in the forties, in the hey-day of Bebop. He could see Dizzy swinging from that lamppost, Monk shuffling towards the piano at the back of another dimly-lit, smoke-filled club. Those clubs – the Five Spot, the Three Deuces and many others – had closed down long ago, but their glamour had not faded in Simon's imagination. And now, he told himself, Alex Petrie might be the perfect reason to get to know the place for real.

Simon wondered how long he should wait before he called Alex again. He didn't want to seem too eager, but then he didn't want her to think that he wasn't interested either. Perhaps tomorrow morning. Or perhaps the morning after. God, he thought, this stuff is complicated.

That evening, Simon trudged to the Underground thinking about Alex Petrie, and trying to work out exactly what he should do next. Despite the success of the previous day, the idea of calling her made Simon go weak behind the knees with apprehension.

Simon wanted to talk it through with Joe. He would have got Simon's message of last night by now. Joe always seemed to relish doling out advice, and Simon was sure that he wouldn't miss the opportunity of doing so again. As he approached the automatic ticket barriers, watching the constant stream of commuters scurry into the bowels of the Underground system, Simon didn't feel quite ready to go home yet. He needed to relax, indulge himself. He turned and walked out of the station and clambered on to a bus instead. It was time for some retail therapy.

The shop, as always, smelled of old cardboard. From the speakers bracketed high up on the wall came the sound of a tenor saxophone in full flight, notes spilling out into the close atmosphere of the shop like a million tiny shafts of light. Simon stood listening for a while, looking around the shop. There were three customers, each lost in his own small world. They stood hunched over the racks of second-hand vinyl, flicking through the battered cardboard covers with a practised eye, stopping to pull out a record and read the sleeve notes, sometimes chuckling to themselves in quiet recognition at a song recalled, an anecdote remembered.

Simon listened to the music on the stereo. The saxophone solo had been followed by a trumpet. Simon recognized the tune. It was a Rodgers and Hart song, 'The Most Beautiful Girl in the World'. As the trumpet flew over the chords, Simon began to move around the shop, stopping occasionally to examine a record. On the walls hung old posters of jazzmen long since gone. There were collections of memorabilia, preserved behind glass, which Simon loved: old photographs, ticket stubs, programmes, even an old record or two.

As the song ended, Simon went over to the counter to see what he had been listening to. It was a live album recorded at Ronnie Scott's club in Soho in the early 60s by a quintet led by the saxophonist Tubby Hayes. Tubby. Jazz musicians did have some odd names, reflected Simon. Jelly Roll Morton. Zoot Sims. Mezz Mezzrow. Dizzy. Anything was possible. He had a record that Stan Getz had cut with a drummer called Milton Banana.

Simon flicked through the ranks of haphazardly filed old vinyl. Finally he went to the counter and inspected the Tubby Hayes album again.

He made a decision.

Some time later Simon arrived home, clutching his new purchase under his arm. He immediately went through to the sitting room to check the answer machine. It was winking at him. Joe, thought Simon.

He went over to the turntable and extracted his new record from its sleeve, placing it carefully on to the waiting black baize. Simon listened to Tubby make his introductory comments to the audience. As the opening notes of the first song began, he pressed the button on the answer machine.

'Hi, it's me.' Arabella. 'I just wanted to say thank you *so* much for looking after Sophy for me – for *us*, I suppose I should say. I hope she wasn't too much trouble. She's been off playing with a neighbour's daughter this afternoon and I've been lying very quietly on my bed with a towel over my face. Anyway. Hope everything's fine with you. Give me a call soon. See you.'

'End of messages,' announced the machine officiously.

Simon frowned. Nothing from Joe after all. That was boring. Simon needed his advice. He picked up the telephone and dialled Joe's number. As the ringing tone echoed down the line, Simon tried to work out what he was going to say. After four rings, there was a click.

'Hi, not here, leave a message.'

'Er, Joe? Hi, it's Simon.' He tried to sound confident and relaxed. 'Just giving you a quick buzz to see if you got my message last night. It'd be good to have a chat, so give me a ring, maybe when you get in, if it's not too late.' Simon paused, worried that that had sounded too desperate. 'Nothing important,' he said unconvincingly. 'Just wanted a chat, you know, see how you are, that sort of thing. Well, I suppose I did have one or two things I wanted to ask you. Nothing important,' he said again, aware that he was now rambling hopelessly. He took a deep breath and tried to compose himself for a strong finish. 'Anyway, it's now, what, about seven. I'll probably be here all evening. So, yeah, give me a ring. Speak to you soon.'

Simon slammed the phone down, and slumped on to the sofa. He closed his eyes and allowed the music to wash over him.

EIGHTEEN

Joe didn't call back.

Simon spent the rest of the evening pacing his flat like a caged ocelot, nerves jangling, waiting for the phone to ring. As the hours crawled by, Simon felt less and less competent to call Alex Petrie without taking detailed instructions first.

Simon's self-confidence was so low, that despite the success of their day together, he didn't know how Alex would react to his call. Instinct and empirical evidence told him that he should still prepare thoroughly before picking up the phone. Simon stared at the telephone, hating it. Life must have been so much more civilized before Alexander Bloody Graham Bloody Bell. You would go round to a lady's house and present your card, and then wait to be entertained in person by your hostess. All right, there was probably less snogging, but romance in Jane Austen's time had a certain appeal to it. It was more elegant, more refined. And there were no telephones.

At around midnight Simon finally went to bed, having successfully argued himself out of leaving another message on Joe's machine. He was so drained after such a prolonged expenditure of nervous energy, that he slept soundly. He dreamed that old-fashioned Bakelite telephones, each the size of a small house, kept crashing out of the sky, narrowly missing him.

By the time he arrived at Station Magic the following morning, Simon was thoroughly depressed. As he pushed open the front door, he caught a glimpse of himself in the glass, and seeing his GI Joe haircut made his spirits dip lower still.

Vick and Brian were standing behind the counter shouting at each other. Dean stood over the cash register, trying to ignore the heated family row being conducted a few feet away. Vick was wearing a turtle neck sweater. As the door opened, everyone looked up.

'You're late,' snarled Brian.

'Simon,' breathed Dean with relief.

'Oh, *God*,' said Vick, and stormed off to the stock room.

'Hello everyone,' said Simon. 'Thanks for that super welcome.'

'Just get behind here and do some bloody work,' snapped Brian, before disappearing with a swish of the velvet curtain.

'God. What was all that about?' asked Simon. 'That looked like an extra-special spat, even by their standards.'

Dean shook his head. 'Dunno,' he said. 'I tried not to listen too much. Something about a boy, I think.'

Simon was immediately interested. 'Did they say which, er, boy?' he asked.

'No. That was the problem. She wouldn't tell him which boy it was.'

'Which boy *what* was?'

Dean rolled his eyes ominously. 'You'll see,' he said.

A little while later, unable to restrain his curiosity further, Simon went down into the stock room. To his surprise, Vick was actually doing some work, checking off delivery orders. Simon casually edged up to her.

'Hello,' he said. 'Is everything all right?'

Vick turned towards him. 'No,' she said. 'Actually it's not.'

'Oh dear,' said Simon. He waited for Vick to elaborate further, but she returned to her forms.

'Has this got something to do with Russell?' he asked.

'Yes,' replied Vick, 'it has everything to do with Russell.'

'And what's the problem, exactly?'

'*This* is the problem, exactly.' Vick pulled down the neck of her sweater to show Simon a monstrous purple bruise the size of a walnut at the base of her neck. Simon peered closely in appalled fascination. He could still see the faint indents of Russell's teeth in Vick's skin. The love-bite seemed to glow faintly as if it was charged with some supernatural form of energy, like a mystical amulet.

'God,' said Simon, trying not to stare.

'Yeah, *God*, is right,' agreed Vick, rolling the turtleneck back up. 'Anyway, I didn't realize it was even *there* until this morning, when Dad spotted it at breakfast. He went ballistic. Through the fucking roof. He wanted to know what had been going on. And who with. I didn't tell him. That's why we've been screaming at each other all morning.'

'I *see*,' said Simon. 'But apart from that it's all going well with Russell?'

'Yeah,' said Vick laconically.

'And you, er, you explained to him that you made up that stuff about you and me?'

Vick looked at Simon witheringly. 'God, Simon, take a chill pill. Yeah, I told him.'

'Oh,' said Simon, relieved. 'Well, that's good.' There was a pause. 'So Russell's behaving himself, then?'

Vick nodded. 'He's all right. Bit too enthusiastic, that's all.' She paused. 'But no more chewing on my neck from now on.'

'You should give him one back,' said Simon, wondering what damage all the metalwork in Vick's mouth could do to unprotected skin.

'Yeah.' Vick nodded. 'Maybe I will.'

Brian came down the stairs. His face immediately adopted a scowl. 'Haven't you got anything better to do than just standing around chatting?' he asked. 'Don't you have any work to do?'

Simon shifted uncomfortably from one foot to the other. 'Sorry –' he began.

'Oh, bog off,' interrupted Vick, before running up the stairs into the shop. Simon realized that the question had actually been directed at her.

Brian watched his daughter go, shaking his head. 'I don't know,' he said to Simon. 'Women.'

Simon tsk-tsked sympathetically.

'Unpredictable lot,' observed Brian philosophically.

'Mmm,' agreed Simon.

'Do you know she's been seeing some lad who's given her a big fucking love-bite on her bloody neck?' demanded Brian suddenly. Simon gave Brian a look of what he hoped was shock, moral outrage and despair, all rolled into one compassionate whole.

'*No*,' he whispered.

'If I catch the poxy little toe-rag who did it I'll pulverise him,' said Brian.

Simon thought of Russell Square's fabulous gym-toned biceps and doubted that Brian would be quite so cavalier once he saw the poxy toe-rag in question. 'I suppose she's just growing up,' said Simon. 'You know, going out, snogging boys. Come on, Brian, you must have done much the same when you were young.'

Brian bristled. 'Me snogging boys? What are you saying?'

'No, not boys, obviously,' said Simon hastily. 'But girls. You know. When you were young. I bet you were at it like a rabbit.' Simon winked in a hearty, man-to-man way.

Brian looked at Simon blankly. 'Not really. I was more interested in model aeroplanes in those days. Didn't have any time for girls.'

'Ah,' said Simon. 'Anyway,' he persisted, without being entirely sure why, 'young people nowadays, they grow up faster, don't they? They're more keen to experiment, you know, have fun.'

'All right,' said Brian. 'Maybe. But they're not going to experiment on my daughter, understand?'

'OK,' said Simon quickly.

'Next thing you know she'll start smoking,' said Brian. 'And then I won't be responsible for my actions.'

Simon said nothing.

Despite the good news that the rekindled romance of Vick and Russell Square seemed to be progressing well, Simon was still preoccupied with his worries about when, and how, to call Alex. He spent the rest of the day listening for the telephone, hoping that Joe might ring. The real difficulty, he was starting to realize, was that this time the initiative lay solely with him. He had been given too much time to think. Now he had ground to a sticky, awkward halt.

There was also the small problem of what to do about Michael. He couldn't stand the idea of Michael gallivanting around town, betraying Arabella's trust. Even less appealing, though, was the prospect of telling Bella what was going on. Simon had to concede that if Michael was a shit, at least he was a discreet shit.

Still, he thought. There had to be a way of rectifying the situation without causing Arabella any pain. If Simon could just make Michael *stop*, then he would be satisfied.

The only way that Simon could think of to make Michael behave in the future was to threaten to tell Arabella everything. However, over the last few days Simon had come to the inescapable conclusion that he would never be able to carry out his threat. His primary concern was to *protect* her and Sophy from Michael's behaviour. Once Michael realized that Simon would never tell Bella, he would carry on as before.

No: something else was needed. There had to be a way of making Michael stop his philandering, without Arabella ever knowing about it. Simon tried to think of a more lateral approach to the problem. How did people generally go about getting other people to do what they wanted? Suddenly the vision of Russell Square's forearms popped into Simon's brain. Of course. He couldn't think why he hadn't thought of it earlier.

As he stood there, Vick clumped angrily up the stock room stairs and walked into the shop.

'V,' said Simon.

'What?' she snapped.

'Could you do me a favour?'

NINETEEN

The bottle-shaped neon sign that Simon was staring at suddenly flashed twice, and then switched off. Simon hoped that this wasn't some portent of what was to come.

If the neon sign had fizzled out, it was the only thing that had. Simon was surrounded by a flurry of activity and excitement as people queued up to get into the pub. By the doors stood three large men with small black headsets tucked discreetly into their ears, who considered each prospective entrant before inclining their heads to allow them in. The whole performance was something of a charade, designed to cultivate a palpably false aura of exclusivity. In the fifteen minutes that Simon had been standing there, not one person had been refused entry. Recent arrivals had included a posse of extremely drunk half-naked football supporters, three women who were quite obviously prostitutes, and a red-eyed, unshaven tramp.

For the most part, though, the clientele was young and irredeemably vulgar. The pub was a down-market version of Slick Tom's, which was really saying something.

When Vick had told Simon that Russell Square had agreed to meet him, and told him where the rendezvous was to take place, she had obviously expected some sort of reaction, other than the blank look that he had returned.

'The Crusty Toad,' repeated Simon. 'OK. Where's that, then?'

'You know,' said Vick, 'as in *the* Crusty Toad.'

'Should I know it?' asked Simon.

Vick sighed. 'It's only the best, most notorious pub in Mile End,' she replied.

'Oh,' said Simon. 'Right. *That* Crusty Toad.'

Simon had been intrigued by Vick's juxtaposition of the epithets 'best' and 'notorious', and had been thinking about his trip to Mile End with equal measures of curiosity and apprehension. Having now stood in front of the establishment for a quarter of an hour watching a questionable collection of people pile through its doors – not to mention the occasional hurried exits of mini-skirted young women for quick bouts of tactical vomiting around the corner of the building – Simon was beginning to form a better idea of what awaited him inside.

Simon was to meet Russell Square inside the pub at nine o'clock. It was now eight-thirty. He took a deep breath and decided to go in. He might as well relax and have a drink while he waited for Russell to arrive.

Simon joined the queue. The atmosphere was heady with the mixture of cheap perfume and even cheaper aftershave. Finally he arrived at the front. He smiled blandly at the trio of bouncers, waiting for the cursory nod. The men all wore black trousers and black poloneck sweaters. Each had a gold chain around his neck, outside the poloneck sweater.

One of the men squinted at him. 'All right, mate,' he said gruffly.

'Yeah, good thanks,' said Simon.

The next bouncer raised his chin slowly towards Simon. 'Not from round here, are you?' he said.

'No I'm not,' admitted Simon, surprised. 'Is that a problem?'

The third man took a step closer to Simon. 'Don't be comin' here with that sort of smart-arse attitude, man,' he growled.

'I didn't mean –' began Simon.

The first bouncer held up his heavily bejewelled hands. 'All right, Troy man. Calm it, dude. The guy's not dissing yer.'

'Fucking stuck up little ponce,' muttered Troy beneath his breath.

'So, my friend,' continued the first man, holding his hands together in front of him and interlacing his fingers in some vaguely pious gesture, 'what brings you to the Crusty Toad?'

Simon blinked. 'I want to have a drink,' he said.

'A drink?' The second man looked instantly suspicious.

'This is a pub, isn't it?' asked Simon. 'I mean, it can't be that unusual, surely?'

Troy took another step towards him, his fists clenched. 'I'm warning you, you little tosser –'

Troy's colleagues waved him away again. 'No,' said the first man, turning back towards Simon and fingering his gold chain as he spoke, 'it's not unusual, as such. I suppose we're just curious as to why you should have chosen this particular establishment.'

'Well that's easy enough,' replied Simon. 'I'm meeting someone here.'

'Who you meetin', then?' demanded the second man.

Simon frowned. 'Just a bloke,' he answered.

Troy's eyes betrayed his suspicion. 'What bloke?'

Simon shrugged. 'Just a – friend.'

Bouncer number one regarded him cautiously. 'A friend, you say.' Simon nodded. 'Good friend, is he, this bloke?'

'Well, more of an acquaintance, I suppose,' replied Simon, mystified.

'Hmm. Now he says he's an acquaintance,' said the first man to his two colleagues. They exchanged meaningful looks.

'Look,' said Simon, who was conscious of the growing line of impatient customers behind him, 'can't you just let me in? You've let everyone else stroll through.'

'Yeah,' countered Troy, taking a step forward, 'but they didn't want to have a *drink* with a *bloke*.' From the look on his face it was as if Simon had proposed something unspeakably kinky.

'OK,' said Simon. 'This is how I see it. This,' he said, pointing at the front door of the pub, 'is a pub, licensed to sell drinks to customers. I am a customer, who wants to buy a drink and meet a friend here, have a chat, have a laugh, and maybe buy another drink. I'm just an ordinary punter.'

Three brows furrowed at once, and the bouncers huddled together to consult. Finally they broke and assumed their previous positions.

'Right,' said the first man, straightening up. 'In you go.'

The second man nodded towards the door. 'Move along, now. There *is* a queue.'

'Oh,' said Simon. 'Right. Thanks.'

Troy said nothing, eyeing him with overt distrust.

The first bouncer bent down towards Simon. 'Sorry, man,' he grunted. 'Can't be too careful nowadays, get my drift?'

'Oh, yes, er, quite. Absolutely,' replied Simon, before pushing open the doors and stepping into the pub.

Once inside, it took Simon a moment or two to orientate himself and adjust to his new surroundings. The management had eschewed more traditional forms of lighting for something a little more exotic. If the neon display outside the pub had been somewhat desultory, the interior more than compensated for it. There was neon everywhere. Brightly glowing shapes hung on the walls. The perimeters of the bar area were delineated by blazing streaks of cobalt. There was not an ordinary light bulb in the place. Fluorescent strip lights illuminated the dark space with a bewildering spectrum of electric colour. It was like downtown Kowloon. The pub's windows had been blackened out so as not to spoil the effect. Simon squinted into the semi-darkness. All he could see were the white shirts of the customers, which reflected the neon with a curious, almost translucent blue-white luminescence.

Simon moved forwards, trying not to bump into anybody on the way. The bar was long and surprisingly empty. A woman with electric blue mascara which clashed badly with the cobalt neon served him a pint of beer. Simon decided to stay at the bar and wait for Russell to arrive. Otherwise they might spend hours wandering around in the darkness looking for each other.

He stared out into the mysterious penumbra that swallowed the body of the pub. He tried, for the hundredth time, to work out exactly how to present Russell with his proposal. It was relatively simple. Simon wanted Russell to indulge in his propensity for violent behaviour by administering a little heavy-handed abuse to Simon's brother-in-law Michael, which would be accompanied by some fairly specific verbal directions pointing out how this sort of unpleasantness might be avoided in the future, viz., by an abrupt end to his extra-marital high-jinks.

Simon sipped his pint and wondered whether this was really the right approach. He didn't like violence, but it was the only way he could think of to jolt Michael's unrufflable arrogance and make him change his ways.

Finally Russell Square approached. He was wearing a light grey suit with a garish tie with a large Mickey Mouse on it. The suit half-glowed in the reflection of the neon. Russell stuck out a hand.

'All right,' he said, grabbing Simon's hand and pulverizing it in an efficient manoeuvre. He did not look particularly pleased to be there.

'Hi,' said Simon, catching his breath slightly as his right hand yet again suffered severe physical trauma. 'Thanks for coming.'

Russell grunted.

'What can I get you to drink?' asked Simon.

'Lager shandy,' said Russell. 'Half.'

'Do you come here a lot, then?' asked Simon as he waited for the drink to be poured.

Russell nodded. 'My local.'

'Interesting place,' commented Simon. 'I had a bit of a problem getting past the bouncers on the door.'

Russell barked an abrasive guffaw. 'Them three? Shouldn't worry about them. They're just for show. Wouldn't hurt a fly. They just take themselves a bit too seriously sometimes, know what I mean?'

'They seemed very reluctant to let me in.'

'Well, they don't know you, do they? It's generally regulars in here. Them boys are very suspicious of strangers. I imagine they thought you were undercover filth.'

'Police?' said Simon, aghast.

Russell nodded. 'It has been known.'

'But why would the police be interested in this place?' asked Simon. 'It's just a pub, right?'

'Oh, of course,' agreed Russell, winking broadly as he did so.

Simon's spirits dipped. He wondered whether his plan was such a good one after all. The shandy arrived, and Simon handed it to Russell.

'Cheers,' said Russell. 'Shall we sit down?' He led the way from the bar to a secluded table on the other side of the vast room. There was scarcely any light at all. Simon could just about make out the silhouette of Russell's enormous frame on the other side of the small table.

'So,' said Russell once they had sat down. 'Yeah. Before we start, I suppose I should say sorry for last week. That little conversation we had.'

Simon waved a dismissive hand. 'Forget about it,' he said. 'Just a misunderstanding.'

Russell chortled. 'Women, eh?'

Simon did his best to look amused. He rolled his eyes. 'Women,' he agreed.

'Nah, V said that actually she wouldn't go out with

you if you were the last remaining man on the planet,' said Russell conversationally.

'Well, that's great news,' said Simon, meaning it. He took another swig of his beer. He wasn't quite ready to get down to business yet.

'Tell me, er, Russell,' he said. 'What is it exactly that you do?'

'Jobwise?' asked Russell. Simon nodded. 'I'm a trader,' he answered.

'A trader? What sort of trader?' Simon thought of the silver Porsche. 'Cars?'

Russell frowned. 'No. A proper trader, you know. I work in the markets.'

Simon nodded. 'Oh, I see,' he said. 'So what sort of stuff do you sell? And which markets, principally? I've been to that one in Petticoat Lane a couple of times.'

'No,' said Russell. '*Proper* markets. I trade auto-annuative cumulative foreign interbank perennial derivatives, with particular emphasis on Far Eastern quasi-systematic proto-industrialist junk bonds.'

'Oh *right*,' said Simon. 'Proper markets.'

'And you,' said Russell, 'work in that stupid magic shop.'

There was a pause. 'That's right,' said Simon.

'Anyway,' continued Russell. 'V said you wanted to see me. What do you want?'

Simon took a deep breath and began to explain the position with Michael. He recounted their chance meeting in Slick Tom's. He explained how he wanted to stop Michael seeing other women without arousing Arabella's suspicions or revealing the truth to her.

'So what is it exactly that you want me to do?' asked Russell.

'Well, I wondered whether, you know, given your, er, performance the first time we met, maybe you might be prepared to employ similar tactics to get my brother-in-law to behave.'

'Right,' said Russell, taking another sip of shandy.

'And, well, I suppose I'd want you to go just that little bit further with your threats and perhaps carry out one or two minor, er, assaults, just to show him that you were serious.'

'You want me to beat him up?' said Russell.

Simon nodded. 'Basically, yes.'

Russell looked at Simon with an amused glint in his eye. 'Well, well. Maybe you're not such a tosser after all,' he said.

'Er, thanks,' said Simon. 'So will you do it?' he asked.

Russell thought. 'Yeah, I suppose I'll do it. It'll be a laugh. Did you say this guy's a lawyer?'

Simon nodded.

'Then I'll definitely do it,' said Russell. 'And you want me to tell him to stop cheating on his wife?'

'Yes please,' said Simon gratefully.

'Now,' said Russell. 'Details. Where and when? And I'll need a description, preferably a photo. I don't want to get the wrong bloke.'

'Right,' said Simon. 'I brought a photo with me, actually.' He pulled it out of his jacket and slid it across the table. Russell looked at it with interest.

'Smug bastard, is he?' he asked.

'He is quite,' said Simon.

'Looks it.' Russell looked up. 'This is going to be fun.'

Simon gave Russell the address of Michael's law firm. 'I suggest you catch him one evening as he's leaving work,' he said.

Russell nodded. 'Consider it done.'

Simon paused. 'You won't hurt him *too* much, will you? Just enough to give him a real scare and something to think about.'

Russell grinned at him implacably. 'Don't worry, mate,' he said. 'He'll still be in one piece at the end of it.'

'Well, that's good,' said Simon uncertainly.

The opening notes of the 1812 Overture sounded from Russell Square's pocket. 'He took out a tiny silver mobile phone and put it up to his ear. 'Hello? Yeah.' Russell nodded and listened. 'Bloody right he should,' he said. Simon sat patiently. 'What, now? Well, I suppose so.' Russell listened, rolling his eyes at Simon as he did so. 'Give me twenty minutes, then.' He looked at his watch. 'Fuck, no. That's bullshit. I swear. Yeah. OK. See you later. Yep. Right. Bye, Mum.' Russell switched the phone off and put it back into his pocket. 'Sorry about that,' he said.

'Quite all right,' said Simon politely.

'Look, hope you don't mind, but I have to go,' said Russell. 'Something's come up.' He frowned, his mind elsewhere. 'So, are we sorted on your thing, then?' he asked.

'Absolutely,' said Simon.

Russell Square stood up. 'Right, then. Cheers.' With a wave he strode off into the surrounding darkness. Simon was left contemplating his glass in the half light. He quickly drank the rest of his beer and got up to leave the pub, thinking about the nefarious connections he had begun to make. He pushed open the front door and made his way surreptitiously past the trio of bouncers who were still standing there. Suddenly he heard Troy shout, 'Oi! I want a word with you!'

Simon's head involuntarily twisted round, and he saw that Troy was gesturing towards him. Remembering Russell's theory about their suspicion that he was an undercover policeman, and reasoning that (a) it was therefore unlikely that Troy just wanted to have a friendly chat, (b) in the absence of friendly chat, some measure of violence could legitimately be expected, and (c) he was in absolutely no position or indeed shape to defend himself, Simon began to run.

There was a strangled expletive from behind him. As he tore down the near empty street, Simon glanced behind him and saw to his horror that Troy was now in hot pursuit, swearing and yelling as he did so.

Like all self-respecting bouncers, what Troy lacked in charm, social graces and cerebral capacity, he compensated for by a magnificently-toned body. Endless days spent in the gym meant that he had both a physique and stamina which Simon could not hope to compete with. By the time Simon had fled a quarter of a mile down the street, he could hear Troy closing in on him, still cursing colourfully. A pain flashed across Simon's chest, and he realized that escape was impossible. He stopped, desperately trying to concoct cunning ploys to persuade Troy not to hurt him. He opted for the direct approach.

'Don't hurt me!' he yelled, throwing his arms in front of his face.

Troy cruised up to him, and glided to an easy halt.

'What'd you run for, man?' he demanded.

'I'm not the police!' cried Simon, hands still in place.

'Yeah, I know,' said Troy.

Simon lowered his hands. 'You what?' he said.

'I know, man,' repeated Troy. 'You're kosher, man. Russell came out and had a quiet word after he'd met you. We thought we'd better, you know, apologize for before.'

'Oh,' said Simon, his nerves still jangling.

'You should of said,' said Troy. 'Russell's well liked around these parts. Any friend of Russell is a friend of ours.'

'I see. Well, that's great.'

'Yeah. So anyway, you'll always be welcome round these parts, yeah? Next time we'll usher you right through. And sorry again.'

'That's all right,' said Simon magnanimously.

Troy nodded slowly. 'Cool,' he said. He waved a languid hand. 'On you go, my man.'

'Er, thanks,' said Simon. 'He leaned against the wall, his chest heaving, and watched Troy amble back towards the pub. After a few moments he realized that in his panic he had run the wrong way down the street and to get to the tube station he would have to pass back in front of the Crusty Toad. There was, he reflected, no way he was going to do that. Cautiously he turned down a side street and began to navigate his way along the back streets of Mile End.

An hour or so later, having become lost, then angry, then sad, then found, then lost again, and finally too bored with his own sorry predicament to worry too much about it, Simon finally arrived at Mile End tube station. He collapsed on to the first westbound train. As it drew into Liverpool Street he began to think about what he had asked Russell Square to do. God, he thought. What have I done?

TWENTY

When Simon arrived home from his meeting with Russell Square, he went straight to his answer machine. He had to get Michael out of his mind now and concentrate on his own problems.

Nobody had called.

Deflated, Simon sat down, opened a bottle of beer and put on his new Tubby Hayes record. As he listened, Simon was struck by the seamless interplay of the quintet. How does that happen? he wondered. Simon could not imagine such nexus, such intimacy of thought and feeling with another person. Nobody understood *him* so well. He felt dislocated. The words of a famous song came to him. He was 'Desafinado' – slightly out of tune.

Suddenly, the telephone rang.

Simon jumped to his feet, a rush of adrenaline screaming through his nervous system. He suddenly felt light-headed with relief. Joe. Thank God, he thought. About bloody time. As he stepped towards the telephone he tried to compose himself. Act cool. Act natural. Ignoring the profound contradiction inherent in these two instructions, Simon picked up the receiver and said, in as bored a voice as he could manage, 'Hello?'

'Hello.'

'Oh. Hello.'

'All right?'

'Fine,' said Simon, trying to hide his disappointment.

'Are you sure?' asked Kate. 'You don't sound it.'

'No, I'm fine, really. How are things in sunny Australia? What time is it there?'

'Come on,' said Kate. 'I'm not stupid. 'What's wrong?'

With a sigh, Simon explained about Alex Petrie and how he was trying to work out when to call her, and what to say when he did.

There was a squeal down the phone line. 'My God! I'm impressed. You actually did it. Good for you.'

'No need to sound quite so surprised,' said Simon in an aggrieved tone.

'Well, sorry, sweetheart, but I suppose I never thought that you actually would.'

'What, all words, no action, that sort of thing?' asked Simon bitterly.

There was a pause as Kate considered this. 'Pretty much, yeah,' she agreed.

'So now we've established exactly what you think about my dynamism and general ability to take control of my life, have you got any good suggestions?'

'Just don't leave it too long, is all I will say,' advised Kate. 'After a while it looks too contrived, as if you're playing games.'

'But that's just it,' complained Simon. 'We *are* playing games. It's one big game.'

'Yes, Simon, I realize that,' said Kate patiently, 'but the point is not to do anything to make it too obvious. Part of the game is pretending that there *is* no game.'

Simon sighed. 'I thought this meaningless sex thing

was supposed to be easy. This is all too confusing for me. That's why I need to talk to Joe.'

'This is the famous new friend with all the answers?'

'That's the one. He hasn't returned my calls. I'm wondering if he's got bored of me or something.'

'God, Simon. Get a grip. Just pick up the phone and ring him.'

'You're right,' said Simon.

'I know I'm right,' said Kate. 'That's what I'm here for. I'm a telephonic trouble shooter.'

There was an affectionate silence for a few moments.

'Anyway, I should be going,' said Kate finally. 'Work beckons in three and a half hours.'

'Jesus. You have the stamina of an ox. I don't know how you manage it.'

'Practice, practice, practice,' replied Kate cheerfully. 'It's the key to everything.'

'Right. Thanks for calling,' said Simon.

'So you'll call this Joe character straight away?'

'I will.'

'Promise?'

'I promise,' said Simon. 'Now get some sleep, you mad woman.' He put the telephone down.

After a few moments, he dialled Joe's number. As Joe's phone rang for the fourth time, Simon's heart sank. He still wasn't there. The answer machine clicked into action. At the beep, he cleared his throat and began.

'Joe, hi. Me again. Simon. Teller. Simon Teller.' Pause. 'Just a quick ring, really, to say hi, and to see how you were. I left a message a couple of days ago. Maybe you didn't get it. Anyway.' Another pause. 'OK. Well. Give me a ring some time soon. If you're back tonight, maybe. Right. See you. Cheers.'

Clunk.

Oh, fabulous, well *done*, said Simon to himself as he went into the kitchen to retrieve another beer from the fridge. Such panache, such fluency. Such winning conversational gambits. And all this with a machine that doesn't even answer back. Well done you. There was nothing now that he could do except sit, wait, and think about Alex Petrie.

So that is what he did.

The following morning Simon came to a decision. He had been thinking about Kate's advice about calling Alex. He didn't want to risk delaying things for too long. He would have liked to have spoken to Joe first, get a few pointers, but he couldn't wait any longer. Today, Joe or no Joe, he would call her.

By about eleven o'clock Simon was too distracted to perform even the simplest trick. He had ruined a potential sale by failing to find the playing card that the customer had chosen, and then he had mistakenly cut up someone's credit card and was unable to put it back together again. When someone came in asking to see the wrist guillotine demonstrated, Dean had hastily stepped forward and offered to perform the trick.

Simon realized that his nerves were getting the better of him, and decided to stop procrastinating. He walked down the road to the nearest public phone box.

He took a deep breath, dialled the number of Alex's hotel and asked to be put through to her room.

There was a rattle as the phone was picked up.

'Hello?'

'Alex?'

'Who is this?'

'Alex, this is Simon. From the magic shop.'

There was the smallest pause, before she said, 'Well, *hi*. Nice surprise. I was wondering what had happened to you.'

Simon beamed. 'Sorry,' he said. 'I've been a bit busy.'

'Well, better late than never, I guess,' said Alex. She sounded genuinely pleased to hear from him. 'Look, I wanted to tell you, I had a really good time last Sunday.'

'Oh, yes, me too,' said Simon eagerly. 'It was really great.' As he spoke Simon noticed a man in an overcoat carrying a briefcase who was waiting outside the phone box, glancing at his watch.

'I loved the walk in particular,' said Alex. 'That was cool.'

'Good, good,' said Simon. 'Well, I was wondering whether you would –'

'Mind you, bit awkward with your niece, wasn't it?' said Alex, laughing. 'I couldn't get out of there quick enough. It just unnerved me a little, you know? Kids tend to have that effect on me. Make me want to run. I'm sorry. It wasn't the best way to end the day.'

I'll say, thought Simon. The man in the briefcase had now approached the phone box and was knocking on one of the glass panes, pointing at his watch, and mouthing something slowly at Simon. 'Never mind,' said Simon, turning away to avoid the man's stare. 'These things happen.'

'Yeah. I guess so. Anyway, sorry for running out on you like that.'

'Well, think nothing more of it. You can make it up to me, if you like.'

'Yeah? How?'

'Well, I was wondering whether I might entice –'

'Excuse me.'

Simon took the receiver from his ear. The man with the briefcase had opened the door of the phone box.

'Do you mind?' said Simon. 'I'm on the phone.'

'I can see that,' snapped the man. 'You have been for quite a while now.'

'Well, I shall be for a while longer,' said Simon, 'so kindly sod off.'

The man puffed up his chest like a peacock. 'You can't talk to me like that,' he said.

'I just did,' Simon pointed out, 'and I shall do again if you don't get out of this phone box and stop interrupting my conversation.'

'Can't you hurry up?' said the man. 'It's urgent.'

'No,' hissed Simon. 'Now fuck off.'

The words startled both of them. The man backed out of the box without another word, and Simon lifted the receiver hesitantly to his ear again. 'Sorry about that,' he said to Alex. 'Some rude man interrupting our conversation.'

'And I thought the English were all so goddamn polite.' She laughed. 'Anyway. You were saying?'

Simon frowned as he tried to remember how far he had got. 'Yes. Sorry. So I was wondering if we could do something else together, you know, see each other again.' Simon realized that the handset had become slippery with his sweat.

'Oh, Simon, that's really sweet.'

Simon breathed a sigh of relief. There, that wasn't so difficult, was it? Everything was going to be fine. The man with the briefcase had begun to flick ostentatious V-signs at Simon through the glass. Simon closed his eyes and tried to ignore him. Alex was speaking.

'The thing is, this week is a bit of a problem for me. Obviously I'm working in the evenings, and then I've got lots of other stuff to do.'

'Well, OK,' said Simon. 'How about the weekend? We can do another weird and wonderful tour of London.'

There was a slight pause on the other end of the line. 'I'd love to. But this weekend is going to be really busy, too.'

'Oh,' said Simon.

The man outside the phone box had now put down his briefcase, and had begun pulling faces at Simon through the glass. People walked calmly by, as if this was the most natural thing in the world. Simon tried to concentrate.

'So,' Alex was saying, 'would you mind if we took a rain-check until next week?'

'Next week. Sure. Why not?' Simon paused. 'Next week would be great. When?'

'Look, I don't know at the moment. Why don't you call me next week and we'll talk about it then?'

'Right,' said Simon eagerly. 'I'll call you, what, on Monday?'

'How about Wednesday?' suggested Alex.

'Wednesday.' Over a week away. A whole bloody week. 'OK. Wednesday. I'll speak to you then.'

'Great. I can't wait.'

'Me neither.'

'See you, then,' said Alex.

'See you.'

'And thanks for calling.'

'You're welcome.'

'OK.'

'OK.'

'Bye, Simon.'

'Yup, bye.'

He put the phone down.

Immediately the man with the briefcase was at the door, tapping impatiently on the glass again. Simon picked up the telephone again, and pretended to dial another number. Out of the corner of his eye Simon could see the man hopping up and down. Simon smiled in grim satisfaction. Spite, he thought, can be very cathartic. As he listened to the dialling tone buzzing in his ear, Simon thought about Alex. Having to wait a week wasn't ideal, but there wasn't really much he could have done, he reasoned. If she was busy, then she was busy.

Still, thought Simon, he had another date with Alex. Sort of. And a date was a date. He had telephoned her, and arranged a date. Unaided. Without safety net. Of that he should be proud.

The rest of the week passed quickly. Simon did his best not to think too much about his date with Alex the following week. Instead he cautiously allowed himself to dream about her in a more abstract, long-term way. There were times when generalized fantasies were more alluring than having to worry about immediate specifics, such as whether or not she was going to allow him a second chance to sleep with her.

During the rest of that week, Joe never called Simon back. As the days wore on, Simon's feeling of mild hurt was replaced by one of concern. It was unlike Joe to ignore his calls, particularly when there was the opportunity to dole out some advice.

By the following Saturday afternoon, Simon had resolved to do something. He had left two more messages on Joe's answer machine, and still there had been no response. Something must have happened to him. Perhaps he had had an accident. A small doubt entered Simon's brain. There *were* more plausible explanations. A holiday, for example. Joe *was* allowed to disappear without informing Simon first. There was no obligation to return calls within a given time period. Wasn't it possible, suggested the doubt gently, that Simon might be overreacting somewhat?

On the other hand, thought Simon, isn't that what friends are for? Friends look out for each other. What if something awful *had* happened to Joe? Wasn't the idea that friends didn't need to be asked before doing the right thing?

Simon picked up the telephone and dialled Joe's number again. Once again, the machine clicked on. Simon sighed. 'Joe? It's Simon. It's Saturday afternoon, and I've left God-knows how many messages. Where are you? I'm worried. I'm coming over.'

He set off for the tube station.

* * *

Half an hour later, Simon emerged blinking from Kennington Underground station into the South London sunlight. After a few minutes' walk, he arrived in front of a red door in the middle of a terrace of well-preserved Georgian houses. Simon peered at the stack of buzzers next to the door. Joe's name was unevenly typed on a dirty piece of paper which had been slid behind the top rectangle of clear plastic.

Simon pressed the buzzer. Nothing happened. After a minute or two, he pressed it again, and waited.

Nothing.

Simon sighed. Now what? There wasn't much else he could do. He eyed the other buzzers beneath Joe's. Perhaps he could check with Joe's neighbours to see if they knew where he was. After a moment Simon shook his head. It would look very suspicious; the neighbours would probably call the police straight away.

Stumped, Simon turned away from the door.

'Simon. Hi. What are you doing here?'

Joe was standing on the pavement, holding his bicycle with one hand and shielding his eyes against the glare of the sun with the other.

'Joe,' blurted Simon. 'How are you?'

'I'm fine. What are you doing here?' Joe asked again.

Simon did his best to look nonchalant. 'Nothing, really. I was in the area. Just passing by. So I thought I'd look in. You know. Haven't heard from you in a while.' He suddenly felt rather foolish.

He watched Joe chain his bike to the iron railings at the front of the house. How was he going to explain the reason for his visit without appearing ridiculous? Then he remembered the anxious message he had left for Joe earlier. He groaned inwardly.

Joe walked up to the front door and smiled briefly at Simon. 'Well, you'd better come up,' he said, digging into his pocket to extract his keys.

'No, don't worry, not if it's any bother,' said Simon hopefully.

'Course not. Don't be daft. Come on.' Joe opened the front door.

'OK,' breathed Simon. He followed Joe up the stairs.

'Here we are,' said Joe, as he opened the front door to his flat, which was on the top floor of the building. Simon followed him in. He noticed the telephone sitting on the hall table. Its red light was blinking furiously. Simon's heart sank. 'My humble abode,' announced Joe. 'Coke?'

Simon smiled weakly. 'Coke would be good.'

'OK. Hang on a sec.' Joe walked into the kitchen, ignoring the answer machine. Simon moved in front of the hall table, blocking Joe's view of the flashing red light.

'So what have you been doing with yourself?' asked Joe from the kitchen.

'Oh, this and that,' replied Simon. 'Usual sort of stuff. Nothing exciting.'

Joe came out of the kitchen, and handed Simon a can of Coke. He opened a second one and drank.

'Thanks,' said Simon. 'How about you?'

Joe shrugged. 'Not been up to much, really.' He leaned against the door, watching Simon, who shifted uncomfortably in front of the answer machine. 'So. Do you want the grand tour?'

'Er, OK,' said Simon.

'Come on, then,' said Joe breezily. 'Through here is the sitting room.' He gestured through an open door.

Reluctantly Simon relinquished his position in front of the answer machine and followed Joe, wondering how best to explain his message. Finally they arrived back in the hall. Before Simon could react, Joe saw the flashing light. 'Aha,' he said cheerfully. 'Somebody loves me.' He walked over to the table and pressed the button. There was a brief pause.

'Joe? It's Simon,' crackled Simon's voice. 'It's Saturday afternoon, and I've left God-knows how many messages. Where are you? I'm worried. I'm coming over.'

Joe looked at Simon questioningly. Simon spread his hands affably. 'Don't worry about that,' he said quickly. 'Nothing to –'

The machine interrupted him with a loud beep, and then another voice echoed through the flat.

'Hi,' said the voice. 'It's me. You've just left on that sweet bicycle of yours. I thought I'd give you a quick ring to say thank you for that magnificent performance. And to check that you were coming around again tonight for some more. I've bought some clotted cream, as instructed. You *beast*. I'll see you at eight if I don't hear from you.'

As the tape whizzed back to the start, Simon stood, frozen, staring at the answer machine.

For the second voice was unmistakably that of Alex Petrie.

TWENTY-ONE

Simon and Joe stared at each other for several moments.

'Er,' said Joe eventually.

Simon shook his head. 'I don't understand,' he said after a while.

'What?' asked Joe.

'That message.' Simon pointed at the answer machine.

'Hmm,' said Joe. He pulled a face.

'That was Alex, wasn't it?'

'Yes. It was.'

'So I don't understand,' said Simon again.

Joe shrugged. 'Well,' he said. 'I got your message last Sunday so I knew things hadn't worked out for you guys. So I went back to the restaurant the next night to have a go myself. She came and did that trick with the handkerchief again. It really *is* a great trick. Anyway, I asked if she fancied a drink after she finished work, and she said yes.' He looked at Simon. 'And things sort of progressed from there.'

'So are you –? Have you –?'

Joe looked embarrassed. 'Um, yeah, I suppose we are. That is, we have.'

Simon tried to stem the nausea rising in his chest. 'But you *knew* I fancied her,' he said, bewildered.

Joe finished his can of Coke and crumpled it in his fist.

He lowered his chin and let out a loud belch of carbonated gas. 'Simon, she's American. She's going back to New York in a week. She was the last person you wanted to get involved with.'

'Oh, really? That's your opinion, is it?'

Joe nodded. 'Come on. Let's face facts. It would have been a disaster. I know what you're like. She would have gone back to the States and you'd be left here with your heart broken.'

Simon shook his head. 'Hold on. Are you trying to tell me that you did this for my own good?'

'Kind of. I didn't want to see you get hurt.'

'*Hurt*?' demanded Simon. 'What exactly do you think I'm feeling just at the moment?'

'You're upset,' said Joe. 'Pissed off, even. I can understand that. But believe me, I've done you a favour. What you're feeling now is a lot less painful than what you would have felt once Alex had gone.'

'So,' said Simon. 'To recap. You deliberately went behind my back to chase after the woman that you knew damn well I fancied rotten and now you're telling me that you did it for my own good.'

Joe nodded. 'That's pretty much it,' he said.

'OK. I have one question.'

'Fire away.'

'Do you think I'm a complete fucking moron?'

Joe held up his hands. 'Look, it obviously wasn't *just* for your sake. I mean, she's a pretty girl.'

'I remember,' said Simon bitterly.

'But Simon, listen. She was *my* sort of girl. She was perfect for me. Transient. Here today, gone tomorrow. We both have a good time, and nobody gets hurt.'

'Nobody? What about me?'

'Well, OK, apart from you, nobody gets hurt.'

'Thanks a fucking million.'

'Come on, Simon. Can't we just forget about this?'

Simon stared at Joe. 'Forget?' he said.

Joe nodded, and tried a brief grin. Simon looked into Joe's eyes, frowning, trying to understand how this could have happened.

'So how about it?' said Joe. 'Still mates?'

'Joe,' said Simon, 'you're full of shit.' Suddenly Simon's right arm was flying forwards. He watched dispassionately as his fist connected squarely with Joe's nose. There was a peculiar crunching noise as cartilage was crushed. Then Simon stepped back, his arm back down by his side. Joe's hands were covering his face, as he crouched forwards. Blood was seeping through his fingers and was dripping on to the carpet.

'I wish,' said Simon, stunned, 'you'd just farted in my face and left it at that.'

Simon went home. He stood gripping one of the plastic handles which hung from the ceiling of the tube carriage like a miniature punch bag. He held on with his left hand. Soon after he had fled from Joe's flat, his right hand had begun to swell alarmingly, and now it was throbbing painfully.

Simon stared at his distended black reflection in the curved glass of the train window. He had been as surprised as Joe when he threw the punch. He had never hit anyone in anger before. It had been a visceral, automatic reaction. He knew that it had been absolutely the correct response, perhaps the only one. And, he had to admit, it had been gratifying. As a means of registering one's displeasure, thumping someone on the nose had a lot going for it.

When the train pulled into Angel station he stepped off on to the wide platform. As he turned to make his way to the escalator, however, he realized that he was not yet ready to face the solitude of his flat. There he would have nothing to distract him from the ugly truth of Joe's betrayal. He needed time to wander with an empty head, to let the facts make sense of themselves.

Barely thinking, he turned and boarded the train again, moments before its doors slid shut. Simon leaned against the door at the end of the carriage, whose window was half open. The stale air of the tunnel whistled through his hair as the train hurtled through blackness. At Hampstead station he got out and followed the crowds to the lifts.

Back in the afternoon sunlight, Simon began to walk up Heath Street, past a stationary line of cars waiting for the lights at the bottom of the hill to change. On Spaniards Road, he stepped into the rough grass on the edge of Hampstead Heath, and began to walk.

Simon kept off the tracks and paths. He wanted to lose himself for a while in the thickets of the Heath. He struggled through dense foliage, climbing over fallen trees, making his way slowly through mazes of entangled branches.

Finally he reached a clear stretch of long grass which rolled into the distance. The vista was punctuated by isolated figures who had settled down for an uninterrupted read, or who were making their way across the expanse of untended heath. The surrounding urban sprawl shimmered in the distance, a quiet reminder that for all this pastoral calm, Simon had not escaped. London, and his problems, were still waiting for him.

Simon pressed on. He passed the mixed bathing pond, where three motionless fishermen sat by the path, cautiously eyeing a small but energetic group of swimmers who frolicked in the water. On Parliament Hill he sat on a bench, and gazed across the rooftops of London. A black Labrador bounced up to him, and nosed his leg inquisitively, egging him into a game. Simon bent down and ruffled the dog's head. Immediately there was a suspicious shout from a middle-aged woman, calling the dog away. The dog's ears pricked up, and without another glance at Simon he turned and raced back to his mistress. Apart from the distant cries of a lazy game of football and the fluting song of nearby birds, there was no sound. A faint breeze cooled his face. Simon breathed deeply, willing the fresh air into his lungs, hoping to drive out some of the stagnant remnants of the city that were festering within him.

On the slopes which fell down towards the running track and the Lido, there was a crowd of people enjoying the sun. Couples lounged casually next to each other, exchanging kisses and soft talk. Small children ran up and down the hill, into the arms of patient parents. Simon surveyed the city which stretched away below him. Somewhere down there, Simon thought, were Alex and Joe. He wondered whether Joe had been with Alex, in her bed, when Simon had called her earlier in the week. Simon shut his eyes. A painful cocktail of anger and self-pity flooded through him. He imagined them laughing after Alex had put the phone down. The pit in his stomach yawned achingly. He inspected his right hand. He was unable to flex his fingers without some pain. It was, he reflected, the second time that Joe had caused him to hurt that hand.

Simon sat staring at the Crystal Palace radio transmitter, alone on top of its distant hill. Alex was gone, lost to him now. He sighed bitterly. He helplessly felt his whole friendship with Joe unravel before him.

He felt a crashing, hopeless, fool.

Simon stayed looking down at the city until the early evening. Finally he got to his feet and made his way back to Hampstead High Street. He realized that he was none the wiser as to what he should do, or what he should think. Put it down to experience, he supposed. File the episode under 'Monumental Fuck Ups' and get on with life.

On his way home Simon visited Charlie and bought two bottles of Chenin Blanc and a frozen lasagne. Back at the flat, he turned on the oven, opened the first bottle of wine, and decided to watch a video to keep himself occupied. He looked at the pile of boxes on the floor and extracted one from near the top – *The Third Man*. Simon put the tape into the video machine and settled back to watch. An everyday story of loyalty and friendship, deceit and betrayal. Perfect, he thought. Just what I need to cheer myself up. He sipped his wine and tried to ignore his aching hand.

By the time the young Orson Welles was explaining his view of the world to Joseph Cotten as they rode the big wheel above the Viennese skyline, Simon had drunk a whole bottle of wine and was feeling very sorry for himself. He listened to Harry Lime's explanation for his amoral, mercenary behaviour with a heavy heart. It sounded all too familiar.

INTERLUDE

'Simon. Hi. It's me. Joe. Look, I'm sorry about what happened yesterday. Really. I shouldn't have behaved like such a twat. [*Pause.*] I can understand if you're angry with me. What I did was out of order, I accept that, and I'm sorry. But I'd still like to be friends. Put the past behind us, that sort of thing. I hope you're well, anyway. [*Pause.*] You broke my nose, by the way. It was a bloody good shot. Hurts like buggery. Give me a ring when you get this. I'll speak to you soon.'

'Hello? Hello? *Shit.*'

'Simon, hello mate, this is Dean. Look, I just thought I'd give you a quick buzz cos we're all wondering where you are, and Brian is screaming blue bloody murder. So, look, I don't know if you're ill or something, but at least call in and let us know. Brian's going out of his tiny mind. [*Pause.*] I never said that.'

'Simon, darling, it's Kate. It's now . . . four in the morning,

Simon sniffed histrionically. There was no justice in the world, that much was clear, he reflected as he opened the second bottle. The guilty go free. The innocent are the ones who routinely get it in the neck.

What's the point? he demanded foggily as he poured himself another glass of wine. Why bloody bother?

Simon didn't watch the end of the film. He had seen it a hundred times before. It was time, he decided, for a tactical retreat from the world at large. He had had enough.

Simon switched on his answering machine and went to bed.

'Simon, *hi*. I don't know if you remember me. It's Monique. From Sophy's party. *I* certainly remember *you*. [*Throaty chortle.*] It was great to meet you and I was wondering whether you might like to hook up some time soon, for dinner, or a drink, or whatever else you fancy. Perhaps you could show me some more of your tricks. I shudder to think what you could do with those dextrous fingers of yours. Call me.'

'Hi, it's me. Hope you're well. Where are you? Gallivanting around town and up to no good, I hope. We're all fine, I suppose, although Sophy has become obsessed with the size of Postman Pat's nose. It's all very strange. Anyway, you haven't called back and I'm trying to make plans. Some of us have shopping lists to construct, you know. So give me a call, you swine. Speak to you soon. Soph says hi.'

'Oh shit. Simon? Hello? Are you there? If you're there, *please* pick up the phone. [*Pause.*] *Shit*. OK. Simon, it's Alex. Er, look, Joe has kind of told me that there's something going on between the two of you, and that it's something to do with me. Now, that's all very flattering, but the last thing I want to do is to come between two friends. Anyway, look, I'm here, still at the same hotel, so ring me and we'll talk.'

'Hi Simon, another message for your answer machine, and for you as well. I don't know whether you're listening to the live performance or if you'll have the benefit of

heure locale, and I wanted to see how everything went with the American girl. Let me know. Fingers crossed. Speak soon. Lots of love.'

'Hi, Simon, Joe again. It's eight-thirty and I was hoping to catch you in. I don't know if you got my message yesterday. Anyway, you haven't called back, so I suppose I'm just phoning to check you're OK and to tell you to ring me when you get a moment. Right. Christ, I hate these bloody machines. God, now I'm rambling. OK. I'd better go. Call soon. Lots to talk about.'

'Simon. It's me. Give me a ring. Something important to ask you about Postman Pat. Oh, and to arrange supper.'

'It's Brian Station. Where the *fuck* are you? If I don't hear from you by the end of today then you can consider yourself sacked. End of message. [*Pause.*] Bastard. Real end of message.'

'*Shit.*'

'Thanks mate. Your call just about saved me from getting killed by Brian. Sorry to hear about the malaria. Sounds serious.'

* * *

TWENTY-TWO

Finally, the inevitable happened. The doorbell rang.

Simon buried his head beneath his pillow. The doorbell went again. Simon pulled the pillow more tightly around his ears and retreated further under his duvet.

Thirty seconds later the bell went yet again, longer and apparently louder. Immediately after it stopped, there was a brisk tattoo beaten out on his front door. With a sigh, Simon hauled himself out of bed. Whoever it was clearly wasn't going to do the decent thing and leave him alone. At the front door he took a few deep breaths. He didn't have to talk to anyone if he didn't want to. If it was Joe, he told himself, he would slam the door in his face. He put the security chain in place, opened the door three inches and stared suspiciously out.

Standing outside was a determined-looking Alex Petrie.

'Oh,' said Simon numbly. 'Hi.'

Alex looked at Simon through the three-inch gap. 'Can I come in?' she demanded.

Simon tried to think. 'OK,' he said eventually. He shut the door and unhooked the chain. As he opened the door properly Alex swept into the flat before he could change his mind. Simon turned and followed her into the sitting room. What on earth was she doing here? he wondered.

enjoying this broadcast in playback mode. I wonder if you're there. Well, whatever. Please call me. It's Joe. Your mate.'

Beep.

led to believe that he *had* asked you first, and that you didn't have any objections. I was rather upset, to tell you the truth. When you telephoned the other day I figured you'd just changed your mind, but it was all a bit late by then.'

Alex and Simon both fell silent.

'Believe me, if he had asked me, I would have said no.' Simon paused. 'Several times, at some volume.'

Alex looked at him levelly. 'I do believe you,' she said.

Simon looked at his hands. It hadn't just been him who had been hoodwinked. 'God,' he said after some moments.

'God,' agreed Alex.

'So what will you do now?'

Alex shrugged. 'Well, I'm seeing him tonight. I may ask him about it then.'

'That's it?' blurted Simon before he could stop himself. 'You'll just *ask him* about it? Aren't you *angry*? He *lied* to you.'

'What else is there to do? It seems a shame to let that get in the way of everything else.'

'Everything else?'

'Look, Simon,' said Alex patiently. 'Let me explain. There's nothing very sinister about it. I've been seeing Joe for these last few days because we've been having some really amazing sex. That's all.'

Simon stood stock still for a moment as he concentrated on remaining upright and functioning. 'Oh, really,' he finally managed to say. 'That's all? Just amazing sex?'

Alex nodded. '*Amazing*. He does this thing with clotted cream –'

'Well, that's marvellous,' interrupted Simon.

Alex frowned. 'Oh, come on. Chill out. OK, Joe lied to us both. But what did you think was ever going to happen

Was she was about to explain that there had just been a terrible misunderstanding? Nervously his heart began to flutter beneath his dressing gown.

'Well,' said Alex, sitting down in the middle of the sofa without waiting to be asked. 'You've been quite a difficult man to get hold of recently.'

Simon shrugged. 'Sorry,' he said.

'I've been a little worried about you.' Alex looked him in the eye. 'Where have you been?' she asked.

'You know, here and there.'

'Too busy to answer my messages?'

Simon paused. 'Pretty much, yes.'

'Nothing to do with the fact that you think Joe and I are humping away like rabbits.'

Simon's heart lurched a little. 'I suppose there is that, yes,' he conceded. There was a pause. 'You *are* humping away like rabbits, aren't you?' asked Simon.

Alex regarded him coolly. 'Oh yes,' she said.

He had to bloody ask, didn't he?

'Well,' he said, trying to hide his mortification, 'that's nice.'

'That's why I wanted to come and see you,' said Alex. 'Joe thought you were upset, and I wanted to talk to you, to see if I could sort things out.'

'OK,' said Simon cautiously.

'First things first. Why did you hit Joe?'

Simon blinked. 'Why? Because he went behind my back, knowing that I was very keen on you, and asked you out.'

Alex frowned. 'But he did check with you first.'

Simon looked at Alex oddly. 'No he didn't. That's crazy. Do you think I would have agreed if he had?'

Alex raised her eyes towards the ceiling. 'Actually, I *was*

Was she was about to explain that there had just been terrible misunderstanding? Nervously his heart began to flutter beneath his dressing gown.

'Well,' said Alex, sitting down in the middle of the sofa without waiting to be asked. 'You've been quite a difficult man to get hold of recently.'

Simon shrugged. 'Sorry,' he said.

'I've been a little worried about you.' Alex looked him in the eye. 'Where have you been?' she asked.

'You know, here and there.'

'Too busy to answer my messages?'

Simon paused. 'Pretty much, yes.'

'Nothing to do with the fact that you think Joe and I are humping away like rabbits.'

Simon's heart lurched a little. 'I suppose there is that, yes,' he conceded. There was a pause. 'You *are* humping away like rabbits, aren't you?' asked Simon.

Alex regarded him coolly. 'Oh yes,' she said.

He had to bloody ask, didn't he?

'Well,' he said, trying to hide his mortification, 'that's nice.'

'That's why I wanted to come and see you,' said Alex. 'Joe thought you were upset, and I wanted to talk to you, to see if I could sort things out.'

'OK,' said Simon cautiously.

'First things first. Why did you hit Joe?'

Simon blinked. 'Why? Because he went behind my back, knowing that I was very keen on you, and asked you out.'

Alex frowned. 'But he did check with you first.'

Simon looked at Alex oddly. 'No he didn't. That's crazy. Do you think I would have agreed if he had?'

Alex raised her eyes towards the ceiling. 'Actually, I *was*

ed to believe that he *had* asked you first, and that you didn't have any objections. I was rather upset, to tell you the truth. When you telephoned the other day I figured you'd just changed your mind, but it was all a bit late by then.'

Alex and Simon both fell silent.

'Believe me, if he had asked me, I would have said no.' Simon paused. 'Several times, at some volume.'

Alex looked at him levelly. 'I do believe you,' she said.

Simon looked at his hands. It hadn't just been him who had been hoodwinked. 'God,' he said after some moments.

'God,' agreed Alex.

'So what will you do now?'

Alex shrugged. 'Well, I'm seeing him tonight. I may ask him about it then.'

'That's it?' blurted Simon before he could stop himself. 'You'll just *ask him* about it? Aren't you *angry*? He *lied* to you.'

'What else is there to do? It seems a shame to let that get in the way of everything else.'

'Everything else?'

'Look, Simon,' said Alex patiently. 'Let me explain. There's nothing very sinister about it. I've been seeing Joe for these last few days because we've been having some really amazing sex. That's all.'

Simon stood stock still for a moment as he concentrated on remaining upright and functioning. 'Oh, really,' he finally managed to say. 'That's all? Just amazing sex?'

Alex nodded. '*Amazing*. He does this thing with clotted cream –'

'Well, that's marvellous,' interrupted Simon.

Alex frowned. 'Oh, come on. Chill out. OK, Joe lied to us both. But what did you think was ever going to happen between us? I mean, all right, maybe it would have been you and me having the amazing sex rather than him and me. But apart from that. It's just a bit of fun.'

Simon remained silent. Just a bit of fun. Joe had been right all along, he brooded. Women wanted sex as much as men. He had been fooling himself for years. He sighed deeply. 'Fine,' he breathed. 'But please go.'

Alex Petrie stood up. 'Don't beat yourself up about it, OK? You're a nice man. I like you. You did everything right. But it's just a game. A game.'

'A bit of fun,' echoed Simon.

Alex nodded. 'Right. A bit of fun.'

Simon rubbed his eyes and led Alex back to the front door. 'Thanks for coming round,' he said as he held the door open. 'Take care.'

Alex Petrie looked at him seriously. 'I will. You too.' She kissed him quickly on his cheek and then turned away.

Simon watched her walk to the end of the street. She didn't look back.

The day following Alex Petrie's visit, Simon finally left his flat.

He did not want to give up the solitary comfort of his duvet, but in the end he was left with little choice. After three days of a televisual diet which consisted exclusively of Australian soap operas and programmes with earnest-looking people sitting on pastel-coloured sofas discussing cellulite, he needed to escape.

Also, Simon needed to eat.

He walked to Charlie's shop. His self-enforced confinement had not done him much good. Each time that he had tried to fathom Joe's behaviour, painful visions of Joe and Alex rolling around in various stages of undress and in a variety of imaginative positions, some of which now included clotted cream, floated before his eyes. He felt raw. To make matters worse, his hand was still hurting badly. The middle two fingers had swollen up and turned a spectacular purple.

Simon crossed the threshold of Charlie's shop, inhaling the familiar pungent smell of curry powder. Charlie was sitting behind the cash register reading a copy of the *Sun*. He looked up as Simon walked in. 'Aren't you supposed to be at work?' he asked, flicking over a page in a bored way.

'Holiday,' mumbled Simon.

Charlie regarded him critically. 'You look as if you should be in bed,' he said. 'You look bloody awful.'

'Thanks very much.' Simon went to examine Charlie's selection of tinned soups. Soup was supposed to be good for you, he thought. It was hearty, warming, life-giving. Optimistically he put two tins into his basket.

Simon continued to tour the shop. By the time he approached the till he had also selected a loaf of pre-sliced white bread and a tin of frankfurters. Charlie closed his newspaper and put it to one side as Simon approached. He examined the contents of the basket critically as Simon put it on the counter.

'You should eat more greens, you know,' he said, pointing at the collection of gangrenous vegetables at the far end of the shop, most of which had been sitting there for at least a week. 'You'll never grow into a big boy if you carry on eating this shit.' He picked up the tin of frankfurters and looked at it with distaste.

Simon did not want to get trapped into one of Charlie's discourses on the nutritional benefits of his wares. He paid for his food and fled.

Back in the flat, Simon opened the tin of frankfurters. He was starving. The sausages bobbed up and down obscenely in a murky sea of brine. He extracted a frankfurter from the tin and washed it under the tap to remove its sheath of glutinous slime. He squeezed a generous dollop of tomato ketchup on to a slice of white bread. He put the frankfurter in the middle of the bread and then rolled it up into a tube, before taking a bite from one end. As he did so, a large blob of ketchup shot out the far end of the bread and landed on his T-shirt. He was too hungry to care. He finished off his improvised hot dog in three mouthfuls and wandered around the flat, chewing thoughtfully as he tried to swallow it.

Finally Simon sat down on his sofa and switched the television on. A group of young Australians were arguing on a beach. This is hopeless, he thought. He went back to the kitchen and prepared another hot dog.

His meal finished, Simon let himself out of the flat again. The sun was shining. He strolled to Highbury Fields, and sat on one of the benches that lined the eastern perimeter of the uneven patch of green. In the middle of the park a group of men kicked a football about. The sunshine glimmered through the foliage of the overhanging trees, and a light, warm breeze carried the muted rumble of traffic on the Holloway Road to his ears. From behind a hedge he could hear the shrieks of young children as they hurled themselves about the municipal playground. Simon stretched out on the bench and relaxed. He let his mind go blank for a few moments.

Suddenly there was a cough next to him. He turned around. A large woman had sat down next to him. Her face was smudged with dirt, and her hair was tied up in a stained scarf. She wore several layers of torn and rotting clothing. On the path in front of her were two bulging plastic bags.

'Spare us a quid,' she said.

Simon looked at the old woman. She grimaced. Perhaps it was an attempt at a grin. It was difficult to tell. The action revealed an irregular and incomplete set of brown teeth.

'Go on,' she said. 'Please.'

'For a cup of tea, is it?' asked Simon.

The woman shrugged. 'More likely I'll get a can of Tennants Extra, if it's all the same to you.'

Simon smiled. He dug into his pocket, and took out two pound coins. 'Go mad,' he said, handing them over. 'Have a party.'

The woman looked at Simon in surprise. 'Thank you,' she said with dignity. 'I will.'

Simon stood up. There was no point feeling sorry for himself any longer. 'I have to go,' he said to the woman.

'Sure you won't join me?' she cackled.

Simon bowed formally. 'Very kind offer, madam, but I shall have to decline.'

'Suit yourself.' The old woman made herself comfortable on the bench, holding Simon's money tightly in her gloved hand. 'Have a good day. You're a nice man.'

'Have a good day yourself.' With a brief wave, Simon turned and walked back towards his flat.

There was a lot to do.

* * *

Simon took the tube to Victoria. He needed to find out whether he still had a job.

When he arrived at Station Magic and cautiously pushed open the door, he didn't know what to expect. Brian and Dean were both behind the counter. Vick was nowhere to be seen.

Brian eyed him suspiciously. 'Didn't I fire you?' he asked.

'No,' said Dean eagerly. 'You were going to, but he had malaria, remember? He was ill.'

A frown creased Brian's forehead. 'Oh yeah,' he said. 'So you're better, then?' he asked. 'Malaria's cleared up?'

Simon nodded. 'Right as rain, thanks.' He looked at Brian. 'So,' he said, 'have I still got my job?'

'I suppose so,' said Brian grudgingly.

'Great,' said Simon. Dean beamed at him.

'Now get back to work,' snapped Brian.

As the day progressed, Simon found to his surprise that he was genuinely pleased to be back. He had missed Dean's silent camaraderie, in particular, but even Brian's bad temper had a reassuring familiarity to it. It felt like learning to walk again after a bad accident. Simon felt like the Bionic Man. He needed to be rebuilt, but would come back, stronger and better than before. By the end of the day, his spirits had lifted considerably.

Simon arrived back at his flat that evening feeling that he had made a creditable start to his reintegration into society. This had been achieved principally by keeping himself too busy to think about Joe and Alex, but if it worked, it worked.

As he walked into his sitting room, however, Simon's self-congratulatory mood vanished. The flat reminded him of his recent internment. He immediately began to feel hemmed in. Instead of its usual comforting atmosphere, the flat now seemed as cold and unwelcoming as a prison cell.

The answer machine was flashing. Simon sniffed, and went to the kitchen to fetch a beer from the fridge. He was no longer interested in his messages. The rest of the world could get on quite well without him. Suddenly it occurred to him that it might be Arabella. It might even be Alex. It might, God forbid, be Monique. He walked back into the sitting room and eyed the machine with loathing. He was powerless to resist the lure of the flashing light. Try as he might, Simon knew that he would succumb to temptation, and press the little button on the electronic Pandora's box. The only question was when. He sighed. Given the inevitability of the outcome, there seemed little point waiting. With a fatalistic sigh he pressed the button.

'Hi, Simon. It's me. Look –'

Simon hit the delete button, cutting Joe off in full flow and erasing the rest of his message unheard. He grunted in satisfaction. Funny how the smallest of victories helped.

He looked around the flat. His eyes finally rested on his Thelonious Monk poster. Perhaps, he thought, it's time for a change of scene. Simon stood up.

He was going to go clubbing.

As he climbed the narrow stairs of the Vortex Jazz Club, Simon felt the familiar tingle of anticipation pass through him. Simon liked the Vortex because it was on the first floor of its building, which was a pleasant, unpretentious change from the traditional smoky basements which jazz clubs were supposed to inhabit. He heard a rim shot crack through the air, a trumpet quietly running through scales, and the languorous low twang of a double bass. He smiled to himself. The band were warming up, each man in his small world, preparing himself for the communal pull, the group effort to come.

Simon settled into his seat at a small table in the shadows towards the back of the sprawling room. He watched the people at the tables between him and the stage. Men with blocky, peppered beards and cardigans sat silently staring at the musicians. Mostly, though, the room was filled with the happy chatter of a younger crowd who seemed more interested in each other than the musicians.

Simon went to the bar and bought a bottle of Pinot Grigio. He returned to his table clutching the bottle and a solitary wine glass. Live jazz and posh plonk: very trendy, very *now*, he thought to himself wryly.

He poured himself a glass of wine and looked towards the front of the room. An old man stood to one side of the stage, saxophone slung low around his neck. He squinted into the lights, peering into the room. Then he slowly made his way to the front of the stage. The other musicians ambled into place behind him.

Gradually the room quietened, expecting the saxophonist to make a few introductory remarks. He fixed the audience with an intense, beady eye for a few moments, half a grin twitching on his leathery face. He turned to the drummer and counted off two bars of introduction.

The band launched into a swinging, up-tempo version

of 'I'll Remember April', racing through the head twice before the sax player breezed into a ferocious solo, all honks, wails, trills and achingly lovely melodic movement, as he created small eddies of notes which spun, sank and rose again as the band pushed onwards. It was quite a performance. Simon sat back in his chair, took a sip of wine, and shut his eyes in unabashed pleasure. The troubles of the last few days began to slip away.

Suddenly there was a clunk on the table in front of him, the sound of glass on wood. Simon opened his eyes, and saw a second wine glass standing next to his own.

'Hi,' said Joe. 'Mind if I join you?'

Simon stared at Joe, momentarily unable to speak.

Without waiting for an answer, Joe pulled out one of the other chairs at the table and sat down. He was looking rather the worse for wear. His nose was swollen and there was a dark streak of purple beneath his left eye. 'May I?' he asked, pointing at the bottle of wine. Simon nodded numbly. 'Cheers,' said Joe affably. He poured himself a glass and took a large swig. Simon watched him, his mind reeling in disbelief. What was Joe doing here? Simon had not replied to any of the messages he had left over the last few days. Could he simply not take a hint? Joe was looking towards the stage, nodding his head in time to the music.

Simon just wanted Joe to go away, but knew that he would listen to whatever Joe had to say. This was due in part to morbid curiosity, and in part to a potent masochistic streak. He didn't expect a happy ending; he had learned that much. Simon looked at Joe warily, and waited.

The band had begun to trade four bar breaks with each other, listening, echoing each other's phrases, quoting other songs, trying it on, making each other laugh, enjoying themselves. Finally they broke into the tune once again and played it through to a rousing finish. The crowd broke into enthusiastic applause. The band leader nodded faintly at the room, and turned his back on the audience to talk to the bass player.

'This is all right, this place, isn't it?' said Joe, looking around. 'Very cool. I've never been before. Do you come here a lot?'

'Joe,' said Simon, 'what are you doing here?'

'I wanted to talk to you,' replied Joe.

'How did you know I was here?' demanded Simon.

'I followed you.'

'Followed me?' said Simon. 'How? From where?'

'Your flat, obviously,' said Joe. 'When you didn't reply to my messages I realized that I would have to come to see you. Only just as I got to the end of your road you walked out of your flat, and I followed you here.' He paused. 'I was wondering whether or not to come in. I'm not a great jazz fan. But eventually I thought, well, fuck it, I've come this far.'

'But what makes you think that I would possibly want to talk to you?' asked Simon.

The band broke into a brisk bossa nova rhythm as the saxophone and trumpet launched into an old Joe Henderson melody, 'Recorda Me'.

'I wanted to try and sort out what's been going on, to see if we can put this behind us,' said Joe, ignoring the question.

Simon sat back in his chair. 'You're going to try to apologize?' he asked in disbelief.

Joe shrugged. 'I'm not sure I'd go that far. I just want to sort this out.'

Simon shook his head in an effort to clear it a little. 'So you're not going to try and apologize?'

'Look,' said Joe, 'it seems to me that we're just coming at this from different angles.'

'Different angles?' said Simon. There was a pointed harrumph from the bearded man at the next table. Simon lowered his voice. 'Which angles are different, exactly?' he hissed.

'Well, look at you,' said Joe. 'You're obviously upset. And I just want to find out why.'

Simon blinked. '*Why*?'

Joe nodded. 'Yeah. I feel *bad* about this. I didn't mean to piss you off, you know. I had no idea that you'd overreact like this. I mean, she's just a girl, right?' He took another swig of wine.

Simon's shoulders slumped. He leaned forward towards Joe. 'That's it? That's your excuse? "She's just a girl?"'

Joe looked at him. 'Well, isn't she?'

Simon sighed. 'The thing is,' he explained, 'I actually quite liked Alex.'

There was another pause as Joe digested this information. An odd look came over his face, as if he'd just bitten into a slice of lemon. 'What,' he said, 'liked her, as in, *liked* her?'

Simon nodded.

'But *why*?' asked Joe.

'I thought she was *great*,' said Simon. 'She was funny, she was pretty, she liked jazz. She was the most interesting girl I've met in years.'

Joe looked at Simon suspiciously. 'You're not having me on?' he demanded. Simon shook his head. 'Fuck,' he muttered to himself.

'So, does that make things clearer?' asked Simon.

'But she's going back to New York in a couple of days,' said Joe, ignoring the question. 'What were you going to do then?'

'That's not the point,' snapped Simon. He wasn't about to tell Joe his dreams of going to Manhattan. That all seemed a long time ago now.

'Excuse me,' came a voice from the table next to them. '*Some* of us are trying to listen to the music.' The crowd on the table behind them were now staring at Simon and Joe with disapproving looks. Simon's face burned with shame. He mouthed an apology and then turned back to Joe.

'That's not the point,' he repeated in a whisper. 'The point is, the points are, as follows. One, I was very keen on this girl. Two, I failed to sleep with her at the appointed time owing to the unforeseen appearance of my niece in my flat. Three, I told you about it. Four, you immediately went out and slept with her yourself. Does that about cover it?'

'I guess so,' said Joe quietly.

'*And*,' continued Simon, 'not only did you go behind my back, but you also lied to *her* and told her that I'd said it was OK.'

Joe pulled a face. 'Yeah, Alex mentioned that last night, too.' He paused. 'Sorry.'

Simon couldn't restrain his curiosity. 'What did Alex say when you admitted it?' he asked.

Joe shrugged. 'She called me a conniving bastard.'

'Was this before or after the latest instalment with the clotted cream?'

Joe paused for the briefest of moments. 'Before,' he replied.

Simon settled silently back into his chair. Women.

'Look, Simon, I just had no idea how you felt about her. I mean, obviously, if I'd realized what was going on in that crazy head of yours I would have left her well alone.'

'Obviously.'

'Come on, Simon, give me a break. I'm not a bloody mind-reader. How was I supposed to know that you were so hung up on her?'

'Well, two things spring to mind. First of all, you always could have asked, rather than just barging in there. Secondly, regardless of how I felt about her, there is also the small matter of general politeness. You can't just jump in without so much as a by-your-leave. There was actually a queue, you know?'

Joe looked awkward. 'I'm sorry. I just didn't think. Anyway,' he said, 'I always thought the one you really liked was Delphine.'

Simon looked at him sourly. 'Well, you single-handedly managed to make sure I didn't stand a chance with her, if you remember.'

Joe ignored this. 'No, come on. *Wasn't* she the one you really liked?'

'Yes. So what?'

'So why did you never even try and get in touch with her?'

Simon looked at Joe in exasperation. He and Joe could converse like ordinary human beings on most topics, but as soon as the subject turned to women, something strange happened. All of a sudden a vast, uncrossable gulf opened up between them. Nothing meaningful could be transmitted across the void. It was hopeless.

'You don't get it, do you?' he said sadly. 'There's no

way I could ever call Delphine. I'm incapable. I've had the requisite cerebral circuit removed. It's a biological impossibility. Unless she magically turns up on my doorstep, I am destined to lead a Delphine-free life.'

A strange look had come into Joe's eye. 'That's extraordinary,' he said.

'Yeah, well,' said Simon, fed up. He looked at Joe. There was no point continuing the conversation. 'You and I are different. Fair enough. But stealing my girlfriend and lying to me is not what I expect from my so-called friends. So if that's all you have to say, then I'd like to enjoy the gig on my own.'

Joe looked at him, astonished.

'That's it?' he said. 'You're dismissing me?'

Simon nodded. He gestured towards the stage where the musicians were still playing. The bass player was in the middle of a solo, and the horn players were standing to one side of the stage listening to him play. 'I want to enjoy the music. That's actually why I came here, rather than to have a pointless conversation with you.'

'But you can't just *dismiss* me,' said Joe angrily.

There was an irritated 'Shhhhh' from the neighbouring table. This time both Simon and Joe ignored it.

'Joe,' said Simon. 'Please go. There's nothing more to say.'

Joe remained where he was. 'There's heaps more to say,' he insisted.

'About what?'

'We haven't resolved anything,' said Joe. 'I mean, yes, we've established that I fucked up with Alex, and I accept that, but apart from that we're no further forward.'

'In terms of what?' asked Simon, who was curious, in spite of himself.

'In terms of *us*,' replied Joe. 'As mates, you know.'

A glacial calm settled on Simon. 'Joe,' he said softly, leaning towards him over the table. 'It's over. End of story. We're not mates any more. I'm no longer interested.' With each word Simon felt himself grow stronger. He picked up his wine glass and drank.

Joe shook his head. 'You can't just do that,' he said.

'Do what?'

'You can't *dump* me.'

'I'm not dumping you,' said Simon. 'You're not my bloody boyfriend.'

'Exactly,' replied Joe. 'That's my point. You can't dump a *friend*. It doesn't work like that.'

'But that's *my* point,' said Simon. 'You see, you are *no longer* my friend. So by my reckoning, I think I'm in the clear.'

'Forgive me for saying so,' said Joe, 'but your reasoning is totally circular.'

'I forgive you. Now please go away.'

'Look, I admit I made a mistake. And you broke my nose, which was fair enough.' Joe paused. 'But I've paid my penalty. I've done my time. It's time to forgive and forget.'

'Believe me,' said Simon, 'if I could forget the whole bloody thing, I would.' He was bored with the conversation. He poured himself some more wine, pointedly ignoring Joe's empty glass, and turned his chair towards the stage so that he had a better view of the musicians. The band was playing a medium-paced blues with oddly syncopated phrases in the theme which gave the piece a jarring, uneven feel. Simon tried to concentrate on the music.

'So anyway,' said Joe after a few moments. 'Where did you learn to throw punches like that?'

'I didn't. Beginner's luck. Or perhaps I was inspired by the circumstances,' replied Simon acidly.

'God.' Joe grinned ruefully. 'I shall have to make sure I don't make that mistake again.'

Simon looked at him. 'Me too,' he said.

There was a pause.

'So where are we, then?' asked Joe.

Simon sighed. 'What do you mean?'

'You know, are we mates again?'

'You get full marks for persistence, but the answer's still no.' Simon paused. 'I can't look at you without thinking about Alex. You betrayed my trust. I have a real problem with that.'

Joe waved a dismissive hand. 'That thing with Alex? It didn't mean anything.'

Simon shuddered. 'Not to you, perhaps.' He looked at Joe intently for a few moments. 'Can I ask a question?' he said.

'Please do.'

'*Why* are you so keen to be friends with me?'

Joe pulled a face. 'Why?' He thought. 'I like you. We have a laugh.'

'But you must have hundreds of friends,' persisted Simon. 'Why go to all the bother of coming here?'

'Hundreds? Hardly,' said Joe.

Simon frowned. 'You surprise me.'

'It's true.'

'What about Angus and Fergus?' said Simon, thinking back to when they first met.

'Oh, God, they're not *friends*,' replied Joe. 'They're acquaintances.'

'What's the difference?'

'Acquaintances are the sort of people who invite you to parties, but only so that you'll invite them back. They're raw material, fuel supply for your social life. You can rely on them to make up numbers. But they're not people you would actually want to spend much time with.'

'But friends are?'

'Of course. Friends are people you actually *like*. People you want to have a drink with. You can talk with them, laugh with them. Like we do,' added Joe hopefully.

'Or you can steal their girlfriends,' observed Simon.

Joe continued resolutely on, ignoring Simon's interruption.

'Friends are people you feel relaxed with, who you can just be yourself with. No need for play-acting or pretence.'

Simon thought. 'What day is my birthday?' he asked.

Joe looked at him blankly. 'I have no idea,' he said.

'How many brothers and sisters do I have?'

'Oh, Christ, I don't know,' sighed Joe.

Simon sat back and shrugged. 'You know nothing about me,' he said.

'Not true. I know you're not a great curry fan,' said Joe. 'And that you're a hopeless romantic.'

Simon snorted. 'Big deal.'

'Anyway,' said Joe, frowning, 'what's that got to do with anything? Is there some sort of test you have to pass before you're allowed to be friends with someone?'

'No, but don't you see that being friends with someone is a bit pointless if you know nothing about them? It just doesn't *mean* very much. It's like recommending a book you haven't read.'

'I do that all the time,' said Joe, frowning. 'What's your point?'

Simon sighed. 'Well, if you don't know anything about the book, it makes the endorsement rather hollow, don't you think?'

'Books aren't like people' replied Joe. 'Even if you believe that you can't judge a book by its cover, that principle doesn't apply to people. I can make judgements about someone as soon as I've met them. I don't need to have known them for ages. That doesn't make me a shallow person. An intuitive one, perhaps. But no worse.' There was a pause. 'Look,' said Joe. 'You and me, we're different people. We expect different things. That much is obvious. And that's fine. But at the end of the day, there's a reason why you and I are sitting here having this conversation.' Simon looked stonily on. 'And that reason is that we actually both like each other. By my reckoning, that makes us friends.'

'Well perhaps you should have thought about that before you jumped into bed with my girlfriend,' said Simon sourly.

'All right,' said Joe, holding up his hands. 'I was wrong. I accept that. And if you want us to get to know each other better, then that's fine too.' Joe smiled, sensing he was making progress. 'You start. Tell me about your parents. What do they do?'

Simon's ears filled with white noise.

'My parents,' he said, 'are dead.'

Joe looked at him, stricken.

'They died three years ago,' continued Simon tonelessly.

'My God, Simon, I'm so sorry. I'm so –' Joe lapsed into silence, and stared at his hands beneath the table top.

Simon nodded. 'Me too.' He paused. 'You're not my friend, Joe,' he said. 'How can you be? You know nothing about me. Nothing.'

'Right. You two.' The voice boomed through the club's loudspeaker system. Simon felt the eyes of every person in the room swivel towards them. There was complete silence for a few moments. On stage, the band had come to a halt and the saxophone player was standing at the microphone, pointing towards them. 'You pair have not stopped talking since we began playing. Now, I've nothing against having a good chat, but this isn't the place for it. The rest of these nice people are trying to listen to the band.' There was a murmur of assent from the surrounding tables. Simon felt a slow burn climb from the base of his neck up towards his ears. 'Now fuck off out of it.' There was a self-righteous whoop of approval from someone nearer the front. Simon shook his head in disbelief. They couldn't throw him out. Throw *Joe* out, he wanted to shout. I just came for a quiet night of music. It's nothing to do with me.

He became aware that everyone was looking at them, waiting for them to move. The band stood on the stage, obviously not intending to play another note until they had left. Pushing back his chair, Joe stood up. His face was a mask. Simon remained seated for a few moments longer as he struggled to come to terms with what was happening. He finally stood up, and began to make his way to the exit, ignoring the smattering of sarcastic applause that chased him out of the room. As he stumbled down the stairs towards the anonymous sanctuary of the street, he heard a brief drum roll from the stage as the musicians prepared to recommence. His head numb with humiliation and anger, Simon stepped out on to Stoke Newington Church Street.

It had begun to rain.

For a moment Simon stood on the pavement, transfixed by the weather's dirty collusion with events.

Joe was looking up at the sky. 'Oh bollocks,' he said mildly. He didn't seem bothered or embarrassed by their expulsion from the club, and his implacability was suddenly an unspeakable torment to Simon.

'Happy now?' Simon finally managed to say.

Joe gave Simon a sardonic look. 'Not especially,' he replied. 'You?'

'What do you think?' he asked. 'Just when I thought you couldn't cause any more damage, you do. All I wanted to do was to lick my wounds, pick up the pieces, and get on with my life. All I wanted to do was to forget I ever met you. But you couldn't let it go, could you? You had to come back and perform one last little trick, something for me to remember you by.'

Joe frowned. 'What are you talking about?'

Simon nodded towards the door to the club. 'In there.'

'What about in there?' asked Joe.

'You had to interfere, didn't you?'

'Simon. What are you talking about?' said Joe gently.

Simon took a deep breath. 'In there,' he said, 'is where I come alive. In there is where I stop being boring old Simon Teller who works in a magic shop. It's like being woken from a deep sleep. Suddenly everything makes sense.

Everything sparkles. Everything connects. It's magical.' He pointed up at the dimly-lit windows of the Vortex. 'In there – I'm the tops. I'm Mahatma Ghandi. I'm the Coliseum. The shackles fall away. I can do anything. It's like some wonderful drug. Hallucinogenic, maybe, but a wonderful drug all the same.' He stopped, and looked at Joe.

Joe shook his head. 'Sorry,' he said. 'You've lost me.'

By now the rain had soaked through their clothes. They stood looking at each other, as cars splashed by them. Simon shivered. 'Don't you see? Now you've sullied all that,' he said.

Joe shrugged. 'But they'll let you back in, surely?'

'Of course they will,' said Simon. 'But that's not the point. The question isn't whether I'll be let in, but whether *I* can keep *you* out. Every time I go back in there, the memory of tonight, and of you, and of Alex, is going to come along, too. And it'll sit there, on the chair next to me, spoiling all the fun.'

Joe did not move. His hair lay flatly against his head under the downpour. 'Simon,' he said. 'Look.' He paused, and took a deep breath. 'I'm sorry. OK? I'm sorry for farting in your face. I'm sorry about the Canadians. I'm sorry about Alex, and I'm sorry about the jazz. And I'm sorry about your parents. I'm sorry I never knew. But I don't know what else I can do. I'm sorry. If I could turn back the clock, then I would. But I can't. We're trapped in the present. We can't wave one of your magic wands and undo what's done. We both have to make do with this shit. I'm sorry. I'm sorry.'

Simon looked at Joe. A raindrop hung from the tip of his nose, but he didn't seem to notice. He was staring at Simon, a look of resigned supplication on his face. He took a step towards Simon.

'You said sorry,' said Simon. 'You actually said it.'

Joe nodded, and smiled a small smile. 'I'll say it again if it helps.'

Simon thought. He shrugged. 'Don't bother,' he said.

He turned away.

TWENTY-THREE

'Ready?'

'I suppose so.'

'Right. Brace yourself.' Dean stood on tip-toe and inserted the long metal sword through the middle of Simon's head.

'Is this where I'm meant to say "Ow"?' asked Simon.

'Depends,' replied Dean, picking up the next sword and banging it on the counter to demonstrate its solidity. 'Whether you're playing it for laughs.' He walked around Simon and stuck the sword through his head from the other side.

'How many swords have we got?' asked Simon, his voice sounding muffled from inside the wooden box.

'About ten,' replied Dean. 'Shall I continue?'

'Please do.'

Dean picked up another sword. He consulted the instruction manual. 'It says that this one should go straight downwards through the top slot,' he said.

'Splendid. Right through the middle of my cranium,' said Simon.

'I'm not sure I can reach,' said Dean.

Simon sighed. 'Here. Give it to me.' Dean put the sword carefully into Simon's outstretched hand. Simon lifted it over the box which encased his head and felt around for the slot. Moments later he found it and the sword was in place, theoretically splitting his skull neatly down the middle. 'Seems to be going all right so far,' he reported.

It was lunch time. Dean and Simon were alone in the shop, trying out a new trick that had just arrived in stock. It was a version of the famous vanishing head illusion. A wooden box is placed over the head of the magician's assistant, and swords are inserted into the box, through the head, at impossible angles. The magician explains how he is able to perform this miracle: he opens the front of the box and – hey presto! – there is nothing inside except for the swords which penetrate the box. The assistant's head has vanished. It was a wonderful trick.

'Everything all right in there?' asked Dean.

'You haven't killed me yet, if that's what you mean,' said Simon.

'Excellent,' said Dean. 'And otherwise?'

Simon stared ahead into the darkness which surrounded him, and thought. 'Otherwise, Dean, maybe not so good.' He could hear Dean walk around him. A moment or two later the next sword appeared. 'I'm glad it's you doing this, Dean,' said Simon. 'I can trust you to get it right and not to hurt me.'

'Hope so,' muttered Dean to himself.

'I mean, is it too much to expect a little trust and loyalty from your friends?'

'Hold still while I do this next one, will you?' said Dean, carefully avoiding the question.

'I mean, not only did Joe sleep with my girlfriend, but

then he expects us still to be friends afterwards. What does he think I am? Some sort of doormat?'

'Don't know,' replied Dean.

'It's a rhetorical question,' said Simon irritably.

'Sorry,' said Dean meekly.

'Anyway, I told him. I made it quite clear. I've had enough. God knows my self-respect has taken enough of a battering since he's come into my life.' Simon paused. He thought about hiding in his bathroom making puking sounds to ward off Rachel Gilbert and creeping out of Slick Tom's trying to avoid the awful Debbie. He thought about Corky and his disastrous haircut, and the humiliation of standing in Joe's flat listening to Alex Petrie's voice on the answer machine. He thought about being thrown out of the jazz club. He shuddered.

'Another one coming,' warned Dean as another sword skewered Simon's head.

'What did I think I was doing?' wondered Simon.

'I don't know,' replied Dean absent-mindedly.

'Excuse me, Dean, do you mind?' snapped Simon. 'There's no need to keep interrupting all the time, is there?'

'Sorry,' said Dean again.

'Where was I?' asked Simon. 'Oh yes. I can't think now why it took me such a long time to work out what was going on. God. Talk about *blinkered*. He confused me so much I couldn't see past the end of my nose.'

Rather than risk further approbation, Dean wisely remained silent and instead merely shoved another sword through Simon's head.

'When I look back now, I can see that I should have realized that something like this was going to happen. I've been an utter berk. I mean, for Heaven's sake, the very first time I met Joe he put me into bloody hospital. He's a sociopath. It was obvious then. But no, no, I had to find out the hard way, didn't I? I couldn't possibly rely on common sense or instinct. The only way *I* could work it out was to humiliate myself completely. I feel such a fool.'

Dean said nothing.

'Anyway,' continued Simon. 'That's it for me. I've had enough. I'm bowing out. I'm taking myself out of circulation. I'm fed up. I intend to stay at home and listen to my jazz records from now on. No more girls for me. Or friends. Who needs a social life, anyway? All it does is tire you out and cost you money.'

There was a pause as both men considered this.

'Now I come to think of it, Joe was a shit even *before* he farted in my face,' said Simon, remembering. 'He made me look a sad bastard in front of a roomful of strangers. I mean, who hasn't had a wank in the bath from time to time? Let's face it, we've all done it, haven't we?'

'Bit quiet in here today, isn't it?' asked Dean.

'But that wasn't the really awful thing. The worst thing was that Joe's stupid story completely ruined my chances with this absolutely beautiful French girl who was at the party. Delphine, she was called. She was gorgeous. Anyway, after Joe told his story she couldn't look at me without laughing, so that was the end of that. God. She was perfect. I mean, really really perfect. I could have just looked at her all day. And she was French.'

'You said,' said Dean.

'Yes, but not just French. You know, she was *French*. In the way that French girls are supposed to be but never actually are. You know, sexy, beautiful, very chic.

Like what's her name, you know, Nicole in the car ads.'

'Oh yeah,' said Dean, relieved to have finally understood something Simon was talking about. 'She was very nice. I liked her.'

'Exactly. Very nice. But have you ever actually *met* a French girl like that?'

'Er, no?' tried Dean, who, as far as he could remember, had never met a French girl at all.

'No. Exactly. Nicole only exists in men's imaginations, car adverts and in glossy magazines. There's nothing different about French girls in reality, except they have a sexy accent and don't shave under their armpits.'

'Er, Simon,' said Dean.

'Except for Delphine,' continued Simon. 'She was the genuine article. She was as sophisticated and sexy as you get. And she was funny, and smart. God. She was amazing.' Simon stared into darkness, thinking about Delphine.

'Simon,' said Dean, coughing meaningfully.

'And so what do I do when I meet this perfect girl? How do I react to this once-in-a-lifetime, never-to-be-repeated opportunity? Easy: I admit to masturbating in the bath and then sprain my wrist playing Twister. Are you all right?'

'Fine,' said Dean, who had been coughing loudly while Simon had been speaking. 'Last sword coming in now.' He thrust the blade through the final hole.

Simon sighed. 'You know, Dean, if I knew then what I know now –'

'Right,' said Dean quickly. 'Let's open up the front, shall we? Ready?'

'Ready,' said Simon.

Dean slid back the two small bolts which were holding the doors at the front of the box shut. He opened the doors. Where Simon's head was supposed to be, there was nothing but a lattice of sword blades. Otherwise the box was empty. Simon heard an astonished gasp. There was somebody else in the shop.

'Who's that?' demanded Simon.

'A customer,' said Dean.

'For Christ's sake, Dean,' snapped Simon, 'you might have bloody told me there was someone else in here before I started rabbiting on like a lunatic.'

'I did try,' said Dean mildly. 'You know, coughing.'

'Oh, great, coughing. Very helpful. How am I supposed to know what a cough means? I thought you had a frog in your throat.'

Dean closed the doors of the box and began to extract the swords.

'Why didn't you just tell me to shut up?' asked Simon.

'Actually,' said Dean awkwardly, 'she didn't want me to.'

Simon froze. 'What?'

'She didn't want me to,' repeated Dean. 'She put her finger to her lips.'

Simon let out a breath. It was Alex Petrie, back again. He stared into the darkness of the box, wondering what she wanted now. He tried to decide how he should play this. Cool, calm and dispassionate? Or dark, brooding, emotionally raw?

Simon turned to where he thought he had heard the gasp come from. 'Hello,' he said coolly.

There was a pause. Then Dean said, 'She's waving at you.'

'Isn't she going to say anything?' asked Simon.

'Er, no. At least, she's shaking her head,' said Dean.

Simon decided to go for the dark, brooding, emotionally raw approach. Apart from anything else, it seemed appropriate since he still had so many swords sticking out of his head.

'OK. Will she at least answer one or two questions for me?'

'She's nodding,' reported Dean.

'Excellent.' Simon thought. '*Why*? Why did you do it?'

There was a murmuring from the other side of the room. 'Why did she do what?' asked Dean.

'Why did she sleep with him?'

There was a pause while Dean and Alex conferred quietly. Finally Dean said, 'She says, Sleep with who?'

Simon snorted. 'Oh, come on. With Joe, of course.'

There was more whispering. Dean said, 'She says, Do you mean Joe from the dinner party?'

Dinner party?

'Because if so,' continued Dean, 'then she most definitely never slept with him at all.'

A little while later Simon and Delphine were sitting in a café drinking Diet Cokes.

'I feel incredibly embarrassed,' said Simon, for the eighth time.

Delphine giggled. 'Don't be. It was funny.'

'I thought you were someone else,' explained Simon.

Delphine laid a hand on his arm. 'Simon, I know. You've already told me lots of times. It's all right.'

'But all that stuff I said. About you.'

'Ah. Now *that* was very interesting.' Delphine's eyes shone mischievously.

'How much did you hear?'

'Not all of it, unfortunately.'

'I feel incredibly embarrassed,' said Simon, for the ninth time.

'No, you mustn't,' said Delphine. 'Actually I was very pleased to hear this, because I was wondering already for some time what had happened to you since the dinner party.'

Simon looked at her cautiously. Her accent sounded wonderful. 'You were?' he asked.

'Oh yes. But anyway, I had a thought that perhaps this was how you felt.'

Simon felt his cheeks go hot. 'You did? How?'

'Joe told me when he called me last night. He asked me to come here today to ask you to forgive him for what he did.'

Simon blinked. 'He did?'

'Oh yes. He was very eager for me to come to see you today.'

'So you knew how I felt about you before you came?'

Delphine nodded.

'And you came anyway?'

Delphine nodded again.

Simon thought. 'Golly,' he said eventually. 'So what exactly did Joe say to you?'

'Well, he tells me that your fight is about a woman?'

Simon waved his hand dismissively. 'A woman?' he sniffed. 'Well, I suppose so. Sort of. But don't worry about *her*,' he said, eager not to get off the far more nteresting issue of what Delphine felt about him.

'But I promised Joe I would talk to you about this,' said Delphine. 'He was upset, I think. Really sad. I think he still wants to be your friend.'

Simon pulled a face. 'So he claims. But I've never understood why he was so keen to be friends with me in the first place.'

Delphine thought. 'Perhaps he is very lonely,' she said softly.

'Too many acquaintances and not enough friends,' mused Simon, remembering Joe's distinction between the two. He looked up at Delphine and smiled. 'I don't need his friendship,' he said, and meant it. 'I mean, what are friends for?'

Delphine shrugged. 'To make you happy? To be there for you when you need them?'

'OK,' said Simon. 'Well, looking back, Joe made me miserable almost all of the time. And when I needed him, he invariably would come and make things worse than they already were.'

Delphine looked at him. 'I think you have already made up your mind on this,' she said.

'Quite right.'

'It is important that you can make decisions and stick by them,' said Delphine. 'I like that.'

'Well,' confessed Simon, 'I haven't always been terribly decisive.' He paused. 'At least, I don't *think* I have.'

'You just need the courage of your convections,' said Delphine.

Simon hid his smile. 'Indeed I do,' he agreed.

'And what about me?'

'What about you?' said Simon.

'Are you sure about what you said about me when your head was in the box?'

Simon blinked. 'Absolutely. I suppose.' He paused. 'If that's, you know, OK.'

Delphine laughed. 'Sure it's OK,' she said. 'I'm pleased.'

'Really?' spluttered Simon.

'Really,' said Delphine.

'Wow,' said Simon.

TWENTY-FOUR

'Wow,' said Arabella.

'Hmm,' said Simon.

'No, really. I mean it. Wow. That's great.'

Simon pulled a face. 'Yeah.'

Bella pushed a bowl of steaming soup towards her brother. 'You don't seem very sure,' she said.

'It's not that,' replied Simon. 'I mean, of course I'm sure. Who wouldn't be? She's wonderful. I'm just worried.'

'You? Worried about a girl? Surely not.'

Simon sighed. 'We're going out for dinner next week. And I don't know what to do. I've had an awful run of luck lately. And I really, *really* don't want to mess up this time. This one is special. This could be something big.'

'Now where have I heard that before?' asked Bella.

Simon put up his hands. 'I know, I know. But this time, it's different. Really.'

'Then why so glum, chum?'

'Well, that's the problem. The stakes are higher this time.'

Arabella shook her head in exasperation. 'What are we going to do with you?' she asked.

'Have me put down?'

'I'll put you down myself. You're an idiot. There.'

Simon grinned. 'Thanks,' he said.

'Do you really like her?' asked Sophy.

Simon looked at his niece across the table. 'Yes, Soph, I do. I like her a *lot*.'

'Is she pretty?'

'Oh yes. Very.'

'Prettier than me?' asked Sophy archly.

Simon looked shocked. 'Don't be silly.'

Bella rolled her eyes.

Sophy beamed. 'Does *she* like *you*?' she asked.

'I think so.'

Sophy frowned. 'So why are you worried?'

Simon shrugged. 'Because it's difficult.'

'What is?'

'Never mind,' replied Simon. 'You'll find out soon enough.'

'Do you love her?'

'Sophy, eat your soup,' suggested Arabella.

'Do you think you'll get married? Can I please be a bridesmaid?'

'No, Simon's not getting married,' said Arabella before Simon could answer. She turned towards her brother. 'She's got a thing about weddings at the moment,' she explained. 'We've moved on from fairies.'

'Ah,' said Simon.

'Luckily there's not much difference in the costumes. It's just a question of removing the wings.'

'But if you *do* get married, can I please be a bridesmaid?' persisted Sophy.

'Of course you can,' said Simon, smiling. He had already decided to ask Sophy to be a bridesmaid. (He had also worked out the menu for the wedding reception, and had compiled a rough guest list.)

'Getting married ish very sshpecial,' said Michael, who had been listening to the conversation with an unreadable look on his face. 'Besht thing I ever did.'

Arabella looked at her husband indulgently. 'Ah, bless you. That's so sweet. My hero.'

Michael shrugged, and glanced at Simon. 'I mean it,' he mumbled through his swollen lips.

Ever since Michael had arrived home the previous Thursday evening, looking rather shaken having tripped and fallen face first into a filing cabinet at work (sustaining multiple minor injuries in the process), there had been an extraordinary change in his behaviour. Suddenly his late night meetings had been cancelled, and he had spent the weekend working in the garden and nursing his broken jaw. He was now a thoroughly docile and attentive husband and father. He had even sat through an epic magic show during which Sophy had eagerly performed every trick she knew for him, twice. Michael had applauded all the more second time around – as best he could, anyway, with two fingers in plaster. It remained to be seen whether Michael's metamorphosis into loving family man was a permanent one, reflected Simon.

He ate his soup and thought about Delphine. While they had sat in the café, she had waited patiently for Simon to summon up the courage to ask her out for dinner. Finally, falteringly, he had managed to squeeze the words out. Now he couldn't help thinking about their imminent date with an inescapable sense of doom. This was nothing to do with Delphine – far from it. It was merely a triumph of experience over optimism.

His mind tripped momentarily back to Joe. Simon k exactly how *he* would approach the problem. Simon sigh He didn't want to think about Joe any more. He had don enough of that. Still, no matter what else Joe had done, he *had* sent Delphine to him. Simon wasn't yet sure whether this was something for which he would be eternally grateful or if it would turn out to be one more reason to forget that Joe had ever walked into his life.

Sophy slurped the last of her soup from her spoon. 'Simon,' she said, 'do you remember that night I came and stayed at your house?'

'Of course,' replied Simon.

'Well, I wanted to ask you something about what we discussed.'

Simon was instantly on guard. The warm fuzzy feeling generated by his thoughts of Delphine dissipated instantly in the face of this new threat. 'Well, Soph, how about later? I'm sure we don't want to bore everyone else with it.'

'It's not boring,' said Sophy, sounding a little hurt.

'No, all right, not *boring*, but maybe we should talk about it later anyway,' said Simon hurriedly.

'Is this about Postman Pat, by any chance?' asked Bella suspiciously.

'Oh, no,' said Simon quickly.

'Yes it is,' said Sophy.

There was a pause.

'Oh. *That* conversation,' said Simon weakly.

'I thought you said you didn't know anything about this,' accused Bella.

'Er, that's right,' said Simon. 'I didn't. Don't. That is, I forgot.'

'*Really*.' Bella raised a sardonic eyebrow.

…nyway,' said Simon quickly. The spectre of Postman … and his Black and White Cat, not to mention his large …ose, loomed over him like the glinting blade of a guillotine, and he wanted to change the subject. He turned to Michael. 'Sorry to hear about the filing cabinet,' he said.

Michael looked at Simon, suspicion lurking behind his puffed-up eyes, which were ringed with magnificent hoops of dark purple. 'Thanksh,' he said shortly.

'Dangerous places, offices,' observed Simon.

'Indeed,' replied Michael.

There was a pause.

'So, back to our friend Postman Pat, then,' said Bella briskly. 'What was it you want to ask Simon, Sophy?'

'Well,' said Sophy, 'I was just wondering. You know what we were saying that night about Postman Pat?'

'Sophy, don't you think we should talk about this later?' said Simon anxiously.

'No,' said Sophy and Bella in unison.

Simon sat back uneasily in his chair. 'All right, then,' he said in a resigned voice. 'What was it you wanted to know?'

'I've been thinking,' said Sophy.

'Yes,' said Simon apprehensively.

Sophy nodded thoughtfully, and then pointed at Michael's nose. 'Daddy's a wanker, isn't he?'

Simon shut his eyes.

DISCOGRAPHY

Saxophone Colossus – Sonny Rollins, Prestige

Jazz Classics, Volume One – Sidney Bechet, Blue Note

Kind of Blue – Miles Davis, Columbia

The Modern Jazz Quartet Plays the Music from Porgy and Bess – Philips

Clarinet Concerto in A Major, K622 – W. A. Mozart, Decca

Piano Music – Erik Satie, played by Peter Lawson, EMI Classics for Pleasure

Conception – Bill Evans, Milestone

Down in the Village – The Tubby Hayes Quintet, Fontana